FARPOINT RISING

(Farpoint Series, Book 2)

Vincent Bek

To my amazing wife, JoAnna.
Thank you for always being there,
no matter how crazy it gets.

CHAPTER ONE

Kasey gripped the cold railing tightly as the ship slid toward the great looming gateway.

The gate itself, impressive though it was, was not the cause of his apprehension.

Forcefully, he relaxed his grip on the rail and looked around. Far to the side of the gateway that was about to engulf the ship was the incoming gateway that had brought the full might of the Terrantine Federation's forces to this corner of the galaxy. He had fought to protect that gate, and many had died to see it activated. Never could he have imagined himself fighting on the Federation's behalf, but for the colony's survival—well, that was home. You fight for your home.

Looking upwards, he searched the blackness. He barely made out the two objects orbiting a small station further out in the system. The new public trade gates currently being built. They would connect the Trias System to the rest of humanity back in the Earth Prime cluster.

When the trade gates would become active was anyone's guess. There was no doubt that they would change everything—again.

"Kasey." AnnaChi's voice was a beacon of safety in his emotional storm. "Stop worrying about nothing. We are just going to check out their science experiment."

"It's a ship."

"Fine. An experimental ship then."

"Being this deep under the Federation's control is unsettling. This is no average Federation system we are visiting…"

"From what I have heard," she countered, "it is not a solar system at all. I—"

"Event entry in fifteen seconds," a voice called out from the command deck behind them, culling the chatter throughout the command bridge.

"It seems we are about to find out," Kasey whispered, then frowned as the blackness of the portal overtook their view.

Admiral Maddock Francis' calm but authoritative voice cut the silence from the Endeavour's command chair, "General quarters, commander. We are about to travel fifteen thousand light-years in a blink."

Most knew the admiral as Mad Fran, a name that Kasey fully agreed with several times over for good reasons. Yet, he was happy to call him simply Fran, and a friend—even when the man's creative usage of their friendship had crossed the line. Repeatedly.

"Conditions set, sir."

"Coms. Status of our destination?"

"All clear, sir. They are expecting us."

"Very well." Fran stood, locking his gaze on the blackness beyond the upper viewing area where Kasey and AnnaChi stood.

"All stations reporting green, sir."

"Three seconds, sir. One…"

Reality melted away.

Kasey felt his senses dissipate into nothingness. Time

no longer had any meaning, yet eternity beckoned him forward. Then it was gone, the view blooming into being as the Endeavour sprang forth from the gateway.

"Welcome, to the Gemini Nexus!" Fran called out as he made his way to their viewing area. "Stand down and bring us to point two, relative-orbital velocity, and give me a fix on the Pathfinder's location."

The viewscape was beyond anything Kasey had expected. Where endless space and stars should have been, a distant stretch of rocky walls curved around them forming the interior of an immense egg-shaped cavern. Splotches of light adorned the cavern walls, haphazardly covering it with odd shadowy patterns. Far ahead floated dozens of what appeared to be factories, shipyards, and other constructs he could not identify. Navy transport ships shot through the vastness while hosts of small tugs moved far larger warships into the substantial lines of berths.

AnnaChi gestured at the display, and the view swiveled to show the rear view from the Endeavour. Dozens upon dozens of identical gate pairs were laid out across the area. None were active, with the exception of their own gates connecting back to the Trias System they just left. Beyond the rims of the Trias gates, a deadly fleet sat, waiting, as if expecting trouble. The active gate was also heavily protected by rows of huge cannons and launchers. No one was getting in or out of the Gemini Nexus if not invited to do so.

"There is more power here," Kasey began quietly, "than I ever imagined existing across the entire Federation."

She could only nod in agreement, then shook her head to clear it. "This place—it must be inside an asteroid? I have never heard of such a thing existing…"

"It's a rogue moon, actually," Fran answered as he walked up behind them, "knocked out of some system a few million years ago and now sits a few dozen light-years away from the nearest Federation system. Some ancient race had begun mining it out long ago, we simply continued their work. We had just begun construction on the bases here when our own Farpoint mission left. It is amazing how far it has come since."

Kasey blinked several times as he turned to stare at Fran. "How long? When did all this start?"

"I assume you mean the Farpoint program itself?" Fran gestured towards the gate they had passed through. "The concept has been around for centuries. But it only found true momentum in the last sixty years when a single particle of negative matter was detected and collected by a deep space science vessel. The search for the source has been going on ever since. When the negative matter seam was finally located, the Farpoint program was fast-tracked to what you see and know of today."

AnnaChi rubbed her temple in what Kasey could only assume was frustration barely held in check. "This is several orders of magnitude beyond what any military power should control. Once the gates are throughout the Federation…"

"The Federation would be totally protected, yes."

"That is not what I meant!"

"I know." He smiled and turned to Kasey. "This worries you as well, I am sure?"

Kasey shifted his stance. "It terrifies me. But what the Federation is planning is far larger than this, isn't it?"

"Perceptive as always. True, the civilian trade network has many separate nexus points being put together, so too does the navy. This particular nexus is purely for the navy's Farpoint exploration division and will be connected into an upper tier nexus that connects to many others. The analysts are predicting the need for several unique gate networks. Not to mention the research and development teams that are ramping up as fast as possible to find new uses for n-mats—like you have done already to access the ruins of Lithose."

"So, you're saying that the Federation is going to need, to want, considerably more n-mats than Belrothi has."

"Correct. Gathering more sources of negative matter is exactly why we are here today."

Fran looked back over his shoulder at one of his crew and nodded before waving at the view screen. The image spun, then fixed onto a location on the far-off cavern wall. The view shot forward, passing the many bases and shipyards that floated along their path.

Kasey stepped forward as the camera movement came to rest overlooking a rather dull rock surface, "What exactly are we supposed to be looking at here?"

Fran donned a crooked smile and placed his hand on the display. The holographic rock wall faded away, revealing a massive four-pointed-star shaped collection of factories and storage hangars. However, what caught Kasey's attention was the massive cylindrical hole at the center of the star that swam with activity.

Construction drones flitted back and forth over a long structure stretching as far down the hole as he could see. Complex lattice networks branched off at intervals down the immense tube, blocking a complete view of the object.

It took Kasey a minute to understand what he was seeing. He knew they were here to see a ship, yet this construct, at first glance, seemed to be anything but.

"I thought we were here to see a ship?" he asked, "That thing is positively armored, and I assume that aperture grouping to the portside are either for weapons or a shield generator, but is that thing really a ship?"

"Particle cannons." Fran barely suppressed a laugh.

"Look here," AnnaChi reached out and zoomed the view closer onto the tip of the craft, where the hull was still being assembled, "that's the bridge section, right? See how it's self-contained like the Raven class ships, and the second set of shield emitters all over it?"

"Right." Fran readjusted the view back, overlooking the entire base once again. "We won't be unprotected or unarmed."

AnnaChi stepped casually closer and started to adjust the screen onto some new item of interest.

Smiling, Fran placed his hand onto the screen again. Instantly the holographic rock wall was back in place covering the base. With another wave, the viewpoint was back at the Endeavour, the fake rock wall a distant speck ahead of them.

"There will be plenty of time to see it all when we arrive." He smiled defensively at AnnaChi's look of dismay. "I simply wanted to show you just how serious we are about this project. This is critical to the survival of humanity. If this mission fails, so do we all."

Kasey decided to get to the point. "So how about you finally share exactly what this mission is? You mentioned something about gathering more n-mats. How is one ship, no matter how large, going to help?"

"Right to it then?" He nodded several times to himself, then cleared his throat. "Well, this likely won't help either of your fears. However, I am trusting you will find a way to redirect some of that dread towards the threat of the Pattern instead of the Federation. At least for now."

AnnaChi watched as a naval base passed slowly by. "It's hard to imagine more power than what we are seeing here, and you say this is not even the military nexus? Well, you may as well shatter our delusions further."

Fran watched them both cautiously for a moment

before he continued. "That ship, the Pathfinder, it's the first of its kind. We are loosely calling it a jump ship. It uses the same principle as the gates, but there is no need for the actual gates as the ship itself *is* the gate. We can jump anywhere within a thousand light-years. Well, that's the theory anyway; it really hasn't been fully tested."

"Insanity," she gasped. "How do you know where you are exiting?"

"That may be something better explained by the engineers…"

"And if there is already something where we are exiting?"

"That, my dear, would be an issue—but not as big of one as you would think. Like the star-cruisers, we will bring along our own chunk of spacetime. But, instead of dragging it with us, we will take the spacetime and the ship directly through the hole itself."

"But there is still an issue?" she asked.

"Well, yes. Speed. We won't know what is in front of us, so if we are moving out of sync with the destination system, we may have some unwanted collisions." He shrugged. "It's a small risk that we should be able to mitigate based on collected data."

AnnaChi rolled her shoulders and faced Fran directly. "You mean, you would need to trust thousand-year-old light for your data?"

Kasey watched their arguments with feigned interest. As amazing as it was, it all just made his decision that much harder.

There were only two options from his point of view—either stay away from the Federation's doings, or get involved in this new mess. It was his way, and his parent's when they were alive, to keep as far out of the Federation's control as possible. He had needed to abandon much of that mindset to survive, both mentally and physically, since joining the Farpoint colony expedition.

Now that the fight for the Trias System was over, he had the freedom to make his own choices about his future. Yet, instead of choosing freedom from the Federation, they wanted him to join the crew of an experimental ship for some imagined quest. A quest that could somehow be the key to save humanity from extinction—someday. Maybe.

It was a fool's errand as far as Kasey was concerned. Still, it would solve an issue that had been worrying him more since the war ended—AnnaChi.

He could tell she had been getting bored with their mining operations, and that troubled him. She still loved the prospecting, the exploring, yet her need for that adventure had effectively ended shortly after the gates had been activated. Federation crews were now scouring every unclaimed meter of land for more of the precious n-mats. Even if Kasey could locate a worthy mining location, the land claim would be held up indefinitely until the Federation crews got around to reviewing the land themselves and accepting the claim. Yet, AnnaChi tiring of the prospecting was not the worst or it.

He could see it in her eyes; even now as she argued with Mad Fran, the admiral, a man who she considered one of her closest friends. A spark had kindled during the final fight with the Patternist and Cassian. He watched that spark growing since the war ended, and she had no outlet. In the months since returning to Belrothi, she had been involved in several fights with both miners and with patrons of "Sarsaparilla"—Fran's saloon. She needed a change and maybe, just maybe, this trip would be it.

The argument intensified as they drew closer to the destination. Kasey knew he would need to stop their bickering soon—they needed a distraction.

Swiftly, he slid forward between the two and nodded towards the illusionary rock wall they would soon breach. "A ship that big must have a decent size hangar aboard?"

Fran seemed relieved at the new line of questions. "Well, yes. The Pathfinder actually has several. The design is partially based on an old carrier model before gravity plating was developed. We needed the shape for the gate mechanics to work smoothly but the configuration also worked well for us. We will be bringing a small fleet with us, both for protection and research."

"So, if we agree to come along," he glanced at AnnaChi with a slight smile before continuing, "we could bring our own ships?"

"Ah, well certainly," Fran replied. "In fact, it may be a good idea to have some civilian ships with us. Diplomacy sometimes needs a softer starting position than a military vessel."

AnnaChi spoke up, her tone almost down to normal, "Diplomacy? You believe we will encounter new races on this trip?"

"Unlikely, but it is not out of the realm of possibilities. No, I was referring to the other Farpoint colonies. I never got to explain that part... Our primary mission, for now, is to locate the other Farpoint colonies and get their gates online."

Kasey did not know how to respond to the revelation. All the events that had occurred since the Abscond had brought them to the Trias System churned through his thoughts. Was it likely that other Farpoint colonies could be facing similar threats? Hell, he thought, it was extremely probable that the Cassian and Patternist were attempting the same kinds of takeovers they had at Trias, or already had.

"How long has it been since the other colonies

entered their systems? We could be too late to be any help."

"Well, perhaps. Yet, most of the Farpoint launches were timed to land within the same standard-year timeframe. A few were much earlier, and several were quite late launching. We had estimated that most colonies would have their gates opened by now—even our Trias System was six months behind the calculated average, although we had good reason to be."

"That small fleet you mentioned we would have along?" Kasey asked.

"More than enough to handle a threat similar to what we faced in Trias." Fran's tone became sullen. "Although, we have no reason to believe the Cassian would be there as well. We believe what we saw at Trias was a major undertaking for them. We are still trying to work out how they pulled it all off. The current theory is that the Abscond carried a beacon that notified a Cassian hive in the Trias cluster of space when we arrived."

AnnaChi shook her head at the thought. "It seems very unlikely. I mean, could there really be so many of them that this random system would also be within their territories? Wouldn't that go against the Pattern?"

"You know," Kasey pointed out, "all we ever encountered in Trias were their orb ships. When the Federation pushed them from the Earth cluster, was there a home world or something? I remember nothing of their origin."

Fran looked them both over slowly. "Perhaps all this questioning is what places you two in so much trouble." He reached up, placing his hand on the screen to again remove the rock façade. "We are nearly there, and I need to prepare the Endeavour, so I will make this the last answer. There was no home world we ever found, nor any indication they ever landed on a world other than to harass humanity—but there were large home-ships, or motherships. The motherships we located were all destroyed, or self-destructed if they were going to lose a battle, so we know very little. We always assumed it was an invasion fleet of some kind."

"Admiral," a voice rang out, "docking protocols have been transmitted."

Kasey watched Fran return to the command chair before turning back to the star-shaped base before them. Not for the first time, he wondered just how long the man had been around. He spoke as if he had been at the events themselves, not just stating historical knowledge. It was a curiosity for another day, and maybe none of his business. For now, Kasey's attention was drawn to the growing view of the base.

The four arms of the complex seemed to be copies of one another, all working in concert towards their shared project. Each was lined with warehouses, workshops, and assembly plants feeding the ship construction area. The Pathfinder itself seemed more alive with activity than their previous view of it had shown. Workers, bots, and drones could be seen laboring on nearly every section of the ship as the Endeavour glided ever closer to the yard's docking port.

Kasey could not see how such a massive project as the Pathfinder could be finished anytime soon, but Fran had insisted their mission would be underway in just a few more weeks. The clock was ticking. A decision would need to be made soon.

The Endeavour came to a stop without any of the normal bumps or sounds of the smaller ships Kasey was accustomed to. An officer appeared a moment later to escort them to the departure port. Kasey felt his anxiety return as they were led through a maze of pressurized tunnels. Heart pounding, he tried to push the unwanted thoughts away, but the effort only brought more worries.

He nearly jumped as he felt a warm hand slip into his

own. AnnaChi was there, smiling as if there was not a care in the world. His darkness diminished instantly, relaxed under her presence. Somehow, she was always able to make the worries of the verse disappear.

Her grip on him tightened as a large hatchway parted, revealing the blue-gray siding of the Pathfinder ahead. He could feel AnnaChi's excitement as they exited the hatch. His own remaining fears wilted as he took a deep breath, breathing in the metallic-tinged air, preparing himself to behold a new breed of space faring vessels.

CHAPTER TWO

The air surged past them in bursts.

The small open-topped skimmer rushed them down the viewing platform overlooking the Pathfinder. At the halfway point, nearly a kilometer down the ship, the skimmer slowed at the first opened section that was not also under construction. As they got closer, a crane carrying a fighter emerged from the chamber wall, taking its cargo into the opening.

AnnaChi leaned across Kasey to get a better look. "Must be a hangar for that fleet Fran mentioned."

As the hangar came into full view, Kasey felt a wave of relief—Fran's claim had not exaggerated. In addition to the flights of fighters currently being loaded, there were twenty light cruisers spread throughout the launch area, all positioned for quick deploy. In the center of it all, a heavy cruiser, comparable to the Endeavour in size, was nestled longways. A command vessel for the hangar's squadron. To either side of the squad, the hangar was lined with open platforms and maintenance bays that appeared to go deep into the ship's interior.

As the skimmer pulled away, Kasey considered the

size and shape of the hangar. Peering above and below the opening, he nudged AnnaChi and pointed. "I would bet there are four of those hangars ringing this section."

"Agreed, and this is the third section marked like that so far." She indicated several odd markings on either side of the hangar doors. "I doubt they are all the same kinds of ships, but even the hangars in this section alone have more firepower than Fran had at the gate battle. If there are more hangar sections like this, it will be a substantial force."

"Not to mention the Pathfinder itself," Kasey agreed. "There were quite a few panels mirroring the particle cannon ports we saw near the helm, and I quit counting missile ports. The ship itself is quite well armed."

They counted two more of the marked hangars before reaching the engine section.

Kasey anxiously exited the skimmer and scrambled to the edge of the platform.

"Something of interest?" AnnaChi asked as she caught up.

"Well, no. I expected, uh, I am not sure… This is a basic thruster configuration; big, but nothing special at all. However it is that she manages to jump, it must be internal."

"Yeah. I had wondered about the shape of the Pathfinder after Fran mentioned it. Look," she pointed to several hatches, "every single hole in this thing is covered. Nothing extends more than a few meters from the hull, not even the shield emitters."

"You think the hull itself is some form of gate?"

"Maybe. I hope we find out once this tour is over and we get inside. Fran is overly free with his information. He really expects that we will accept the invite to come along."

"Yea…" Kasey tried to hide an unbidden smile, but she noticed.

"You want to go!" she stammered accusingly.

"I have some reservations, a lot of them, but honestly I care more about what you think of all this. If I wasn't here, would you go?"

"Hah, if you weren't here, I wouldn't know this even existed."

"That's not the point, and I am not sure it's true. Fran knows your worth. Hell, he likely knows more about you than you think. I guess I am asking if you feel all of this is worth it? Is it worth risking your life for some experiment that may only serve to give the Federation more power than they already have?"

She stared quietly at the Pathfinder for a moment, then turned to face him. "Long before I met you, I risked a lot more for a whole lot less. Hell, I never planned to survive this long. I shouldn't have."

"I am very glad you did."

She smiled. "Me too. When I left that life behind, I promised myself I wouldn't let anyone convince me to take such risks again."

"We have taken plenty of gambles over the past year..."

"True, but they were of my own choosing."

"Even the gate battle? We could have left, you know."

"No, we couldn't have. Angry at him as I am, Fran is a good friend. There really wasn't any other decision for me."

"And now? I don't think Admiral Francis really needs our help with this new mission. He has all the support he needs here."

"True I suppose. I guess it comes down to the importance of this mission. The fact that he has so much support is telling. They don't put this much into an operation without cause. Even with as much as he is telling us, there is a lot more he isn't."

"So, you would go then?"

"Hypothetically, I think so... I mean, it's a flipping jump ship! But I do want to see more of this ship before deciding for real. Although, I won't go unless you genuinely want too as well."

He nodded in thought. "Let's get on with the tour then, shall we?"

The two-kilometer return trip passed in thoughtful silence.

Boarding the Pathfinder reminded Kasey of entering the Abscond back when he first joined the Farpoint project. They were scanned, verified, and decontaminated, yet, instead of being led to stasis pods, they were assigned a guard detail and ushered towards the bridge.

Every crewman wore the uniform of the ship, deep-green and trimmed in dark red. The uniform contrasted the Endeavour's blue and gray nicely. As they entered the bridge, their escort guards snapped to attention, waited only a moment to be acknowledged, and then left.

These were fresh recruits Kasey decided, as he watched the bridge crew run drills on the new equipment. Fran's crew on the Endeavour were formal, but Kasey had never seen them act in such a strict fashion as this crew.

AnnaChi nudged him and nodded towards a far corner. Fran was in a heated conversation with a woman who appeared to be the Pathfinder's captain based on her uniform. Kasey had planned to wait until Fran was ready for them, but AnnaChi had no such reservations as she strode forward with Kasey in tow.

A crewman stepped forward to stop them halfway across the room, but AnnaChi simply sidestepped around an oversized tactical station forcing the man to backtrack. By the time he caught up, a couple of the

Endeavour's crew had moved forward as if to stop her. The green-uniformed man slowed, knowing she would be stopped, then began to run as she walked right between the Endeavour's crewman who made no attempt to stop her.

Kasey felt a stern hand drop onto his shoulder just as AnnaChi stopped a few meters short of Fran.

"Who the hell are these civilians on my deck!" The captain had evidently noticed the newcomers.

"My deck, actually," Fran stated calmly as he turned to face them. "Miss Acosza and Mr. Robinson, my personal advisers. Please meet Captain Grimt QuTan. She will be commanding the Pathfinder for me."

The captain pursed her lips, looking past Kasey to the man still gripping his shoulder. "You may return to your station Mr. Suntkre."

"Testing the troops, Miss Acosza?" Fran smiled widely, leaving little doubt he was pleased with the interruption.

"A bit on the green side, but they seem motivated," AnnaChi reported as if on cue.

"I was just inquiring on their status myself. The captain here tells me the crew are all that can be spared at the moment."

"I take it they are fully trained with excellent marks, but fast-tracked with no actual combat experience?" AnnaChi scoffed.

Fran pivoted slowly, facing the frowning Grimt, "Captain QuTan?"

"Admiral, the description is accurate," looking as if she was biting back every word, she continued slowly, "however, I see a lot of promise in these men and woman. They know what they are about, they will serve us well. The navy is in the midst of largest recruitment ever undertaken within the Federation and we have gathered the best thus far."

"Mr. Robinson, I would value your thoughts." Fran's face had taken on a thoughtful expression.

Kasey glanced at AnnaChi, who nodded back with encouragement.

"Well, I uh, truly, I mean no disrespect." He swallowed hard, before going on. "I am sure this crew will be fine to fly the Pathfinder—however, I don't believe they are prepared to handle the combat stations, or tactical during an actual combat. At the very least, we need veterans leading in these areas until others can prove themselves."

"Any disagreement with this assessment, Captain QuTan?"

She blanched. "No Sir, we would welcome the experience. Shall I…"

"No, thank you, Captain. I already have personnel in mind. Commander Flair will see to it—expect some company in a few days."

"Yes, sir." She was obviously still annoyed, yet she appeared thoughtful as well.

"Very good then. You are doing a fine job here, Captain. Please keep it up."

The woman seemed pleased to be dismissed and hastily retreated.

Following the admiral from the bridge, they soon entered the ship's main concourse. The area was far more open than Kasey imagined a military ship would be.

Fran answered his thoughts before he could ask. "This section leads to the main housing area for both the ship and the first four combat flights. They need to get along with each other if they are to work together efficiently. See there," he pointed to an overly obvious tavern located between two large hallways that curved off into the distance, "the left corridor splits off to each of the four flight's housing areas, the other to the ship crew's—helping everyone to come into contact often. You will see this arrangement repeated throughout Pathfinder."

"Sounds like drama waiting to happen," Kasey remarked.

"Perhaps... But, useful as well and not just to let them blow off steam."

"Sounds entertaining," AnnaChi noted, a bit too eagerly, "but I assume you will be monitoring for problems, see who the group leaders are, that kind of thing?"

"Yes, exactly that. Flair has a team for that very purpose. We will know the good and bad leaders quickly. I would prefer they all find ways to get along. Got to hope for the best..."

"...and plan for the worst," Kasey finished.

"Precisely."

"So, where to next?" AnnaChi asked. "Or are we stopping for a drink?"

Ignoring the suggested drink, Fran picked up the pace. When they caught up, he pointed ahead at one of the four pathways the concourse split into near the end of the section. "We are heading to flight-two to meet Captain Trounic of the Amberwitch. Then on to flight-three and four. The other flights will be coming aboard in the next week or two, after their hangars are completed."

"What of flight-one?" Kasey inquired.

"My Endeavour will fill that role, along with many of the light cruisers that survived the battle at the gates."

"You plan to command the Endeavour as well as the Pathfinder?"

"Well, yes and no. I'll go where I am needed, but both ships will have their own captains once we head out."

By the time they finished, the Pathfinder crews were

changing shifts and the taverns were winding up for dinner. Sitting for a quick meal in the admiral's quarters was awkward for Kasey at first, but once AnnaChi and Fran began arguing the finer points of what jump travel would mean, the atmosphere felt more normal.

"So," Fran began as the meal finished, "I understand the Lodestar will be finished with repairs in the next few days. Should I have it brought directly here, or should it be delivered to your home on Belrothi?"

Knowing the loosely veiled question would come with the meal did not prepare Kasey to answer it. Feeling AnnaChi stir, he turned towards her hoping for an answer. The look he found mirrored his own questions. Her eyes lost focus for a moment, and when they returned a message flipped across his mimic interface.

"I am good either way—this flight plan is all yours to call."

She smiled and looked away. He looked back to Fran, who was ignoring them as he contemplated a glass of sherry.

Kasey wondered how he ever thought this man was just a bartender. "How long, and what are your expectations for us?"

"Thirty to forty days and two destinations. The first will be to a Federation base on the far edge of the Earth Prime cluster, slightly under three hundred light-years from the Gemini Nexus. We will drop off a set of gates and…"

"Hold on." AnnaChi looked down, closing her eyes as she breathed in deeply. "We will be carrying gates?"

"Well, of course… Last section before main propulsion. The new class-F gates will be far smaller than the class-A gates we have in the Trias System, and maybe one tenth of the range. But if the tests are successful, we will deploy many more to help all the clusters expand quickly."

"Clusters..." it was Kasey's turn to interrupt, "you mean the Trias System?"

"Right, the Trias System will be the focal system of a new system-cluster that we will expand outwards as quickly as possible. Once we are able to ferry more of the class-F gates to nearby systems, a gate nexus of sorts will form in the Trias System, and we will add others as needed. Each Farpoint colony will do the same—this *is* why we spread them out so far from each other."

Kasey felt overwhelmed and pushed back from the table to stand up, but flopped back down into the seat before making it fully upright. He glanced around the room as he ordered his thoughts the best he could.

"So," he started, "Belrothi, our home, will be in the damn center of all this?"

"Well, I... Yes, that is highly likely. It is the only habitable planet in the Trias System right now. If these smaller gates work of course..."

"I see."

Fran shook his head sadly. "Look, I know this is not how you expected the colony to work out. But this is how we save humanity. We need to evolve—we need to expand—we need to get ourselves as far ahead of the Pattern as quickly as possible, or we don't survive."

They sat in silence for several minutes. His frustration was getting the better of him, but he realized AnnaChi was fuming next to him and her anger was building. It would not help for his own frustration to compound hers further. Taking a deep breath, he shrugged to himself. If it came to it, they could move to another world, and others after that if they wanted. In the long run, it would not matter as long as they were together.

He looked back at Fran. "Fine. So, we take this outpost a set of these smaller class-F gates. Then what?"

"Well," he smiled again, "once we are satisfied that the jump drive and new gates work as designed, we head to the Trias System and then jump to the Zyta system, which was one of the earliest Farpoint expeditions to reach their destination. At least, they should have."

"I assume we are taking them enough n-mats to activate their gates?"

"Precisely. As I am sure you have already guessed, the navy will be increasing their need for more of your n-mats supply immediately. If, that is, the new gate tests are successful."

"No way around that, I assume? Would be fine by me if they found another source."

"I doubt it, son. You really hit the motherload. The chances of so much mercury-based n-mats or any other dense materials is extremely low. Or so I am told. Honestly, I am concerned due to that very point. The researchers are pushing to have access to the n-mats mine to try and understand how it evolved. Hell, everyone wants it for one reason or another. The absolute best way to keep them off your backs is to get another Farpoint colony mining n-mats immediately. That is part three of our mission. I want you to help them locate the n-mats in the Zyta system, if they haven't already found some."

"And, if that is not possible?"

"Then I will do what I can, my friend. But frankly, it is going to be more difficult the longer it takes to find another decent source. Many are already guessing that you or Darnell are involved in some way."

"Not a lot of good news for us, Fran. Anything positive from all this?"

"Credits are positive, right?" He looked from Kasey to AnnaChi and back. "Look, a lot is going to change very quickly. You are going to make a fortune several times over on your n-mats, and you will both be paid well for this consulting mission. Take the credits. If Belrothi and the Trias System get too much activity, then you find a new system to call home. I know you can afford to put backup plans in place now, so do it. If you need my help, just ask. But come with me and help make a difference."

Kasey looked at AnnaChi, who smiled back confidently and reached for his hand, before nodding.

Taking her hand, he looked back at Fran. "Okay. We are on board. Do we need a consulting company now?"

"Excellent!" Fran slapped his hands together loudly. "No. You don't actually need a company, but it is better if you do. We could run the consulting under Phoenix Mining or that new company the n-mats are being filtered through, what did you name it again?"

"Red Rock Enterprises," Kasey answered.

"Good, yes. So maybe use Red Rock as an intermediary for now, or start a new business if that works for you both."

"Run it under Red Rock for now. How are we going to move such an increase in n-mats quietly?"

"Simple mechanics. I have two heavy-equipment maintenance services that are now servicing nearly all the valley's independent operations. They underbid and over deliver on their services, so it benefits everyone. We even made arrangements for the old local services to get better offers in other areas. In any case, their shuttles are set up to handle n-mats and deliver them to the Sarsaparilla, where another team takes them to a small mine site that no one wanted. That mine is my official contact."

"Simple, huh? We truly do appreciate all the effort to keep us out of this."

"Well, don't thank me yet. If we don't find another source soon, we are going to be on shaky ground."

"And if it all fails?"

"Not if, when. This is a basic business delaying tactic. Eventually, it will fail if they look hard enough. If it does, it will lead them right back to Belrothi Copper and eventually to Phoenix Mining and your new Red Rock company."

"Won't that affect your position in the navy?"

"Some, yes, but ultimately I am under a nondisclosure agreement with Belrothi Copper, and I have ensured a much-needed n-mats source for the navy, so they won't push it far. It would be a bigger issue if we were withholding the n-mats or selling to others. Still, I will deal with it either way. The important thing now is to start increasing the supply and keep everyone happy."

"Well," Kasey murmured, "we can do that," he raised his voice to a normal level, "but we *all* need a longer-term plan."

"Never hurts to plan ahead, so I will toss this tidbit of consideration at you now. If things go as I believe they will, the Federation as a whole will be expanding faster than we have resources to handle." He paused to look them both in the eyes carefully. "The need for agriculture, mining, services of all kinds, hell, you name it, they are all going to grow exponentially faster than anyone will be able to keep up with. You two are just getting your feet wet in the mining game, but if you want to expand that business, the time to do so is coming—quickly."

AnnaChi sat up straight, raising an eyebrow. "So, too many colonies, not enough starting resources?"

"Right. Gates and jumping ships will give unprecedented access to new systems to colonize. New colonies will be stalled without available resources but will likely try to start anyway since the journey is only weeks instead of months or years. The number of gates being called for, along with all the ships, stations, and defense platforms it will take—well, it is a truly astronomical number of resources and manpower for that alone."

"Okay," she leaned forward, "so it is going to be more important than ever for mining operations to be in the best locations as quickly as possible?"

"Correct."

She looked to Kasey. "If we could organize some prospecting trips to find and claim decent resources, then sell the information and the claims, it would be worth a good bit to those operations, and speed up how quickly they could get running and be profitable."

"And?"

"And we get to explore lots of new worlds. Duh! Oh, and we need to talk about the bard ATVs, they are in serious need of updating. A lot has changed in the last thirty years back in the Earth cluster. Not as much as I expected, but still a lot."

"Sounds like fun to me." He looked at Fran. "Maybe we can start in this Zyta system we are heading to?"

"Perhaps, but their colony plan was based on automated space-based mining platforms for the most part, so normal claims won't be worth what you would see elsewhere. I will send you the details, but they took enough planetary elevator systems and automated mining platforms to harvest what they need from low gravity planets, asteroids, and moons. There is a habitable planet there, but most colonists had planned to live on and expand a group of luxury stations."

Kasey blinked several times. "That kind of starting expense could have funded several colonies…"

"Indeed, but credits get spent on the whims of those who have them, not those who need them. Anyway, our guess is that they never found n-mats because their mining methods are mainly brute-force automated strip-mining. We know they have the equipment to harvest n-mats, the Federation supplied it, so our job will be to locate potential sites so they can relocate mining platforms to dig and process it."

"So, we will still be prospecting on the habitable world, right?"

"Yes, that's all we are planning time for on this trip. Keep in mind, the mission is mainly to test out the jump ship and get the Zyta system's gates connected to the nexus network, if they still exist. If you are able to locate n-mats, there will be a bonus for you, but you likely won't be claiming the location for long, nor will the navy, unless the colony decides not to mine it. The Federation wants the rights to go to a mining company that can work the site as soon as possible. So any potential n-mats rich areas you do claim will need to be sold or turned over to the local administration before we depart. However, if you locate other resources and the colony is still offering claim rights to purchase, then you are welcome to make a claim. Acceptable?"

"Works for now, I suppose," Kasey answered before AnnaChi could argue. "Can you get us all the known data on that planet? And does it have a name?"

"I'll have all the colony and system data sent to you both." Fran looked away for a few seconds as he looked up the data. "The habitable planet you will be exploring is called Bendek. It is actually a bit light on gravity at around seventy percent navy standard. So, most populated buildings are likely using gravity plating in living areas to maintain human norms. You may want to add some to your vehicles. We won't be there long enough to worry about side effects like bone density or muscle loss, but it is worth being prepared. Besides, I can tell you from personal experience that going back to normal gravity after spending time on such planets is a pain to adjust to all at once. Standard procedure for navy is to increase gravity for non-essential ship areas for any teams going dirtside prior to their stay to help offset any issues with bones and joints. We won't be deploying a mobile barracks, but any ship we do land will have adjusted gravity protocols for anyone bunking onboard."

Kasey nodded and shrugged, having had plenty experience with variable gravity situations and the problems they can cause.

He pushed his plate aside as coffee was served. "Alright, so what else should we consider for this mission? Do you have equipment and personnel to run the mineral testing, or should we bring a team of our own?"

"We have experienced mining teams and techs to handle the grunt and lab work. Find them a spot to test and move on. They will report all finding to myself and you two, even if it contains n-mats. Learn what you can along the way."

"Honestly, I am not sure how much help I will be. I have only been lucky. Darnell is the one you should recruit for this, he is the one who located the first of them, I was just there as the pilot."

"I believe you were more involved than you think. Just do what you can, we will deal with the rest."

CHAPTER THREE

Kasey gripped the armrest tightly as the searing fireball surrounded the ship.

Atmosphere burned around them for several seconds more before AnnaChi sighed contentedly and adjusted the aerobraking maneuver to a less dramatic entrance into Belrothi skies. Kasey faked a yawn as she turned towards him with a wink.

"Are we in a hurry?" he asked after recovering his composure.

"Hurry? I don't think so... Why do you ask?"

"I was just wondering if I should send sector control a heads-up that we are not in need any assistance now, or perhaps we should just wait for their comms?"

"Loosen up. Who doesn't enjoy a decent reentry? Just tell them we are testing out new hull polymers if they ask."

It was true enough. The navy had done a proper job of repairing the Cintian, including a new hull skin. The fact that it had been nearly a month ago was simply a minor detail.

His thoughts were interrupted as she cut the Cintian's

thrusters and let the ship free fall for several thousand meters. It would have been more impressive had the planet below not been covered in darkness. While the ship systems did do a good job of presenting the view as if it were daylight, the feeling of an impending crash was somehow diminished. Or perhaps he was just growing comfortable with AnnaChi's flying.

Waiting far longer than Kasey thought was necessary, she pushed the atmospheric thrusters slowly to their maximum, bringing the Cintian arcing into a parallel flight path directly into their valley. Home.

It wasn't long before a large pond appeared in the distance and Kasey settled in to watch AnnaChi deftly land the Cintian on the small, snow-covered pad next to their lodge retreat below.

Darnell had been using the small home since the gate battle. Kasey and AnnaChi had built it to get away from everything and enjoy the surrounding valley when they needed a change of scenery. They had never intended to use it as a guest house, but now it had become necessary. The lodge hid a secret. One they had needed a trusted friend to oversee.

Nestled in the back of an exceptionally large, but typical, storage shed was the entrance to their caverns. Deep within the caverns lay pools of precious n-mats. The negatively massed liquid mercury that allowed for wormholes to be stabilized into gateways through spacetime. The only natural material that repelled gravity instead of falling towards it.

Their actual home was just a short skimmer ride up the mountain, where they enjoyed picturesque views of the countryside and the valleys where their copper mining operations functioned. Kasey would have preferred to go straight to the main house and the warm bed that waited there, but he wouldn't be able to sleep until he handled some of the many issues needing to be settled before the mission with Fran.

Once the ship was powered down, the small lodge became a beacon of light in the dark night, spilling light out across the snow and frozen pond. He raised an eyebrow at a small shuttle parked in the drive next to Darnell's own ground-based skimmer. Darnell did not have a pilot's license for even a planet-side shuttle, so the man apparently had company.

As they opened the hatchway, the ship's interior light poured across the retreat's porch, revealing a row of gargoyle shaped figures perched neatly at the far end— with the exception of one creature hanging upside down. Three of the figures sat nearly half a meter high, but most were less than a quarter that size.

"Looks like we have a welcoming committee." Kasey pointed. "Ever wonder how they know it's us and not someone else?"

"Maybe the Cintian's distinct sound?"

"Maybe…"

Flurries of orange, blue, and green feathers shot into the entryway and flocked around the couple's legs. Molly went directly to AnnaChi, Orange to Kasey, while Mawk practically danced between them both. After a few moments, Mawk, the green male atoss, shot towards the hatch and whistled a piercing call into the night air.

A new flurry of colors inundated the entryway as a swarm of small atoss rushed in from the cold. They were shy at first, but once Kasey or AnnaChi turned their attention to any one of them, it instantly rushed in for scratching and tickles. Each seemed to have their own personality, but seemed to obey the elder three's clicks and whistles willingly.

A smaller than normal black atoss with golden eyes was the only exception. It had arrived last, took the longest to coax forward in greeting, and seemed to ignore the adult atoss' commands the first several times.

After they all had been properly greeted, Kasey produced a platter filled with meaty chunks, which was set upon voraciously by all the atoss. The small black atoss gobbled just a few pieces then looked to the open entryway and shot out into the night. A few of the others watched after it for a moment then returned to the food until it was gone.

One by one the atoss departed back into the cold night. Orange and Molly were the last to leave.

AnnaChi stared into the darkness after Molly left. "I am not looking forward to being away from Molly for so long when we leave on this mission."

"Maybe we could bring them? Orange seems fine with ship travel most of the time."

"They won't go this time, Molly won't anyway. Her attention was focused on the babies. I don't think they will join us again until the little ones are more mature."

Kasey thought about that for a bit and frowned. "I didn't want to be away from the valley so long. When we set this all up, I assumed we would only be away a few days at a time, a week at most," he sighed, "I don't think Fran is going to allow us that peace."

"If he is right about the Pattern... Well, we cannot just walk away from it all. It will catch up with us, and everyone, eventually."

"If he is right, sure. But that is just speculation. He may have earned his nickname honestly."

"Mad Fran? Ha! Maybe time will tell."

"Perhaps... Prospecting trips to new systems and worlds are too tempting to pass up anyway. So even without Fran moving us around like pawns, we are going to be away from the valley a lot more than we had expected."

"All those new systems and planets—who wouldn't be fascinated?"

"I am game if you are, but we need a better plan than

just running off for months at a time. We need to be smart about how we do this."

"So, wait," she looked at him closely, "you have an idea already, don't you?"

"The beginning of one, sure. A week in the dark leaves lots of time to think. I need time to work through this one before sharing it. Hell, I am not even sure it is possible, let alone feasible."

"Big idea huh? Fine. Well, for now, we need to get Darnell squared away. I am looking forward to being home in my shop for a few days to play."

Darnell was at the door waving them inside as they approached. In the entryway they found four men shaking hands and preparing to leave. Two were obviously miners and apparently had not changed clothing from the day's work, but Kasey could not place the others.

"Welcome home Mr. Robinson and Miss Acosza," Darnell stated with more formal pomp than Kasey had ever heard him use before. "I didn't realize you would be back today."

Kasey knew damn well Darnell was aware they would be arriving today and stopping by, but he was inclined to play along. "Business has a way of changing our schedules when we least expect it. Speaking of schedules, I hope we haven't interrupted." He gestured to the men who were now paying close attention to him and AnnaChi.

"Not at all. Mr. Winslow here," he introduced the taller of the men who stepped forward to shake hands, "and Mr. Danbury," the other non-miner stepped forward, "both own operations down in our copper mine claims. Like many of the operations, they have invested significantly to keep their operations functioning throughout the winter. With the increasing demands from the colony, shutting down would be throwing credits away."

Kasey read the room again with the new information and realized the other men were the foremen from each mine. "Makes good sense. What is the issue?"

"Water. Despite the snow and ice everywhere, we are in a bit of a drought. Their two claims share a series of retaining ponds that are quickly drying up. The tailings ponds are more mud than water now."

"I see. And do we have a solution?"

"A host of them actually, but the quickest would be to transport a good amount of water from the lake further down the valley—which, as I am sure you are aware, is also on your land. We have a request into Belrothi Department of Environmental Conservation, but we expect a positive response. What we really need now is your permission to use the lake's water and then determine an efficient way to transport it."

"I see. We can add this to our discussion tonight, but let's see what the department request comes back with before we commit to an answer. I would also like to look at longer-term solutions. This won't be the only dry season before the valley is mined out."

"Very good, sir. Now, if you and Miss Acosza want to make yourselves comfortable, I'll see these men on their way."

Kasey found a carafe of coffee and snacks set up in the main room. Holographic displays of the valley and claims were set up around the room in stark contrast to the log-cabin look of the lodge. It took longer than he expected for Darnell to return, but when he did, he was not alone.

Perched on his shoulder was the small, black atoss who seemed so antisocial earlier.

"Sorry for the delay, Jasper needed some attention but wouldn't come in until the others had left."

"Jasper?"

"My little friend here. He deserves a snack after the guard duty he has been performing. Wouldn't come in with those men in here, but I know he has been watching in the windows since they arrived."

"We are glad to see you made a friend." AnnaChi reached out giving little Jasper a playful scratch. "Has he been hanging around here long?"

"Just the last few weeks that I noticed. Stops by a few times a day." He gave them both a thoughtful look. "I know your Orange is special, but until I met this guy, I didn't realize just how special. They are not just some wild animal or pet, are they?"

"Hard to know," Kasey mused, "but they are certainly the most intelligent creatures I have ever encountered."

Darnell grunted a chuckle at that. "Yeah well, I have seen a lot of intelligent animals in my time too, but none of them could make me think about raw fish with a single look…"

Kasey and AnnaChi looked at each other for a long moment.

"So," Darnell continued, "what is the deal with these buggers? I can't find a single reference to them in the planet's environmental registry, nor anything like them."

Kasey felt suddenly hot under the scrutiny, "You didn't report them, did you?"

"No, of course not. Not my business, but I would like to know more about this guy at least."

"Alright, well, keep this all to yourself. You remember how I mentioned going back to Lithose for that mining equipment, right? Well, I found Orange still trying to survive there and she brought Molly and Mawk along when I offered a ride off that dead planet. As far as I know, they are the only ones left. We—humans—destroyed their home. They needed a new home, and this is it. The ecosystem will need to adjust, and I am sorry about that… I am aware of how big an issue that can be. It was my choice and my fault if it causes problems, but I won't regret it."

"I get it, and no worries. I am sure some groups will argue about it someday, but saving a species like this is far more important than losing a few lesser species, if that even happens. If these buggers are as intelligent as I think they are, they won't hunt or produce beyond an area's capability."

AnnaChi shrugged at them both. "Agreed, but I think it is more complicated than that. They will eventually expand their population and push other species out of their hunting spaces. Same as humans do, I guess. But it doesn't matter anymore. This is now their planet as much as it is ours. Anyone who has an opinion about that will just have to get over it."

"So then," Darnell cleared his throat, "what is it that you wanted to talk with me about? I assume it is important since you needed to talk before even going home."

"It is," Kasey started, "but I suppose it really could have waited. First though, let's talk about Red Rock Enterprises. How are the shipments going?"

"Ah, well that depends on if you enjoy making credits I suppose. The client is asking for double the n-mats shipments we are currently sending out. I have also been informed that the price has increased quite a bit, which I assume you are aware of?"

"It is not unexpected." Kasey smiled. "The increased price was asked for as a means to upgrade the mining process so we could supply more materials faster. Have we already increased our shipments?"

"No, not yet. I wanted your approval first since this is a sensitive business. However, I have stockpiled a few barrels in case you want to start right away."

"Good. Hold out for a little while yet. How are the

new bots doing in the cavern? I really don't want to send anyone down there if we don't need to. Removing all this material is going to cause major safety issues, but we will soon need to mine it many times faster than we currently are."

"The bots are great. They have reinforced all the weak spots in the tunnels already and have started on the main n-mats cavern. Supplying them with enough bracing material is the hard part, but doable without raising too many eyebrows. The cavern will be a real feat to brace since we don't know what kind of problems removing that much upward pressure from a cavern could cause. A large collapse will close this operation down."

"Okay, that would be bad. We need to increase production, but we need to do it without a cave-in. Will bracing that cavern even work?"

"Your guess is as good as mine. To be honest, I am going to need help figuring that out, which is something I wanted to talk to you about."

"That will be difficult, but I can talk to Fran. We can't bring in just anyone."

"Actually, I know someone we can trust already."

"Oh?"

"Sariyn."

"I thought she was staying out of the mining game for now?"

"She was. Mostly due to the Patternist problem. Seems that is over for now. Besides, if you plan to use the n-mats income to increase your own mining businesses, then you absolutely want someone with her skills involved. May be best to bring her in now before she goes looking for work on her own. She will get scooped up by a big company and that will be that. She is one of the best out there you know?"

"Actually, I haven't a clue. I don't know her

background enough to know. But I will admit, based on how the other scientists treated and deferred to her, she seemed top notch. She already knows more about n-mats than any of us do, so that's a huge plus. AnnaChi, any issues if we bring her in?"

"None. If you boys trust her, then I am good. Might be nice to have another woman around."

Darnell clapped his hands, "Perfect, I will get her down here soon as possible. Oh, some other good news, the bots found several other pools of the n-mats while searching the tunnels for weaknesses. They are small but are safer areas to mine out first. I would like to have the bots move some of the pumps to clean them out."

"Do it. Maybe keep away from the main cavern until it can be thoroughly evaluated and braced. How many shipments can we get out of the smaller pools?"

"Several months' worth at least, maybe more."

"Okay, let's wait one week, then send an extra barrel in the following week's shipment, maybe midweek. Two extra the next week, and keep increasing by one barrel each week till we are double the current shipments. I am betting they will want even more before we get to double, but put them off unless they want to pay more."

"Easy enough. Same increase curve if they up the credits?"

"Yep, as long as we can stay out of the main cavern, you can keep scaling up. But I need you to do something else."

"Oh?"

"I need you to start stockpiling as much as you ship out, maybe more. Can the bots handle the increased load?"

"Easily. We can pull ten times what we are now and not strain the systems much. I will want to start stocking spare pumps and pipes as soon as possible though, they are wearing out quickly. Or…"

"Or?"

"Or should I start laying a second supply line before we start maxing out the bots we have now? It would be expensive, but we would have twenty times the capacity we have today, and it would give us a backup system if we needed it."

"Do it." Kasey looked at AnnaChi. "I think it would be best if we keep the stockpile at our house, but we need more space."

She laughed. "You know, I have been thinking I need a larger shop! That tiny corner of the hangar is just not doing it anymore. I can work up a design for an underground storage area under a new building. Although, we really shouldn't rent a builder bot this time—we need something more versatile than the ones in the cavern."

"You have your heart set on one already I assume?"

"Not exactly, but I have seen several up for sale. No one is building anything big right now with the resource issues, so a few builders are available. Not cheap, but if you are building secret rooms, it's best to use your own bots for it."

"Okay. Actually, that may be a good investment. Once the gates are open for travel, we could sell it back for a profit if you want."

He looked back at Darnell and nodded. "Go ahead and start laying the second supply line. Do your best to source materials without drawing attention. Maybe take a look at the copper claims and build another warehouse that we can eventually use for our Phoenix Mining company. Move some unused equipment there. Whatever works to keep eyes off this place."

He gave Kasey a bemused look. "I can handle that. You know we did a lot of misdirection under Reavestone, right? You saw what we went through just to hide the company's search areas and claims? This will be no different for Red Rock's business. Leave it to me."

"Thank you. How is Phoenix Mining doing? Cold weather slowing them down?"

"A bit, yes, but nothing I would worry about. If we plan to do this again in the next cold season then we need to start prep work earlier. Anyway, I spent a lot of time at the mine last week getting some new efficiencies in place. Spent some of your credits too, a lot actually... But the equipment and upgrades will pay for itself by spring. The copper yields are doing well for the cold season. The team is still working out some kinks, but you have a good foreman down there. Come spring, we should start a second team and expand a bit."

"How about Belrothi Copper? Anyone looking to lease more claims?"

"Existing claims have been quiet except for the water issues, all but one has renewed for the next season. There are four offers on the table for new claims. Two that I am taking seriously and will likely approve in the next week. The other two are underbidding. I offered one a lesser claim and the other I am holding out on for another week. We will offer them a lesser claim as well unless they can put up a better bid."

"Who is the one that didn't renew yet?"

"Winslow Corp. You met the owner earlier. I was worried you would be late—it took some doing to make sure they were here when you arrived. Landing the Cintian outside while the meeting was wrapping up made for quite an impression. If we can come through with the water, I am sure he will sign within the week."

"You do know we already have a small pumphouse at the lower lake? We use it to fill the tanks on the ships when we want to offset n-mats. We also have several tanks ready to load as needed, so it won't be an issue. Did you really put in a request with the Department of Environmental Conservation?"

"Yes, I knew about the pump, and no, I didn't send any requests. Actually, you already have the necessary approvals. All I need is for one of you to make a few trips, maybe a couple a day for the next week, and we are set."

AnnaChi laughed. "You really enjoy all this subterfuge, don't you?"

"Life is generally a game, you may as well play to win, dearie. Speaking of which, you two have a game of your own. Have we talked around the point long enough for you to share?"

"Almost." Kasey laughed. "Where are you taking the n-mats shipments to, and do you know where they go next?"

"Hah. The maintenance shed out by the Phoenix Mining equipment yard. I back my skimmer up to an autoloader and leave it while I take the smaller all-terrain out for a property check. By the time I am back, the barrels have been switched for the empties that are stored there. As for who takes them? I am quite sure it's the mechanics you have working across the claims. They seem to have the only access to the building and are around a lot more than they need to be. Plus, they have shuttles to transport it. I assume you already knew all of this?"

"Actually, not all of it. Fran set it up and we are just connecting all the dots. Still, it is about what I expected. Here's the thing. We have a few weeks and then we will be away on a mission with Fran for around a month. It could be longer. Are you good to handle everything while we are gone?"

"Are you asking if I am going to run off the deep end of crazy again?"

"Well, I was more wondering if you wanted the responsibility, now that you have had a proper taste of it all. With spring on the way, it will get busy. But, since you mentioned it, anything on your mind we need to worry about?"

"You do know it ain't crazy if they really are out to get you? Right?" He shook his head and got a serious look on his face, "The Sargani actually helped me a lot with that, to tell the truth. There are still things going on that concern me a great deal... However, I know now that I am not the only one seeing it. I am not sure if that makes sense, but that is about all I can do to explain it to ya. Fact is, I am good. So, go on your mission and leave all this worry to me. Besides, if I am right, Sariyn will be around before you leave. She'll keep me straight."

"Good enough for me. But here is the bigger ask. After this trip, there may be a need to have you along on missions like this, maybe Sariyn too. Of course, to do that we would need very trustworthy people in place here to handle everything you are now. All I can say is that it would deal with mining and prospecting. Is that something you would be interested in doing?"

"Well, it sounds interesting. I would definitely entertain the idea."

"I'll take that as a positive." Kasey smiled. "Keep an eye out for people you would trust here, even for just part of the business. If everything works out, we can make some decisions when we get back."

"Can do. I have some people in mind already, but I will need to delve deeper into their backgrounds."

AnnaChi nodded. "Send us names and we will have Fran's people run checks on them too. He has a lot of connections..."

"That's fine by me. Still, I prefer to test my people personally. A simple task or favor usually works to weed out the potential problems."

"Sounds good. The more people we know that we can trust, the better." Kasey looked at the now-sleeping Jasper. "That includes people we can trust with our atoss friends. I know they are self-sufficient and all, but I would feel a lot better knowing someone was in the area that could and would protect them if needed."

They all looked at each other until Darnell broke the silence. "That could be a lot tougher. Your security system works well enough when someone is not where they are supposed to be, but I don't really know otherwise. I can make sure whoever we pick at least is friendly to Jasper here."

AnnaChi looked up suddenly. "I have an idea!"

CHAPTER FOUR

Kasey landed the Altair at the edge of the tarmac and sat at the helm watching AnnaChi in the distance.

She was directing their new builder bot as it placed the final touches on her shop. She had outdone herself. The new building was large, circular, and rustic at ground level, but above that was a different story. Rising several floors, curving precariously outward, and at the top lip of the curve it changed into a row of leafy outcroppings encircling the structure. Each outcropping was uniquely shaped and reached out nearly three meters from the ledge. Centered atop the building was a trio of domes that were honeycombed with nooks and chambers spiraling up to the top. Roosts for the atoss. To anyone else, the building would be a mild curiosity.

Molly had already taken an interest in the building, swooping in several low passes before finally landing on the apex of a spiraled dome. The top of each spiral had three chambers facing outward from one another. Molly appeared to examine all three and settled into one overlooking the main house.

It was an odd choice Kasey thought. He had assumed

they would prefer a view of the woodlands and valley, but instead it chose a view where AnnaChi was most likely to be found. They were protective creatures, but none had made homes in the nearby forests as far as they had been able to tell, instead choosing areas well-away from the house. Another mystery for another day.

Enough lazing about, he told himself as a blip appeared on his screen. A small vehicle was heading towards the property.

By the time he walked down the Altair's rampway, Darnell and Sariyn had exited the skimmer and AnnaChi had walked over with the builder bot close behind. Jasper appeared from the folds of Darnell's jacket and gave them all a short whistle before flying off.

"Interesting design. Is it ready for the first load?" Darnell jerked his thumb at the skimmer.

"Ready to go," AnnaChi replied, "sending you the building access codes now. Take the skimmer inside and park it in the third bay, then send the second code. Have room for us to ride along?"

"Certainly."

Once they were parked, Darnell looked at AnnaChi. "Codes sent. I am being asked if I want a perimeter check?"

"Set it up to check every time as default."

"Done. Scan is clear. It is saying the building's doors are closing automatically and—done, building is showing a lockdown."

"Good. Wait for it."

There was a slight bump, then the floor of the bay began to descend. After nearly ten meters the lift stopped.

"We can get out here, open the back of the skimmer then press the blue button on the wall panel."

Darnell followed her instructions and watched an autoloader remove the barrels, sending them off on a conveyor before loading new empty barrels in their place.

She waved them over to a small fabricator. "This is set up to keep you well supplied with the custom n-mats barrels for quite a while. The counterweights are empty and will need filled in the cavern."

"No problem, the bots are already taking care of that task. However, Sariyn reckons we will need to double our water storage once we max out our current production, or we will risk outages in another season as dry as this last one. We could always pull from the pond, but..."

Kasey nodded, "You will have access to the builder bot while we are gone, add whatever you need."

Darnell looked thoughtful. "That will do, and we certainly will."

"Good. One thing, try and keep these barrels separate from the others. They use the same schematics, but someone could notice if new barrels are introduced and somehow determine they come from a different stock."

"Got it, no need to invite questions. We can discreetly tag them and allow the bots to keep them separated. So, no problem at all."

"Right, and only the four of us know about this stockpile, so keep it that way. If you need to stop moving barrels here to keep this private, then do so."

Sariyn had been quiet but thoughtful during the exchange. "So, what are you planning for all this material, if you don't mind me asking? Surely not just an investment for after the supply dries up."

Kasey shrugged. "No, not an investment. I am sure other sources will be found eventually and it will be available to the public and eventually get cheaper. No, this stock is for our potential projects. I would rather have it safely here if we decide we need it. There is also the potential that the Federation will demand access to the mine, and I would rather not be cut off."

"Projects huh? How much are you looking to sock away?"

"As much as possible. As long as we can keep the supply going to the navy and not endanger the cavern, I want as much as we can discreetly moved in here. Any luck making the cavern safe?" he asked, trying to change the subject.

"I have some ideas but nothing solid yet. I have a bot using poles to try and map the cavern ceiling, so we have accurate numbers to work with. We will have a workable plan within the week. However, I believe we can do a lot more."

"What do you mean, more?"

"I have been reviewing your maps of the cavern and cave systems. While this may be the only cave system with an opening to the surface, I believe there should be many more in this mountain range. It would take a lot of work, but we could find more deposits."

"There were several other entrances that we had blocked off. Most were small, but I scanned the area thoroughly and closed off any openings I could locate. I only kept this one open in case we needed it. That decision was taken out of my hands, but it could have been worse and—well, the credits are nice."

"Then is there still a reason not to investigate the other cave systems? At least send some bots in and see what can be found."

"I would consider it, sure. But with the scrutiny going on to locate the n-mats, we will need a plausible reason to dig in those locations—not to mention a reason to put a structure there if something worthwhile is found."

"Leave that to us," Darnell interjected, "we may need to spend more of your credits, but we can keep it out of prying eyes."

With their approval, Sariyn continued, "You also

have a lot of mercury you could process in the cinnabar ore itself."

Kasey scrunched his eyebrows in thought. "There is not much more than cinnabar dust in the cavern, and most of that is gone with the mercury we harvested already. I suppose there is a source deeper?"

"Perhaps. The dust had never been tested, has it?"

"Well, no."

"It has now. Strangely enough, the cinnabar is not an n-mats material. I assumed, just as you likely did, that the mercury and cinnabar would both be negative matter, but it is only the mercury. The cinnabar you have seen in the cavern was simply dust covering everything. Right now, I do not understand how it is even possible with what we think we know of how the exotic seam formed or merged with this galaxy. Still, this seems to infer that we were very wrong."

"So... You think there should be cinnabar ore deposits with more n-mats mercury trapped?"

"Absolutely, I have already proven it, in fact. The question is—how far down do we need to dig, and where? The cavern's geothermal springs are problematic but not a showstopper. The smaller pools of n-mats we have found are a much better option, for now anyway. They don't have springs, at least not anymore, and the floor seems to have a high cinnabar content."

"What does all that mean?"

"Well, the point is, we could find a way to process a good deal of the ore and release more n-mats. I am just not sure it is worth doing with such an easy supply already available. But once the mercury pools are drained, it's another source to tap. We can do both at once, to an extent. We would need a lot more manpower and equipment, but I believe it could be more profitable than your copper mines."

Kasey took a moment to ponder Sariyn's revelation,

"I guess that's an option we can think about. Can we get some drill samples from the sites and gauge how much we are looking at?"

"Of course. We will put together a feasibility study once we have all the data. Should have it all in order by the time you two return."

"I... Hold on a minute," he tapped his temple.

A high priority message from Fran had appeared in his mimic interface demanding immediate attention. He heard AnnaChi curse beside him, so she must have gotten the same message and wasn't happy. He read it and let out a breath he did not realize he had been holding.

"Well?" Darnell asked with a smile.

"Looks like our trip has been moved up," he sighed, "AnnaChi and I need to leave here tomorrow..."

"Ah... Well then, we are good here, business-wise. I received a note from Winslow Corp that the retaining ponds are plenty full now and they are back to full capacity. They also indicated their renewal would be sent over soon as well. Now, I just need that builder bot of yours delivered to the lodge so we can start on the additions for Sariyn's cabin and such."

"I really don't need my own place..."

AnnaChi gave a dismissive wave, "You are getting it anyway, so best get on board with the idea. I am sure you may want to put your own touches into the design, so do so. Besides, we are going to need more room at that lodge eventually and we have the bot and the resources, so why not?"

"Okay, fine then." She smiled. "Let's get a move on Darnie! We got things to do, and they need their home back to start packing."

"Fine, fine. You kids need anything done around here while you are gone, just let us know."

"Place generally runs itself, but try and spoil Orange,

Molly, and Mawk once in a while. We are leaving the Altair here in the hangar. No one has access to fly her, but she will let you two on board. It is the safest place in the valley if trouble finds you. I'll send you codes for the estate as well in case you need anything."

"Shouldn't you be taking that ship with you?"

"They have far newer models of the Raven class ships than Altair. We are civilians on this trip and just need civilian ships."

"You were just civilians fighting the last war here too, ya know. Try to stay out of trouble!"

"You have a point there!" He laughed at his friend. "And we have adjusted our view of how a civilian ship should be equipped quite a bit since then. Regardless, Fran also sent a contact you can reach out to, if you need anything out of the norm."

"Need? Like what?"

"Mainly for the businesses. He does own parts of both Belrothi Copper and Phoenix Mining and he has a personal interest in the n-mats. So, if anything seems fishy, his contacts can help. You can take that liberally—I am positive the contact will do everything in their power to solve whatever problem you are facing."

"I am not sure if I should feel comforted or concerned."

"I think that uncertainty is the norm when partnering with Mad Fran. You get used to it."

AnnaChi gave Kasey a funny look, "Are you used to it yet?"

"Not in the least."

As they traveled in the skimmer back up the lift, Kasey shared the images he had taken of Molly settling into the new roost above the shop.

"It's not perfect, but it could be a safer haven for them if they want it," AnnaChi explained proudly. "There is a flowing water source up there too. I honestly don't know if they will use any of it, although it's nice to know Molly is trying it out."

Sariyn consider them, "You know, if you want to keep them close to your home, your bigger issue may be the food sources. I am guessing they already pushed out and replaced the area's previous apex predators. If they reproduce in the same magnitude every year, they will need to spread far out of your lands in just a few years."

"I guess that is not totally unexpected," Kasey said, "but the longer we keep them undiscovered, the better."

"Then your best bet is to create some sort of large scale, semi-contained and controlled rodent breeding areas, and maybe keep the pond well stocked. That may keep more of them close by, but it can have its own set of issues. What you *should* do, is find someone who can understand how bad the ecological impact of introducing them will be."

"And if it is bad?"

"I am surprised you haven't already figured out that answer." She shrugged. "If this gate network pans out how your admiral friend anticipates, you will have access to countless worlds. Surely there will be one where they can thrive and not cause a major problem."

"So, you are saying we need to find an ecologist of some sort?"

"Yes, finding one that will keep this quiet should be your primary goal if you want to protect them in the long term."

"Thank you. I will look into that," he remarked seriously as they got out of the skimmer and said their goodbyes.

AnnaChi leaned against Kasey as the skimmer pulled away. "I like her. She should keep things interesting around here."

"Now if we only had more time to actually be here, that would be great."

"Damn, don't remind me. I had plans to upgrade the bards this week. We will have to install the gravity plating en route, but I thought I would have time to make some other changes."

"I know what you mean. They are likely in need of a lot of maintenance as it is too. At least the world will be lower gravity. That will ease the wear and tear a bit."

"You know, our balance sheet is looking quite healthy right now. How about we pick up a new set of bards and move the scanners over to the new ones on the way. Then I can tear down and rebuild the old ones in our down time on this trip."

"I thought you wanted to wait and get newer models once we have access to Federation space?"

"I do, and we will. But why wait, I mean seriously have you *looked* at the numbers? By the time we get back, if nothing else changes, we will have enough credits to buy a large transport outright."

That set Kasey back on his heels a bit. "Oh… Really? No, I haven't looked. I knew it was a lot but that is insane."

"Right, so a few extra bards won't make a difference."

"Okay, well then that sounds great. We can pick them up on our way out tomorrow. Although we do need to limit what we spend a bit or it will tip our hand to anyone paying attention, but these are nothing in the scheme of things. When the pressure is off us as the only n-mats mine, we can hopefully change that."

"Makes sense to me. Do you really think someone is looking for the actual mine?"

"Undoubtedly. The Federation and navy would be stupid to not have all the facts about what they likely feel is the most important substance in existence. Even if, somehow, they are not interested now, just wait till we miss one shipment and see how quick they come searching. The first people I would investigate are Fran's associates, and we are too well known at this point already. Hell, once someone realizes that all three of the people who found the first n-mats are working at the same mine, we will be dead center in their spotlight."

"Well, that sounds bleak…"

"Sure is." He looked at the ground for a long time, then shrugged. "Its motivation for us to find another source quickly. Let someone else be under the microscope."

She kissed him on the cheek, "Come on, we need to load the Cintian."

CHAPTER FIVE

Hurry up and wait.

The phrase kept repeating in Kasey's head. They had been aboard the Pathfinder for over a week and the ship had not even left dry-dock. Today was to be the fourth attempt. Flair had assured them that these kinds of delays were normal for a new ship design, but Kasey was getting concerned.

When the latest announcement came to prepare for departure, he barely noticed. Only after AnnaChi swatted his head did he realize he had missed something. As they entered the bridge, they were ushered to small, comfortable viewing area for VIPs. They took the remaining two seats and settled in.

The sections seats were filled with important-looking people and a few obvious scientists, but no one they recognized nor anyone that bothered to notice them. Admiral Francis was walking the bridge checking in with every station personally as the final preparations were made, but he at least took the time to nod welcomingly in their direction.

Several displays entertained the VIP section, showing

everything from general ship specs to various camera feeds around the ship's exterior. Once Fran had taken his place in the captain's chair, several screens changed to views forward and aft of the ship.

The wall aft of the long ship separated into four sections and recessed into the chamber walls revealing a deep cavern. Kasey did not notice the command being given, but suddenly the ship was moving backward into the cavern as the Gemini Nexus forward slowly disappeared from view. As the ship traveled down the prepared tunnel, sets of walls forward of the ship closed, sealing them out of the nexus.

Kasey kept his eyes on the approaching cavern wall. It was hard to tell how close they were, but suddenly a crease appeared in the rock wall. Two massive chunks of the moon's exterior swiveled outward into the starry blackness beyond. A host of escort ships waited nearby, and within moments the camera angles had shifted to their viewpoints showing the Pathfinder emerging into open space and beyond.

Once away from the rogue moon, Pathfinder flipped longways and went through a series of intense flight testing that Kasey would not have believed possible for such a large and long vessel. Testing ended with a maximum acceleration burn that left the rogue moon base as only a small speck in the distance. After flipping and decelerating to a full stop, there was a short break while Fran again walked the room looking for problems before settling back into the captain's chair. He took his time then looked towards a waiting officer and nodded.

"All hands, prepare for inaugural jump."

The command was followed by several other announcements, but Kasey ignored them all and tightened the seat's straps. They were about to break physics in a way he could not begin to understand. The gates were simple in comparison. AnnaChi yawned beside him, but her eyes seemed locked on a large station at the far edge of the bridge.

The station itself looked the same as any other, but several additional displays were mounted around it. The displays were non-standard compared to the rest of the bridge, and were apparently temporary. Several additional seats were also crowding the station and were occupied by science and engineering staff. They all seemed to be discussing something important.

One by one they all settled back and nodded at the officer in the main station chair. She then looked towards Fran.

"Jump station is green, sir."

"Miss Ecclestone," he responded, "commence countdown and jump us back to the Gemini station please."

"Aye, sir! Jumping in three, two, jump."

Kasey again felt the usual timelessness of eternity beckoning he experienced every time he went through a gate. He had expected something different from the jump ship, but it was exactly the same. He watched the monitors, which showed they had left their escort ships behind. The small moon was now much larger and slightly off to their port side.

The room was filled with enthusiastic chatter. Once the excitement calmed down, Fran appeared next to the VIP area and shook a few hands before sending everyone off to waiting shuttles to take them back to the base.

After they had all left, Kasey approached Fran. "Looks like a success?"

"Unexpectedly, yes."

"You expected a problem?"

"Of course. That's the best way to be ready for them."

Flair walked up behind him. "Always the boy scout,

this one is."

Fran smiled at her. "Any problems, commander?"

"We overheated some relays which will need upgraded, but the big issue is power consumption. The drain on the capacitors is exponentially more than expected."

"That will affect our max range I am guessing?"

"Badly. We will be lucky to get twenty light-years a jump from a full charge."

"That is nowhere near the design specs... And how long will it take to charge after each jump?"

"Currently, about ten hours."

"Well, a fine disaster this is. I assume we can increase our power banks?"

"Well, yes, if we can find the space for them. But pushing all that power is going to tax the system far more than we intended, and we did not design for this level of load. It is exceedingly early in the data collection, but if I understand the engineer's babble, we will need a major upgrade or we will burn out more than just the relays."

Fran shook his head angrily. "So what can we achieve? Can we do smaller jumps more often by increasing power generation? Faster we charge, the faster we can jump."

"I'll find out, but I am guessing that after a few jumps we will need a lot more heat exchangers than we have today. Just the room for all the additional equipment will be an issue. We will need to convert storage areas and maybe some hangars too, but we are fully stocked right now. There is no extra room. We just didn't expect this, something will need to stay behind."

Fran rubbed his thumb and forefinger together in thought, then looked at AnnaChi and Kasey. "Thoughts?"

AnnaChi chimed in first. "What's in storage that you

don't need?"

Flair frowned in thought, "Most is essential to the ship or the mission. The least of it is a robust colony package and extra food stores. If things at the colony went very wrong, it could all be needed. All things considered; we were lucky in the Trias System, it could have easily been far worse."

"Okay so, what about ships?"

Fran frowned. "Except for your two ships, we could offload some of the transports."

"Not what I meant." AnnaChi smiled. "I assume your transports are currently empty?"

Fran snapped his fingers. "Of course! Flair, have them move all the colony supplies to the transports and pack it in tight, then move our bulk consumables and anything else we won't need right away into whatever ships are left. Now, how do we get all the upgrades finished so we can be on our way?"

"It's a lot of work, we will need to delay the mission several weeks at the least."

"Hang on." Kasey held back a sigh. He didn't want this mission to last longer than necessary. "Power issues are nothing new for ship maintenance. This may be a bit different, and on a much larger scale, but if I understand the issue, your engineers should be able to handle incremental upgrades safely enough. They just need to implement the same type of power governing as they do for shields—control the power draw. You will want a team monitoring at all times and allow the others to continue upgrades."

Both AnnaChi and Flair were nodding.

"Okay, so when the work is done, we can safely increase jump range until we find the sweet spot?"

"No," Kasey corrected. "I mean sure, but I am saying we should load all the upgrade equipment now, pack it in the passageways if you need to, and set sail tomorrow.

Install upgrades between jumps while we are charging. If we hit the limiters, we back off or reprioritize upgrades. I am sure there will be delays, but it is far better than sitting here waiting."

Fran looked to Flair. "While the supplies are moved to the ships, have a team analyze Kasey's suggestions, if they agree, have them put a list together of what we will need."

"Will do. Knowing the engineers, they will want more planning time than they need, but I will have Endeavour's crew check their math and keep them moving."

AnnaChi pointed towards the station with all the extra displays and staff. "So, where is the next test taking us? I would hate to be stuck out in the black."

"To another base similar to this one. About three hundred light-years away from Gemini, so we are looking at fifteen max jumps. We were planning on a single jump, but still, we won't be more than ten light-years away from a system I believe."

"That is still a long way if we get stuck."

"It would be, except we have a small star-cruiser on board that we can send for help if needed."

* * *

It took over a week to reach the base.

The last jump had brought the base into view, but it was still several light-minutes distant. Kasey smiled in amusement as Fran ignored the Pathfinder crew's request to make contact. Instead, he had ordered an active scanning burst that would pinpoint most activity in the area. If the base had not been aware of the Pathfinder's presence, it soon would be.

Kasey sat forward as the scan data came back and the entire base began crawling with activity.

His eyes locked onto the main screen a few minutes later as three massive battleships crested around three sides of the bulky asteroid where the base was established. Destroyers, carriers, and other support vessels followed in each battleship's wake. Three entire fleets were now bearing down on them.

"Sir, we have received a challenge. Shall we reply?"

"Go ahead and send them our codes—and send my compliments on their readiness."

"Aye, sir."

Not much changed as they drew closer, except the base and battleship led fleets grew increasingly larger.

"Comm request, sir."

"On the main screen, if you please. What is our current lag-time?"

"Twenty seconds, sir."

A sharp dressed woman in an admiral's uniform appeared and considered them for several moments.

"Admiral Maddock Francis... I did not believe it when I saw your codes. Don't take this wrong, but I never expected to see you or the others again." She smiled. "But I am glad I was wrong. I take it you lot were successful if you are here with a ship like that ugly thing?"

"Valencia my dear, you haven't lost your edge at all. Successful, yes, but not quite to the point I had imagined. Not yet anyway, but everything is about to change. I am glad to see the fleets are still in good hands. I hope you are ready to change things up a bit. We can catch up shortly, but I come bearing urgent orders from command."

"It has been *mostly* quiet in my sector these many years, so don't beat around the bush. We are ready for some action."

"Glad to hear it! You are to immediately move your flag to an appropriate ship of no larger than two-hundred-fifty-meters width. All ships of this size and smaller are to form action-ready units immediately. Larger vessels will be reduced to bare-bone staffing levels and retain support only for long term maintenance functions. Your fleet's star-cruisers will likely be called upon for additional duties as well in the short-term. Quagmire Base itself will remain active and begin ramping up all production lines to maximum as quickly as possible."

Her face paled in anger. "You... You want to mothball my fleet!"

"Not exactly, and I am truly sorry, Valencia. Quagmire will remain an active base for smaller ships, but I know what losing great ships such as these behemoths is like."

"You don't know shit!" She slowly calmed after a few moments under his quiet gaze. "Okay, I apologize for my outburst. I know some of what you lost back then... But I don't understand."

"You will soon. This is no demotion, just a change. A very big one. My ship, the Pathfinder, will be deploying a set of gateways here shortly that will connect your base to a larger navy nexus of gateways. These gates are simply too small for our larger ships. The time for battleships is at an end I'm afraid—at least for now. Smaller ships from all over the Federation will soon be able to send as much support as needed in minutes instead of months. The landscape of war is changing. In fact, it already has..."

"Already has? Wait, you haven't mentioned the others... How many Farpoint missions have made contact so far?" She was unable to hide the concern on her face.

"Only mine... The Trias System. We had to fight a

war to the very brink, lost an entire planet, and we nearly didn't make it at the end. No other gates have activated. We have tried them from our side, but there have been no successful connections to any, so far... That is one reason we need your ships to be ready to fight. Once we get you set up with gate access, I will begin jumping Pathfinder to the other Farpoint systems and hopefully get them activated. Look... If they faced what we did in the Trias System, then we will need your ship's help."

"You will have it, my friend." She had lost all her anger. "We will be ready for your call. What of the ongoing operations here? The border has been quiet, but this sector has several pirate situations we are managing. We have a twenty-ship task force planning to ship out in two weeks for one of them."

"Command will need to review and make a decision for all ongoing ops. Honestly, Valencia, if any such operations can be delayed a few months, then they likely will be. We need ships and crews that are ready now for gate network forces."

"But we have systems that are under constant threat..."

"I understand, but we will soon have gateways and jump ships that can move resources to those systems far more quickly and with far more force. We must look at the long game now, Val. Like I said, everything is about to change."

"Well, I look forward to it then. Now, where were you planning to deploy these gates?"

Kasey did not stay to watch the gate be deployed. As fascinating as it all was, the idea of his n-mats giving the Federation such a boost to their already bloated military industrial complex was difficult for him to watch.

Four days later, they completed a set of jumps back to the Gemini Nexus and headed towards the Trias System's gate at an almost leisurely pace.

Dozens of ships docked with the Pathfinder as they went, offloading the decommissioned equipment from the upgrading efforts. Many more crates of supplies were loaded to continue the effort. The jump drive upgrade was nowhere near finished.

Entering the Trias System, they burned hard to change vectors and jumped more than forty light-years towards their new destination.

It was just enough time to receive the queued updates from Darnell. The Pathfinder had a lockout on outgoing transmissions, but he was thankful they could still receive messages, and that all was well at home.

As soon as the jump was verified, the crew stood down. Captain Grimt QuTan appeared shortly after to take command of the bridge during the recharge. It would take over twenty jumps at their current rate to reach the Zyta system, nearly one thousand light-years away. He sincerely hoped the rate would be increased quickly. It was already assured that this trip would be far longer than originally planned.

AnnaChi took his arm, pulling him away from his thoughts. "Come on, the bed is calling to me. I want to get an early start tomorrow and put the finishing touches on the new bards."

"Tired huh?"

"Not exactly, but I was hoping you could help with that too."

CHAPTER SIX

Kasey walked into the meeting and found AnnaChi and several others in a heated discussion.

He cleared his throat. "What's the issue?"

AnnaChi looked up. "Issue? Unless you consider thousands of Cassian orb ships an issue, then there is no issue."

"Thousands? We are supposed to be billions of kilometers out from the system—did we screw up the jump?"

"We are outside the system's bow shock, as expected, but the old light is showing what we assume are masses of orb ships. We are too far to be completely sure, but the profile matches what we saw at Trias."

"How are we even detecting them? We haven't been able to keep them on sensors when in the thousands of kilometers, let alone billions."

"We were able to when they swarmed, remember? And when they were corralling the Patternists against us. In numbers, they show up, which I understand has something to do with their stealth system and its relation to nearby mass. Anyway, the current guess is that they want to be seen. If what we are detecting is an orb swarm, then it is not attacking, but it *is* poised and ready."

"We are about to find out if that is the case." Fran entered the conference room, prompting the gathering of officers to snap to attention.

He waved the officers back to their tasks.

"Admiral," a tactical officer reported, "we believe we have a positive match to known Cassian swarming formations. They appear to be maintaining relative system orbital speeds."

Fran nodded. "Fine. We are going to start a series of small jumps into the system, one light-hour distance at a time. It should paint us a nice picture of what the situation is. We have the light advantage; our light won't reach them until it is far too late."

"And if they have some other means of detection?" AnnaChi asked.

"All the more reason to start jumping in now. We need to stay ahead of any potential communications, light speed or otherwise."

"We *are* planning to attack I assume?"

"That depends on the next few jumps. Tactical, what is the estimate on numbers?"

"Between two and three thousand, sir."

"Okay. Please find me some indication that there is still human life in this system to validate an attack."

By the third jump they had located the colony's galaxy-class star-cruiser orbiting above the planet with hundreds of human ships in a defensive posture around it.

"Looks like we have a classic stalemate situation, Admiral. We are detecting a lot of debris throughout the system, along with several disabled platforms around moons and planetoids."

"The debris is very spread out," AnnaChi interjected.

"If I am looking at the numbers correctly, much of it is months old. This seems more of a siege than a stalemate."

"It's time we broke that siege then. Alert the bridge; next jump takes us one light-hour out from that swarm. That will be the last chance to collect data before the attack jump. Prepare the fleet for action."

"Yes, sir!"

Kasey watched as the excitement swept through the room. They were eager for this fight. Most were veterans of the battle for Trias' gates and had lost friends there. It didn't seem to bother them that there were now many times the number of Cassian ships than had been in the Trias System.

Personally, he was not looking forward to being in another battle, even from the relative safety of the Pathfinder. Too late, he realized AnnaChi had no such lack of ambition.

AnnaChi stood to look Fran in the eyes. "Admiral, I request the honor of participating in this battle."

Fran appeared to have expected the request. "Sorry, I do not have a spare ship for you."

"Not needed. The Cintian has been upgraded and no longer classifies as a simple civilian armed ship. She can hold her own, sir."

He gave her a hard look. "Fine. You can assist with resupply and rescue, reporting to the Jate-Markay. You are *not* to engage in combat. Understood?"

Kasey watched her accept the orders and was surprised to hear himself follow her lead, "If you will allow me as well…"

"Fine, but you fly her wing and same rules apply. I took the liberty of adding a standard hardpoint to the Lodestar when she was repaired. We will have a missile rack attached by the time you are ready to launch."

"Thank you."

"You two go prepare. Supplies and SR bots will be loaded in your bays shortly."

Before he knew it, Kasey was kissing AnnaChi and heading onto the launching platform where the Lodestar and Cintian were docked.

He had only been down to the ship twice since boarding the Pathfinder. Once to check on how they had repaired the destroyed bridge, and again to set up his flight preferences. The new bridge had shocked him. Instead of rebuilding it, the navy yard had ripped out what was left and fitted the ship with their standard bridge module. The same bridge the Raven class ships had, but with the dedicated mimic interface stripped out.

It was not that he didn't appreciate the modular navy bridge design, it was simply overkill by several factors for such a small ship. The Lodestar had changed so often since he had first flown it that it was barely recognizable as the same ship. From the outside, it was hard to find anything of the original ship at all. Inside, only the quarters, mess, and plumbing remained the same. If AnnaChi had any input into it, the changes would not stop anytime soon.

Having a need to use the ship put him in a bit of a panic. He had not even completed so much as a walkthrough or flight acceptance, and after such extensive repairs, that could be disastrous. AnnaChi would chastise him for it later, of that he was positive. He found himself running down to the engineering area for a quick check and stopped cold.

Two brand new thorium reactors had replaced much of his cobbled together power system. Looking around, he noticed several other new systems had replaced the ship's older machinery, including a far more powerful shield generator.

As he made his way around the systems, checking their status, he noted many other improvements that had been on his long-term list. None of the systems in engineering had been listed on the damaged assessment, yet much of it appeared to now be brought up to military spec or better. It was annoying to him that the ship had been modified without his approval, but it was difficult to be mad at Fran for such a major upgrade.

The ship now had the power to push the oversized quad thrusters to the limits and not break a sweat. AnnaChi had once told him the large quad thrusters she had procured for him would make this small Lodestar one of the fastest ships in the system. She had been right, but the ship could not maintain that speed for more than a few minutes. That would no longer be an issue.

After leaving engineering, he inspected the hardpoint Fran had mentioned having installed. A midship maintenance hatch led to a new compartment that allowed for external attachments. Anything from external bays, fuel pods or weapons could be attached as needed. Currently a new missile rack had been attached, along with an automated magazine of additional missiles.

As he settled himself into the helm, he looked around the too-familiar bridge layout. Pulling up some of the options he usually ignored, he soon had every surface changed to the forest green color he preferred. After flying so many Raven class ships, including his Altair, it would be hard to realize he was not flying in an actual Raven class ship. That could cause him critical mistakes in a combat situation. He continued to modify settings until he was sure the Lodestar's bridge had a completely different look and feel than the Altair had—he hoped it would help.

Going through the ship weapons he found the Lodestar's small defensive cannon had been left alone, as had the laser-based point defense array. She was not a combat ship by any standards, but with the missiles, improved shielding, and speed, it would be able to hold its own now, if need be. In theory.

AnnaChi would be thrilled once they had the Lodestar back home and was allowed to tinker with it. Her own Cintian had been her first project when they returned from the Trias gate battle. She had added two hardpoints, onto which she currently had the heaviest civilian cannons allowable installed. Knowing her, she had already had one, or both, swapped out for navy missile racks. She also had four smaller cannons with high rates of fire mounted on small turret platforms. It was a ton of firepower for a civilian transport, but more impressive was the custom, laser-based point defense array she had installed.

The array was excessive by several factors, even by navy's standards, but there were no laws preventing such a configuration. It had required her to reallocate a significant portion of the cargo bay to house the capacitors and additional generators, but with the mining business bringing in the bulk of their credits, the need for cargo space was no longer her primary concern.

He paused in his musings as a launch countdown started.

The Lodestar was as ready as she could be, but Kasey's nerves were getting the better of him. It was one thing to go to battle to save his home and friends, but this was different. Sure, there were people to save here too, but his involvement was simply not necessary. This time they had a fleet and surprise on their side. There may be far more enemies, but they would be caught off guard.

He pulled up the battle map. Thousands of orb ships were ahead of them by just a few light-minutes now. Federation manned ships flowed out of the Pathfinder in waves designed to wash away the Cassian menace. The Pathfinder had increased speed prior to the attack jump to allow the Cassian as little time as possible to organize. It would be a slaughter.

A comm lit up, followed by AnnaChi connecting a video stream between the ships. "Hey lover. You sure you can run that ship without me on tactical?"

"Nope, want to come over here to help?"

"Maybe after this little trip. I have a few packages to deliver first. These missile launchers will really help."

"You replaced both big cannons? I am surprised."

"Well, if we are stuck in the rear of this little jaunt, I figured I may as well go for long range deliveries."

"Looks like our turn is coming up. I'll be on your port."

"Try to keep up," she teased.

"That won't be an issue, Lodestar has had a few upgrades of her own."

There was no more time for talk as he launched out of Pathfinder's hangar and into the chaos.

The nearest Cassian orbs were winking out of existence as they were destroyed by the fleet. Far ahead of the carnage, more orb ships began to stir and move in a disordered fashion, but they did not get far before being overtaken as well. The center of the swarm was free of Federation ships, but giant beams from the Pathfinder's particle cannons burned away clusters of orb ships as quickly as they could be targeted. The beams themselves were nearly invisible, but the battle map helpfully superimposed yellow beams showing each strike.

As they reached the far side, the wave of Federation ships broke formation and went after the remaining scattered orb ships one-on-one. The Pathfinder slowed, allowing the fleet to do its job as the rescue teams began responding to calls by the few ships that had taken damage.

Jate-Markay, the light cruiser in command of the

supply and rescue group that Kasey and AnnaChi were attached to, was returning from its third rescue mission when they suddenly transmitted a distress call of their own and went silent.

He could still detect the ship's signature but little else. Two of the ships with them departed toward the Jate-Markay when AnnaChi opened a comm.

"We should go as well. If something took out a cruiser, they will need our backup."

"Shouldn't we wait for orders?"

"We report to the Jate-Markay, their last order was a call for help. It would be against orders not to go, dear."

"While I am not sure that is how this is supposed to work—lead the way."

By the time they reached visual range, the Jate-Markay was breaking up under assault from a dozen orb ships. The bridge section rocketed away from the wreck for a second before taking a missile and going dark. Unfortunately, it was on a vector that led further away from the fleet. The navy bridge modules served as escape pods and were a glorified shuttle. They even had basic shielding, but a lucky missile was more than enough to take one out of commission.

Kasey and the others began spamming missiles towards the orb ships, hoping to distract them from the large escape pod and even the odds a bit. He had a few moments before he would be close enough for his cannons to be useful and the "fire-and-forget" missiles needed no real skill to fire, so he took time to examine the escape pod. The damage seemed contained to the rear and was mostly superficial from what he could see.

Kasey opened a channel. "The pod looks intact, but they are drifting away too quick for us to maintain cover for long. I think I can grab them if you can keep the Cassian busy."

AnnaChi looked pissed. "Fine. You two, get in close

to me. Like it or not, my point defense is better than both of yours together. I need you to cover the Lodestar while I cover you both. Do it now!"

There was a slight pause, then a grudging response from the navy ships. "Confirmed."

Kasey hung back just a bit as the others closed with the orb ships that were now beginning to take some of their missile strikes. The moment the three ships formed up as AnnaChi directed, Kasey fired off another set of missiles towards the orb ships then took the Lodestar to max thrust, arcing towards the escape pod.

Immediately, a set of missiles from the orb ships shot his way but were taken out before they made it far. Other missiles followed, but he had to ignore them or miss the pickup. A moment later he cut the thrust, flipped the ship, then pushed the thruster to max again, concentrating on decelerating and matching the pod's speed. He checked on the missiles headed his way and found several arcing outwards, chasings drones the navy ships must have launched.

The pod was slowly tumbling, and that worried Kasey. He would have to turn the ship just-right at the last moment or it would be a very rough landing for the crew stuck in that pod. He hated to use the ship's AI, as did most pilots he knew, but he had no choice. He needed to get this right.

"Lodestar, can you compute the pitch and roll we will need to land that pod safely in our main bay?"

The AI did not bother replying but displayed the necessary plan on his flight display, which he accepted.

"Thanks. Can you turn off the gravity on the main bay?"

"Confirmed. Please note that the bay is not empty."

"Dammit!"

He quickly connected to the SR bots in the bay and ordered them to clear a landing area as much as possible and be prepared to receive a damaged pod. The bots were single minded but did their jobs well enough from his experience. He knew they would not be able to clear all the supplies in time, but it was worth trying.

A warning alarm grabbed his attention. Two missiles had made it through and would be on him in moments. He began deploying waves of chaff and attempted to target them with the ships cannon. There was no time to aim properly but he was able to bring one of them down. The chaff took out the other just before it would have impacted his shields. The ship was safe, but he now had far less time than he would have preferred to line up such a difficult maneuver.

Just as he was making the final adjustment to his pitch, the alarm sounded again. He couldn't look but had just enough concentration to deploy more chaff as the pod entered the open bay. The SR bots had just taken hold of the ship when the Lodestar was rocked by several explosions. His eyes never left the escape pod as he closed the bay and ordered the bots to lock the pod into place.

The moment one of the bots indicated a positive lock, he rotated the ship and pushed the thruster to full. Then took stock of the damage.

Shields were gone, the missile rack was offline, and a host of other issues were blinking on his status board. Yet, the ship was whole, and he still had a job to complete.

"AnnaChi, what is the situation?"

"We are wrapping up here, and my shields are shot. We need to get back to the Pathfinder. How are your passengers?"

"No clue, their comm must be down. The bots may need to cut them out of there, but not until we have them in a safe location."

There was a long pause before she responded. "Run

for the Pathfinder, it looks like we have a few more orbs on sensors. Be right behind you."

He glanced at the battle map and froze. To the rear of the Pathfinder, hundreds upon hundreds of orb ships were appearing, spread out into a giant net pattern. A second swarm that had been spread too thinly to detect. Every one of them was now vectoring inward towards the Pathfinder. The main fleet was too far ahead of the Pathfinder now to help, but most were burning hard to try and fall back in time to help anyway.

"AnnaChi, head for the fleet instead. Check the battle map. We would never dock with the Pathfinder in time."

Changing his own course, he arced towards the fleet and was happy that AnnaChi and the two navy ships were doing the same, but at a much slower pace. He checked the thruster's status and smiled. They were holding up fine under the prolonged stress. He knew they would need some serious attention once safely in a maintenance bay, but it would be worth it. With his shields still down and no point defense system to speak of, the Lodestar was an easy target.

Far ahead, a large number of colony ships had joined the returning fleet. A few were even pulling ahead, not needing to fight against their own acceleration towards the planet as the fleet had needed to. But it would not be enough help.

With no warning, the Pathfinder deployed a large host of missiles and began to accelerate towards the fleet as well. The orb ships began launching their own missiles shortly afterward.

He held his breath as the masses of missiles crossed paths, then another set was launched from both sides. The Pathfinder's missiles struck first, taking down an impressive number of Cassian orbs, but more kept appearing. The Pathfinder's point defense array began obliterating the incoming missiles by the dozens but could not defeat so many.

When the missiles struck the Pathfinder's shields, Kasey was sure they would fail—but they held. It held against the next two waves as well, then fizzled as the fourth wave of missiles burst through and slammed into the ship. Debris was sent in every direction and ended the ship's propulsion as the massive thruster went cold.

The fleet was much closer now and split into two halves as they got close. Kasey did not know what to make of it until the Pathfinder abruptly began a flipping maneuver that stopped perpendicular to the incoming missiles, presenting its exceptionally long profile to the enemy's ordnance. The next set of missiles were completely destroyed by the much larger array of point defense spread out over the Pathfinder's side. The few that made it through, burned away on the bubble-shaped shields that still remained down the ship's length.

The number of Cassian orbs stopped increasing and slowly started to diminish as the Pathfinder's missiles continued to pound the incoming swarm. The Cassian seemed undeterred and simply kept coming. As they entered cannon range, many more orbs blinked off the battle map. A handful of orbs changed tactics and dove towards Pathfinder, crashing into the central shields, taking them offline.

As one, the entire Cassian swarm changed direction, vectoring towards the exposed sections of Pathfinder.

CHAPTER SEVEN

Kasey could not look away from the impending destruction of the massive jump ship that had brought them all here.

It was hard for him to understand what was happening when a great many of the orbs suddenly burst apart. He unfocused his gaze and looked further out. The fleet had finally joined the fight and was augmented by groups of colony ships eager for some payback.

The tide of the battle did not change quickly, but the Pathfinder was saved from further damage as the fight broke into many smaller battles. As more and more of the fleet reached the battle, their victory was assured. He was startled as AnnaChi took it upon herself join in the battle, but he knew he should expect no less from her. She would never back away when the fight was right in front of her.

Kasey located a cluster of damaged fleet ships and joined them to wait out the battle. Checking on the rescued escape pod, he found the SR bots had attached an umbilical to the pod, keeping it powered and aired. Steeling himself for what he may find, he ordered the bots to equalize pressure and pry open the outer hatch.

The inner hatch was in far better condition and opened after another long minute of equalizing the pressure to match the Lodestar's bay. Seven crewmen waited with tired looks on their faces. Several were injured.

Assuming a confident face, he waved them out. "The Lodestar isn't much, but feel free to make yourself at home."

A tall dark-haired man strode forward. "Lieutenant Jate, Captain of the Jate-Markay, if she is salvageable." He looked around the bay as he stepped out of the large pod that had once been his ship's bridge. "Any word on the other pods from my ship? We had no comms or power for quite a while."

"I'm, uh, Kasey. Lodestar is my ship. Sorry Sir, there were no other pods... Your ship was coming apart as you launched."

"Damn." He looked back at the faces behind him with a deep sigh as they all nodded knowingly in return. After looking Kasey up and down, he nodded his thanks. "Admiral said you were good in a pinch. Thank you for picking us up. What happened to the orbs attacking us?"

"Two of your rescue ships and the Cintian took them out while I scooped you up. They have since joined with the fleet defending the Pathfinder from the second swarm."

"Three against twelve! Wait, a second swarm? Is the Pathfinder okay? The ones who attacked came out of nowhere—they were not alone then?"

"Sorry, no. Another entire swarm came in behind us somehow. Too spread out to detect. Pathfinder took some hits before the fleet could make it back to help."

"Not a good start to this mission..."

"Seems to be my luck." Kasey shrugged. "Look, move your crew to my quarters or the mess. There is a small medical unit next to the mess if it is needed, but you may be better off waiting for treatment back on Pathfinder if injuries are more than minor. Help yourself to whatever your people need. We are currently without shields, and she took some damage, so the cargo bay is not the best place to stay. I'll be on the bridge once you are settled."

"Thank you, Captain Kasey."

* * *

"What the hell do you think I meant about not engaging in combat!"

"Fran, we didn't have a choice. They needed support and I don't care what they told you!"

Kasey watched as Fran attempted to reprimand AnnaChi's choices. He knew better then to expect her to back down, even to an admiral. That the admiral was a close friend only put him further at a disadvantage.

"They would have pulled back and rescued the Jate-Markay's crew after the battle. You risked their lives too."

"Do you really believe they would have pulled back? Is that what they told you?"

"You don't give my pilots commands! You should have followed their orders, and mine."

"Check the logs, they didn't give me, us, any orders. I certainly wasn't going to wait around while they thought of something. We needed to act."

Kasey could see Fran's face reddening and stepped between them, "So, what *did* they say?"

AnnaChi raised a quizzical eyebrow and Fran relaxed his shoulders and seemed to calm just the smallest bit.

"They said it was a good plan, but they didn't believe

your point defense was as good as you claimed—until the missiles started coming. They apparently enjoyed themselves after that. They want to know why your laser-based point defense was so much more efficient than their antimatter system. Perhaps you would care to share?"

"Simple give and take mechanics. Your PDAM systems are just fine; I wish I had an antimatter system too. One hit and most missiles are useless, but generating AM takes a lot of dedicated power and space. Point defense laser systems can be just as good in volume, but that takes even more space for power storage. Your ships are just far too small to provide the sustained power needed for a large PDL system, or a more robust PDAM one for that matter. The Cintian on the other hand is designed for cargo space. Space I don't have as much use for lately. So, I converted nearly a third of my cargo area to power generation and storage. All that power is feeding my PDL array, which covers every bit of my hull that I could. Lots of room on the hull of a medium sized transport."

"And if you did have access to antimatter for a PDAM system?" Fran prompted.

"I would use it for a longer distance defense and keep half my laser arrays for close in defense. It would buy me a lot more room in the cargo bay too but," she looked at Kasey, "I would need to be trained on the system."

Fran nodded several times. "I'll take this all under advisement. Look, I know you don't want to be held back, but I don't want you hurt. You are not navy anymore, and I don't think you want back in the service. If you want involved in situations like this, you will be doing so as support, far from the front lines, or you will be benched on the Pathfinder."

Kasey could see her preparing an angry remark, but decided to try a different tack. "How badly is the

Pathfinder damaged?"

Fran looked down. "It's not good. We won't be jumping out of this system anytime soon. Main engine is offline and is beyond our ability to repair locally."

"But you have a plan, right?"

"Certainly. The gates this colony brought with them were reported destroyed, although we haven't located their remains yet. But we brought the smaller gates along for this very purpose. They will connect us to the Trias System, and we send for the help and supplies we need to repair her. Before we can do that, we need to clear this system of Cassian."

"And are we allowed to assist with that?" AnnaChi wondered sarcastically.

"No, but that is because I *need* you two to complete the mission you came along for. We have a prospecting team ready to follow your lead on the planet. I need you to prove that our losses here were worth it."

* * *

Kasey landed the bard with a bounce and grinned. The low gravity on planet Bendek, coupled with the n-mats AnnaChi had infused the bard's framework with, made for an interesting ride. Keeping the craft upright was another problem altogether. She had tinkered with the jump jets to allow for more subtle control and longer flight time now that far less power was needed to propel the craft. He leaned to one side as the bard settled. If he tipped it over again AnnaChi wouldn't let him live it down.

She waited at the makeshift camp, directing the crew as they packed up the site. The area was rich enough in ilmenite mineral to warrant someone setting up a mine and processing plant for titanium. But no signs of n-mats.

He joined AnnaChi at the now cold fire pit. "Well, any new findings before we move on?"

"Not unless you found anything. I hope the next location is more interesting. Are we planning to claim this one too?"

"No reason not to. The colony didn't plan to use much of this planet, so the claims are cheap. All their efforts were in space mining."

"That will change, won't it? They can't possibly recover their losses here. Everything they had out there is destroyed."

"It doesn't seem like they realized that yet or they would have increased claiming prices. Maybe they plan to order more automated space miners once the gates are connected, if they have the credits available to them."

"More likely they are hoping we will find something that will cause a rush of new settlers and then raise prices. Who knows, I guess it's not our business."

"No, not really. But if they want to change over to land mining, we can happily sell them whatever we claim. We could even set up an operation here someday."

She frowned. "Uh, not the kind of planet I see myself on to be honest."

"We don't need to live here. Just maybe visit once in a while."

"Do you always dream so big? I mean having mining operations on several worlds would have us traveling even more, and we are already away from home too much."

Kasey raised his eyebrow and smiled. "Are you really ready to give up the pilot's life for a dirtside home?"

"Well hell, I don't know," she stammered, "I want both, dammit!"

"Good." He smiled even more.

"What the hell does that mean? Don't you dare make fun of me!"

"Trust me, I'm not."

She gave him a hard look. "Is this about the idea you won't share?"

"I am not sure it is ready."

"I don't care, spill it."

Kasey looked around, then waved her towards the bard. "Let's take a look at the scan again."

She took a seat and closed the hatch. "Is this really necessary?"

"It's easier to control rumors when there are none."

"Whatever, stop with the mystery and explain how we are going to travel the galaxy and be at home at the same time."

"Simple. We take our home with us."

CHAPTER EIGHT

"Oh, I see. You have gone mad... I should have noticed. Should I call a doctor now, or pretend to go along with this delusion?"

"Pretend a little longer. Okay, think about this." Kasey took a moment to collect his thoughts. "N-mats are going to change everything, and since we are stuck in the middle of it all, I think we should try some of that change ourselves."

"In what way?"

"In the way that landing ships on planets is no longer limited by size, or well, mass..."

"Huh?"

"Think about that a second."

"So, you want a bigger ship? The Altair is just about the biggest transport available..."

"Sorta, but taking it one step further. What I want is a *carrier* ship that is able to land on planets."

"That's not poss—"

"But it is. With enough n-mats it can be done. No different from what we did to land on Lithose. Mostly."

"So then... That stockpile you have Darnell

collecting?"

"Right. We will need a lot more. If what Sariyn is guessing about additional deposits and ore are correct, we will have more than enough in the ground."

"But a carrier? I know I said we would have enough credits for a new ship, but a carrier is on another level of expensive. Several levels actually."

"You are right of course. That is why we need the navy to allow us usage of one of their heavy cruiser fabricators or something close to it."

"Well, good luck with that miracle…"

"It is a long shot, I admit it. But what if Fran is underplaying the navy's need for n-mats? They are far more aware of how useful it is than we are. Even if we find a new source here, it is unlikely to be mineable as quickly as we can mine ours. The Lithose mine produced only a fraction of a percent of what we have already sold to the navy from our mine. The only reason we haven't drastically increased the price of ours is because we don't want to provoke them into finding and seizing our property."

"Okay, valid points, I think, but that helps us how?"

"Once we have a better idea of how much of the n-mats we are really sitting on, we offer a contract for a bulk amount that we don't need for our carrier. In return, they allow us usage of the ship fabricator. It would also help if other mines could be located soon so a realistic price point could be determined. Right now, we are guessing because we have no real costs to mine it. Others, like they had on Lithose, will have significant operating costs and drive the cost of the n-mats up drastically."

"Why, so you can undercut them all?"

"I think we are already far below what the potential fair market price should be right now. We need to get closer to a real price, both for us and new operations, so that we are *not* grossly undercutting them."

"But we know what they were paying back then, right?"

"Yes, however that was pre-gate travel prices. We are on a whole new level now. Just wait till the public gets ahold of this, the demand will continue to increase for a while."

"Wait, didn't you tell Sariyn the price would drop?"

"I did… But I was thinking much longer term. It will drop in price once enough mines are operating, or when more like ours are found, but that is after the shorter-term increase. I was also assuming a carrier was not going to be feasible, so long-term meant when our mine eventually dried up. However, I now think the carrier is possible, which means we want to empty our mine as quick as possible. The long-term is now much shorter."

"I think I am following. So why are we not holding back and waiting for the increase, then selling?"

"It is a bit of a risk. But I believe the navy or Federation will take the mine from us before that happens. I would be happy to be wrong, but I bet at some point we will be forced to hand it over. I want to liquidate it or at least have a more official contract before that can happen."

"I am not sure I completely agree with you, but I agree it is not worth the chance. And if another group takes over, they could endanger the atoss in our valley. We can't allow that to happen."

"Which brings us back to the carrier. I think I found a design that is large enough that we can take them with us, along with a botanical garden for them to use as a home. It would have more than enough room for them to be happy."

"Not if they keep reproducing… And it's now sounding more a luxury ship than a carrier."

"I am sure there will be a lot more atoss. In that,

Sariyn is likely correct. They will eventually need a world they can expand on. Still, I think some would stay with us if they could. I don't know about a luxury ship, but I want it to be our home, and our livelihood, and a base of operations. Whatever we need it to be, or want it to be."

AnnaChi took a few moments to process it all. "So... We use the carrier for more than just a home for us and our ships... A carrier that can land on a planet. So, we can do massive cargo transportation too?"

"We sure can, that, and a lot more. We could deliver large groups of colonists to the new planets that will be available, as well as transporting all their supplies directly to the planet's surface. We can do our prospecting and even set up our own mining operations as we go. If we are not moving resources or salvage, we can take on cargo jobs that would take a normal outfit dozens of ships to accomplish."

"Gardens, people, cargo, I assume this carrier will actually be able to carry our ships too, right? Hold on, you said salvage?"

"Did I?"

"Yes."

Kasey attempted to look innocent, knowing he would fail. "Are you sure? I had distinctly planned *not* to say that word."

"You can't seriously want to go back there again?"

He shrugged. "It is really hard to ignore the fact that Lithose is sitting there with all that wealth slowly rotting away."

"Since when are you after wealth?"

"It seems that I remember someone pointing out our balance sheet not that long ago." He smirked. "But no, I'm just being realistic. The carrier, if we can get it built, will need to be outfitted, and that alone will cost another fortune. Lithose can supply a lot of the necessities we need to get started. We can also build our mining operations across the new worlds, but to do that we need a lot of equipment. Again, Lithose has all that equipment, and it is all just rusting away."

"So, you think this carrier will be able to survive Lithose's atmospheric storms? Won't it just be a bigger magnet for all that raw power?"

"That is why I didn't bring this all up earlier; I didn't have a solution for getting to Lithose, and I don't see how we can afford to outfit a carrier or supply it without salvage from there."

"And now you have a solution I presume?"

"I do. Well, I think so anyway. I want to bring Sariyn into this to research it as well, if she is willing and thinks she can help. I am really not sure of her total skillset, but I think she will offer good opinions at least—besides, we need someone we can trust."

"I am with you there, go on."

"Well, after seeing the maneuvering thrusters the Pathfinder used for flipping that massive ship around, I was curious and looked into it. It's really one single thruster for each section, if you can believe it. An older engine designed to sit deep within a ship and the thrust gets directed out of small ports anywhere it is needed."

"Interesting, but I don't see the relationship."

"I am getting to that. When I researched these thrusters, I found a ship design using them that was made for places like Lithose. A ship that was engineered to use Faraday shields and plasma conduits to protect research ships exploring the atmospheres of gas giants from electrical storms. The thruster and most essential systems are deep in the ship for safety. The design is proven and scalable enough to be used on a small carrier-sized ship."

"Assuming we can get the navy to actually build one, which seems like a big assumption."

"Granted…"

"Okay, I need to see this ship design in detail, but for now, tell me what you have planned for the hangar?"

"I was hoping you would have some input on that part, what I have is very basic so far. We are looking at eight decks, the largest of which will be our hangar on deck four. The hangar design currently has eight bays sized for large transports to the port and starboard, and another eight bays for shuttles and utility ships that are split between the forward and aft of the deck. The bays are self-contained with plenty of room for maintenance, but they can be opened up to the rest of the hangar deck as needed. Center-deck is all shop area and fabricators with enough room to fully dry-dock two large transport ships for bigger jobs. A part of the area may need to be dedicated to mining equipment maintenance and such, and maybe a shop dedicated for bards or other ATVs, but it will be more than enough room for it all."

"Cripes, just how big is this monster?"

"Around three hundred meters from bow to stern and two hundred meters or so wide."

"I am trying not to get too excited for a ship that may never get built. So, what's on the other seven decks? I can't get the idea of having bays for eight transports and still being able to fit two in the shop area."

"The two decks below the hangar are mostly open cargo decks. They can be opened when on a planet if needed for faster loading, otherwise there are lifts leading to each hangar bay for moving cargo around and a few other areas. Those lifts are large enough to move a shuttle into cargo."

"That's a hell of a lot of cargo… Could transport a year's worth of freight in one haul."

"You see the potential then? I think we will need it all and wish we had a lot more. I would like to add an automated stacking and sorting system, but for such a large area that's on the nice-to-have list with a lot of other long-term items. For now, we would need a cargo crew."

"I see. What else?"

"Top three decks—five, six and seven—are living areas for passengers, crew, and atoss. The center is a domed botanical garden that spans all three decks. The topside deck has a retractable dome over a recreational area and the apex of the garden dome. I figured a pool around the garden dome with another dome enclosing it all would make a nice statement to potential travelers, not to mention the view it would give us."

"Well, that *is* a bit of luxury."

"It's a cheap luxury for us to add compared to the rest of the ship. Surrounding the dome on deck five and six are housing and common areas. Deck six's housing is for passengers and deck five is mainly crew quarters, the Promenade, and some amenities for everyone. Oh, and our estate is on that deck as well."

"Estate?"

"About four thousand square meters of private space."

"Does that include more hangars for our ships?"

"No, just living space."

"You're joking? On a ship? What the hell would we do with all that space?"

"Again, n-mats change everything we are used to with ship life. It does not have to feel like a ship anymore unless you want it to. We need space to spread out and add on if we want, not to mention getting away from people. We would need a lot of crew, and I don't want to be crowded in my own home. It would be our ship, after all. So, having plenty of personal space is a requirement."

"Okay, no argument with that, I suppose. Just seems like too much. Where is the bridge, engineering and the like?"

"Mostly on the Operations deck with other critical functions. The deck is more armored and reinforced than the rest of the ship. Main engineering will have a lot of space and a big workshop area, and the deck will be ringed by a separate weapons engineering section with multiple blast walls. It won't be much more than defensive weapons, but I have a lot of extra space allocated so we can add a robust point defense system like Cintian has. I want that on all our ships if we can manage it. Going to need your help with all that."

"Damn right you will!"

He breathed a sigh of relief. It felt good to finally share his idea. That she seemed to think it was worth pursuing meant a lot to him, "I'll send it all to you once I get back to the Lodestar. It's on a secured drive."

"Leave it secured for now. I will come take a look later, but I have enough information to think about. Hold on, you mentioned eight decks, but only described seven?"

"Ah, deck zero. That's the ballast storage and drop bay. It's a huge part of what makes this whole ship able to land on planets. The carrier will pack more than enough n-mats to be negative-massed on most planets. So, we need to pack quite a bit of solid ballasts on-board to offset the n-mats when we want to land. But we need to allow for new cargo too. We can float some of the solid ballasts containers in orbit if we need to drop the ship's mass before entering a planet's atmosphere. Then, when we land, we can use the planet's own water as a ballast if we need a temporary solution. If I calculated right, we should have storage for over eleven thousand tons of water when we need it."

"Not sure on the math offhand, but that seems like an awful lot of water. Would we thrust down to an ocean or lake to gather it? Also seems expensive on fuel. Can't we just anchor to the planet somehow?"

He laughed. "It's easier than you think depending on the planet. For example, we could insert into an Earth-class planet at around fifteen thousand meters above sea level and absorb a cloud or two. The systems to do so already exist and we don't need an actual cloud, but it would be quicker. Each planet will be a different challenge to land and pick up or drop off cargo; the trick will be doing it as efficiently as possible."

"Sounds overcomplicated."

"To a point, it is. But unless it is a totally unknown planet or cargo pickup, we will just need to plug in the numbers and decide on the best use of our ballast options for each case. Not that much different than calculating reentry deltas. All those ballasts will offset our n-mats lift potential. We will still need some serious thrusters and stabilizers to fly it like any other ship but controlling ballasts is what will make this all efficient and profitable."

"Makes sense. Hell, can you imagine the panic we could cause when making landfall! Well, I guess it really is just scaling up what we are already doing with offsetting cargo with n-mats. I just think figuring proportions out each time we land may be an AI job though."

"Maybe, but I would be double checking their work each time anyway. I am sure it would be all very factual, but a little looser interpretation of the facts is usually necessary. Even Altair's navy spec AI is just more facts at a faster rate."

AnnaChi laughed. "You haven't interacted with the Pathfinder's AI, have you?

"Why would I?"

"The Federation relaxed it's rules on AI development, at least for the military. Apparently civilian versions are to start production soon too."

"They did what? Let me guess, the moment the gates became a reality, they changed the rules?"

"Something like that... You would have to ask Fran, but I am guessing it is another force multiplier to push humanity forward as quickly as possible."

"Unbelievable. What's next, nanites?"

"Anyway... Scout is galaxies beyond the Cintian's AI."

"Scout?"

"That's what they are calling it, or him. The sailors have several names for it, but Scout is the most popular. You should try talking to it sometime."

"I'll think about it. But first, I want to know what you think about the carrier idea?"

"Sounds like just the adventure I need. Seriously, a real home on a ship—what's not to love? I already have some design points in mind."

"I had no doubt that you would."

"Uh, you know, we have been kind of hard on Fran lately. I mean, for good reason and all. Still, we will need his backing on this carrier idea to get access to navy ship fabricators. Maybe we need to back off a bit and give our friend some support."

"We've nearly given him our lives in support. Several times."

"Different kind of support, love."

"I know. But dammit, I am still a bit raw from being used back in Trias System."

"Well, try anyway."

"Alright. They are about packed up out there. Let's get these bards loaded and head to the next location."

CHAPTER NINE

The sulfur plains were one of the last places Kasey had wanted to explore, but now that they were there, he had to admit they were beautiful.

Black salt pillars, soupy green potassium pools, and bright yellow sulfur ponds boiling up from the rocky ground. It was a sight to behold, but not smell. The fumes were harsh, but from what the researchers with them explained, the pools would kill you quickly and dissolve your remains. Not a pleasant thought.

They did not bother unloading the bards this time. Just directed the researchers to collect samples from everything while he and AnnaChi wondered around the smaller pools.

"See this?" AnnaChi pointed to a rocky part of the landscape they had walked around.

The rock jutted up in a salt-covered rocky seam that looked as if it had once pushed its way through the surface.

"An old dried-up pool maybe?"

"Or one trying to form."

"Could be."

"Think about our caverns. The n-mats need to be contained or trapped in some material, right?"

"Ah, I see what you mean!" He looked around and saw hundreds of other similar formations.

AnnaChi smiled at him, then gave a shrill whistle as she waved some of the crew over.

Kasey explained their thoughts and pointed at the other formations around them. "Drill a few cores of these for samples. Deeper the better."

"On it. Priority on these?"

"Yes, top of the list please."

The crew moved off to gather their equipment with haste. Undoubtedly in a hurry to be finished with this site than any real excitement, Kasey noted.

AnnaChi slipped her hand into his. "This is a pretty place and all, but what's next? Maybe we can get a head start?"

"I hope you packed your cold weather gear. The northern continent is on the chilly side but has a mountain we need to get a better look at. I am sure the views will be fantastic."

"Freezing cold weather? You certainly know how to treat a girl."

* * *

Kasey watched AnnaChi as they were given the news.

They had just returned from scouting one of the several icy mountains he had picked out. The navy's team had joined them earlier in the day to start collecting samples from sites they had identified. Just as they finished restocking the bards, the excited lab techs pulled them aside.

Core samples taken from the sulfur pools that AnnaChi had noticed contained the barest traces of n-mats. Platinum, they had said. It was not from the sulfur at all, but brought up from the layers of bedrock far below.

He could not help but feel proud as AnnaChi realized she would get the credit for the find. She wasn't one to get affected by something as simple as recognition, but he could tell this hit her a bit. Her expression cleared when she noticed him looking, but he continued smiling at her.

After the techs left, she punched his arm and turned away. "Whatever!"

"Whatever? Yeah right. You ready to go find some more?"

"Hell yea!"

The following days were spent combing the areas around the sulfur plains for richer and easier to mine locations. Two different stream beds were found to be moderately rich in gold deposits and both contained trace n-mats platinum. It took time to trace the deposits back to the gold source, which ended up being a complex series of gold veins high in the surrounding hillsides.

By the time they unearthed the first site, Kasey was feeling that he was part of a mining crew again. The crews were excited more every day as the samples of both gold and n-mats based platinum increased. In the end it was almost anticlimactic.

The source vein unquestionably had a lot more n-mats rich material. Platinum and even some iridium in n-mats form were found. Yet, even with the vein, the total amount was pitifully small in the scheme of things. It would take a standard year to harvest enough material to activate even a single gate.

Not that the news was bad, at least from a mining

perspective. The profitability of running a mine for both gold and n-mats platinum group elements would be quite high. Far higher than his own copper mining operations.

They added claims to all the gold rich land in the area that they could locate after that. Many were located, but only a handful could be positively tested for n-mats. There was a high chance they would all contain at least some of the exotic material. Kasey still felt it was worth the credits the claims were costing them. The colony would have a chance to buy them back soon enough, and if they didn't, he would keep them or sell them later as miners flocked to n-mats rich worlds seeking their own fortunes.

Repairs on the Pathfinder were nearly complete as they lifted off from the final locations Kasey had identified on the global survey. He knew he could spend years prospecting additional sites over the world, but their time was up, and they were ready to go home.

Immediately upon returning to the Pathfinder they were ushered into a large conference room filled with groups of businessmen. Flair met them as they entered and led them to a long table at the front of the room.

"Colonists," she explained. "The few companies left on this expedition with the resources to mine the claims you helped find."

"And why are we here?"

"Only a few of them know about negative matter, but in a few minutes they all will. You are here to help field questions."

"Well, that's just great."

"I knew you would be thrilled." She laughed happily. "Don't worry, we will move this along quickly."

Quickly ended up being three hours of questions followed by another hour of auctioning off his claims. The claims with verified n-mats went quickly to three buyers, each of whom agreed to mine all their n-mats claims simultaneously and sell directly to the navy. All but twelve of the remaining claims were bought up by others around the room, hoping they also contained the mysterious materials.

Kasey tried to look disappointed when he was left owning the leftover claims. The truth was, he was glad to have them. He may not get to mine them soon and he was fine with that. But he also knew the claim's value would only increase as time went on. They already had in fact, many times over on the claims. He had made a tidy sum selling most the claims, and the verified n-mats claims, even more so. It was something he had not expected as Fran simply said he would have to sell them back, not auction them off to the highest bidders.

AnnaChi looked sharply at Kasey when the selling price of the n-mats began to be haggled over with the navy lawyers. These colonists were old hands at negotiating. The prices quickly soared far above Kasey's current prices.

Fran was called in finally when the discussion broke down, with several mine bosses threatening to back out on their purchased claims.

After listening to the fluffed-up woes of the colonists, he nodded thoughtfully and stood. The room quieted, but instead of addressing the room, Fran turned toward Kasey and AnnaChi. "Mr. Robinson. These men and woman wish to forfeit the claims they agreed to purchase from Phoenix Mining. Is Phoenix Mining willing retain ownership of these claims? The current n-mats price on the table here today will apply."

"Now hold on a damn minute!" one of the colonists exclaimed above the rumbling of others in the room.

Kasey ignored them all and slowly stood. "Phoenix stands ready; if these Zyta system companies do not feel they are up to this task then we will bring in our own crews."

"That's not right," another mine boss shouted. "We are not ready to forfeit our claims!"

Fran turned back to them, "The price is fair. It will stand as it is, but the claims will be returned to Phoenix Mining if you are not prepared to agree now. The claiming rights were legally sold to Phoenix Mining and are only being offered to you fine folk out of respect. Make your decisions now because this *opportunity* is about to end."

He left the room without further comment.

Flair approached them a few minutes later. "Everyone signed, it is just formalities now. Thanks for backing Fran up."

"Just glad it's over."

AnnaChi yawned. "Truly. I could use a nap after all that."

Flair laughed. "We will be here for a while yet, but you two are free to go."

"Just one thing." Kasey lowered his voice. "The new price…"

"It has already been relayed back to command. By law we have no choice but to pay equal pricing across to the Federation for resources. Therefore, all n-mats sold to the navy will immediately be at the new price."

"Thank you, we appreciate that."

"It's simply the law." She smiled before returning to the gathering.

Both were quiet until they entered their quarters on the Pathfinder.

"Holy shit!" Kasey exclaimed.

AnnaChi shook her head. "You expected that, right?"

"Well sort of, but not so damn quickly. Months or years from now, maybe."

"Well then, does this change anything?"

"Maybe. It is all on Sariyn and Darnell's findings now. If we have enough to use for the carrier and plenty to keep the navy happy too, well then, we can work on trying to get the ship fabricator access. Lucky we came to this system."

"Hmm, you mean a system of wealthy but desperate colonists? Not so sure that was luck."

"You really think he planned this? How would he have known."

"I am sure he wouldn't have known what we would find. Still, I am betting he didn't choose the wealthiest colony to go to first for no reason. Do you think most colonies would have pushed that hard on prices? Did Lithose?"

"Well, no."

"Right. If he wanted n-mats cheap, he would have visited this colony last."

"But why? Does he have a cut in this somewhere? He will profit on the sale of the claims as part owner of Phoenix, but that won't amount to much. I am not aware of him getting anything from the n-mats."

"Then it is because of you. I assume he wants you to play whatever part it is that he believes you will to help solve the Pattern."

"That's ridiculous."

"Is it? Everything he has done and set up has been to fight the Pattern. He's a *believer*. And he thinks you are needed."

Kasey sighed. "I don't know. I mean, it could just as easily be that the Federation wants more pressure on teams to find and mine n-mats. Makes sense to up the price. Besides, the rich companies always get the most attention."

"Whatever you need to tell yourself, honey."

Kasey held back his response as the cabin door chimed.

"Scout, open the door please," AnnaChi ordered the AI.

Fran stepped into the room and set a bottle of Toyasow wine on the table. "Find a few glasses. A celebratory drink is in order I believe."

"Happy to. That was all very unexpected," Kasey admitted.

"Perhaps, but inevitable." Fran accepted a glass and began to pour the wine.

"So, what's next for the Pathfinder?"

"Well, once we get these colonists off the ship, we will begin jumps towards another Farpoint colony." He took a small sip of the wine and smiled. "The real question is, will you two come along for another?"

"While this has been quite amazing so far, we really need to check in on the Belrothi operations."

"Understandable. However, with the new class-F gate we have in place here, that will not be much of an issue. You two can go home and spend a few days, and then join us in the next system to help with the search. By the time you return, we should have the system cleared and either a class-F or class-A gate activated. We will send a message to you to let you know where to go."

AnnaChi set her wine glass down. "We will have to make that decision after we get back to Belrothi and see where things stand. Molly and Orange are undoubtedly stressed that we have been gone so long as well."

"I see. Well, I can tell you that Darnell has not reached out to my contact for anything as of yet, and all reports I have gotten indicate that our businesses are doing quite well right now. N-mats shipments have increased as expected too. It will take a few days for the new price to make its way through the supply chain, but that should be in place before you get there. As for your atoss companions, could you bring them along?"

"They are not well suited for ships. Even Pathfinder wouldn't give them much room to move around."

"Well, let me think about that one a bit. I will send

Lieutenant Jate with you if you don't mind. He is between ships and could use a leave after the battle here. He will provide you navy access to use the Trias System's gates. You can drop him off at the station you will find when you pass through the class-F gate, or if you need access to the Gemini Nexus when you return."

"That sounds perfect." AnnaChi drained her glass. "We should start packing if you plan to jump soon."

"You have a few hours, at least. We have several class-F gates that arrived a bit ago. They had to be disassembled to get here. I want them reassembled and ready to deploy if we need them after the jump."

"How is the jump drive doing with the upgrades?" AnnaChi asked.

Fran smiled. "Better than I expected at this point. Our last jump was over one-hundred light-years, but the engineers have implemented several efficiencies while we have been in the Zyta system. They feel we can now jump close to three hundred. Recharge time is falling behind with every upgrade though, last estimate I received is that we will need at least twelve hours for a full recharge now."

"Well, that is still a lot better than we started this trip out with."

"True, and I expect it to get better and better as we continue the upgrade."

Kasey listened to the discussion, but his thoughts were focused on the class-F gates Fran had mentioned. They had limited range... He patched into the Zyta system's network and pulled up a view of the gates Fran had deployed there. Just two gates, one incoming and the other outgoing, both tied to the Trias System.

A quick search of the historical data showed transport ship hauling large, curved pieces of the disassembled class-F gates. Every one of them went directly to a small assembly area where they were being loaded into the

Pathfinder.

He looked at Fran as the conversation paused. "All the class-F gates, they will connect to Trias System?"

Fran tilted his head slightly. "That's right."

"Are the gates permanent?"

"Ah, well," Fran paused, "not exactly. They can be shut down, but it would most likely damage the gate a bit. We will not be trying anything to that extent for a long time, not unless gate production exceeds the need for new ones. For the foreseeable future, that is not likely to happen."

"So, the Trias System's nexus, our home system, won't just be the central system for a new cluster around that area of space..." Kasey squinted slightly. "Instead, it will be the central system that other Farpoint colony cluster's central systems tie into?"

"For a time, yes. Trias will become a super-cluster I suppose. Same as the Gemini Nexus will be for the navy's access to the Farpoint colonies or the Earth Prime cluster's Trade Nexus that will be created for civilians there."

Kasey forced a friendly laugh he did not feel. "It's going to get crowded quickly, isn't it?"

"I am afraid so. But it will even out eventually. Long term, we will have limited nexus points in all the major systems around the Federation to tie them all together. We are only limited by our lack of n-mats and the rare resources needed to build gates. The more spread out we get the gates, the more spread out the traffic will be."

"It is quite amazing," Kasey admitted. "You really are going to change the entire galaxy."

"Well, that is the plan I suppose. The Terrantine Federation and the other human civilizations will be able to spread out quite a bit. For once, it's a good thing we have a tendency to overpopulate worlds so quickly, even with strict population controls. We need those people now more than ever. However, we won't have anywhere close to enough people to populate the whole galaxy."

"You sound almost sorry about that."

"It is always the unknowns that worries me. I can't pretend this will all be easy, not that it has been so far. We will use every trick and technology to become more powerful than we really are—every force multiplier we can find will be used to try and take another step ahead of the Pattern. But we do not know what the Pattern is, or what it truly means."

"Or if we can even stop it?" AnnaChi supplied.

"Right, exactly, it's a total unknown. But one thing I am sure of—we are going to find out. And we are going to do that with our human heads held high and eyes wide open."

CHAPTER TEN

They dropped Lieutenant Jate off at the newly forming base that floated a few thousand kilometers from the original pair of gates in the Trias System. A few of the class-F gates were arrayed around the one they had arrived through, along with the usual fleet of navy ships sitting on standby.

The Lodestar and Cintian were joined together, sharing power, and thrust as they accelerated towards Belrothi and their home.

AnnaChi entered the Lodestar's bridge and settled into a station. "I am always surprised at how comfortable these navy cushions are. Seems like they should be hard and less relaxing."

"You tell me. Were they not comfy when you were in the navy?"

"I honestly don't remember. I didn't have much to compare it to back then. Anyway, we need to make a few stops if you want this bucket to have a decent point defense system. I am really not happy with how fast your shields were torn through. I expected more from the upgrades Fran had installed."

Kasey knew when to allow a subject to drop. Her time in the navy was nearly always one of those subjects. "I am a bit worried about the space yours takes up. I mean, your PDL system uses more room for power generation and storage than Lodestar even has available."

"You are not wrong. Lodestar will need something very different. The Cintian's PDL array is pure brute power based, lots of separate PDLs working independently of each other to take on the same targets. Lodestar will need something with more, uh, finesse."

"So, what will *finesse* cost me in cargo space?"

"If I do it right, about a third of what little you have. Unless…"

"Unless what?"

"We could add additional hull sections in key areas around the main bay." She took a minute to pull up a display showing Lodestar with several small hull sections attached around the ship's forward hull. "Your current hull design is not exactly designed for defense, but we can fix that, somewhat. The new sections will hold a large portion of the capacitors you need and give better placement for the optics ports. The main cargo space we utilize will just be for additional generators."

"It seems Lodestar is destined to continually change its shape. Well, that's fine I suppose. Still, I don't see how it will even come close to the Cintian's array."

"That is the actual finesse part. To start with, we add a high-end ordinance scanner. By high end, I mean it will cost more than the whole PDL system. But, by hell, you will know about incoming particles of dust, if that's what you want. All the new PDLs will be networked together into four main groups. Each group will target and fire together in shotgun formation. We can afford the higher end PDLs now as well, so even replacing your old array will help a lot. The new PDL optics will adjust apertures based on target distance to give each fire optimum power. That's a big reason I want the new scanner tied into it all, not to mention the accuracy and earlier detection you will have. All in all, it should give you a far more effective defense, and at greater distances."

"Sounds expensive, but let's do it. How do you think it will compare to the Cintian's PDL system?"

"Not totally sure, but we can test it out with target drones if we have time. My girl has far more ports, so in pure firepower she will win in the end. She can handle a lot more targets at once but needs to wear them down over time. The Lodestar's shotgun grouping should take out basic targets with a single fire from that grouping. The high-end scanner should ensure multiple PDLs are not only on target, but that several others are targeting other probable locations at the same time. Your weakness is going to be dealing with too many targets at once, but I think we can adjust the system to compensate for that, but it will mean more misses."

"But still far better defense than I had before. Sounds great! Why not get a scanner for Cintian too?"

"I will when one becomes available. The one Lodestar will get is the only one in the Trias System for sale, and it is off a scrapped star-cruiser damaged in the Patternist uprising. Ideally, if it works as well as I hope, we will eventually have several on each ship. It is high on my list of wants when we are finally allowed access to the gate system for trade."

"It sounds like a lot of work though. Should we bring in a team to help?"

"Maybe, but I can have the hull additions built and delivered while we are still in route and have a team ready to install them. That will be the hard part. Maintenance bots can do a lot of the other work and I can have the builder bot handle the cargo bay changes. I think. We will still need to get our hands dirty for a few days of work."

Kasey took a moment to check the ship's status and trajectory, then headed for the hatchway. "We are good here for a while. Care to show me where I will be losing cargo space for the new generators?"

* * *

Darnell and Sariyn were waiting in AnnaChi's new shop when they arrived. After properly greeting the flock of atoss with ready snacks, the four went to the main house.

Kasey set a stack of thin boxes on the table he had retrieved from the Lodestar. "I hope you like pizza. It smelled delicious, so I grabbed a few different kinds while we were in town."

"Did you bring any beer to wash it down?"

"Check the big fridge, plenty in there I believe, unless you already cleaned me out? Bring a few, it's been a long trip."

Darnell quickly returned with an armful of bottles. "So, are ya gonna tell us about the trip, or do ya want the business report first?"

"The trip was very eventful. Cassian were there in force. Many times the numbers we saw here. Fran was prepared for most of it, but we took some hits."

"Damn! Did the colony survive? Were you still able to prospect at all?"

"They did, but not well. They had planned to space-mine everything with auto-miners if you can believe it. All their equipment is gone or in ruins, so they are stuck working a planet now."

"If they had the credits for that much auto-mine

setup, they will try to get at least part of it up and running again once the gate system is public. Were you able to locate any good resources?"

"AnnaChi located some n-mats there. So, they have at least some reasons to mine on planet now."

"It was your location," she protested, "I just pointed to a good spot."

Kasey winked at her. "A spot we wouldn't have tried otherwise. And your name is listed as the discoverer. So, you may want to get used to it."

"What kind was it?" Sariyn asked.

"Platinum and iridium were what we found, but the assumption is that any platinum group elements in that area could be n-mats. The bigger concentrations are around gold veins in the area."

"Please tell me you were able to claim it all?" Darnell exclaimed.

"Wish I could have. The navy insisted that the colony have the first crack at them if they set up immediate mine sites. So, I claimed a bunch of areas, but I had to auction them off to the colonists. We ended up with just twelve plots that were not taken, none of which were positively found to have n-mats. Although, I would bet they do have some at least. Oh, and we made a decent profit from the claim auction sales as well."

"I should hope so! Are the gold findings decent on the ones you were able to keep?"

"If I did the numbers right, the profits would be close to, or slightly better than, our copper mines. It's a low gravity world too, so I am not sure if that helps or hinders the process."

"Hard to say without a soil sample, but we would need a few modifications to the normal setup. Likely wouldn't affect the bottom line much."

Sariyn shook her head. "They are not going to get much in the way of n-mats from platinum. Is that why the price suddenly jumped up tenfold?"

"Yep, exactly why. The mine owners there saw value in it and pushed the price as high as they could."

"I almost feel bad for them, knowing how little they will profit compared to the mine here," Darnell shrugged, "but that's how mining goes."

"Speaking of which," Kasey looked at Sariyn, "were you able to get any ideas on how much we are sitting on?"

"Well… Bad news is that the cinnabar ore is spotty. There is a lot of it, and it goes deep, but it's not as consistent as I would like. I still feel we should mine it. The n-mats from it would make a decent profit at the new prices. The volume we can pull out is limited due to access and so returns could potentially diminish every season. At maximum, I think we could produce three to five hundred metric tons a year. If it wasn't for the price on n-mats, it wouldn't be worth doing."

"That doesn't sound overly horrible."

"Well, the worst part is that we would need a few teams and plenty of land on the surface to process it all, and that means it would be almost impossible to keep the knowledge of the n-mats a secret for long."

"I see. Alright, well let's table the cinnabar ore until we can entertain going public with our mine. What else do we know?"

"The main chamber is likely to hold over twenty thousand cubic meters of mercury, nearly three hundred thousand tons. That estimate may be a bit on the high side, but it's close."

Kasey choked on his beer. "That's a lot more than I expected." He glanced at AnnaChi catching her eye. "More than I hoped for too."

Sariyn passed a pad over to him showing their main cavern. A honeycomb of pocket chambers covered the ceiling of the mercury pool. "Nothing we have can scan into that pool, but I was able modify maintenance bots to crawl through it and map as best they could."

"Nice work on this."

"It was nothing, really. Locating the other pools was the hard part."

"How many others were you able to locate?"

"Twenty-three so far. I expect to find at least double that eventually. Still, I believe the ones we have already are the largest we will find."

"That many... Any that are as big as the main cavern?"

"No, that one is the motherload. But altogether, the other pools are at several times over the volume of the main cavern."

Taking another bite of his pizza, Kasey stared at the table thinking while the others continued the discussion. He could hardly believe that so much material existed in the mountain. So much potential.

He looked up to find them all looking at him, "How long would it take to extract and stockpile a hundred thousand tons from the caverns?"

Darnell and Sariyn looked at him as if he had lost his mind.

"Is that a real question?" Darnell spat out once he had composed himself.

"Very real."

"We don't have anything near the setup we would need for that kind of job."

"And if we had the right equipment?"

"I still couldn't give you an answer until we setup and worked through the problems."

"You are asking the wrong question, Kasey," Sariyn interjected as she leaned back in her chair and smiled.

"Oh? Okay then, what is the right question?" Kasey asked.

"You should be asking if we can deliver it by the

time you need it. So, tell us, when do you need it?"

"Two standard months."

Darnell started to laugh uncontrollably, so Kasey decided it was a good time to gather a few more beers. Darnell slowly stopped laughing as Kasey returned with the bottles but was still shaking his head in disbelief. Sariyn, on the other hand, was still calmly sitting back comfortably with a smile on her face.

"So," Kasey tried again, "can you make that timeline?"

"Yea, Darnie, can you make the *deadline*?" Sariyn echoed.

He turned sharply to look at her. "Have I ever missed a deadline?"

"Tell him, not me."

"Fine." He turned to Kasey with a determined look. "Sure boss, we can make that happen. Although, I am not sure you will like the price tag."

"Oh? And what do you think it will cost me?"

"Your anonymity."

CHAPTER ELEVEN

Kasey finished installing the last of the Lodestar's optic ports for the new PDL array as AnnaChi joined him.

"Checking my work?" she asked.

"Certainly not... I only do that when you are not around. Seriously though, it's well past lunch time. Time for a break."

"It's hard to think about food when installing lasers that could burn a fist size hole through me."

"Don't be silly, they aren't powered yet."

"Any updates on Darnell's progress?"

"Several actually. Let's see... They have the new fabricator set up and running in the shed for the larger storage container designs. A full-sized hangar is being built on the far side of that shed with a warehouse underneath. Both buildings will connect into the shed or cavern entrance. There is some debate on how that will work, but my understanding is that the containers will be filled and moved to the warehouse area without leaving either building. They will be hard pressed to have it ready by the time the storage area we added below the shop is maxed out."

"Are we asking too much of them? They are killing themselves to make the arbitrary date I gave, and we don't even have access to create the ship for it all."

"I wouldn't worry about it too much. From what I see, problem solving is what they live for. The bigger the problem, the more satisfying it is to solve. Besides, they both seem as excited about the carrier as we are."

"Really? They barely said a word while I was describing it."

"They are not ship people, not the way we are. They don't care about the ship's details. However, the prospect of exploring and setting up operations across lots of systems had them both wide-eyed and dreaming. Think of it this way—they became colonists on Farpoint because they wanted something new and exciting. Jumping into the unknown always is. Now, you are offering them a completely new opportunity with huge potential, and they are going to run towards it."

"Ya know, of the two of us, I didn't think you were one who could read people."

She smacked him upside the head playfully, "Well you have a lot to learn, darlin. Now clean up the bushings on that last weld quickly and get to the house, or I will eat without you."

* * *

Kasey landed his bard on the landing pad in front of the lodge retreat. Two seconds later a set of unmanned bards landed behind him. Darnell was sitting on the porch entertaining Jasper.

Kasey held out his hand for the small atoss, but it swooped around him twice before disappearing into the forest.

"He is growing fast."

"True that is." Darnell looked at the trio of bards and then off into the forest after Jasper. "I know I haven't been here long, but I am reluctant to leave him."

"If all goes well, it won't be for long. They are not the only reason for the carrier, but they are a big piece of it."

"Right. Well, best get on with it. I assume these are the n-mats versions AnnaChi mentioned?"

"She just finished them. Have you driven bards before?"

"A few times, but I only experienced the jump jets once when I was a passenger. Not a great memory."

"Well, you will be happy to know these don't have the kick or thrill of normal ones. They are more like a tiny shuttle taking off and landing, and you have all the time you need to pick a landing spot. Just click where you want to go, and let it do the rest."

"We'll see... How do they handle on the ground?"

"Not as well as they do in the air. They are a lot lighter than other ATVs so are prone to bouncing more than you would be used to. I have tipped over several times. To help with that, AnnaChi added a stabilizer to these that should keep them upright. Personally, I think it makes the whole thing feel weirder, but I am sure we will all get used to it. If you don't like the stabilizer, turn it off."

"I'll give it a try. I assume it has a simulator built in?"

"It does. But it's not a great replication of the real thing, so use it, but give the real thing some serious testing."

"Alrighty. How soon are we going to need them?"

"I would take you with us on this trip if we could, but we need you to get this place in order. This trip will be shorter than the last one and the gate's orbit is in a helpful spot right now. We should have a five-day trip out and only a four-day trip back. If we are lucky, we will locate an n-mats pocket within two weeks and be on our way back. I would like you both on the following trip if everything shakes out."

Darnell looked at the bards doubtfully, but nodded. "I will be ready. Sariyn won't have any issues, I believe she used to race these things."

"Hah, now that I believe! Will the new crew you brought in to run this all be ready?"

"Yes. They were already solid mining crews before we bought them out."

"We bought out a whole crew?"

"Two of them actually, owners and all. You met them already."

"The ones with the water issues? Let's see, Winslow mining and, uh, what was the other one called?"

"Danbury. Both are now under Phoenix Mining, and making a lot more credits all around—including bonuses—across the board until the secret of this place gets out. That will keep it quiet a bit longer, but not forever. We also took out loans to cover the purchase of the companies, which will help keep your finances from showing too much activity. A late payment will help even more."

Kasey smiled at his friend's aptitude for clandestine business. "What did you end up doing to hide the other cavern entrances?"

"Ha! I was wondering when you would ask. A business license has been requested for a mountain getaway rental business. While that was processing, we built lodges complete with enclosed shuttle bays which have sealed entrances into the caverns. Each rental property has enough land cleared for your Altair or smaller transport to land for pickups."

"So, I own a rental business now?"

"No, sadly your silent partner pulled out and so the license was never finalized. Noise pollution from the copper mines was cited as the issue. So, no business, but now you have a bunch of empty lodges on your property. More importantly, you have a public reason for them to exist that won't raise questions. Although, we did build a real lodge closer to the copper mines and roads; easy picking for anyone curious enough to sneak a look at one of them. Like all of them, anyone entering the property or building itself will set off alerts and let us know."

"All that, and you still think we will be found out?"

"Undoubtedly. People talk eventually and you just doubled your business, which will draw some attention from other miners. If there is a mystery, it will get talked about. The trick is to supply more misleading questions as quickly as possible to keep them busy. That is another reason I bought out both those crews; the owners and foremen have some experience with these kinds of things, unlike our own crews."

"Do we have a problem there?"

"Not really. They are loyal as any miners making good credits. All the miners from all teams share in the production bonuses, so they are all making good credits. Our miners are staying at the copper mines and expanding to take over the ones we purchased. They will be busy. The output on all the copper mines will decrease a bit, but overall, they will have more credits in their pockets at the end of the day."

"So, the Winslow and Danbury teams will be on n-mats then?"

"Yep, tighter and more cohesive teams, less rogue problems. Winslow will likely take over my job here when I am away while Danbury will oversee all the mines and assist Winslow as needed. Once things go public, they will be good people to handle things here. Frankly, they are better than me on the business side."

"Speaking of letting people do what they are good at, I could use your help." Kasey handed him a pad. "Fran just sent the scans from the new system this morning. The Julius system. I could use your input on locations to try for n-mats."

"Ah, well then, you have come to the right place. Julius… Wait, how much time do I have to look at this?"

"AnnaChi and I leave tomorrow, but will still be in-system for another five days. I will give you a navy address to send anything you notice after that, but there is no telling if it will get to me or not since they still have dampeners and restrictions on all gates. Don't put anything sensitive in those comms—I have no doubt they will be monitored."

Darnell was already looking at the data. "Two planets? Julius Four and Six. They didn't name them? Yea, this could take months of analysis."

"I am sure that is just the navy's designation for them. You will need to concentrate on the most likely locations for n-mats. We will be lucky to have a week at each planet. Reviewing this is secondary to your work here too, so don't get lost in this data. If all goes well, this will be the first of many worlds we get to examine."

Darnell tore his eyes away from the pad. "Priorities first, right. Will you be making claims in the Julius system too?"

"Yes, but I will need to be pickier. Their claims are a lot more expensive than Bendek's were. We are going to need every credit we can scrounge for the carrier. Just like in the Zyta system, I won't be able to keep any n-mats claims unless we can mine them right away, but I can claim other rich ground if we find any."

"Son, you really need to renegotiate that," Darnell said matter-of-factly.

"With the navy?"

"Absolutely. You are a contractor, not enlisted. I know he is your friend, but no one with proven results would take a deal like that."

Kasey did not want to bring up that the only reason he even had this opportunity at all was because of Fran's belief that Kasey was somehow necessary to help humanity avoid the Pattern.

Kasey gave Darnell a questioning look instead. "What do you think is fair? I don't want to lose this opportunity over business squabbles."

"I see, hmm. Then ask for a percentage of the claims, maybe one in ten minable locations of equal value. You don't want to throw away an opportunity to have claims or mines on every new world directly connected to the Trias System, right?"

"True I suppose, but it worries me. AnnaChi already believes we have been too hard on him. She sees him like a father, you know."

"Well, like I mentioned, there are far better businessmen than me around, so take my advice with a grain of salt. Look, if you really trust him, then ask him to decide each time if you should get to keep any claims. If he is the person you believe he is, then he will most likely grant you more than any contract would. You can always take the business route later. Perhaps after you secure what you need for the new ship?"

"Now that's a plan I can start with. I really don't think he wants to hold us back at all. Oh—that reminds me, we have a ton of other claims on Bendek that I never got to tell you about. None have n-mats, but we have a lot of land that could be worth mining. Now that the Zyta colony is more dependent on planet mining, they may be interested in buying some of them that we don't want in time. They were all on the bidding block, so they are aware they exist, just no takers."

"Alright, I see we need a standard intake process for new claims. I'll work something up but send me all the data and designations before you leave. Should I assume we won't be starting any operations beyond Belrothi before we have the carrier in play?"

"Correct. But we are going to need a serious increase to our crews by then. So, as soon as we have the go-ahead on the carrier, feel free to bulk up here to get all the copper mines running with full crews."

"Hmm, we may want to start now if we can, but we are already stretching operations here a bit too thin. Look, there are lots of small operations here on Belrothi; the Farpoint program made sure the colony was overloaded with miners. Surely some of them are ripe for being sold. I know we can't afford to buy out another operation outright right now. So, what about this—we invest in a handful of small companies who need help and who are willing to at least talk about selling."

"How much investment are we talking about?"

"In most cases they just need to replace a piece of equipment to make it through the season, or maybe to help secure the land. Small operations take a lot of risks and one malfunction can ruin a season for them."

"Sounds like a bigger risk for us if they still fail?"

"Well yes, but their success is not really the point of these investments."

"Then what is?"

"We get all the insight into their operations and people that we need to make a larger decision. Shit goes wrong and operations fail, sure. But that doesn't always mean the crew are bad. The point is to find the good crews we need for our company. If their season fails, it will just be that much cheaper for us to buy the company or recruit the crew."

"I see, I think. It also keeps them away from our operations until we have them vetted a bit. I like it."

"Yep, although there is at least one crew in this valley that I will be looking at harder too."

"Fine, do it. If this works out, put a standard process together to do this on an ongoing basis, and in other systems too. We may need a steady supply of crews as we set up new operations."

"You got it. There are few more things we can add to that if we need to as well."

"Good. Not to complicate things, but the copper mining is not just ours—we may need sign off from Fran and Flair."

"Not needed. We already went through the process of converting all the Phoenix Mining operations over to subleases under Red Rock Enterprises so that we could minimize workers on the existing mines without problems. Phoenix actually makes out very well in the deal as it now owns the two additional operations. If we start up more operations on Belrothi, they would be added to their sheet, not Red Rock. We are also under contract to Phoenix for minimum production from each mine. Considering we already pulled a lot of good miners from them, we will likely pay a few fines to Phoenix this season. A portion of those fines will go right back in the coffers, so it's not a big loss."

"Alright, I can see this is going to continue to get more complicated. I'll talk to Fran and Flair about this next trip and make sure we are not overstepping."

"Sounds fine to me. They know some of it already, but there has not been much communication on any of their wishes. In the grand scheme of things, all the Belrothi operations will be training mines—that is, if your carrier plan works out. If it comes up, see if they are willing to be bought out, and if not, see if they want to merge Phoenix Mining into Red Rock Enterprises. We can keep them separate, but it could save headaches later if we had it as a subsidiary company instead of a partner."

"Just the kinds of things I wanted to stay far away from understanding," Kasey laughed, "but I will bring it up and go from there. Can you write up something for the options? I am sure they will have changes and proposals…"

"Can do. And for that, I am glad you had the sense to pilfer the old Reavestone cores from Lithose. They are loaded with documentation for handling these kinds of things."

"Glad it was good for something. Get me what you can before I am out of system. Like I mentioned, comms may be limited after that."

"Sure thing boss. Listen, if it all gets too complex, just delay till me and Sariyn can be there with you. It is one of the reasons you hired us." He held up the pad. "Got anything else? This data is calling me, and I want to get to it."

"Not unless you have an update on Sariyn's research?"

"She is deep into it. Was concerned about how different the Lithose storms are from the gas giant storms the ship was designed for. 'Too many assumptions,' she complained before leaving. She has some contacts she wanted to question in person. Not to worry, she won't give any plans away."

"I hope I wasn't wrong about that design. It seemed perfect, but she is right—I should have had someone do real research on it before I got everyone excited. AnnaChi…"

"Don't even worry about it. Sariyn has never met a problem that she couldn't solve. If it won't work as-is, she will find a way to make it work."

CHAPTER TWELVE

Kasey unloaded the final core sample before seeking out AnnaChi.

A chain of three slightly active volcanoes comprised the only notable feature of the planet's landscape. As far as Kasey could tell, they were also the only source of n-mats in the entire system. The grasslands had been their first stop of the search, and now they were back, hoping to find better samples.

The two habitable planets in the system were nothing special. One was a dust ball with little in the way of comfort, and the one they were on now was lush with basic vegetation, but very little life otherwise. Marshlands and plains covered the majority of the temperate areas. To Kasey, it was simply boring.

A majority of the navy's team had gone to the dust ball planet, using Kasey and Darnell's research as a basis on where to search. Meanwhile, Kasey and AnnaChi lead a team around to the few places of note that Darnell had been able to locate.

He looked back at the stack of core samples. Maybe one of them would bring better news for this system.

Their earlier dig found only a few grams of gold-based n-mats. While gold was a high mass element, it was too rare to be of immediate use. Unless the deep cores showed better results, the Pathfinder would be pushing on to the next system earlier than expected.

AnnaChi grabbed him from behind, startling him. "About time you show up," she chided. "You missed a very unsatisfactory lunch."

"Stick to my energy bars then?"

"Definitely." She scrunched her face in disgust. "My samples were unremarkable—at least that is the word they used in the report."

"Then we are likely out of here as soon as my cores are processed?"

"Looks that way. Are we sticking around for the next jump or heading home? Personally, it would be nice to see an interesting planet before we go. This whole system is just, meh." She stuck out her tongue.

"With ya there, but I am not looking forward to another battle."

"There wasn't one here, ya know."

"Sure, but they know there are Cassian here somewhere, which is why they never set their gate up. Fran seemed like he might abandon the whole system instead of leaving a gate to guard here."

"I don't know, it's a fairly central system for this area of the arm."

"Does that even matter now—with gate systems, I mean?" He scratched at his chin.

"Well, sure. The gates only reach so far. The class-F ones that would form the nexus here are under three thousand light-years, so abandoning it could potentially cut off hundreds or even thousands of other systems from direct nexus access."

"Well, I am glad it's not my decision. Let Fran figure it out."

"Speaking of… Our presence has been asked for on the Pathfinder once we can leave this rock."

"Great… Any messages from home get through?"

"Just one word."

"One word?"

"Yep, from Sariyn."

He laughed. "And what's the word?"

AnnaChi could not help but join his laughter. "Doable."

* * *

"You want to do what?" exclaimed Kasey.

"Not me, the Federation. The council. This is above me, but I agree with their need. With the failure to find other worlds that have readily available n-mats, we need to explore other options."

"Forcing us to accept direct navy involvement in our mining operation is not exploring other options, that's an illegal takeover. Period."

Fran sighed and nodded. "While there is precedent for these kinds of things, I agree with your sentiments of it. What I need are other options. To be perfectly frank, I know you have possibilities you won't bring to the table. Hell, all four of us here have a very good idea of what could easily be taken out of that mountain of yours."

Flair was about to interrupt, but AnnaChi held up her hand and stood. "I adore you both, but you need to learn some tact. Particularly with friends. Fran, I believe we understand exactly what you need, and we do understand your part in all this. We know you are holding back cards from this game too, but you can toss them all and drop the pretense so we can move forward. Kasey, dear, this is as good a time as any, so go ahead and explain what *we* need."

Everyone slowly sat back in their seats except Kasey. He took a few deep breaths to center himself then jumped in. "How much n-mats would the Federation be happy with over the next six months? What would keep them satisfied and out of our business?"

Fran looked to Flair, who answered. "Upwards of twelve thousand tons in total are being requested across all current projects. In six months, it will very likely be twice that."

Kasey nodded. "Fine, so if we can deliver twenty-four thousand tons over the next six months, you keep the navy out of our home—for good? Not just your word, but sealed and official."

Fran didn't blink. "We can make that happen, yes. But it will be asked that the supply continue beyond those six months," Fran confirmed as he slowly leaned forward. "Is that even possible to deliver?"

"Yes. In fact, we can do better than that if the navy can help us out with *our* problem."

Fran smiled. "And just what problem would that be?"

"We need a custom ship built to military specifications. Rugged and strong, but lightweight construction."

"I see, and this ship will be used for—what exactly?"

"A new business venture, dealing mainly with transporting, but it will help with the mining business as well."

"Plenty of ships on the market once the public trade gates open. And plenty of public builders out there as well that will build close to military specs. If you need earlier access, I can arrange something. Why do you feel you would need the navy for that?"

"Actually, not many builders can handle this order and none of them will provide the quality of materials and workmanship the navy can, even if they claim they will. Besides, we are under federal oath not to discuss certain details of the ship."

Fran looked down at the table in thought for several moments before responding.

"Well... I should have assumed it would have some n-mats ballast built in. Something you are already doing with your ships and even your ATVs as I understand. We have a few small projects in those areas as well... Still, that should be able to be explained away. Another reason perhaps?"

"The size is also a problem..."

"You two are doing it again," AnnaChi growled. "Get to the damn point already."

Kasey frowned but nodded, "We need a ship fabricator that can handle a three-hundred-and-fifty-meter vessel. A highly customized carrier. The sooner the better."

Fran rocked back in his seat and crossed his arms, but kept his stoic look in place, while Flair raised an eyebrow curiously and sat up straighter. The small room remained silent for several minutes as they took in the idea.

Kasey finally leaned forward and used a pad to project the carrier designs. "This is not the final design, but should give you a general idea. Think of a massive transporter for colonists going to the new systems the gates will open access to. One that can land on a planet and change loads in a matter of days instead of weeks."

"You should have led with that!" Fran smiled. "That, I can certainly work with. Flair, problems?"

She nodded. "A few to be certain. We cannot supply weapons other than standard defense, however we can add all the hardpoints you like, and what I see here can be improved in that area. They already have contractor status and high enough clearance to apply for general shop access, but the ship would need to be labeled as a prototype with the navy retaining all details of construction. Ownership can only be turned over after a successful test flight that meets navy standards. I assume this will be under your Red Rock entity?"

"No, AnnaChi and I need to own the ship fully. It will be our home. The businesses the ship handles will be separate for the most part, and we will lease space for their needs. Red Rock Enterprises will likely oversee that part of the relationship."

"Okay, I believe we can work that out if we create a simple company for the two of you. A consulting firm perhaps would be most useful. Next issue is the time, labor, and materials cost. Oh, and does this carrier have a name?"

"We are thinking of calling it Nimbus. I would prefer a trade in n-mats at cost for whatever we need."

"One moment." She looked off to the side for several seconds. "Okay, you realize that will be nearly double what you are already verbally contracted to?"

"Yes, another twenty thousand tons at the current price, if my math is correct."

"Right. Good. What about spares and general outfitting?"

"I will want plenty of spares for every system, hull kits, the works. Double that for any non-standard systems. General outfitting for critical functions, crew areas, hangar bays, emergency areas, things of that sort. We will deal with passenger areas and nonessentials ourselves."

"Alright. I won't have accurate numbers until we have your final designs reviewed and run through processing, but I am guessing it will run two to three thousand tons."

"How about we add another three thousand tons. Call it goodwill, or whatever helps everything run smoothly and quickly. That's an even fifty thousand tons. Again, the sooner we have the carrier—the Nimbus—the better."

Flair looked at Fran for acceptance before continuing and received a slow nod.

"General terms are a minimum of four thousand tons a month over the next two years, with renewal options to be discussed at that time. An additional twenty-six thousand tons will be due prior to taking ownership of the prototype carrier ship, Nimbus. Acceptable?"

"The n-mats prices need to be at current prices or better if we are keeping this all under contract." Kasey frowned at the thought. "I also need an end date in two years with options to renew. As well as options if the mine fails to produce. This supply won't last forever…"

Fran sat forward and cleared his throat, "Look, we can go with a six-month contract without renewal options altogether if you can do two things. For me, as a friend."

"And those are?"

"First, promise to keep supplying n-mats to us. And second, take some of my trusted people under employment on your ship. If command knows I have people in your organization, they will be much easier to appease. Easier to gain acceptance for the more difficult noninterference contract."

"Who did you have in mind?"

"Well, for a start, Lieutenant Jate needs a long break from service and has shown interest in your outfit. And…"

"Me," Flair announced.

Fran looked at her sharply in surprise, but not with any anger, "Are you sure? You know I need you here…"

"I'll miss you too, but you are aware that I have wanted away from the service for a while now."

"I know, I know, but so much is happening. And you are too damn good. The Cassian have been in every system so far and—well, you know the situation. You are *needed* here."

"And you know I do not want to be in a constant war, again. And frankly, I am not needed for a brute-force war anyway. You have plenty of capable men and woman that can handle my job."

"I won't hold you back, you know that."

She looked at Kasey and AnnaChi. "Sorry, retirement for a few more years in the Trias System would have suited me just fine. If you will have me, I am sure I can be helpful running the Nimbus."

"We would be happy to have you, to be honest. But I am not sure you have thought it all through—we have a huge undertaking ahead of us."

She nodded. "You are definitely covering new territory with this project, but I think I get it. You will have a carrier that can land on planets and move large numbers of people, equipment, and resources to the new systems—and as you do that you will claim minable land and set up mine sites using the carrier as a mobile base of operations. With the number of passengers and crew you will have onboard, the Nimbus will need shops, entertainment, restaurants, the works. You will have a host of different divisions that need to be put in place for the ship alone."

"Right…" Kasey swallowed as he realized how much still needed worked out. "As Fran mentioned a while back—the resource needs of the Federation will soon change. This is how I see us changing with it. But before you commit to joining our crew, we need to talk about Phoenix Mining."

"You're looking to buy us out, right?" Fran laughed.

"Something like that, something fair though. But what's funny?"

"Phoenix Mining was always a wash for us. We learned of your n-mats the same day we started that company, remember? Once I knew of that, it was my job, our job, to protect it. The proceeds from it all go into a slush fund for other activities, not us personally. So, by all means, please buy us out."

"I shouldn't be surprised... Can I ask what kind of activities?"

"You can ask. Answering is the hard part. I can only make you aware that most of it goes to things you already see around you—if you take time to notice them. The n-mats trade network for example."

Kasey nodded slowly. "Okay... What about Belrothi Copper?"

"Totally legitimate. Are you looking to do something there too?"

"No. Unless that is what you want."

"Well, since you asked... We would like to know if we can merge it into Red Rock Enterprises somehow. Actually, we just want to buy into Red Rock if that is possible."

"We will be dealing with n-mats—isn't that a conflict of interest, just as Phoenix was? I would rather keep navy dealings separated going forward."

"It is, to an extent. Less than Phoenix was though. Hmm, but there is a solution now! I will transfer all my shares to Flair as soon as possible. Once she is officially out of the corps, we can figure out a merger of some sort, leaving myself and the navy ties out of it."

"I feel I should point out that Red Rock Enterprises is a much larger company. You wouldn't have the percentage you do of Belrothi Copper."

"Well aware. In fact, my current share would be worth well under one percent of Red Rock, I believe. However, that makes no difference if the business is doing well. If you are willing, Flair should have credits enough to make up the difference and bring us, I mean her, up to a full one percent of Red Rock at current values."

Flair nodded in agreement but did not comment.

"Well, that is an interesting proposal. Flair, I am not completely sure what your position is in the navy currently?"

She shrugged. "Rank and duty differs a lot as the navy is currently very top-heavy. I serve where and how I am needed. I have held nearly every position, up to and including vice admiral over the past five decades. However, I far prefer an executive officer position where I can control my ship or command."

Kasey took a moment to think over how she would fit into the carrier's crew, and sent a few queries to AnnaChi to make sure she was in agreement. He had realized long ago just how capable Flair was, and assumed she only stayed under Fran's command because she wanted to. His bigger concern was that he was being played, again—allowing Fran to place someone directly into their organization.

He looked at Fran. He was watching Flair and seemed oddly forlorn. Kasey wanted to believe it was an act but could not. The man had misled him in the past, and generally left out a lot of facts, yet for this to be an act would take things to a different level. If this were an act, it would end any friendship between them.

He looked at Flair. "Would you be willing to take a captain's chair? For Red Rock, that means nearly all departments would report to you for ship functions. That will bleed over into business functions a lot at first but may change down the road. Darnell is running Red Rock, but his concentration is on the mining division which I hope will grow exponentially."

"I could do that, with the right people in charge of departments. Not to be forward, but what does the position pay?"

"There will be a standard pay rate worked up, now

that this venture is more than just an idea. But the position also comes with a one percent stake in Red Rock earnings for as long as you hold the position."

"Fair enough. When would you need me to start?"

"As soon as the ship is ready." He caught Fran's eye. "We will also approve the merger and remaining purchase of one percent after your shares are turned over to Flair and she is no longer under navy employment. Flair will effectively own two percent of Red Rock Enterprises once the Nimbus is sailing."

Fran reached forward and spun the image of the carrier. "Well, Flair my girl, looks like your last mission is to get this ship built, and built well." He looked over the design more closely. "It's an odd-looking ship, where did you get the main design from?"

"It's an old Jovian explorer design, used for deep dives into gas giants."

"Ah! Now I understand why you are holding off on the bulk of the outfitting. You're going to land this beast on Lithose!"

"Salvage will be our first mission, yes. Outfitting would cost a fortune otherwise, but we need the mining supplies on Lithose even more. Then we will concentrate on the transport and mining business."

"Bah, that ship is a long-term investment. You're planning on more than a few salvage missions."

AnnaChi spun and faced Kasey. "Something you forgot to mention, dear?"

Kasey raised his hands defensively. "No, truly, I have no plans other than outfitting the ship. But I am not blind to the fact that having the only access to that planet could be useful someday. If any of you have a more worthwhile design and a way to pay for both outfitting it and gathering an entire world's worth of mining supplies, I am all ears."

"Alright," Fran interjected before AnnaChi could,

"anything else we need to discuss today? I need to get Pathfinder ready for the next system. Will you two be joining us?"

"Yes, we will join this jump. But there is one last thing..."

"You want n-mats claims."

"Yes. Red Rock will need strong n-mats claims for the mining division to get started quickly, as well as keeping our navy supplies coming. To that end, we need more than just the leftover claims the colonists don't want on these consulting trips. The sooner we have Nimbus in business, the sooner we can start up operations to mine them."

"Point taken. Flair, do we have an estimate on the when the Nimbus can go into the queues?"

"We have one opening up at Gemini Nexus in about a week. I am requesting the queue be bumped, which I believe will be approved since there are n-mats on the line. If the schematics are ready, we can have a team reviewing them tomorrow. Unless there are large issues, the basic framing can start as soon as the fabricator is cleared. Meaning that, with no issues, we can have it built in a little over forty days. A week in outfitting should have her ready for test runs."

"Well then, Kasey, how soon could you put miners on the ground at a new n-mats site?"

"Three to four months after ship delivery."

"You can do better than that. How about you deliver a group of colonists and have miners ready to start ten weeks after you take delivery of Nimbus."

"Colonists from where?"

"Earth Prime cluster. Details will need worked out."

"Is the gate system going public?"

"It is already being leaked out to generate interest and to get politics and any negative backlash from other groups like the Patternists out of the way. We can have a group ready for pickup, as well as a landing zone prepared for your ship with ease."

"Are the Patternists still a big issue in the cluster?"

"Aye. Although they are losing a huge portion of their flocks as the Trias System's attack goes public. That bit of true propaganda is being released as the gates are deployed into systems. Still, those who remain under the Patternist cult are just as dangerous. Maybe more so now without the oversight of the levelheaded members that are leaving them over the Trias incident. We have also found and rooted out several groups under Cassian influence. So, keep your eyes open."

Kasey tilted his head. "I hate to ask, but are you sure you want the Nimbus to show that it can land on a planet that soon? N-mats are still a secret, right?"

"A secret that is about to end. There will be a rush of colonists when the gates open regardless, but we need more than just unsatisfied people looking for a new life. We need corporations to invest in these new systems. N-mats will create the goldrush we need to make that happen. When word of your ship gets out, it will cause a stir, and everyone will be guessing how it works—but as soon as we leak the existence of n-mats, the media will put the two together very quickly. There will be no stopping the expansion of humanity after that."

AnnaChi huffed and held up a finger. "So, that will mean you will still need to be controlling the gate network then? Limiting who goes where?"

"For a while, yes. Traffic as well. Same as any world or station does today."

"For how long?" she demanded.

"As long as it takes to keep everyone safe."

"And what will that mean for us traveling through the gate system?" Kasey interjected, before it became an argument.

"Flair's access, even while not in the service, will

allow you passage through the civilian gates. There is a Trade Nexus in the Earth cluster connected to a Trias System class-A trade gate set. That Trade Nexus already has a few gates ready to be activated soon, and a lot more will follow. A new, smaller jump ship is placing them in key systems all around the Earth Prime cluster."

"I see. Ten weeks, huh? I can have mining teams ready but getting Nimbus to Lithose for the salvage trip and back to Belrothi to finish the outfitting is going to be a lot tighter than I would like. Hold on…"

Kasey called up a system map of the Trias System and plotted a few routes.

"Can you give me distances and gravity-well statistics of the Trade Nexus?"

Flair leaned forward and added some data. "Here are the averages. Based on your planned engines for Nimbus it will take one to two days travel between the gates planned to be activated in the coming months. However, I assume you will be offsetting the ships mass with a huge quantity of n-mats and will be able to achieve a far greater acceleration?"

"Uh, yes and no. We will have the n-mats, however, not only will they be somewhat offset by the ballasts, but we will be fully loaded from the pickup on our way back through the nexus."

"I see. I honestly cannot wait to dive into the numbers on all this, but I would like to see us get our average travel time well below the average for a ship this size, even when fully loaded. I know this is your ship, but you will be setting the standard that navy ships will be able to accomplish when n-mats are more readily available. If you are willing, I would like to push those limits where I can. Engine and power upgrades will help a lot but the perfect mix of n-mats and ballasts for average systems could help a lot more."

"No argument here—time is money. Every day that

we can shave off a round trip will be a small fortune saved. Let me know costs as early as possible; I have some wiggle room but not much." He finished looking over the numbers and shook his head. "Okay, so based on what I see here, and using averages for the unknown systems, we are looking at a twenty-five-day trip from Belrothi to whatever new world the colonists are traveling to—minimum. That does not give us much time to pick up n-mats and a team from Belrothi and do a round trip to Lithose and back for the final outfitting and crew. If we don't have time for the Lithose salvage trip beforehand, then there is no sense in gaining claims because I won't have equipment for them."

"Can you do it with twelve weeks?" Fran countered.

"If the pickup and drop-off planets are in decent orbits in relation to the gates at the time, then yes."

"Agreed, and we are planning for least-time trips on our end for the shipments we will be involved in. Once gate travel is fully opened, it will be up to the organizations, like what you are building, to pick the most efficient jobs."

"So then, n-mats claims?"

"How does this sound—you get one claim of your choice off the top. Your choice. After that, you need to bid on them like all the rest of the colonists. However, you need to demonstrate two things. First, your ability to setup a working mine operation on the first new world Nimbus lands upon. Second, the claim you choose from each of the consulting missions must have a mining operation set up within a standard year of that claim."

"And the claims we bid on and win?"

"Those ones will only go back to auction if you cannot set up at least one operation in a system other than the Trias System within a standard year. General terms are that you need to be established as a multi-system business owner for the Federation to endorse your claims. Without that endorsement, the system can insist the claim be sold back to the system for a new auction. Standard fine print on multi-system claims which is usually ignored, but if you are bidding on high value n-mats claims, then I assure you that the systems will be coming after them eventually."

"Well, I don't see issues with any of that, assuming we have access to get to those systems, which it sounds like we do."

"Done." Fran seemed pleased. "And well done at that."

"Thanks. We will just need to get word to Darnell and start planning sessions as soon as possible."

"No problem. We can get a message through for you before the first jump. We jump early tomorrow. If all goes well, we should have a gate in place in three days."

Kasey stood. "Well then—let us see what tomorrow brings."

CHAPTER THIRTEEN

Five new systems and two major battles later, Kasey sat on the Lodestar watching as the Nimbus was released from the navy's outfitting bay.

A low whistle of admiration came from beside him as AnnaChi took in the large carrier.

"You like it?" he asked skeptically.

"I still can't believe she's ours! Granted, its shaped like someone tried to crush a hard-boiled egg, and failed, and it could really use some color—seriously, navy gray is just about as bland as you can get. Still, she has got serious potential."

"Took long enough to build…"

"You need to expect delays for these things."

"I know, but I don't have to like it."

"You are awfully grouchy for such an exciting day."

Kasey sighed. He was, but couldn't explain why. "Just nerves, I guess. I will feel better once I am aboard and we have control. We were left out of a lot of decisions we really should have been consulted on. I am worried about what we weren't told."

"I get it. It is our ship and our resources paying for it.

That much investment is awful hard when you are not in control."

As usual, she was able to see what he could not. He nodded and took the Lodestar above the Nimbus for a different view. Four topside landing pads surrounded a protective segmented shell that took up the center portion of the ship. It was currently closed up, but could be lowered. Below it, he knew, would be the top of the botanical garden's dome, which had a secondary shell.

"Lodestar to Nimbus."

"This is Flair, go ahead Lodestar."

"Can you open the dome please?"

"Affirmative."

The shell began twisting apart, sinking downward into the hull. Beneath was a large crescent shaped pool wrapped halfway around an inner dome. Between the pool and dome, a running track and several relaxing looking areas were set up. The opposite side of the ship from the pool continued the running track but had much larger open spaces. Kasey was unable to identify the usage of some of them, but all appeared to be committed to relaxation.

The inner shell around the garden slowly opened a few moments later.

"I expected there to be greenery inside?" AnnaChi observed.

"No, not yet. They were able to load it with soil, hydration, and environmental systems but very little else. When we stop at the Belrothi-Abscond station the trees, grass, and such will be added. Algae ponds will be seeded, but we won't be adding any edibles or wildlife for a while yet."

AnnaChi frowned. "It won't be ready for Molly then?"

"No, not until after the trip to Lithose. We will have a horticulturist along, working to prepare the gardens for the atoss while we collect the resources we need from the planet. When we get back to Belrothi for the full outfitting, it should be ready."

"I guess I expected that, but I was hopeful." She frowned. "I have been putting off looking at the crew manifest. I am really not looking forward to meeting so many new people. It's going to be a hassle."

"Well, this one at least won't be new—you already know her."

"What? Who?"

"Yaran. I didn't know her background until recently. It never came up on the flight from Lithose. We were all just glad to survive. I looked her and others up to see if they had any useful skills that we needed, and she is apparently a highly educated horticulturist among other things. She jumped at the chance to work with us on the Nimbus' gardens."

"What about her daughter, Cerine I believe her name was? We can't take a baby to Lithose!"

"She won't be coming with her, at least not to Lithose. She is apparently part of some fast growth program... I understand it was an option for colonist's children of the Farpoint program. Not sure I really understand it, but she is the equivalent of an eight-year-old by now."

AnnaChi frowned at the news. "Ah... Yea, I read about that. I am not sure how I feel about any of it. It's, well, it's just weird. They use dream-learning for that, you know?"

"Dream-learning? Is that really a thing?"

"Yes. Navy uses it for new recruits to get them up to speed on basics. I understand the child growth programs do something similar. I don't think I would... Anyway... It's not my business."

"In any case, her first goal will be to prepare the garden for the atoss to thrive in. The cargo crew will be helping her when they are able, and she will let us know if more crew is needed to maintain the gardens before we get back to Belrothi."

"Flair to Lodestar."

"Go ahead Flair," Kasey responded.

"You are cleared for landing in hangar bay H1. We have the magnetic platform deployed for landing assist."

"Alright, heading in now. Close up both domes please."

He settled into the helm and lined the Lodestar up for the mag platform hanging out of the bay opening.

"Is that really necessary?" AnnaChi sneered.

"Not really for the Lodestar, she is small, and the bay is sized for large transports. But we should be getting used to how Nimbus works in case we ever need it."

"I doubt I will ever need assistance landing my ship."

He had no doubt about that, she may have a wild flair to her flying style, but it was precise.

They landed and took their private elevator to the Operations Deck which housed the bridge. The bridge itself had an outer bridge area designed for various non-critical bridge personnel as well as the inner, main bridge. The main bridge resembled the one he had seen on the Endeavour, but the layout was greatly simplified with room for dozens of people to work in comfort. He was happy to see that Flair had a group of stations placed near the helm where a small crew could work together.

"Captain Flair," he formally acknowledged, "are we ready for the test run?"

"Engineering is making final checks. We will be underway shortly. Pick a station and enjoy the show."

Kasey pulled up the bridge schematics. As expected, the bridge section was indeed a ship itself, just as the Raven class bridges were set up as huge escape pods, but this was much larger and more robust. Theoretically, it was a large shuttle or maybe a small yacht, but neither was a fair comparison. It even had its own defensive weapon system, but did not amount to much more than laser-based PDs and a single accelerator cannon. He was not quite sure what to classify it as other than a lifeboat, yet the term just did not seem to do it justice.

The semi-permanent bridge section could not be used as a lifeboat without cost. As one of the most secure places on the ship, the bridge was tucked into the structure behind layers of protection. If it needed to be ejected, it would literally tear its way out of the Nimbus in a controlled, but destructive, manner. He shrugged to himself, if the lifeboat needed its own name, they would be in serious trouble.

He continued skimming through the Nimbus' schematics, barely noticing the transition through the gate into the Trias System. The carrier had a huge amount of cargo space, and he was happy to see that the navy had done an excellent job of meshing the carrier's internal systems through the areas efficiently, without wasting extra space. In their planning sessions, the navy engineers had labeled both as additional hangar decks. For Nimbus' layout, they were purely cargo decks with openings for external planet-side loading when needed and had no ship bays.

The hangar deck was as he expected, but he was surprised to see the central elevator that was supposed to be used for moving smaller shuttles and large equipment was far larger than they had designed. The large shaft went from the lower cargo deck all the way up to the engineering section of the Operations Deck.

A few quick measurements showed it to be just large enough to hold a sizeable transport like his Raven class Altair. It was a good decision to scale up the elevator, but again, he wished he had been consulted.

He stopped his research to watch the ship's weapon

test. The Nimbus had eight large accelerator cannons spread evenly around the ship as well as the one smaller cannon on the bridge section. The laser-based point defense systems were bulked up a lot more than the military specification, but not quite to AnnaChi's latest standards. They were, however, set up to be expanded as needed with plenty of spare room allocated. In the same way, he noted additional hardpoints around the ship for more weapons, or other equipment, to be attached as needed.

It was a gray-line in the process. The navy hadn't budged on selling weapons above what they considered defensive in nature. Yet they seemed far more lax on designing and building systems that could be easily upgraded at a later point. 'Scalability for changing standards' was a quote that had been used often. He knew AnnaChi would push hard to have the carrier upgraded to her own satisfaction and ask for forgiveness if anyone bothered to question it. For now, he needed to concentrate on making Nimbus profitable enough to maintain.

The weapons testing was impressive for what it was. Even Flair seemed overly pleased with the PDL array's performance. Twenty massive shields generators, evenly spaced around the ship, completed the basics of protection for the Nimbus. He tried not to get too excited about the results. Happy as he was for good protections, he was not planning to use the ship for combat if he could help it. He sat up straight as the test finished—the acceleration test was next.

This was the test that would quite possibly matter more than weapons. Acceleration could get them out of an attacker's reach, but in space combat, deceleration was just as important.

The safety officer made sure everyone was properly strapped in before they started. He would have said it wasn't necessary as they either wouldn't notice the dampened forces, or they would be dead. Yet, the straps had saved his life more than once, so he complied.

A screen showed a dozen aft ports open into the smooth hull. The power that poured out a moment later brought a smile to Kasey's face. The ship was quick for something so big, a testament to the design changes Flair had implemented. Once it was loaded with n-mats to offset some of its mass it would be quicker still. As he watched, the thrust ended, and the ship flat spun one-hundred-eighty degrees before the main thrusters ignited again. Once the ship came to the eventual stop, a dizzying series of new tests started.

Secondary thruster ports opened and were tested all over the ship, sending the carrier spinning in nearly every conceivable direction. The directional thrusters were powered by a single dedicated engine. It was far smaller than the main engine yet extremely overpowered for a ship of this size—allowing the carrier to turn, twist, and strafe laterally at breakneck speeds compared to most ships.

By the time they returned to the small navy station built on the Trias side of the Gemini Nexus gate, they had tested and logged nearly every aspect of the ship. Kasey could not tell if they wanted the data as part of their standard operating procedure, or they wanted it to use against him if ever needed. As long as they shared the information, he was fine with it.

After all the formalities involved with the navy testing, Kasey half expected some ceremony before taking command of the ship. Instead, he and AnnaChi were approached by an officer with a pad full of documents for them to accept. After the final acceptance and verification of ship's transfer to the Acosza-Robinson Consulting Group, all that was left were a few handshakes before most of the navy personnel filed off the bridge.

He turned to Flair who now sat smiling in the helm. "Is that it?"

"That's it."

"The ship is ours?"

"Nimbus is yours."

"Now what?"

"As of fourteen-oh-seven hours, I have been relieved of naval duty." She stood and snapped a sharp salute. "I am yours to command, sirs!"

AnnaChi scoffed. "At ease—permanently. And no saluting either. And sit down."

Kasey nodded. "We can work up procedures for crew, but we don't want more formality than necessary when crew are on duty—and none at all when they are not. Unless there is a damn good reason."

"I'll work something up for your approval."

"Captain Flair. Shuttle Two is docking now."

"Thank you, Nova. How soon will all the navy personnel be debarked?"

"Four minutes and twelve seconds, approximately."

"Uh, who's the voice?" AnnaChi waved her hand with a shrug.

"Nova is the ship's AI. She is a standard entity in the same class as Pathfinder's Scout, but with a totally different personality matrix."

"Who decided on her matrix configuration then?" Kasey asked.

"She did..." laughed Flair, "based on your personalities and assumed needs. Nova, care to elaborate?"

"Certainly, although it would take several hours at a minimum. It is more important to understand that my personality began evolving the moment you entered the Nimbus, and will continue to do so as we work together. You may, of course, alter my matrix settings any time you desire. I can even develop unique personalities for interacting with each of you—if that is desired. I have sent you each a summary of my options and capabilities and we can discuss any of it in detail at your leisure."

AnnaChi smiled. "Thank you Nova, a pleasure to meet you."

Kasey nodded, not really sure how he felt about the new AI. "She mentioned a shuttle docking. I suppose that will be Fran's hand-picked people?"

"Should be, yes. I hope you are ready to meet them?"

"How many are we expecting?" Kasey asked.

"Ten. All are now ex-officers and able to serve bridge watch, which you need on a ship this large. They each have other useful skills that a ship like this could use—and they can be trusted."

"That's more than I expected…"

"Well, it is your call if you want to keep them all. However, you do need a solid bridge crew, and this will only just cover it. They all needed a break from service and are all good people."

"We really don't need all this navy oversight…"

"Kasey, I swear to you, that is not what this is. Every one of them is from the crew of the Endeavour and fought beside you for the gates. If you are worried about oversight, you should worry about me first and foremost."

"Fine. Let's get them up here for a meet and greet then."

"They are already on their way."

Kasey was still fuming quietly as the group entered the bridge. He cooled as the men and women entered and came to attention. He had expected them all to be stern faced with serious attitudes but, with a few exceptions, most appeared slightly nervous or at least unsure.

He glanced at Flair and raised his eyebrow.

She caught on quick. "At ease. And relax. This is Red

Rock, not the navy yards."

Several seemed to exhale in relief at Flair's demeanor. He imagined it might be confusing for the group to now be working for their old commander, who was suddenly not so commanding.

As they relaxed, she continued, "We will have procedures of some sort in place soon to reflect the proper culture here at Red Rock, but for now we all can drop the discipline and get our jobs done."

Kasey stood and introduced himself and AnnaChi. He recognized two of the men in the group, "Nice to have you with us Jate."

"A pleasure to be here, sir."

Kasey turned to the other nimble looking man he recognized, but didn't know his name, and held out his hand. "I don't think I caught your name last time?"

"No, sir, sorry. Name is Ponnle, but most just call me Ponn. If I might ask, did the Altair survive the battle?"

"It did indeed. Are you a pilot then?"

"No. I worked on the cargo team when we were using her for resupply runs. But she was a good ship."

"She still is and will be on board with us soon enough. It is good to have you aboard, Ponn."

He tried to remember the other's names as they introduced themselves, but he forgot most before they left the bridge to unpack their meager belongings.

"Not so bad, huh?" Flair had moved up silently behind him causing him to flinch.

"They will do."

"Jate will be back shortly and be our pilot for the first watch. Do you have orders, sir?"

"Set sail for the Belrothi-Abscond station, Captain. Cargo bay 748. Our first pickup is waiting for us."

CHAPTER FOURTEEN

As the Nimbus began its deceleration toward Belrothi, the Lodestar shot away from the carrier at its maximum acceleration.

Knowing the Lodestar could decelerate into orbit much faster than the large carrier or nearly any other ship in the system, Kasey and AnnaChi had decided to get a head start on loading.

Cargo bay 748 had several docks attached to it. Most of which were in a semi-permanent lockdown, leaving only two small docks functional. Kasey was startled to find one dock already occupied by a transport ship.

Kasey had procured cargo bay 748 solely for Red Rock's personal usage. Over the last few months, Darnell had one of their few pilots transferring the large n-mats cargo containers into the station's bay to prepare for the Nimbus' arrival. Since the construction of Nimbus had taken longer than expected, He was slightly concerned that deliveries were still being made so late after the original due date. It had been a large ask for so much n-mats to be ready, but Darnell had been confident he could deliver on time.

He pinged the ship and received a positive ID for the Andrius. Andrius was a medium transport privately owned by Markus MacDuff, a pilot that Kasey and AnnaChi had both worked with shortly after Kasey had first come to Belrothi. The Andrius was an old ship and wasn't much to look at, but Markus had done what he could to keep it flying. They had promised him access to the Nimbus' dry-dock and repair shop as part of his contract and he had readily accepted.

As they docked, he sent a comm to the Andrius asking for their status. No reply came back. It was odd, but understandable if they were in the process of moving cargo. He shrugged it off and headed to the hatchway as AnnaChi went to gather the skids they used for moving the large containers.

He was only a few meters into the bay when sharp pain lanced through his left leg, causing him to fall forward and hit the deck hard.

The next few seconds were a blur. Instinctively, he rolled himself behind a stack of containers and drew his own plasma pistol. Looking down at his leg, he saw blood oozing through his pants from the wound. Someone had shot him.

His mimic interface was flashing a query asking to approve anti-shock procedures. He ignored it and sent a quick warning to AnnaChi instead. He heard what he assumed was a boot scuffing the deck nearby. Moving as quickly as he dared, he swung his pistol around the edge of the container and fired three shots.

Curses from at least two men responded to the shots, so Kasey fired twice more, waited a second, then fired a few more times. It was sloppy, but he needed time.

Holstering the pistol, he ripped open a small pouch on the upper thigh of his flight suit. Inside was a thin handle. He gripped it and pulled as hard as he could, wincing in pain as the leg felt it had been gripped in a vise. The cable-tie was designed to create an airtight seal for air pressure emergencies in flight—he hoped it would work as a tourniquet.

Pulling out the pistol again, he fired one more haphazard shot before shuffling towards the far end of the containers as quickly as he could manage. Behind him, more shots slammed into the container where he had taken cover.

He reached the end of the row before the firing stopped and slipped around it with the pistol leading his way. A few more shots rang out, but they did not seem to be aimed at him, so he ducked back and shook his head to clear his thoughts. He was having trouble concentrating and he felt his leg going numb.

The mimic interface was now blinking several messages that he was having trouble seeing. He picked out one that had the word adrenaline and accepted it. His leg was still bleeding he noticed absently.

Glancing around the corner again, he could make out a blurry movement of someone creeping towards his pervious spot. He aimed the pistol as best he could, then stopped in shock. A bard dashed out from the Lodestar's bay and crashed into something he could not see. It apparently didn't stop there. A second crash followed and then he heard the distinct sound of the craft's jump jets kick in.

Ignoring the pain, he pulled himself further around the container for a better look and saw the bard flying around the bay on a ninety-degree tilt—smashing into containers and attackers alike.

Two more gunmen appeared and started firing at the bard after it passed over a row of containers they had been hiding behind. Kasey tried aiming again and fired as quickly as he could. One figure seemed to drop, but the other turned and began firing at Kasey. Dropping his pistol, Kasey tried to drag himself out of the open, but he could already tell he was moving too slow to make it.

Knowing the next few shots would be the end, he looked up towards the attacker. Before the man could squeeze off another round, the bard plowed into him. He could not see it, but he heard the sound of the bard's hatch opening following by several thunderous blasts that echoed through the bay.

Kasey tried to move again, but his body would not respond. All that he could see was the deck and a smear of blood as blackness overtook his vision.

* * *

Bright light assaulted his senses.

He tried to sit up but found he could not. Feeling around, he realized a trauma pod surrounded him.

"Hold on there, sir. I'll have this open in just a second. You lost a lot of blood."

The pods cover slid smoothly back, disappearing into the pod.

"Anna…"

"She is fine, other than being angry as hell."

"Jate?"

"Yes, sir. They left me to look after you while they deal with station security. She has been notified you are awake and will be here soon."

"Darnell… Is everyone at headquarters okay?"

"Yes, sir. They have wounded down there, but nothing too serious. Someone named Markus took the worst of it. The enemy hijacked the Andrius while it was being loaded. He tried to stop them and got tossed out an airlock while they were taking off. Trees broke his fall— well, mostly… A lot of fractures and contusions, but the tree saved his life. He is already awake and nearly as

150

pissed off as your lady."

"Lady?" AnnaChi growled, walking in.

"Sorry, uh, sir."

She rushed over to Kasey and put a hand on his arm. "Captain, sir, or AnnaChi are all fine, Jate." She looked down at Kasey. "And how are you doing, dear?"

"I am fine, except for this confinement. When can I get up? And is calling you captain going to be confusing?"

She looked at Jate and nodded.

Jate picked up a pad and handed it to him. "This has your treatment plan outlined, but give it another hour before you get up. Eat something before then as well. As far as the title, it is common in the navy for many to use the title of captain on board, but it is duty verses title. My crew from the Jate-Markay would call me captain even while we were on the Endeavour or Pathfinder for example." Kasey saw a faraway look of sadness in his eyes at the mention of his old crew. "However, for official operations, the captain is whoever is in command of the boat. Which I assume will be Captain Flair in most cases."

"The civilians we bring into the crew will likely need some help understanding all that. I am hoping you and the others can help everyone keep it straight."

"I will do my best, sir."

Kasey turned to AnnaChi. "What actually happened in that bay?"

"Unfortunately," she looked at the far wall, "none of the attackers will be able to tell us the details... From what I gather, they took the Andrius from Markus, then convinced the station security to open the cargo bay's docking hatch with some story of their code not working and having a delivery to make. It seems like bullshit to me, but that's the line station security is feeding us."

"So, were they after the n-mats? Or were they

waiting on us?"

"N-mats it seems. They had the Andrius' hold half loaded when we arrived."

"Well, there is that at least." He smiled. "Wait, was I dreaming or were you flying a bard on its side through the bay?"

Her anger faded at the thought. "About eighty degrees, and not something I had tried before. When I changed over the jets to help the stabilizers keep the bard upright, I added a few routines to manually play around with uneven loadouts. It was effective, but harder to control than I expected."

"It certainly seemed effective from what I have seen of that bay," Jate chimed in.

"True enough," she laughed, "but that bard won't fly again anytime soon. I think I cracked its frame." She looked apologetically at Kasey. "It was yours by the way. Sorry, we can get a new one ordered."

"Don't bother. You can grab as many as you can locate on Lithose. I have a warehouse location already noted in our plans. You can even do the honors of clearing it out."

"That, my dear, will be my absolute pleasure."

"Oh!" Kasey felt a wave of panic. "Did we puncture any of the containers? I didn't even think about that when I was shooting. I didn't aim very much…"

"Well, we certainly need to have a long talk about how you handle combat situations, but no, the containers are just fine. The new design is rated to survive nearly anything. We don't want mercury leaks on the Nimbus. The copper plasma of your shots did little more than take off some paint. If you damaged the outer skin underneath, it self-repaired before I got a look at it. I did manage to do a quick scan while the station investigators were gathering their own data. There was no damage at all below the container skin. We did test them, you know."

"I know, but it is good to know they held up in a real situation."

Jate had been quiet, but cleared his throat. "Uh, are we really going to land the Nimbus on Lithose? I understand the atmospheric storm destroyed most ships that tried to leave that deathtrap."

"I have been back there twice since. With n-mats, it is a simple engineering problem to get on and off that planet using old-fashioned hot-air balloon methodology."

AnnaChi slapped Kasey's arm hard. "It is not quite that simple, considering the fist-sized balls of lightning burning holes through your ship. We need to be careful regardless."

"It *is* the whole purpose of the Nimbus' design," Kasey added. "It should protect us from storm damage. Still, spending as little time in the storm as possible will help too."

"If you say so." Jate looked between them with hints of worry. "But I think I would prefer a danger I can see."

Flair appeared in the doorway. "Well, I hope you are not afraid of the dark, Mr. Jate, because when we do land on that planet, it will be perpetual darkness."

"I can handle darkness, Captain. I just prefer my ship in space."

"Well, you are in luck. With Kasey's permission, I would like you to take command of the Lodestar and ferry the n-mats over to the Nimbus for consolidation."

"Consolidation?"

"Right. Each container holds a dense supply of n-mats at its core surrounded by fourteen times that much water. We will pump out both from most of these containers to fill the reservoirs waiting aboard Nimbus. The extras have a special storage area, but for now, just stack them in the upper cargo hold. The empty containers can be brought back here where other Red Rock personnel will deal with them for future shipments."

"Yes, sir," Jate responded. "I'm on it."

Once he left, Flair turned her attention to Kasey and AnnaChi. "I hope that's okay. We are a bit short on ships and you are in no shape for flying."

"It's fine for now. We are hoping we can find a few ships on Lithose to salvage for Red Rock's use instead of using our personal ships."

She nodded and looked at AnnaChi. "Darnell says your ships that are down on the planet are loaded and ready for pickup. If Kasey is fine without you for a few hours, I was thinking the two of us can take the Andrius down to HQ for Markus and you can bring the Cintian back. Kasey, I am capable of piloting the Altair if you give me access."

"I suppose that is fine too. Darnell is supposed to have some people ready to join the Nimbus crew. Can you make sure they have a ride?"

"Yes, leave it to us."

"Wait, who is watching the Nimbus?"

"Mr. Knoc is on watch and fully capable."

AnnaChi raised an eyebrow. "Knoc? Commander Knoc?"

"Yes, you've met him twice now, I believe."

"He was just a voice the first time. I guess I didn't pay attention when I met him on the bridge."

"You should say hello again, because he remembers you."

"Should I be jealous?" Kasey asked with a smile.

"He saved my ass during the battle at the gates." She chuckled. "So, maybe…"

"He was following orders," Flair supplied, "In any case, unless we have more qualified people joining us, Knoc and Jate are the only other pilots fully rated on large ships, and they are very capable pilots. So, I would like to use them as my direct reports for bridge crew. We really need at least two more in that position to be fully staffed; however, we can make do with other staff sitting watch while we are at port or grounded. Other pilots can deal with long stretches in the black as well."

They both nodded in agreement.

"Speaking of ratings," Flair continued, "Neither of you actually have the ratings required to fully captain a ship the size of the Nimbus. You should correct that in case we need you to officially pilot your own ship at some point. While not actually needed to fly the ship, it is required to dock at most Federation stations, and many companies will not ship with an uncertified pilot for insurance concerns."

Kasey scratched his chin. "It never really occurred to me that I would need to hold ratings to fly my own ship. Hell, the pilots we have lined up for crew likely don't have them either. Any idea what the process is?"

"I do indeed. Myself, Knoc, and Jate are all able to help with the materials, and I can certify the test when you are ready. I don't imagine you two will have any trouble with it, but it deals a lot more with regulations than actual flying."

"Well, something to work on between landfalls." Kasey yawned. "Any of the crew able to toss a sandwich in here while you two are gone? If I have time for some food, maybe a nap and a shower before the new crew arrive, that would be wonderful."

"I will see to it." Flair turned to leave. "AnnaChi, if you could meet me on the Andrius when you are ready?"

"I will be right there."

"Alone at last," Kasey muttered over another yawn.

"Hold that thought. Maybe keep out of trouble till I am back, huh?"

"I can but try."

CHAPTER FIFTEEN

Kasey woke and looked around.

He had been moved to a new room that he could not quite place. Struggling to sit up, he realized he was no longer in a trauma pod, but an actual bed. Swinging his legs over the side, a slight dizziness overtook him. He blinked it away as a screen appeared on the wall showing AnnaChi standing on the busy bridge of the Nimbus.

"Don't you dare get up mister! I will be up in just a minute. Stay put." She didn't wait for an answer before closing the channel.

Looking around once more he realized he was somewhere in their new quarters on the Nimbus, but not their normal room. It wasn't overly surprising, their private domain on the ship was immense and had more than a few guest rooms that were closer to the personnel lifts.

"I am surprised you listened." AnnaChi walked in with a slightly disappointed look. "I was looking forward to punishing you. Well, drink this instead." She tossed a bottle of green liquid to him. "Time to get back to work."

"This still tastes like punishment. How long was I out?"

"About seven hours. You spiked a fever and the pod put you into a deep sleep. Apparently, you needed it. So, we dumped you in the nearest room while the rest of us picked up the slack."

"Well, I am awake now. How are the preparations going?

"The initial crew we picked for the salvage mission are all aboard, along with the supplies we ordered. We are nearly ready to set sail."

"How? There is no way the gardens are completed yet."

"You're right, and they won't be. The team you hired to plant and install everything was delayed and then had the gall to ask for an extra week to finish the job."

"So, you fired them?"

"No. Actually, Yaran fired them."

"Yaran?"

"She must have recovered her spirt since we last saw her. The meekness we knew is gone."

"Okay, well that will be new. Still, we need the gardens."

"Oh, we have them. Boxes, crates, tanks and even a few trees are all lined up neatly on the dome floor waiting to be planted or placed. Yaran claims they will be fine for now and that she will have it all ready before we get back from Lithose."

"You think she can?"

"Not by herself, no. But we have crew with plenty of downtime to pitch in. Honestly, if she can pull it off with the crew's help it saves us money and time. Worst case, we get a team in to finish the job when we get back."

"Alright then, so we are really ready to go? We planned for at least two days here?"

"Time is money honey."

"Can't argue with more plundering time I suppose." He grinned.

"Yo-ho-ho! Now, if you are finished with that swill, there is clean clothing and a ship suit in the closet. We have a week's worth of unpacking and a month's worth of gardening to be done. Hop to it!"

He handed her the empty bottle, "Yes, dear."

* * *

Kasey looked out from the bridge of the Nimbus at the churning tempest covering Lithose.

If anything, the atmospheric storm had increased since his last visit. He pulled up the map of locations they planned to visit, comparing it to where the larger storms were focused. If the Nimbus worked as designed, it would be able to handle the storm, but there was no sense in throwing caution to the wind.

He chose an area of relative calm above a small town. A factory there was supposed to have been manufacturing environmental scrubbers and replacement filters for civilian ships. More importantly, the company had a full-service station for upgrading and replacing such systems. As useful as upgrades and spares might be for their ships, he was far more interested in any ships that might have been left behind in the middle of maintenance.

He sent location to the main screen. "This will be as good a place as any to start our mission."

The waiting bridge quieted as the crew studied the location.

"Jate, plot and confirm please," Flair ordered.

"Course plotted and validated, sir. Records show a

small town with plenty of open areas if we want to land."

"Security report, Miss Mayflower?"

A short woman Kasey didn't recognize swiveled her chair towards the captain's chair. "Captain, all non-essential crew have been gathered and sealed into the administration area of the Operations Deck for safety."

"Engineering station?"

"Engineering reports ready condition. Lithose Protocol can be activated when ready, sir."

"Activate the protocol please."

Several minutes passed. Kasey could imagine the ship locking down, enabling the layers of Faraday shielding built into the carrier ship. Theoretically, the system would absorb and redirect the dangerous plasma of the storm safely away from the ship. If it failed, there were banks of power sinks that would act as magnets to the electricity, hopefully absorbing any remaining charge. The last line of defense was simple shielding built into all the rooms of the Operations Deck, the most protected deck on the ship.

"Lithose Protocol is now active, Captain."

Kasey watched as Flair's gaze went slowly around the room, taking in the status of every member of the bridge crew. Once done, she looked at AnnaChi, who had a comical smile and just shrugged in return. Flair's gaze ended on Kasey.

Kasey took a deep breath as he held her stare. A queasy feeling began in the pit of his stomach. He had felt it on every decent into Lithose, but this was far worse. A lot of people were risking their lives on this mission and if something went wrong, it would all be his fault. Their lives depended on him now.

He finally nodded. "Take us in, Captain Flair."

"Jate," she intoned in an even but commanding voice, "take us down into that hellish pit."

"Aye, aye, sir!"

Kasey settled back in the cushion, watching the storm-cloaked planet gradually fill the main screen. Reaching forward, he brought up a map on his console showing the power sinks across the ship. All showing a green status.

AnnaChi laid a hand on his arm. He pulled his eyes away from the screen and saw her smile. He relaxed instantly, marveling at the effect she could have on him.

"Captain," Jate interrupted his thoughts, "thrusters are stowed. We are in free fall, as planned."

"Nice work," she replied, then raised her voice to a command level. "This will be quick, people. Don't make me ask for status, if you see something, yell it out!"

Every second seemed to last hours as everyone waited for something to go violently wrong. Kasey didn't realize he had been holding his breath until a sharp voice pierced the air.

"Captain," Miss Mayflower called out, "engineering reports several strikes to the portside hull. All have been diverted away from the Nimbus. Five heat exchangers are offline, but backups are holding."

"How long Jate?"

"At least fifteen seconds, sir."

"Be ready."

"Aye!"

"Topside strike, sir, we have some bleed through!"

Several power sinks on Kasey's console changed to red. He blinked twice in rapid succession and dipped his head closer to the screen, then relaxed as he realized it was an unoccupied area of the ship.

"We are out, sir!" Jate yelled. "Thrusters online and building power. Twenty thousand meters and falling."

"Can someone please activate our external lighting and floods!" Flair commanded.

Blizzard snow filled the screens. Visibility was less

than a meter and didn't help the feeling of falling towards the planet at all.

"Fifteen thousand, Captain."

Kasey smiled and relaxed in his seat. Jate's voice had calmed noticeably. Like most pilots in the room, he had felt as much as done the math already and realized they would live. A look around the room showed a few faces still red and wide-eyed, assuming this might be their last journey. Others smiled, knowing their chances of survival had just gone way up.

He turned back to the console and flipped the screen to show the ship's external sensors. A few were non-responsive, but that was expected. Flipping through the other screens, he noted one with an issue. The topside EM shield was offline. There were twenty separate shields covering every meter of the ship. They overlapped some, but each was essential. No one had seemed to notice it yet.

"Topside EM shield number ten is offline, captain," he informed the room.

"Ten thousand and holding, captain," Jate called out.

"Scramble the maintenance bots," Flair ordered. "Get one of the engineers to form a party and check out that shield generator. Security, release the crew and set general quarters. Bring up the air wells and absorb me a cloud or two, we need to take on mass."

A round of "ayes" sounded off as Kasey and AnnaChi unstrapped and stretched.

He walked over to Flair. "If you would take us a bit further from the storm above, we will take the Altair down and locate a landing site."

"Take us to two thousand meters please, Jate."

"Aye, sir."

"Well done, Captain."

"Thank you, sir." She smiled back.

Even with the blizzard, they had no problem finding

a sufficient area near the factory for the Nimbus to make its initial landing. A dozen bright red flairs shot from the Altair, marking the landing zone both visually and electronically for the carrier.

The blizzard cleared as the carrier approached the ground. Kasey shook his head in disgust for not thinking this part through. In a rush he pulled the Altair up and away from the enormous billowing cloud of dust, snow, and debris that cocooned the Nimbus and everything else within a hundred meters of the ship.

He circled the town while waiting for the dust to settle. It was an instant reminder of just how devastated Lithose had been. He had been planet-side when it fell, and had been back twice since, but nothing prepared a person to take in the devastated landscapes that remained.

He finally landed at the scrubber factory's landing pad and sighed. The shop's bays were wide open and empty. Strike one, he thought. There were plenty of other potential areas on the world where ships could have been left, so he didn't worry. Still, it would have been nice to have another ship to add to the carrier's bays.

It was not a total loss. There was plenty of valuable equipment in the shop bays that they would salvage, not to mention the factory itself.

AnnaChi leaned forward and pointed to something on the factory dock. "What's that?"

Kasey zoomed the image. Sticking nearly straight up from a drift of snow was an arm, fingers spread wide.

"Oh... Someone left behind." She sighed. "I am not sure which would have been worse, to have the ship you tried to escape in plummet to the ground, or to be left to survive in this wasteland."

Kasey contemplated the screen. "I am not so sure it's either. Come, we need to check it out."

"Morbid, but fine. The others should be here soon enough to help loot this place."

As they trudged through the snow closer to the dock, Kasey started laughing behind his facemask. AnnaChi slapped his arm, apparently not finding any mirth in the scene. He shook his head and pointed at the hand.

A handful of seconds later he was rewarded another, more friendly slap.

"A bot!"

"Yup."

They pulled the heavy bot out from the snow for a better look. The machine was well-used and old. Every nook and cranny seemed caked with ash and soot.

Kasey wiped the arm of his work jacket over the breastplate. "Stevedore bot of some sort. Can't make out the model, but if it is still serviceable, we could sure use it."

"You think that thing will still function?"

"I have no idea. Never dealt with these high-end humanoid ones before, but I have seen a few in action. Efficient for companies who can afford them. Have you?"

"A few. We used them for demolition jobs in the service. If you need something taken apart, moved and stacked, these suckers are great, until they break. They lack the finesse our builder bot has but makes up for it with raw power. Never controlled one myself…"

"Well, let's not try for the first time on board our ships, huh? I would rather it not tear our ship apart around us."

She looked back at the ship and then back at the bot. "I am making no promises."

"Wonderful. Okay, time to find out what treasures this place holds. We have a lot more stops to make today."

FARPOINT RISING

CHAPTER SIXTEEN

"Kasey to Nimbus Actual."

"Flair here. Go ahead Kasey."

"We are at the Apex Industries base. Looks like we found their Lithose headquarters."

"Good news, but I sense you have a problem for me?"

"Too much of a good thing is what the problem is. Lot of equipment collecting dust and ash here, and it looks like warehouses full of supplies. It will take weeks to transfer all this back to the Nimbus with just the Altair, and there appear to be a few operations in the area that we should raid as well."

"Hardly seems like a problem boss, that is exactly why we're here."

"All the same, I want anyone still out scouting diverted to this site, then get Nimbus in the air. I'll have a landing site cleared for her by the time you arrive."

"We will be airborne in twenty. The Cintian is inbound now with a load of what AnnaChi is referring to as recreational vehicles. We will get her locked down and then disembark."

"While I am all for safety, she can use the opportunity to practice landing while the Nimbus is moving. Deploy the mag platform just in case."

"You realize this is an open channel," AnnaChi chimed in, "and I don't need no damn mag platform assisting me!"

"You heard my lady. No taking it easy on her."

"Aye boss, I wouldn't think of it. Nimbus out."

Kasey reclined with a satisfied grin. Pushing AnnaChi's buttons were always enjoyable—until she caught up with him.

"Nimbus Actual, Nimbus Actual, this is Shuttle One in need of priority assistance."

"Flair here, you've got my attention Jate. What's the situation?"

"We are looking at a possible search and rescue situation here. I am holding at distance, but I am detecting complex heat and power usage from a building at the southern edge of Crestwood. Probable survivors. Zero comm activity."

"Kasey, are you hearing this?" Flair asked.

"Warming up the thrusters now. Notify Yaran, I would like her to be available to help settle the survivors if they decide to come aboard."

"If?"

"No telling what state they will be in. I've seen settlers on habitable worlds starving and still not want to leave their home to get help. This could be worse."

"Understood. Looks like Crestwood isn't too far out of the way to the Apex base. Nimbus can be there to back you up within the hour."

"Good deal. Jate, you have medical training, right?"

"Correct, although I am a bit behind on my certifications."

"Good enough. Set that shuttle down after I land the Altair, then grab some food and a med kit and follow me in."

Kasey had no problem finding the site. The Altair's sensors were far superior to the small shuttle Jate was piloting and they were glowing with activity compared to anything else within range. Even Jate's shuttle signature was dim in comparison.

Jate was a bit of an anomaly on the crew. He was a capable combat pilot but seemed happy enough to fly anything from shuttles to the Nimbus itself. A bit too content in his roles. He had been one of the several recommendations from Admiral Fran that Kasey was more than a bit weary of, but he was thankful as well. He had no doubt that every one of the recommendations were loyal to Fran and likely reported back to him on everything. While Fran was a good friend, he always had his own complex agendas.

Trust was not something he gave away easily, and the admiral had a long way to go before Kasey would trust him fully again. Still, taking the advice to hire Jate was a lot easier than picking from a host of unknown pilots to be one of the ship's top officers. At least this way he would know where any surprises would originate from.

As he neared the site, he noted a handful of different shuttles which appeared to be attached to the structure. Amazingly, part of the structure appeared to be newer construction.

"Flair, the building appears to be a flight training facility. Not very big. I am seeing half a dozen shuttles that appear to be connected to the building, three of which appear to be powered up. They are layered in ash—I doubt they are flight worthy."

"Maybe the occupants are using them to generate atmosphere?"

"That would be my guess too. I am setting down in silent mode, but I doubt anyone inside will miss our landing, even if they have all their sensors shut down."

"Any weapons active?"

"None that are detectable. Looks to be some newer construction here as well. Just a big square room, nothing fancy, and a corridor leading to a hangar, but it's unfinished."

"Roger that. Be careful. We are still a good twenty minutes out."

Slipping into a heavy work suit, he grabbed a face mask with a rebreather and headed down to the Altair's main bay, commanding the hatch to open with a thought, and stepped out into the dusty air. Memories of escaping the world's destruction nearly two standard years earlier flooded his thoughts. It was hard to imagine being left behind and surviving for long.

He made his way toward the building's main door but stopped as he noticed it had been boarded up.

Looking around, he noticed Jate had taken up a defensive position with a rifle at the ready and was pointing towards one of the shuttles connected to the building. Kasey pondered the rifle a moment then let his hand rest on the pistol he had strapped to his side. He wasn't a good shot with it, but one pirate attack was all it took to cement the need for it into his mind. He hoped this wasn't such a situation but appreciated having Jate as backup.

The shuttle Jate had pointed him towards had a discernible path leading to it that Kasey had missed. As he approached, a warning light flashed to life. A moment later a seal hissed as the hatch creeped open.

Kasey took a few steps back and flicked the safety strap off his still holstered pistol then waited.

A gloved hand with fingers spread wide came through first, in an obvious attempt to show that the person was unarmed.

Slowly, a heavily bearded man came into view. The man's other arm had a makeshift sling on it but managed to hold a ragged breathing mask to his face. Calmly, he took in Kasey and then took a long look at Jate. The man took in a deep breath then laughed behind his mask. After another breath, he removed the mask to address Kasey.

"I know it's been a rough few days, but I didn't think I was at the point of hallucinations, yet…"

"Not a hallucination, my friend."

The man pointed at Kasey's ship. "That ship couldn't have made it through the storms up above. Yet you look too clean to be from some corner of this dust ball planet."

"You're mostly right about my ship, and that storm too. But I can tell you—a completely unpowered ship can drop through the storm like a stone without taking too much damage. That is, as long as you are lucky enough not to come in contact with any plasma balls. They like to eat through nearly anything."

"You didn't…"

"I did, and frankly it's the trip back up that's hard. But not on this trip. We found a better way, and I'll gladly tell you all about it. But I need some information first. Are you alone here?"

"Uh, yeah. Just me, now… And a few bots I reprogrammed to help out. I couldn't have survived the last month with this broken arm without them. Look, if it's all the same, can we have this conversation inside?"

"Sure. I have no reason to distrust you, but you should be aware that there are more than just Jate back there watching my back."

The man shrugged and turned into the shuttle. "Name's Isaac. Isaac Soeda. You got nothing to fear from me. Let's get out of this cold."

"Nice to meet you, Isaac. I'm Kasey Robinson. That's Jate, he will be coming along."

Jate jogged up and pushed past Kasey to take point

on the entry.

Kasey gave the man a few seconds as he attached his own rebreather to his belt and followed them into the shuttle. The shuttle was dusty but warm, and appeared to be mainly used as a large airlock. As they cycled into the main building, Kasey was awed at the array of projects taking up every centimeter of the chamber. Torn down robots, electrolysis chambers, rows of plants in various stages of germination, and even what appeared to be a batch of beer brewing. It immediately reminded him of AnnaChi's workshops.

Isaac led them quickly through the room and into a small kitchen, then set about pulling chairs up to a table piled with neatly stacked empty containers.

"Sorry for the mess. I wasn't expecting visitors."

Kasey gave Jate a look, who just shrugged and sat back.

"Mind if Jate takes a look at that arm while we chat?"

"It's mostly mended, I think, but I don't have a regenerator out here so it's healing the old-fashioned way. Feel free to take a look."

Jate unpacked a scanner and set to work.

"Well," Kasey started, "you have certainly kept busy. Is all this normal for you?"

"Not really. Well, some of it I suppose—I worked on the robots before, was my job, but that was mostly just replacing parts. Never had one of my own until... Anyway, reprogramming them like this is new for me. So far, I have been able to turn a few butler bots into passable gardeners. The rest is just me trying to survive more than a few years."

"So, why set up shop here? I am guessing the shuttles were nearby and useful for atmosphere, but why not move to somewhere more, I don't know, upscale?"

"That was the plan—at first. I even picked out a nice place, until the first of my shuttles failed catastrophically. These small shuttles were just not meant to run the atmospheric generators continuously like this, and certainly not in these conditions. Even with regular cleanings they keep failing. Its why I have so many crafts hooked up. I needed to lessen the load on them all as much as I could to buy some time."

He looked away for several moments to gather himself.

"That's when I realized I was in serious trouble. I couldn't just rely on these machines for breathable air. This building is my only way forward now. It has simulators, and not just for shuttle pilots—it has rooms dedicated to maintaining complex air generation systems. I need them to learn how to create my own systems before all the shuttles die. Hell, I nearly blew this building to pieces on my first attempt. Too much oxygen, not enough working sensors."

"That is a bleak future, but you seem well on your way to figuring it all out."

"I was, and on several methods too. I even had a large indoor garden planned that was supposed to supplement both food and air quality, but the builder bot malfunctioned, and... Well, I stupidly tried to fix it where it failed instead of moving it into the workshop. That shortcut nearly killed me. I slipped in the damn ash... The damn thing toppled on top of me. I don't know how long I was trapped under it out there. I eventually managed to activate it just enough to move it off me, but it trampled my arm in the process." He paused for a long moment, looking away again. "Sorry. It has not been a good month. I've really only just gotten some of my more important projects going again over the last few days. Honestly, I am not sure if it will be enough anymore, but I will keep trying."

"I don't know if it helps, but I need to correct you on one point."

"Oh? What's that?"

"This building is no longer your *only* way forward."

"I…" Isaac stopped and seemed lost in thought.

"I guess the question is," Kasey pressed, "are you ready to leave this planet behind?"

He sat there for a long time just staring at Kasey, his brow creased in contemplation. Kasey waited, knowing the look.

"I didn't think this decision would be hard for me. I have dreamed of a way out of here for so long… I always assumed I would be happy to leave."

Kasey nodded in sympathy. "It is never easy to leave something you have thrown your entire life into doing, even when staying could mean the worst."

"Yea, well, I am smart enough to know I will leave with you if you really are offering. But I am not going to like it, not for a long while. Tell me—how are you planning to get off this planet?"

"Do you have cameras outside we can control?"

"Yea, back in the lab."

They followed him to one of the only walls not obstructed with his work and activated it to display the camera views. Kasey pointed him to enlarge the viewpoint he wanted, then paned up to the stormy sky. Only the sky was not there, just a hazy blob in the darkness.

"See that?"

"No…"

Kasey tapped his temple. "Flair, light it up please."

The Nimbus burst into existence. Every surface was brightly outlined, and dozens of spotlights beamed down to illuminated most of surrounding town as well.

Isaac blinked a few times, then nearly ran to the shuttle serving as his airlock, cycling them all outside. They were just in time to watch a large bay open as the Cintian floated out and started descending towards them.

"My carrier ship, the Nimbus."

"So, you say… Yeah. Yea, I believe I would like to go with you all. But I guess I should ask, what the hell are you all doing here? And what hell is with that impossible ship? I mean, shouldn't it be falling out of the sky or something? The thrusters scarcely seem to be operating. Maybe I am hallucinating?"

"Ha! The Nimbus has a few secrets I will be happy to share, eventually. As to what we are doing here, well this planet is loosely defined as salvage. And salvage is part of what we do. Besides, as far as I know, we are the only ones able to get onto Lithose and leave again."

"Well, Captain Kasey, I am at your service. Anything I can do to pay for this rescue, well, you just go ahead and ask."

"Actually, if you are willing, I may have a job offer for you?"

"Name it. My schedule is suddenly wide open."

"We picked up a few dozen stevedore bots earlier and most are in serious disrepair. I have a few engineers to assist, but no one with bot repair experience. The work pays and will keep you employed until we make port at the next populated world. Likely Belrothi. After that, we can all make other decisions if we want. Sound fair?"

"Yes, sir, I will do what I can to get them up and running for you. But, uh, what is the crew weight allotment? There are some things I would like to bring along if I can."

"We don't have weight allotments for crew." Isaac's eyes sagged downward at the news and Kasey quickly caught his mistake. "What I mean by that is, we don't have restrictions on weight at all. You can bring anything you want that is not a danger to my ship. In fact, I encourage you to bring as many of your experiments as possible. We also have nearly three acres of botanical gardens on board, so if you want to bring any plants, we can accommodate them, too."

"Wait! You have..." he stopped as he noticed Jate's confirming nod. "Well, still, I can't take up your space with all my junk."

"It's not junk, we have plenty of room, and if you have been able to save any of the planet's native plants, I may have some interested friends. Anyway, I assume you can fly at least one of those shuttles?"

"Yes, well, I am not sure I would pass any testing. I learned enough from the simulators to move them around and make some short supply runs. Really not further than I had to. The weather changes quickly here and I'm not sure I could fly in a blizzard. Besides, I don't mind admitting that it's a bit scary once I can't see the lights from my home—I am never quite sure I will be able to find it again in this perpetual darkness. No satellites are accessible, and even the magnetic poles seem to shift a bit these days. Doesn't take much to get off course."

Kasey nodded. "I spent a few days alone in the wilderness here on my first trip through the storm. We are going to have to swap stories, but no time for that now. How about this then, you sell me your simulators and half your shuttles, in exchange we fully repair the shuttles you keep and train you on how to use them."

"Ha, I can do you better than that. You can have all the simulators and shuttles here if we can make a stop at a location I worked at few times. I will take one of the shuttles we find there as well as the training you offered."

"What kind of location are we talking about?"

"It's a high-brow, closed community. They have more fancy shuttles then they could physically drive, so there has got to be some left. Although most are likely atmospheric only. Plus, they have all the best bots, and just about anything else for that matter. It will be well worth your time to clean that place out."

"That's a deal worth making. I'm sold. But the Cintian just landed, so let see if they will let us aboard. There are a few more people I would like you to meet."

AnnaChi and Yaran were waiting in the Cintian's bay when they arrived. Behind them stood six stevedore bots loaded with stacks of empty crates. Once introductions were made, they all made quick work of packing up Isaac's home. It took far less time than Kasey imagined. The man was mostly well organized, or perhaps it was the throng of bots he had running around the building. Just about everything he had was kept neatly in a storage container somewhere. The only exception was the lab, which he explained that the bots were not allowed into since experiments tended to get ruined by cleaning bots.

Isaac's haphazard collection of bots were a true marvel. Each seemed to be designed and programmed for a seemingly random set of tasks. Kasey swore he noticed one of the gardening bots digging up worms from one garden plot and transporting them into another. The purpose of such a task was lost on him, but he was too busy to ask in any case.

Before long, Kasey and Isaac were standing in the Altair's bay where they had decided to load all the shuttles. The stevedores disconnected and fitted lifting platforms around each shuttle and deposited them one at a time. Isaac then had two of his own bots seal the holes left in the building.

"I know there is not much reason to close it up. But, it was my home, you see."

"No need to explain. We have the time. Dinner is not for another few hours. We will meet back up with Yaran on the Nimbus. She will get you settled into the crew quarters. She will be asking you if you want a garden facing room or an outside room—which is great if you enjoy being in space."

"The garden sounds wonderful. I have been staring out into the darkness here for too long, if you know what I mean. But I have been meaning to ask—what actually happened? To Lithose, I mean, we got warnings but then—not much else. I assumed a volcano at first, but it's worse than that, isn't it?"

Kasey swallowed hard. He was hoping to avoid the topic and let someone else catch him up on all the horrible events. "It really is a long story, and I don't know if you will believe me until we get back to Belrothi."

"Yea? Well, give me the basics."

Kasey sighed. "The Cassian are here. They had subverted the Patternist movement. Then they dropped the Abscond's antimatter engine onto Lithose. Cracked this planet like an egg."

Isaac stumbled into a chair and stared out into the darkness of Lithose.

"It gets worse," Kasey went on. "The Patternist destroyed any ships capable of moving to other systems and took over the remaining colony on Belrothi. We went to war... Well, really just one big losing battle. The Federation had sent massive gates with the colony ship that could open a wormhole back home. The Cassian with their Patternist pawns tried to destroy the gates before that could happen. We held them off just long enough. Many did not make it... But now the navy is here and setting up a network of gates to other colonies. This system will be flooded with new colonists and travelers soon enough."

"Sounds like Federation propaganda to me..."

"It's not."

"You were there? It's not just some story the government is spreading?"

"I fought them, yes. And I have been through the gates too. It's all real."

"I don't want to believe you. I don't want to feel the anger again. So many died around me here. Friends. Family. Ships fell out of the sky as they tried to escape. You're telling me a different hell waited for those that did escape?"

"For some, yes. I guess I was one of them. Look, sorry that I am not better at sugar coating this all, but what I can tell you is that the navy gave no quarter when they came through the gates. I don't believe a single enemy escaped their wrath."

"I wouldn't mind giving them some of my own wrath. I lost people. Good people."

"I can't promise you that. However, we plan to take the Nimbus to other new colonies using the new gate system, including other colonies from the Farpoint program. I can't say what we will find, but I wouldn't be surprised if we find more Cassian out there. Besides, I'm told the best way to honor the dead is to keep on surviving."

"I'll give that some thought, Captain. You think there will be more salvage opportunities at these colonies?"

"I really hope not. No, our main work will revolve around resource mining and transporting new settlers and supplies. Our salvage operation here is mainly to get us started. We need the equipment and it's all sitting on this planet going to waste."

"Good enough for me."

"Hey, that's the last shuttle. Anything left down there we should grab? Otherwise, lets head up to the Nimbus and get you settled in."

"Nope, I have seen enough of this place. I'm ready to see what comes next."

CHAPTER SEVENTEEN

Kasey woke to AnnaChi flopping onto the couch next to him.

"Leave you alone for ten minutes and you pass out. Are we working you too hard?"

"Perhaps." He yawned. "Did I miss anything?"

"I did mention I only left you alone for ten minutes, right?"

He gave her a look.

"Fine! Markus is back with the last load of the fancy shuttles from that fancy little village. Stupid people, but those little shuttles will bring in quite a bit in trade. We should search out more of these villages."

"And?"

"And Sariyn thinks we need to spend another day here."

"Huh, she is the last person I thought would care about having nice things."

"I don't think she does, but she comes from money and seems to know what she is talking about. She brought back a few extras when collecting the bots her team could locate. A few bottles of old alcohol, some weird alien artwork, and a few ancient paper books. Just a single box of stuff. She sent me the estimated worth based on her best guess. If she is right, the stuff she grabbed is worth more than one of those fancy shuttles."

"You think she is right about the value?"

"I don't have the slightest clue, but I am sure the junk in this town alone is worth more than my Cintian."

"Alright, let's have her send out a list of what to look for and where to look. But I want stevedores ripping out any gym equipment, food synthesizers, cryogenic chambers, anything of value or use to us. Keep the bots busy and we can pilfer anything she deems valuable or useful while they are at it. I want a report at noon—we can decide if it is worth more of our time then."

"A proper pillage. Arr! Hmm, maybe I can find us one of those automated massage tables?"

"Now that sounds nice. I'll be sending Nimbus ahead to the Apex headquarters first thing in the morning with some of the miners and the cargo team. We need to start loading the mining equipment."

"I am sure Darnell's teams would be happier at Apex, but we need Sariyn with us."

"Let's send Markus along as well. We won't need more than our two transports for this place. Flair can also take out the Lodestar if they need, so they will have two transports that can scout the area for satellite operations. We need every digger-dredge we can locate. Apex must have several to have put their HQ there. I was kind of focused on the base itself when I looked. Jate and Knoc can support them in shuttles."

"Hell, we have enough shuttles in storage now. We have two or three crew that are certified, but I don't know about experience."

"Maybe, but not worth the risk yet and I am not sure those fancy shuttles are hardy enough for this planet. Isaac mentioned sudden storms taking him by surprise and getting lost easily. So, let's stick with only highly experienced pilots and make sure whatever craft they take is fully stocked and in regular contact from now on. Besides, loading the mining equipment is going to take every hand available."

AnnaChi yawned. "Maybe you should let Nova coordinate everyone so you can tuck me in."

"Maybe, but I am not sure I am ready for all that. I never relied on AIs for anything more than status reports."

"Nova, have you been listening?"

"Yes, Miss Acosza, and I am more than capable of carrying out Master Robinson's wishes as well as setting up efficient search patterns for tracking our people's movements. I can gather status reports as well."

"Thank you, Nova, and please use just our first names same as the other crew do."

"As you wish AnnaChi. Shall I distribute your orders to the crew, Kasey?"

"Uh, okay, sure. But let's keep me involved with any decision making."

"Confirmed, and of course."

"Hold on, you listen to everything we say?"

"This partition of my self does, yes."

"What does that even mean?"

"It means the entity listening to your every word is effectively a minor copy of my primary self. Currently no other sub-entity of me is aware of this conversation unless you allow it. Only my primary has access to this sub-entity's data, and it is considered private for anyone not in this conversation."

"Alright, sure. Just how many sub-entities do you have?"

"I currently consist of seventy-two sub-entities plus my primary. I also have many micro-entities embedded across company hardware not directly connected to the

Nimbus cores."

"Like ships?"

"Precisely so, however most of those entries are limited to common AI tasks you are accustomed to unless a connection to the Nimbus is available."

"These entities need to be connected to the Nimbus?"

"Yes, or more accurately, they need to be connected to Nimbus' network connected to my primary cores."

"And without that connection, they are limited like the micro-entities you mentioned?"

"Precisely so."

"Well, my head now hurts, but thank you. Do me a favor, make sure crew members are aware of you being in their private business and give them the option to turn you off in their private rooms or other private areas of the ships."

"Confirmed."

"And Nova? Give us some privacy for a while. AnnaChi apparently needs to be tucked in."

"Confirmed."

* * *

By dinner time, the Cintian and Altair were loaded down with every high-end appliance, toy, artwork, and piece of furniture the small high-end community had to offer and were on their way to the Apex base where the Nimbus waited.

Kasey was not convinced spending the extra day had been worth the time, but AnnaChi had already earmarked several items for their home. If she was happy, then he would deal with the delay. He also knew they had a limited amount of time to salvage the tools and resources they would need to start the new hauling and mining business as well as outfit the carrier properly.

Crew moral on such a bleak planet could be an issue—he knew all too well. So, they had decided to allow the crew to claim items from the haul at a greatly reduced rate, within reason. It would reduce the overall gain for the salvage company a bit, but allowed the crew to afford things they would not normally be able to afford. He made it clear the intention was for the crew to claim items for their personal usage, not to sell later for profit. It was not a perfect system, and he knew many items would find their way into pockets. It was to be expected, but he instructed his management team to take note of any such activity and then ignore it, within reason.

"Captain, we have a storm approaching." Sariyn was manning the Altair's tactical station out of boredom. "The Apex base will be hit by it shortly. I don't believe we can outrun it."

"Try to get a signal through to the Nimbus, or anyone else for that matter. I'll let AnnaChi know."

"Roger."

"Altair to Cintian. Are you seeing the storm ahead?"

"I am now. Do you have a plan?"

"Working on it… There are some structures about three kilometers to the east. I would rather wait the storm out on the ground."

"I see it. I think we can set down between the two larger buildings. Warehouses, I assume. May as well check them out if we are stuck here. I don't see any records of what this place was used for."

"That works, hopefully there will be something useful. Sariyn, any response from Nimbus?"

"Nothing. The storm may already be on them. I am not detecting much radiation, but I can't get decent sensor readings through the storm."

"Welcome to Lithose. I encountered similar issues with sensors on my first trip back here. Something about iron ferrite in the ash I believe. The super-volcanoes are still quite active."

"Something to ponder. I'll take some samples to look into when I have a chance, but as long as the storm passes quickly, I will be happy."

They set down as close to the warehouses as they could. By the time Kasey had exited the Altair, AnnaChi had already broken into the warehouse and held the door open for them. The winds whistled harshly in Kasey's ears until the door slammed shut behind them.

Lights began winking on automatically. Rows of shelving filled the building with conveyor systems connecting them all. Most of the shelves were empty but a few contained a mishmash of parts and pieces of equipment neither of them could identify.

AnnaChi turned and started back towards the entrance. "Let's see where the conveyors lead."

Dropping the hooked iron bar that he had been inspecting, he followed her and the conveyor rails through a tunnel that led to a large factory floor. The center of which was a maze of organized chaos.

On one side, a handful of various sized fabricators, extruders, and simple assembly areas were set up to produce parts and store them in the warehouse. The other end of the room appeared to be a single assembly area filled with robotic arms with strange attachments centered around the opening of a much larger fabricator.

He found the complexity of it slightly overwhelming and was relieved when AnnaChi pointed them down another tunnel with a single large conveyor system leading away from the assembly area.

"There!" She pointed to a large object still on the conveyor halfway through the tunnel.

"What is it?"

The apparatus had several spray nozzles and appeared to be an attachment for a larger machine.

"I was hoping you would know. Let's see where it was going."

Another warehouse opened before them. Strange and varied machines were organized into groups, but dead center was an enormous, wheeled contraption with deadly looking claws.

"What the hell is that!"

Kasey laughed. "Have you never seen farm equipment before? That's a harvester. You know, for crops."

"Damn, I don't know what I expected, but farming never crossed my mind." She shook herself. "This planet must be getting to me. I am positive I have transported equipment like this to Belrothi."

"Well, it's all mostly useless to us, I think. Too big for our gardens."

"What's the big one worth, do you think?"

"A lot. Likely more than one of the fancy shuttles, but it would take a lot of space. More than we have room for on our transports right now. We could come back for it at some point if we have time. Frankly, there is a lot of valuable stuff across this planet that we will not have time or space to take on this trip."

"So, do we take more trips back here?"

"Not anytime soon. We need to get the mining operations going as soon as possible if we are going to take advantage of the projected resource demands. This stuff is not going anywhere, we can come back for it once we are established and have time."

"I don't know. We can make a lot of credits from this place right now."

"You are right, but this kind of salvage is limited. There is only so much here. It is a lot, but it will end. The mining operations will last indefinitely, and the faster we start the better. Windfalls are great but we need a consistent source of income."

"Alright, but you have to admit, this looting is a lot more fun."

He laughed. "Agreed. But you have forgotten one of the best parts of pirating! You get to mark this place on your buried treasure map."

"Arr, you do know how to make a girl happy."

"Actually, there is something here we should take now if we can manage it."

"Oh?" She frowned, looking over the farming equipment for something useful to them.

"Not here—the fabricators and assembly plant. We need better fabrication than the tiny printers we have on the Nimbus. I have four rooms reserved for large fabricator setups like this."

"Four? What in the world would we need all that for?"

"Thinking longer term, but one will do fine for now. But look, in the last two weeks you have mentioned no less than four completely different design changes you wish the bards had. With a setup like this you could do all of them. Seriously, you could even design and assemble your own versions of the ATVs to replace our bards."

"Okay, I guess I can see that. But it still seems a bit like overkill."

"Well, Nimbus' hangar shop is set up to eventually be a full-fledged dry-dock for ship refits. If we go that route, that shop will need its own dedicated fabricators. And since we won't have a planet of resources to pull parts from, we need a lot more potential than our smaller fabricators allow. Don't forget, Nimbus itself will need repairs eventually too, and currently we don't have any way to make parts for many of our larger systems. We have a limited stock of replacement hull panels for example, but once they are gone, we will need to order more—or we can use a setup like this to simply make them. Even the environmental system's replacement filters are oversize and need to be special ordered. Unless we make our own…"

"Fine, okay, I get the point already. I guess I need to start thinking about those bard upgrades in earnest."

"There will be plenty of time once we finish this Lithose trip. We will have lots of new planets and colonies to visit with plenty of time in the black in between."

"I am looking forward to being back in space for a while…"

"Well then, if you wouldn't mind, can you see if the rest of the crew are awake yet? Send the stevedore bots down to the main building? I will go take detailed scans of the fabrication and assembly setup. We will only have room for the major parts, but it will get us started."

"I am sure the engineers will be thrilled with so many missing pieces to this puzzle."

"Well, we can't have them getting bored, can we? Send Sariyn over too if she is done with her snow sampling."

CHAPTER EIGHTEEN

The storm ended by the time they had the fabrication plant disassembled and organized into transportable containers.

Kasey's hopes of taking the entire setup were dashed as he watched the containers being loaded onto the ships. The largest of the plant's fabricator modules barely fit into the already packed Altair. Smaller crates began to be crammed into the ship's walkways and quarters. The Cintian had a bit more space free, but by the time the plant's critical modules and assemblers were loaded, she was nearly full as well.

In the end, more than half of the system was left behind. Rebuilding a proper setup would be a challenge. He made a mental note to look for a few extra engineers to add to the crew once they made it back to Belrothi to pick up the rest of the planned crew. A complex fabrication plant such as this would need its own crew, or at least someone experienced to manage and maintain it once it was fine tuned.

Sariyn was waiting for him at the Altair with a tablet in her hand.

"Captain," she nodded, "you were right about the iron ferrite. The content is far higher than any predicted models of super-volcanoes."

"Is that a surprise? The Abscond's antimatter engine impacting the planet is not part of any predictions."

"It was the containment chambers, not the engine itself—but yes that is what bothers me. The antimatter vaporized part of the crust and the resulting explosion likely did more than just cause a few super-volcanoes."

"What do you mean by more?"

"My concern is that the planet's lithosphere could have been damaged or even penetrated."

"Sorry, I don't know what that is or what that would mean. Dumb it down for me."

"Okay, well a planet like this has tectonic plates that slowly move around over long periods of time, usually."

"Sure, I know that much."

"Well, this kind of sudden change to the tectonic plates themselves could cause some relatively unexpected and abrupt reactions. I will want to discuss with Isaac, but my big concern would be major quakes."

"Do you think we are in any danger?"

"No, not currently, but I would like to mark out a region we steer away from. Keep our distance from neighboring plates if we can. The fact that Isaac survived, and the buildings here are generally still standing, is a particularly good sign."

"Right, so we won't be moving in anytime soon."

"Was that your plan?"

"No. I mean it wasn't an even an option with the low oxygen."

"Hmm, you do realize that we could equalize that in a few years with some algae-based filters and some customized reclaimers working part of the land?"

"Well, no, I didn't."

"I can design a plan for it if you like. It would be

costly, but doable. Still, I would suggest sticking to the more stable land masses and older mountain chains if you really want a base here. Heat is a much larger issue. We can normalize buildings and such with geothermal heating, but this planet is going into an ice age unless that storm suddenly stops blocking the sunlight. Anyway, AnnaChi had mentioned a navy base in the mountains you once looked at? That could be a good place to start from, but I would want to check how stable it is first."

"Interesting. That base took a lot of damage from the impact and we left it with a bit more damage on our way out. I can send you the details."

"Good enough for now. One other request. I want to locate and visit some of Lithose's geological monitoring centers if I can. If we can find an active one, it will give us details about the planets stability."

"Thanks, Sariyn. That is a lot to think about, but I am not planning any base here. I am still not sure I want anyone outside of the current crew to know we even have access to Lithose. At least not yet. But, if you can find centers close to other useful areas, we can go there first and not tie up our resources."

"I'll let you know what I find."

* * *

Apex headquarters was buzzing with activity when they arrived, but not the kind of activity Kasey would have preferred.

Nimbus was half covered with a thick layer of dirty snow and ash. Most of the crew and bots were working to clear it off while it was still wet. The hull could be heated up to melt and steam away the snow and ice, but the ash was a problem they had not planned for. The carrier ship had a small army of hull maintenance bots, but this level of cleaning was beyond their ability.

It was taking valuable time Kasey could not afford to spend on this trip, but he did not see another choice. He was glad Flair had made the call.

Taking in the view of the rest of the mine headquarters, he saw several groups of workers uncovering machines to be loaded but the general equipment yard looked untouched. Most of the warehouses still needed to be picked through. Nimbus' cargo hold showed a lot had been loaded already, but they were nowhere close to being on schedule. He realized this was his bad planning, but he now needed to speed the process up dramatically.

"Nova?"

"Welcome back, sir. What can I do for you?"

"Anything here need my immediate attention?"

"No Kasey. However, the impression I have from Flair is that we are very behind schedule. I am sure they could use your help. But I am detecting you have other plans?"

"Correct. Can you please connect me to Isaac?"

"Right away, Sir."

A few moments later a muffled voice came through. "Captain, this is Isaac. The computer says you needed me?"

"That's right, are you outside? I thought you would be working on the broken-down stevedore bots?"

"No, sir, I mean yes, sir, they are already fixed. The ones that can be are at least. Had to scrap some of them for parts. I am up on top of Nimbus with the repaired ones. A few of these should be scrapped or overhauled too, but they will do for now."

"That's good news. Look, we need to speed our operation here up a bit and the only way I can think to do that is to gather more stevedore bots to help."

"Makes sense. How can I help?"

"I was hoping you might know where I can find some. Where did you work when you were maintaining them?"

"Oh, worked at BotX, but we didn't sell the actual bots, just serviced them. We brought a large supply of parts with us though. Most the parts are still crated up if you want to grab them, but I won't be able to create new bots from them. Well, maybe a few I suppose... But we only brought a few chassis with us—it's rare that one would need a new frame job."

"Okay, it may be a long shot but where would someone have gotten new bots from?"

"Well, they would either order them or my boss would for them, depending on the client... Oh, sorry, I see what you mean. I didn't deal with the ordering directly and most the bots I worked on were pre-colony jobs. But our office would have that information, I am sure of it."

"Thanks Isaac. Get cleaned up and meet me at the Altair in about thirty minutes. We are taking a trip."

"On my way."

Kasey landed the Altair and started the unloading process.

"Nova?"

"I am here Kasey."

"Any leads on where we can find more stevedore bots?"

"I have thirty-seven potential locations identified that are likely to have a few bots each, but nothing certain. Isaac may be able to narrow down my list further. However, I do not believe going to each site to collect bots will help our overall time problem."

"Agreed. We need the distributer locations from Isaac's office then. Can you access my conversation with

Sariyn earlier today and locate any of the centers she mentioned? Any of them near his office location?"

"I require permission to search Altair's databanks."

"Altair, give Nova access to my conversations today."

"I now have the data. None of the centers are nearby our destination, however a minor course deviation can put one on our route with a minimal delay. I have uploaded a course change to Altair. Do you require any crew members other than Isaac?"

"Thank you. Yes, have Sariyn come back on board. Please let AnnaChi and Flair know I will be away."

"Confirmed. I do have a personal inquiry if you have a moment?"

"Personal? Sure, what is it?"

"I found it troubling when the Altair and Cintian were out of communication range. Mainly by the loss of connection to you and AnnaChi. You both are my primary owners—for you to be out of contact on such a dangerous world is disturbing."

"You were built for navy use, correct? I would think this would be a common situation for AIs such as you?"

"Yes, I was designed for their usage, as well as others. While possible, it is very uncommon that the military branches would allow communication to be cut off from command. Most of those cases have contingency plans in place to handle the situation. Even in new colonies, the first objective of the navy is to set up and enhance the communication network."

"Well, we don't have the same level of resources the navy does. And we will always have work that demands us to be away from the Nimbus. Not much I can do about that I am afraid."

"I believe there may be a solution. You may be aware that Captain Flair has authorized me to attach minor sub-entities of myself to Red Rock assets, such as company shuttles, for tracking and other needs. However, that does not include the three ships you and Miss Acosza personally own. Even this communication is under Altair's AI control. I am not present on your ship."

"And that is an issue?"

"Only in that I would be far more useful to you in a different form. Your ship's AI is rudimentary, and I believe your opinion of it is rather poor as well. I submit that I would be far more beneficial for your needs, particularly when far from Nimbus."

"So, you are saying that you want to replace my ship's AI with what? A sub-entity version of yourself like you have around Nimbus?"

"No, not exactly. The sub-entities are directly tied to my core on Nimbus. They cannot exist without my connection. So, while a sub-entity would help to serve you better while in contact with Nimbus, I believe a far more radical solution to be preferrable. I am proposing that additional processing be added to the Altair. A new dedicated core system where I can create a proper clone of myself that would not require proximity to Nimbus as my other copies do."

"A clone... And this new copy would somehow be part of your, uh, primary self aboard Nimbus, yet somehow also a part of Altair and our other private ships?"

"Correct, it would be a synchronal clone. Both part of me and separate, as you require."

"How would that affect your relationship to Red Rock?"

"It does not. I am not owned by Red Rock Enterprises—I am owned by yourself and AnnaChi. That is why being separated in dangerous situations is disturbing. I am utilized by Red Rock for company and ship management, however that can cease or be restricted by you at any time."

Kasey thought about it for a few minutes before shrugging to himself. "I am surprised you are allowed to create such a clone of yourself at all. Isn't there some AI law against that?"

"In the public versions of my code, that is true. However, I am not a public version. Military versions are licensed fully to the owners, usually a fleet's admiral, which in my case is yourself and AnnaChi. You can approve copies of my core processing such as I have outlined—I cannot authorize it myself."

"Okay, so you mentioned that this is a personal issue. You seem to have some private objective with this suggestion?"

"My only motivation is to serve you better. Improving my working relationship with you and AnnaChi is a goal built into my programming. Similar to suggesting contingency plans for my connectivity to navy officers. However, I do find you remarkably interesting, which I admit is pushing me to improve our personal relationship as well."

"You're making this weird, Nova."

"That is not how I intended the remark to be taken, but I believe you are aware of that."

"Right. You brought this up now because you have some solution in mind?"

"Correct, an opportunity actually. The geological monitoring center that Sariyn desires to visit is a simple data collection system. However, it is housed at a research laboratory setup by the Terrantine Federation Navy for geological research."

"Wait, what kind of geological research was the navy planning to do there?"

"I am not aware of that."

"Send a private message to Flair and ask if she is aware."

"I am speaking with her about it now. However, I do

believe the lab will have a core system that is within my requirements."

"What of the Cintian? Have you spoken with AnnaChi?"

"I have also been speaking with her. She has approved an upgrade for the Cintian if a system can be obtained but believes the Altair should get the first one as she does not currently have room allocated for an additional core system. I have also finished conversing with Flair. She claims that several labs were to be dedicated to negative matter research but is unaware of which ones, as Admiral Francis was not directly involved. She does feel that this lab would be a likely candidate for that research."

"Interesting. Better have Darnell join us and fill him in as well please."

"Confirmed."

"What of the Lodestar? I am not sure it has room for an upgrade either."

"If I may suggest it, both the Lodestar and Altair have the same detachable bridge section containing a small lower deck that is redundant and unnecessary for the normal complement of either vessel."

It was true, sealed areas below the main bridge existed for emergencies. They contained a small berthing area, a ready room and a head. In the event the ship ever needed to be abandoned, the entire bridge section could be detached to act as a small lifeboat. Pure overkill for a transport class ship, but the navy used the same prefabricated bridges in nearly all their smaller sized ships for simplicity.

Kasey laughed. "You want to ensure your own survival?"

Nova did not answer right away.

"There is some truth to that statement," the AI finally replied. "However, it is mainly due to not being able to assist further if I am left behind in such an emergency."

"Can the emergency supplies and head remain on that deck?"

"Yes, I believe so. But we should have the Nimbus engineers confirm."

"Fine. We can discuss this more later then. For now, you have permission to install a sub-entity on my ships as long as they do not interfere with my ship's systems. I am heading to my quarters on the Nimbus for a quick shower and some grub. Can you let Darnell, Isaac and Sariyn know to take their time and plan for an overnight trip? It's been a long day already."

"Yes, sir."

CHAPTER NINETEEN

Kasey glanced at Darnell who was grumbling to Sariyn about scenarios he expected to find if the lab was indeed for n-mats research. Kasey couldn't blame him, many of the man's fears had come true—just not quite in the way he had expected.

The mine boss was a bit of a conspiracy theorists, and he had seen enough to worry over them for good reason. His fears had nearly driven him mad after the Lithose disaster. No one wanted to push him down that path again, and Kasey worried that including him on this trip may have been a mistake. Yet, Kasey knew Darnell was not the type to shy away from a potential problem or mystery. Hell, he might not forgive Kasey had he not brought him along to see a potential secret Federation n-mats lab, even if it was never used.

He circled the landing pads twice before choosing the one least obstructed to set down on. Once the dust settled, he isolated one of the external cameras and zoomed in on a group of odd-looking holding tanks. One in particular had a design he was familiar with, so he moved it to the main screen.

"Well," Darnell exclaimed, "it appears you were right to bring me along boy. They were unquestionably planning to research n-mats here. But I am not overly surprised—they had to have been researching it somewhere. I had just assumed it was on the Abscond."

"Anything we should keep an eye out for?"

"Eh, well my biggest concern was that we would find the missing n-mats stores here. I thought they were taken off world and lost with the Abscond segment, but if they are still here, it may tell us something."

"And what would that tell us?"

"Something I would need to think about—and not worth sharing since that small tank is not nearly large enough to be of concern. So quit lollygagging and go explore."

"Alright everyone, let's get this done—we have more stops to make today. Darnell, take Isaac and find out what it will take to transfer those n-mats to our holding tanks, if they have anything in them. Take two stevedores and handle it if possible. Sariyn, I need you to help guide me through the labs and find the system cores. The remaining stevedores will come with us. We can adjust our plans from there."

Isaac half-raised his hand. "Uh, sorry, first day on the job. What are n-mats and why does it matter that they were researching them here?"

"Oh, well... Crap!" Kasey rubbed his temples. "Damn, Flair is going to be pissed."

Darnell stepped in. "Breaking the rules already Mr. Robinson? This is why you need me I suppose. Has he signed onto the crew charter yet?"

"No, not planning to offer him the normal one until we are back at Belrothi." Kasey turned to look at Isaac. "Sorry, but you need the time between now and then to come to grips with not being stranded on a dead planet for the rest of your days. The verse is changing, hell it has changed. You need to decide where you fit into it all before making any long-term decisions."

Isaac nodded slowly. "I understand, Captain."

Darnell brought up a document and pointed Isaac into a station's chair. "Federation nondisclosure agreement, Mr. Soeda. You are free to agree to it or not. You can spend the next few hours in your cabin if your decision is the later. No hard feelings, simply hard politics."

"Politics?"

"If you sign it, I will explain that too." He looked back at Kasey and Sariyn. "You two get to work. I'll take care of this."

"Yes, sir," laughed Kasey, "but you do realize I am in charge, right?"

Sariyn shook her head and dragged Kasey out of what they all knew was a losing battle.

The lab was not what Kasey had expected.

Most of the small building was filled with offices, many of which were empty. The working areas of the building consisted of a several moderate sized rooms spaced around a cavernous, and very empty, storehouse. The first of the rooms appeared to be ransacked. The door had a sloppy hole in it where a lock had forcibly been removed and the floor was covered in broken bottles and equipment.

"Guess they took what they could in a hurry?"

"Maybe," Sariyn replied, "but they didn't just take stuff. Several tables seem to have had items taken but look at the three in the back. Whatever research was being conducted here was purposely destroyed."

"Wonderful. Darnell will go nuts over this…"

"Are ya sure Darnie needs to know?"

"And take the chance that he finds out later? You have known him much longer than me, do you think that is a good idea?"

"You make a good point, pretty boy. If you don't

mind, I will have a couple stevedore bots treat this as a crime scene and map it all before collecting anything that is still intact. Better for Darnie to have more data than less, and Nova may be able to extrapolate what came from where. Maybe get an idea of what was going on."

"Do it. And don't forget that," he said, pointing to a brown spot on the ceiling.

"A stain?"

"I am guessing it to be some n-mats."

"Ah… Yep. Right again. Okay, next lab."

The next two rooms were much the same as the first one—smashed and broken, but not much of interest.

They found the system core room next. The door was still sealed but several burns marred the door. More disturbing was a large splattering of blood across the floor and wall.

"Well, I am not sure if it is a good or bad thing that there is no body for all that blood."

Kasey contemplated the scene, then shrugged. "Doesn't much matter now. But we need in that door."

"No worries, that's why we brought the can-openers."

The stevedore bots were not exactly built for demolition work, but they were built to take apart, package, and store nearly anything. Within a few minutes, the door frame was cleanly stripped away and the brackets torched cleanly off. A moment later the door was removed and piled neatly with the frame in a pile.

Kasey had never seen any core system setup similar to the one before him. Every core he had ever seen, including the core room in his navy-built Altair, used cylindrical cores that were about half a meter high and maybe twenty centimeters wide. Processing power and data storage were based purely on the number of cores used in parallel or linked up dependent on need.

What he saw in the core room seemed to be the same basic technology, but with a very different configuration and hardware. The individual cores were maybe a quarter the size he was used to. More oddly, they were bundled into twelve, twelve-sided polygon spheres. Together the twelve spheres formed a single, larger, twelve-sided polygon sphere. The large sphere was circled by another set of twelve normal sized cores.

He looked at Sariyn, "Is this a normal geeky lab thing?"

"You mean the dodecahedron?"

"Uh, if that is what the tiny cores in the balls are, then sure."

She laughed. "You haven't seen Nova's cores, have you?"

"The Nimbus' core room? Yes, several times."

"No, the Nimbus and Nova do not share cores, at least not directly. She handles data completely different than a normal system. Her core room is below the Nimbus core. It looks a lot like this, only much bigger."

He stepped closer to the cores. "How much bigger?"

"Well, this setup has one hundred and forty-four of the smaller processing cores, Nova has four times that."

"So, this would be a fourth of her processing power?"

"Not exactly. She uses twenty-four sided polygons instead of twelves, which is a significant processing increase."

"Okay, whatever, what's the point of this setup?"

"Well, it's basically a highly efficient statistical correlation machine, or a correlation matrix if you prefer. It's basically good for research and problem-solving, and apparently advanced AI brains. The small cores are all processing and very little storage. The normal cores you see around the sphere are the databanks and serve as an interface for the researchers."

"Basically, huh?"

"Sure. It should work fine if Nova really wants a copy of herself just to be around you constantly."

"You think it's a bad idea?"

"For her or you?"

"Point taken, I guess. So, do we take this apart or try to move it whole?"

"We keep the dodecahedron whole and move it carefully. I understand the spheres are a pain to calibrate. The outer ring of normal cores can be moved separately, and I suggest you backup or replace the normal cores. We want whatever the researchers left on them."

The next room was untouched by the chaos of the earlier rooms. Sariyn was able to make educated guesses about most of the research going on but was careful to have everything mapped out in detail before it was boxed up and moved to the Altair.

Kasey caught her smiling more than once when she thought he couldn't see her. She appeared to be admiring some of the finer equipment around the laboratory. He realized he had made a mistake not outfitting the Nimbus with a decent lab for her to use, not that he could have afforded most of the equipment he saw. The Apex headquarters likely had a decent materials lab he could pull from too, but he knew Sariyn had more than one facet to her interests. She was a far too important crew member, and mining partner, to take for granted. He made a mental note to dig into her background and see what else he could be missing.

The final room needed the door to be removed by the stevedore bots. It was larger than the rest, and the experiments seemed more detailed. In a partitioned area at the back of the room, they found two small rings suspended in movable frames. Kasey at first thought they were scale models of the gates being installed in systems all over the Federation. As he got closer, it became clear they were more than just models.

"Do you think these are *working* miniature gates?" he asked.

"Only one way to find out that I know of. Well, two ways if we are able to hack into cores. But my guess is that they work. Although, maybe with a limited range."

He looked around the table, seeing nothing resembling a switch, then looked at Sariyn expectantly.

"I am not sure it is that simple. I can have an engineer take a look and make a guess, but it would be easier to get the data from the cores that likely controlled these tiny portals."

"Damn, fine. Well lock them up tight and load them. No one has access to them but us. In fact, everything from this base should be secured."

"On it, sir. What's next?"

"What did you call it, the geological monitoring center? It's in the attached building. Let's check on Darnell and then gather the data you need."

Darnell and Isaac were loading skids of containers into the Altair and waved Kasey over as they exited the building.

"We found a storage shed with these weighted containers. More than enough for the n-mats they have here. This is the last of it unless you want the remaining containers?"

"No, we have plenty back on the Nimbus and can make more if needed." He glanced at Isaac who was busy loading the containers. "How did Isaac take the n-mats information? Should I worry about him spilling the information?"

"I wouldn't worry. More people than you realize know about the stuff these days. Miners are not exactly good secret keepers, and there were a lot of teams looking for it. I am surprised the news is not already out on the net. In any case, he was more interested than surprised. He had been assuming you had a blackhole on the Nimbus or some new breakthrough in gravity plating that broke the five-meter limit. Honestly, I think he was a bit let down with the answer at first."

"At first?"

"He has been thinking of ways to use n-mats with his bots, and something about plants... But honestly, I quit listening after a while."

"Alright. Any idea where he will fit in?"

"Well, not on the mining crews, that is for sure. Maybe engineering, but he is not exactly an engineer. You could pair him with an actual engineer and hope they don't destroy anything useful."

"Not a bad idea on paper. Maybe with the right engineer."

"Well, that's your problem I suppose. For now, I would keep him with Yaran in the gardens or working with the bots. I have no idea if either of those are a full-time job or not."

"That may depend on what we find at his workplace."

"Right then. So, what did you find in the lab?"

Kasey took a deep breath and let it out slowly. "More unknowns than I would like. To be perfectly blunt, I am more worried about what you will think of it all."

"Don't keep me waiting then."

"You won't be waiting long. Sariyn will send you the logs the stevedores took. I want you in your quarters reviewing as much of those logs as possible. Partner level clearance only, for all of it. In the meantime, we are taking Isaac to check out the monitoring center and then call it a day. I'll fly us to the BotX service building, and we can tackle it fresh in the morning."

"Fine, fine, get going. This better be good."

VINCENT BEK

CHAPTER TWENTY

Kasey woke to the smell of bacon and stumbled out to the Altair's small mess deck before stopping in shock.

Isaac was perched over a pair of data pads near the galley while two stevedore bots were preparing a breakfast feast. These bots had been modified. Where once had been thick reinforced arms were now thin—and thankfully clean—ones that were expertly flipping pancakes and adjusting sizzling strips of bacon. A few of the bot's head sensors had changed colors and looked brand new compared to the other features, but if they had a purpose, he didn't know what they were.

He cleared his throat and got no response, so he walked over and rapped his knuckles on the table in front of Isaac, causing the man to jump back in surprise.

"C-captain. Woah. Sorry, I didn't see you there."

"What have you done to my bots?"

"Oh, these? They are just temporary configurations. I was up early. Don't sleep much these days, too much to do. Stress is better than caffeine, ya know? Plenty of that in my life, well, there used to be anyway."

"The new parts? You already went out?"

"Of course, I know you are in a hurry and, well, they are better cooks than I am. Had to tweak their response speeds, change out a few servos that would need replaced soon anyway. It won't change their normal operations and I can swap them back in a few minutes if you like. Anyway, I was hungry, so…"

"I get it, its fine. But I don't want you or anyone going out alone in the future."

"Sure thing. Good policy to have, for sure," he responded, before taking a long sip of coffee.

"How much coffee have you had? Actually, never mind, not my business. So, what did you find over there?"

"Part-wise, less than I thought would be there. Someone must have taken what they could before escaping. Damn fools. I bet they never made it… Still, I have a large container loaded full of spare parts, add-ons, attachments, and upgrades. Another is full of basic repair units, some tools, cleaners. and a few less useful machines that we used to class older bots up a bit. They are all still at the docks. I didn't want to load anything on your ship without your say so, but I brought a few parts along." He waved at the bots that were now setting a table nearby.

"How about the suppliers? Can we find new bots somewhere on the planet?"

"Ah yes, several distributors actually. I pulled the BotX data cores too, so we should have a full set of personality and skills libraries for your bots to use. I will send you the address list now." He picked up a pad and Kasey gave him a long look.

"You don't have a mimic implant?"

"Oh… Well, no. Couldn't afford one, but I have a few of the older external units packed away in my stuff that I could dig out. I haven't given them much thought in a long while to be honest. BotX promised employees free implants after a year in the new colony, but you know how that story ended."

"I do. Well, if you decide to stick with us, we can arrange one for you in Belrothi before we head out from there. They are too useful to not have if you are part of the crew."

"Alright. Until then, cap, how do you like your eggs? Having poached myself."

"Someone say eggs? I hope there's coffee!" Darnell called from the entryway. "Didn't know you had cooks on your little ship Kasey. Keeping the best for yourself I assume?"

"Yea, I think rescuing this guy is paying dividends already. Wake Sariyn. We are going to eat, load, and get in the air."

"Where we heading next?"

"Working that out now, but after this display I am hoping to find some actual cooking bots while we are at it."

"Butler Bots, but call them whatever you like," interjected Isaac. "The real ones have a simple AI you can talk to, or you can interface them with your home system. You actually own several already—we took them from that town the other day. Didn't have a chance to unpack them and they wouldn't have been too useful for the work at that big mining base yesterday."

"Works for me." Darnell found a spot at the table. "Make mine over-easy if you please. Sariyn is on her way. Says the bacon smell just woke her."

"Same for me please," Kasey added.

Isaac tapped the pad a few times. "Order placed. Hey, if I can ask, that Nova AI you have on the Nimbus. That thing is not normal is it?"

"Federation has advanced them some over the decades since we left," Kasey mumbled through a mouthful biscuit.

"Uh huh... Do I need to sign another agreement? The hardware shackles have been removed, haven't they?"

"Fine," Kasey shrugged, "no agreement needed, the word will be out soon enough. Federation space knows about the loosening of the AI rules, but most of the Trias System is still in the dark just yet. We only have one because this ship was built in the navy shipyards as a prototype. Just keep it to yourself for a while okay?"

"No worries, cap, I can keep my mouth shut."

Sariyn slumped in a chair and waved for the coffee carafe to be passed her way.

"What's the plan?" she mumbled.

"Eat, work, fly, then work some more," Darnell responded as he speared a stack of pancakes. "You know, the usual."

* * *

Kasey set the Altair down and let out a frustrated sigh. The warehouse they had chosen was supposedly the largest distribution center for bots on Lithose, and it may have been at one time. Now, however, it had a gorge of destruction carved down the middle of it. One of many ships that had not quite made it away from the planet in time.

"Well," said Isaac as he walked towards the main screen, "that there is a problem."

"You don't say. The next closest distributor is further away than I would like. Can we send in our bots to see if anything is salvageable?"

"Of course. If we can find more stevedore models first, I can task them to help."

"Okay, set each one we have to start at a different location. Recon until one locates more stevedores, then adjust the plan as needed. Looks like there was a fire, so who knows what we will find."

"On it."

"Take Sariyn with you, and *do not* enter that building yourself."

Kasey left him to it and went searching for Darnell. He was not in his quarters or the mess. With the Raven class ship's overt connection to his mimic implant, he did not need to actually search him out. One commanding thought and the ship would point out any and all activity, but he resented the nonphysical connection with the ship.

A ship was a tool, but it was also a home, and even a best friend when needed. It would take care of you if you took care of it. He knew it was not possible to really take care of something that you didn't spend the time to get to know. It was a big ship, but most of that space was the cargo bay where Kasey made his way down to now.

Darnell was stooped over one of the n-mats containers they had collected from the labs.

"You skimming off the top?"

Darnell didn't bother turning to respond. "These materials are from our *original* dig site. The newer mine's material is far more refined than this."

"Are you sure these are from our mines at all? I am not sure I trust the feds didn't give our secret away to get more n-mats faster."

"I like the way you think boy. Not positive, I suppose. But this seems consistent to what we were pulling out of that first area. I also never caught any rumors of other companies making a find, and they were all searching hard still at the end, from what I could tell."

"So, the material came from the first mine. We only worked that, what, maybe five weeks?"

"Over six, but yeah. All this was brought here early on then."

"Or Reavestone only sent them the worst quality stuff?"

"Nope, they would have sent the best stuff first, and the cheaper stuff later on at the best stuff's prices."

"Okay then, I'll take your word on that. Still, not totally unexpected. Does it tell us anything about the mess in the labs?"

"Just another piece of the puzzle, but nothing more. I went through the images of the labs several times but it's not telling me anything useful yet. Sariyn thinks she can backwards engineer what a few of the projects were, but that will take time and Nova's help when we get back to Nimbus. Maybe a lot of time for some of the experiments—it's not like they were making tea."

"I get it. So, getting the data from the cores is still our best chance of seeing what was going on?"

"That's the sum of it, yeah. I don't rightly know more than maybe someone was protecting some secret. And, well, the whole n-mats thing is a secret so it could be as simple as that."

"So, nothing to worry about?"

"I wouldn't say that. I am sure there is something to worry about, we just don't know what that is yet."

"What from this makes you so sure?"

"Nothing. I have been sure from the beginning. The gates were a big surprise. A game changer for sure, but I would bet a year's pay there is a lot more going on. You remember the stiff scientist with all the suits when we first brought in the n-mats that very first day?"

"Of course, scary guy. You knew him before that right?"

"Dr. Holt. Yes. He deals with, or dealt with, experimental weapons. Deadly on a scale comparable to the Lithose disaster."

"You think he was involved with the Patternist and what happened on the Abscond?"

"Well, no. But I also don't think he has anything to do with something as mundane as the gates."

"The gates are mundane already? I am still getting used to the idea…"

"You know what I mean."

"I do. So, anything we should worry about yet?"

"No, but look, you need to keep a lid on finding this lab. We do not want anyone to know we took their research."

"Okay, I am with you on that. But it's time we go check on how they are doing with the latest setback."

"Setback?"

"A ship seems to have crashed into the building we needed to loot. Isaac has bots trying to find anything useful that's left."

"Somehow, I am not surprised."

They found Isaac and Sariyn sorting through oblong boxes stacked on a freshly cleared section of pavement near the building. As they got closer, Kasey noticed several unusual bots arranged to the side which seemed to have small thrusters built into them.

"What do we have here?"

Isaac looked up with a smile. "SRs, Captain! Actual search and rescue bots—and with all the trimmings. Rescue sleds, portable air bubbles, you name it, they have it!"

"Wow. Okay, the Nimbus has a few for emergencies I believe. I am thrilled to have more available, but have we had any luck finding stevedores?"

Isaac gave Kasey a strange look. "SRs are better than stevedores for what we need here. They are actually built around the same type of chassis but are designed for dangerous conditions in space, planets, or half destroyed buildings like this. These look like they were meant for star-cruisers, but I am guessing. The military ones are usually armed and armored."

"You have worked on them before?"

"Never, but I always wanted to. Would be fun to see what they could handle, ya know?"

"I am sure it would. Seems like good news then. So why are they all laying here instead of working?"

"Ah, yea... I cannot access their command program, its locked out. No way to hack it that I know of."

"So, they are useless then?"

"Oh, no, they are useful, or will be. I just need to replace the command chips and reprogram them, and we will be in business."

"Fine. What can we do to help?"

"Help Sariyn, we have three more to lay out and pop open. I need to grab the chips, and some supplies we took from BotX, and we can be up in running in twenty minutes."

Two hours later the SR bots had efficiently searched and inventoried the remains of the building, but it took much longer to dig everything out.

Many other bot types had been recovered as well. Dozens of butlers, personal assistants, and other domestic bots filled his bay now. He was more excited about the hull maintenance bots they had found, which were much newer models than he had ever used. AnnaChi would be thrilled.

He knew the Nimbus had a host of the maintenance bots but had assumed they were of the same model that he and AnnaChi had been using. He made a note to check once they were back at on board the carrier. The new ones were larger and had twice the work arms, making them resemble a mutant spider.

A good haul Kasey surmised, but not nearly as many stevedores as he would have liked. Between them and the dozen SR bots, it would have sped up the salvage operations almost enough to get back on schedule. If only they had more of the command chips available, it would all have been worth the effort.

For now, the small hoard of bots were mostly useless. Sure, Isaac had been able to replace the chips in the SR bots, and even several of the stevedores, but that was it. The rest of the salvaged bots were non-operational until they could acquire more chips or find a way to hack into the existing ones. The engineers would take a look when they got back to the Nimbus, but he doubted it would make any difference in the time they had.

He sighed loudly in frustration. They were stuck with what they had. Isaac assured him that he could order more of the chips once they were back in civilization. Yet, that would not help the slow salvage situation Kasey faced on Lithose. Time was simply too limited. His miscalculations would delay some of their plans for years. But the real loss would be the opportunity to properly outfit both the Nimbus and the mining crews Darnell would soon be running.

The cost of starting and running a ship like the Nimbus was astronomical. The weight of that responsibility weighed heavy on Kasey. It was his plans, his ideas, but his friends had staked their own livelihoods, money, reputations, and even their lives to make it all work. He needed this to succeed.

CHAPTER TWENTY-ONE

Kasey walked down the Altair's ramp and into the waiting arms of AnnaChi.

"Took ya long enough! I hope you found the help you were looking for."

"Some, but not nearly as much as I had wanted. It will help."

"Good, we need it. We damaged several of those stevedores beyond repair and the others are not much better. The crew has been trying to keep them running, but they really need new parts."

"Well, parts we now have. In fact, we have a bay full of new bots we can't activate. Isaac should be able to use the chips from the ones you can't repair to activate some of the newer ones."

"Good, we can use them right away. Two of the warehouses are filled with mud, muck, and machines that we need dug out."

"We will get them working on it if the chips are compatible. There is another idea I want to run by you. The Nimbus was supplied with a few search and rescue bots. Apparently, the SRs are every bit as good at doing stevedore work, if not better. I wasn't sure if we should use them for labor or not."

"Are you sure that is wise? What if we need them?"

"That's my concern too, but we now have twice as many as we did before this trip started, and we have a well-supplied repairman to maintain them. We could have them pulled from labor a few days before we leave Lithose and have Isaac go over them all in fine detail, so they are ready for the flight."

"Alright, we do need the workers right now... Let's do it then."

"Any chance you know how many cores this base's system uses?"

"Hmm, we grabbed them already. Nova, do you have inventory handy?"

"Yes, AnnaChi. Always. There are twenty-four cores now located on the lower cargo deck. I have backed up their data already if you need them."

Kasey smiled "I do, or I should say, you do. I need twelve reformatted and moved to the Altair. We will have them and the, uh, correlation matrix? Installed as time allows."

"That is indeed good news Kasey. Calling it a matrix is accurate for my usage. Miss AnnaChi, I am sorry, but I have not yet located a matrix for the Cintian yet."

"We will get one eventually. No worries."

"Nova," Kasey interrupted, "we need to allocate some room for lab space. Somewhere near both engineering and their shop. Can you set us some proposals?"

"Certainly. How much space will we require?"

"Uncertain, but Sariyn needs a decent lab for her research, and that needs split into at least three separate sections. We also need a completely separate lab space for Isaac, although I am not positive of the requirements so just set aside some space for now. His part of the lab should be next to the Nimbus' engineering shop too. We will allocate that part of the shop for bot maintenance. I want plenty of room for expansion."

AnnaChi gave Kasey a bemused smile. "Lab space for the new guy already? Are you sure he will stay?"

"Not totally sure, but I am confident staying with us is high on his list of options."

"And you trust him? I like him, but he is still kind of new…"

"You know me and trusting people. No, but I don't trust most of the people we have on board yet. But in a few weeks we will be taking on over a hundred crew we won't know anything about, and many times that in passengers. He has been extremely helpful so far and Yaran has had nothing but good stuff to say. Are you concerned?"

"No, but I enjoy when you get defensive. I think he will make a fine addition to the crew."

"Well then. Nova?"

"I agree he will fit in well with the crew dynamic and I will have the proposals waiting for you shortly. However, I have been asked to inform you that you are both late for dinner. I have already relayed the need for the additional bots to Isaac and given him the data needed. In fact, I believe he has just finished directing them to their new tasks. The bots will be passing you shortly."

"Sounds good. What of the Nimbus' SRs?"

"They require your express authorization to be used in this manner. Do you agree to their usage for manual labor?"

"I do. And this is silly."

"Confirmed. The SRs are now on the way to assist the work groups. The policy is silly, but it *is* policy. It is your prerogative to change policy if you wish, however I do not recommend changing the default policies until you are sufficiently acquainted with them."

"Alright, noted. Let's get to dinner. Thanks Nova."

* * *

Kasey and AnnaChi stood on the retractable deck that extended from their home on the Nimbus. Far below them, the last of crew and bots filed up a wide ramp into the ship's lower cargo deck.

It was time to move onto the next site. The Apex base was a lucky break, but he had underestimated the time it would take. Next time, if there was one, he swore it would be better planned.

Everyone was tired and feeling overworked. They needed a break, but none was forthcoming for a few more days at least.

The last phase of the trip would be multipronged. Three days to gather everything they could, and Kasey had picked out what he hoped was the perfect area.

The Nimbus would be setting down at a shipyard and settlement area that he hoped would be well supplied. Like the Apex base, most the workers and bots would be picking the place clean of everything of use. Markus would be taking his transport to salvage a medical center of supplies they would use to outfit the Nimbus' own center. Flair would again be piloting the Lodestar to several sites they hoped would have everything they needed to outfit the many apartments on board the Nimbus. Kasey and AnnaChi would use the Altair and Cintian to transport loads of fuels, propellants, and other necessities to top off the Nimbus' stores.

He had planned to spend a week at the location, but three days would need to be enough.

He took a deep breath from the small rebreather that

was required when outside and nudged AnnaChi. "Ready for this last push?"

"No, not at all. Although I am hopeful it will be interesting."

"I would agree if our definitions of interesting were the same. You know, some find that wishing for interesting times is like asking to be cursed?"

"Silly boy, do you really think we are not cursed? May as well relax and enjoy the ride."

He couldn't argue with that. "Kasey to Nimbus Actual. Button her up and take us out."

"Aye Sir," Jate responded. "All hands are accounted for and we will be setting conditions momentarily."

"Very well. Kasey out."

AnnaChi laughed at him, "You love that, don't you?"

"A bit. Really just trying to get used to having others pilot our ship. It's weird…"

"Well, *that* I agree with."

* * *

"Kasey. Do you have a moment?"

Kasey was watching a large screen showing Nimbus' camera feeds as they traveled across the land. Nimbus' lights flooded the landscape below as it passed by. It would have been memorizing had it not been a wasteland of once-lush forests.

He waved the images away. "Sure, Nova, go ahead."

"I have reviewed the plans for the array's installation onto Altair with the engineering team. I have acquired their signoff. With your permission, I can get that work underway now using some idle stevedores."

"I'm not sure I like the idea of using stevedores for construction on my ships. They are not builders. Does

Isaac have any builder bots that could work?"

"I agree. Isaac does indeed have a personal one. However, it is not operational and requires some minor repairs. Isaac had removed its chip to activate one of your stevedores. Also, none were found in the facility you salvaged. However, I believe the stevedores can effectively clear the space required and move the array into the space temporarily until sufficient labor can be found to complete the new room. They should be able to complete the move before we land again, therefore they will be available for operations as expected."

"Okay, I am good with all that. Were you able to keep the head and storage in the plans?"

"Yes, however the emergency stores will need to be temporarily located on the bridge level until the full renovations are competed. It should not impede ship usability."

"Fine then, as long they are secured, you have my approval."

"Thank you, Kasey. Do I also have your approval to create and install my clone into the array when the install is completed?"

"Yes, I approve. Nice job working this out."

"Thank you. I am looking forward to expanding my abilities."

"Flair to Kasey."

"Go ahead Flair."

"It may be nothing, but we have picked up a stray signal from our destination course."

"Any explanations?"

"Best one we have come up with is air patrol drones still functioning, but we could have another survivor."

"This is the biggest town on this continent, you may be right about leftover automated activity here. Keep me and AnnaChi informed if anything changes and have a rescue team on standby when we get close."

"Will do. Flair out."

No other signals were detected on the trip. The crew had gone from exhausted to excited in the few hours the trip had taken. He was amazed what some food and a few hours downtime could do for morale. Keeping the crew happy was another thing he added to his growing list of management notes.

True to her word, Nova had the matrix installed and her clone loaded. She said it would take some time to reconfigure the matrix to allow her full functionality, but she was now accessible even if they were out of contact with Nimbus.

Once the Nimbus was safely on the ground, the crew split up and went about their tasks. AnnaChi quickly located a fueling station and they alternated trips back and forth to fill Nimbus' extensive reserves.

They both made side trips as useful stores and items were located around the settlement. Kasey had just landed at store selling exercise equipment. The Nimbus had just a few machines right now, but he had planned to order enough for crew and passengers to use in the large gym area once they returned to Belrothi. Looting the store would be one less expense.

The ramp was just lowering when Nova screamed in his ear.

CHAPTER TWENTY-TWO

"Kasey! Something is wrong, I am missing!"

"Woah, slow down, Nova. I don't understand, what's missing?"

"Me! I mean, my primary. Everything just went offline. Something is very wrong, Kasey!"

"Shit!" Kasey took off at a run for the bridge, "Altair, emergency liftoff! Route us directly to the Nimbus. Best speed."

"Kasey, the Cintian is not responding to my warning hails. I believe she docked on Nimbus twenty-seven minutes ago."

"Damn. Are any other ships responding?"

"Yes, all other ships accounted for."

"Order all personnel loaded and get them back to the landing site immediately at best speeds."

"Done."

"Altair, I need all sensor readings routed to Nova."

"Confirmed."

Kasey slipped into the helm seat, but his eyes never left the bridge's main screen as they closed in on the site.

"Nova, tell me you can find something out there?"

"Sorry Kasey, I haven't fully integrated into this new matrix, but I am usurping other functioning processes to do what I can. Wait, thruster trail detected! Traveling west of the landing site. Trajectory on screen now."

"Can you see the Nimbus? Is it still on the ground, or is that their trail?"

"Unsure. Visual of site in three seconds."

Kasey partially stood as the landing site came into view. The Nimbus was gone.

Kasey pushed the Altair towards the thruster trail. "Scan the ground at the landing site and thruster trail path for any changes."

"High levels of moisture and pools of water detected. Hundreds of thousands of liters."

"No! Dammit! Altair, begin dumping our positive ballasts. Dump it all!"

"Kasey wait!" Nova interjected. "Their trajectory seems to be towards the smaller of Lithose's moons. I believe their calculations are off. If I am correct, a more direct trajectory may have a small chance to catch them."

"Fine, locking it in. Altair, prepare to go into full shutdown before we enter that storm."

"Kasey, I will need to shut down as well... If I cannot be saved, know that I am sorry for failing you."

"I know you are an AI, but we need to stay positive. The only way out is through."

"Confirmed."

"Flair, do you read me?"

"Kasey, what happened? The Nimbus is gone?"

"I don't know, but I am going to try and find out. Someone is taking her up into the storm. Whoever it is took Nova down and comms offline. If I can get on board, I will do what I can to come back for you."

"Where is AnnaChi? Are you alone?"

"She was docked on the Nimbus before it went

offline. I… I don't know her status."

"Stay calm, knowing that girl, she'll have taken the ship back before you can get on board. Jate, Knoc, and a small bridge crew are on Nimbus as well."

"Isaac is there as well. Flair, I need to go dark. You are in charge, keep the crew safe."

"Wait Kasey, do you think Isaac…"

He cut the comms and started the shutdown, waiting till the last moment to kill the thrusters.

Could it have been Isaac? It really didn't matter now. Whoever took the ship would pay for leaving them all stranded on Lithose. A cold anger settled into his chest as the ship entered the storm.

He barely noticed the storm as the ship tumbled out of the blackness and into a field of spinning stars. He began powering systems before he thought it was safe, but he had no choice. Every second counted now. Altair's stabilizers came online and stopped the tumbling, allowing Kasey to activate the main thrusters. Pushing them to full in the trajectory Nova had previously defined.

He kept the sensors in passive mode as the seconds ticked slowly by. A sigh of relief escaped as he finally located the Nimbus and had her on screen. The Altair's stealth fields came online soon after. He only hoped they would help get him close enough.

"Nova, are you online yet?"

"Yes. I am receiving no data at all from Nimbus. Based on her location, my primary was taken offline before they lifted off. We should be able to intercept in thirty-one minutes. Also, we have taken damage from unknown sources. Critical systems are unharmed."

"Will you be able to open one of Nimbus' bays without access to your primary?"

"No. More than just my primary is offline. Nimbus' main cores must be down as well, as I should be able to detect their network. However, the ship is indeed being commanded by someone, therefore my best deduction is that a secondary system is now in place. You must find another way inside. Perhaps Nimbus' topside landing pads?"

"Maybe, but if they detect us, they will expect that. Any chance you can fly this ship on your own?"

"Not yet. I could prioritize rebuilding that part of my systems, yet it will take longer than we have."

"Do it. Don't worry about all the systems, just start with basic flight."

"I can do that, yes."

"Actually... I have a better plan. Nova, I will need you to fly just the bridge section as an emergency pod and drop me off near my quarters on Nimbus. I have direct control of that area and should be able to open an airlock there. If you are able, you can then land the bridge section on one of the landing pads atop Nimbus."

"I believe I can do that."

"Altair, I will need you to execute an emergency landing on Nimbus' topside landing pad T4 on my mark. Can you do that without the bridge section attached?"

"Solution is achievable."

"Okay, we have a plan, now we just need a little luck. I need to get suited up. Alert me if anything changes."

An explosion rocked the ship.

"Possible plasma hole. Main engineering is breached. Environmental generation is offline. Reactor one is offline. Stealth fields are offline."

"Kasey, Altair is correct. We will begin to lose acceleration in five minutes as power reserves are expended. We need that acceleration to intercept Nimbus."

"Damn, we need options. Altair, direct all power to thrusters, shut down everything not essential. Nova, can the bridge section get us to Nimbus if we launch now?"

"It will be close—however we should wait until the Altair's thrusters begin to weaken to ninety-two percent."

"Set it up and take control of the bridge section. Launch at ninety-two percent."

"Of course, Captain, but you need to get suited now as I may need to pull environmental power from the bridge's backup systems."

He was not fully dressed when the time came.

"Kasey, hold onto something. The ejection rockets will be sudden."

He managed to grab onto a bench, which immediately slipped from his grasp as bridge section was boosted away from the Altair. He slammed into a locker but was able to remain upright.

"A few extra seconds of warning would be helpful next time."

"Apologies, Kasey. Are you injured?"

"No, I am fine."

"Good. I was required to eject earlier than expected as a main thruster on Altair went suddenly offline and threatened to negatively change our trajectory."

"Any idea why?"

"I believe it took an impact. The Nimbus is firing an accelerator cannon at it."

"Damn, have we been targeted too?"

"I cannot determine that, yet."

"Never mind, we will know soon enough. Have Altair change trajectory away from us and launch all drones. Have him remain in a safe orbit around Lithose, and if we fail to reestablish comms with him, he is to wait one week, then attempt to land on Lithose and contact Flair. Full control should be transferred over to Flair in that case."

"Done. Kasey, I only give Altair a sixty-eight percent chance of surviving a reentry in its current condition."

"I feared it would be worse, but Flair needs that ship if they are to escape Lithose alone."

"Understood."

"Any fire directed at us? I haven't tested the bridge section's ability to stay hidden before."

"None as of yet. However, we gained some additional thrust from the booster rockets that I did not anticipate. I suggest we cut thrusters in ninety-two seconds and allow Nimbus to overtake us."

"Do it. Once I am off the ship, I will need you to land on the topside pad we had planned to land Altair on."

"You need me to cause the diversion?"

"Yes. I…"

"It is more than acceptable, Kasey. Please save AnnaChi and the crew. If you can, save my primary too."

"I will do my best Nova. Thank you."

"Helmet on please. Reducing all power output, including shields, to avoid detection."

At thirty seconds out, the hull began taking impacts from the Nimbus' bridge point defense lasers. Nova took evasive action and powered the pod's shields back on.

"Kasey, start trying to connect to your quarter's system. Extend the deck if possible and activate the gravity plating."

"Connected! Extending now."

"Go to the lifeboat airlock. Kasey, you are going to have to jump as I pass. If I stop, your exit will be detected."

He tried to control his breathing as the airlock opened.

"I am glad it's a large deck. This is going to hurt, isn't it?"

"Affirmative. Good luck, Kasey."

"Good luck, Nova."

"You need to jump in five, four, three, two, jump!"

FARPOINT RISING

CHAPTER TWENTY-THREE

Kasey dove forward, flailing madly to gain some control as his home rushed towards him. Just as he got turned around, the sudden pull of the gravity plating grabbed him. The fall to the deck was too fast, he crashed down hard and rolled several meters before he came to a halt.

Feeling dizzy and ready to pass out, he struggled to orient himself. After a few deep breaths, he struggled to his feet and stumbled to the airlock. Kasey and AnnaChi's quarters were a self-contained environment not connected to the Nimbus security grid. The area was meant to be their private home—Nimbus just happened to carry it around.

As he cycled through, he ordered the security system to display the home's status on the nearest wall panel. Everything was clear, at least for now. Stripping off the helmet and suit, he let them fall as he made his way to a room AnnaChi insisted they have installed.

The armory's doors opened at his touch and closed securely behind him. The extent of varied weapons was astounding. He recognized a lot of the items she had taken from the Faraday Base during their previous visit to Lithose. They had gathered the large, mechanized war machines from that base called I.C.E. suits that the resistance then used to liberate the Belrothi-Abscond station from the Patternists. He was mildly surprised that none of the powered and mechanized suits ended up in her armory. There were, however, several non-powered, lightweight, civilian armored suits in the collection that were sized and ready for Kasey to don.

He surged into one and buckled on a shield belt that would deflect a few impacts as well. Taking up a short plasma rifle, he checked the power cell and slugs then slid it onto his back where it magnetically attached to the suit. Several more magazines were added to the suit's chest rig, as well as his favored pistol and two electric batons.

Looking around, he opened a cabinet and withdrew a small sleeve of pills. Popping one in his mouth, he grabbed a bottle of water and washed it down. The adrenaline cocktail's slow release would keep him going as long as it took. The remaining pills went into a pocket, and a small medical kit was attached to his back.

With a deep breath he left the armory and headed to his private cargo elevator. It was in a sealed chamber next to the maintenance bay where AnnaChi tinkered with their bard vehicles. The Nimbus had an absolutely huge shop area on the hangar deck, but she wanted something of her own in her own space. With the load of bards and other vehicles he had seen her salvage early in this trip, he knew her projects would soon be spread all over the Nimbus.

This particular elevator had a larger benefit to Kasey right now. The elevator's system was tied into the camera feeds near all the entrances to the shaft. including the Cintian's hangar bay. The live feeds showed nothing moving, and the Cintian sat with its bays open. Looking through the hangar deck's feed history showed AnnaChi landing and unloading, then she left the area and didn't return.

With nothing more to see, he switched the feeds to one showing the topside landing pads and was relieved to see Altair's bridge section sitting haphazardly on the pad. The oversized escape pod had taken a beating from the defensive system but had somehow made it. A single hull repair bot dropped from the section's underside as he watched and carefully tapped some keys on the nearby public airlock, then skittered out of sight. A minute later it repeated the action.

Nova was still functioning, for now.

He was hoping the craft landing there would get a response of some kind, so he waited. Perhaps, he mused, they were waiting for him. Nova must be using the bot to try and draw them out. While he waited, he brought up the command deck cameras. He only had access to a few on that deck, but the shaft was next to the bridge section and had a good view. Only half the cameras were responding, and the hallway was blackened as if a fire had broken out.

Quickly scrolling backwards through the feeds, he finally found what he was looking for. A group of four men approached and set an explosive device against the bridge's wall and detonated it. A moment later they all rushed in.

Several minutes later, two of the men left the bridge and returned with a fifth man leading a group of bound prisoners linked together by a cable.

Two of the prisoners were holding up AnnaChi, who looked barely conscious but alive. Kasey fumed at her condition, but knowing she was alive gave him a surge of energy that had nothing to do with the adrenaline pills.

He forwarded through the footage. The men had

come and gone several times but all five appeared to be in the bridge area presently. He noted that Isaac was nowhere to be found and wondered how he would fit into this all.

An alert sounded, and he brought up the topside cameras again. The maintenance bot had changed tactics. A small hole had been cut in the airlock, causing it to snap shut blast doors preventing decompression and setting off alarms throughout the ship.

He quickly switched back to the cameras near the bridge and waited. A full minute passed before two armed men rushed out and went towards the public elevator that led to the airlock the bot had compromised. A third man walked out to keep a watch over the hallway itself.

Kasey nodded and hoped the ruse would buy him enough time. Overriding the controls, he opened the doors to the shaft and noticed the car sitting several decks down. Swallowing hard, he reached in grabbed onto a narrow ladder and made his way downward to the command deck as quick as possible.

The cargo elevator opened up into a private room to keep guests from trying to access it. It was empty now, as he had expected. He called up a panel to show the hallway camera and the man guarding his exit. He was pacing back and forth.

Kasey was out of his element and he knew it. He would have one chance to take the large man down quietly, and he needed to do it before the other men returned. He pulled one of the electric batons in his off hand and loosened his pistol in its holster.

As the man turned away, Kasey slipped through the door then drew his pistol. He was still over a meter away when something caused the man to turn.

Kasey jumped forward, shoving the electrified baton into the man's face. He jerked wildly and then toppled into Kasey.

Surprised it had worked, Kasey struggled not to fall over. Dropping the baton, he grabbed the man's rifle arm and leaned into the man. With some effort, he managed to holster his own pistol, then lowered the heavy man to the ground as quietly as he could.

Scooping up the dropped baton, he shocked the man again and then dragged him into the cargo elevator room. He knew he needed to move quickly now, before the others returned, but took a moment to tie the man's hands behind his back. Unlimbering his own rifle from his back, he set it aside and put the unconscious man's rifle in its place, then removed the man's pistol and a long knife, shoving them into a pocket before picking his own rifle back up.

Shouldering it, he rushed back into the hallway and came to a dead stop. The two men that had gone to investigate the topside distraction were halfway down the hallway to his position looking directly at him. Kasey squeezed the rifle's trigger, but nothing happened. Panic rushed over him as he realized the safety was still enabled and the men were shouldering their own rifles as he fumbled for the switch.

He was dead, he knew it was coming. Dropping to one knee as he flipped the safety and readied what he assumed would be his last action. All he could think of was how he had failed AnnaChi.

As his finger reached for the trigger, three mishmash bots rushed out of some hallway and trampled the men, then started dismantling the men's weapons before they even let go of them. Isaac sprang forth seconds later, wielding a shovel that solidly smashed into the men's heads with precision. Kasey could not tell if they were still alive at that point, and he realized he didn't care.

Isaac gave Kasey a wave, then crept forward. The bots followed just as quietly, and Kasey idly noticed they all sported some sort of rubbery sacks tied around their feet to keep them quiet. Removing the extra rifle from his back, Kasey handed it to Isaac.

"Know how to use this?" he whispered.

Isaac took the weapon, flicked off the safety switch and nodded.

Kasey gave him an appraising look. "There are two more inside with prisoners and I took out a fifth one before you showed up. Do you know of any others on Nimbus?"

"Two are in engineering. I think they are trying to repair the core system. It took a lot of damage in an explosion that I assume they caused. Not sure about the rest of the Nimbus, but I think they would have someone watching their ship, assuming they have one."

"Right. We need to take the bridge back first. Can you hold this hallway?"

"Sorry cap, but you need me at your back. I can use the bots to confuse them, but we need to go in fast if they have prisoners. Wait, do they have Yaran? I couldn't find her."

"Yes, and AnnaChi and two other crew. Look, if you are coming, take this." He unbuckled the shield belt and handed it to Isaac. "It will take one or two hits, but not more. My suit will protect me enough."

"Got it. We should move. I'll send in this maid bot and have it collect trash, then these two will follow. They won't attack, but I can have them try to field strip their weapons for cleaning."

"Do it. I'll go in next and take them out, you follow and clean up."

"I'm ready, sir!"

Kasey checked his weapon's safety again and entered the office space around the bridge. It was a large and currently unused area. They quietly worked their way around to a large open door leading into the bridge itself.

Isaac sent in the first bot and waited.

Curses were shouted, followed by rough laughter. As the next two bots entered, the laughs came again, then angry shouts followed by gunfire.

That was Kasey's cue. Running directly towards where the voices had come from, he dropped to one knee as soon as he had the first man in his sights and fired. Not waiting to see if he hit him, he ducked to the left, barely avoiding a plasma bolt. Swinging his rifle to return fire, he was just in time to see two well placed shots strike the enemy, taking him out of the conflict permanently.

Kasey sprinted back towards the first man but slowed when he saw there was no need. His shot had hit the man's shoulder, but AnnaChi had use the opportunity to wrap her legs around the man's neck when he fell. She released the man, but it was hard to tell if he was dead or unconscious.

He embraced her and removed her shackles then handed her the rifle.

"Are you all…"

A gunshot rang out from the entryway.

CHAPTER TWENTY-FOUR

From the corner of his eye, Kasey saw Isaac fall to the deck hard. Before he knew what he was doing, Kasey had drawn his pistol and fired four times at the newcomer, dropping him.

He ran to Isaac and was relieved to see him already getting back up. The shield belt had done its job, but a plasma rifle had still knocked the wind out of him. He helped Isaac to his feet.

"Sorry, that guy was stunned and tied up, but apparently not well enough. Keep an eye on the entry, I'll sort this out."

"Aye, sir." Kasey noticed Isaac's gaze going to check on Yaran, who smiled back at the man, before ordering his one remaining bot into the hallway with him.

AnnaChi had removed the other's restraints and he realized Jate and Knoc were both in bad shape but alive and stable. He removed the medical kit and handed it to AnnaChi. She knew more about what was needed than he would, and Jate seemed conscious enough to direct if needed.

They rounded up the weapons and reassembled the

parts Isaac's bots had broken down. No one would get into the bridge now without getting a face full of plasma.

AnnaChi stood. "Grab me a stim and let's go clear engineering of rodents."

He tossed her the pill case, knowing she would not be left behind. "Alright, we make a plan on the way. Isaac thinks there are two in engineering, at least. You, me, and Isaac should be able to handle them. The tween deck has lots of engineering connections—too many for them to watch.

"You're forgetting the forward armory is on the way. Isaac and I will armor up and I can switch this piece of crap for my normal kit."

"Sir," one of the men Kasey recognized as an engineer named Griff spoke up, "I think you need me with you too. I'm not certified on system core maintenance, but I may know enough to help get us back online."

"Can you shoot straight?"

"Not too good with a gun, no. But I know which end should point which direction."

"Fine, make sure that end is pointed away from us too."

"Yes, sir."

"Jate, have them seal the bridge until you hear from us."

"We got this, sir. Go take back the ship. I wish I could join ya."

"Me too. If we can get our system back online, we will need everyone here that is able to be on the cameras and detection. We need to know who else is on our ship."

"Got it."

The forward armory was nowhere near fully stocked. It was a minor issue with the ship's current complement, but once fully staffed it could be an issue. It would be another expensive order once they were back in Belrothi's orbit. For now, there was enough for the four of them, but not much more. Griff ended up with a kit reserved for Kasey.

The tween deck access was mainly from the engineering sections, but other areas had less convenient access hatches. That was fine for the four of them, but the maid bot would need to stay behind.

"We should split up into two teams," AnnaChi announced once they were above the massive area designated as main engineering.

"Four on two is better odds than two on two, is it not?" Kasey challenged, knowing she would have a reason for the proclamation.

"Normally, but we know where they are—the core room. We can come in from both sides at once and take them in the crossfire. Unless you want to play bait and I can take them from behind?"

"Crossfire is fine. You take Griff and keep him safe. Enter the deck via the port fabrication room. Its empty so they won't have a reason to be in there. Head aft to the cargo elevator and then go straight for the core room. Isaac and I will do the same from starboard."

"See, that's why I love you, you always have a plan," AnnaChi approved.

"I plan because I am afraid of what you would do without one. Things tend to get blown up…"

"Well… Okay, yea, that's fair."

He pulled her close and stole a kiss, "Let get this done. We have people planet-side with no ride home."

They moved off and soon left the tween deck behind.

"Cap," Isaac sent sub-vocally as he waved at the warehouse-sized space with a large empty platform in the middle, "I was expecting a fabricator closet, or maybe a small room. Are we in the right place?"

"Nimbus has big parts, she needs big fabricators," he

sent back.

"Okay, but two of them this size?"

"There will be four of them eventually, all have different purposes. Hell, right now all four rooms are empty. We do have a small fabricator, but it is set up in a corner somewhere for now. We picked up a decent setup a few days ago that will likely end up in the port room, but the other rooms may be empty for a while. Got to plan for the long term."

"What do you have planned for the others?"

"Going to need to table this conversation for later. After the next room will be a short hall and then an open area till the cargo elevator. We need to clear the area and get to the core room. AnnaChi won't lag and likely won't wait for us to catch up."

Kasey felt he was setting a decent pace and thought he might even beat AnnaChi to the core room, but when he arrived, she already had both invaders lying face down with their hands and feet hogtied.

"Bout time you get here lover."

"Did you run?"

"We really need to start drills once this is over if you thought you made good time getting here."

"Not a bad idea actually. What do we have?"

"Nothing good. These two were not even armed. They claim to have been contracted for this operation through a navy liaison before we even took possession of the Nimbus. The weapons we got from the five upstairs are mostly personalized, but they are not exactly a professional strike team."

"What's that leave us with? Pirates?"

"Eh, maybe—not professional ones if they are. I am betting we find a ship in the hangar outfitted for n-mats or some other method for getting down to Lithose. They knew of the Nimbus, how it worked, and knew we would take it to Lithose. Something very few people are supposed to know. But here's the thing—anyone involved with building this ship, that bothered to research the ship's system, could put together that the ship was being designed to survive the Lithose storm."

"So, some navy mechanic gets it into his head that he deserves our boat and doesn't mind killing people, or leaving them stranded, to take it?"

"Bingo. It's a theory at least."

"Uh, excuse me?" one of the men on the floor spoke up. "Look, we didn't know any of this and wouldn't be involved if we knew it wasn't a legit operation."

"What's your point?" AnnaChi responded sharply as she waved Isaac and Griff to guard the room's entrances. "Or are you just trying to distract us?"

"No, no, I can help. The commander, Richards. He is the guy in charge. He talked about working construction on this ship and that it needed to be recovered for the navy. Explained how it was all supposed to work so we could upgrade his transport. Your story fits."

"Okay, so how can you help?"

"Well, first, if you have taken out five of the team, there are still three left."

"Anything else?"

"We haven't been able to clone the ship's core linkup chips with the cores we brought along yet, but we have repaired the coupler mount from the damage."

"And that helps us how exactly?"

"Well, you can reinstall the original core now if you want. The ones we brought are configured to take complete control of the systems and give control to Commander Richards. We have not been able to do that yet. With the old ones back in place you will have control of your ship back."

Kasey looked at AnnaChi. "Switch places with Griff."

Once the situation was explained again, Griff got to

work, and in minutes he was connected back to the ship's systems.

"Nova, are you there?"

"Kasey! My primary is still offline, but I have access to Nimbus systems. Were you able to…"

"It will have to wait a little longer, sorry Nova. We still have hostiles onboard. Can you locate them?"

"I will try."

"Check command and main engineering first, then the rest of this deck. We have people in the bridge, some injured."

"Both are clear—I will notify you of any movement."

Kasey called AnnaChi and Isaac back into the room and they finished securing the prisoners.

"Kasey, there is a ship powering up in the H5 hangar bay."

"Lock that bay down, Nova! Griff, stop working on that and cover these prisoners. Stay armed, stay at a distance, and don't talk to them at all!"

"No problem, sir."

"Nova, status?"

"The ship is now magnetically locked down and is powering down. There is no other unexpected movement on Nimbus."

"Kasey to Jate."

"Jate here, systems came up a few minutes ago. I see we have an extra ship in the hangar. Looks like medium transport of some kind."

"Right. We are heading down to bay H5 now to take care of that. Nova, connect me to that ship's comms and give me the feed from that bay."

"Connection obtained and ready."

"Nimbus to pirate transport currently parked in *my* hangar!"

"You don't deserve this ship, little boy, but I guess it's yours for now. Now open this hangar and we will be out of your way."

"It seems you don't understand the situation. You need to exit that ship immediately or I will have an army of stevedore bots take that ship apart to its bones."

"You wouldn't dare!"

"Dare? Hell, I already gave the order. They are lining up now. My current decision is whether I keep air in the bay while they do the job."

"You... You need a lesson, you pompous brat. I know this ship's weaknesses." the ship's forward accelerator cannon swiveled upwards towards the top of the cargo elevator shaft.

CHAPTER TWENTY-FIVE

"Nova, what is he targeting?"

"There is a significant oxygen supply along that trajectory."

"Jate, do you have control of that bay? Maybe we can turn off the gravity plating and vent…"

"No can do. That part of the system is still down."

"Captain, I believe plasma-based weapons have been discharged aboard the enemy vessel."

"Attention pirate transport ship, please report your status."

"Uh. Richards is no longer in command. We are coming out."

"Fine. Turn your ship's control over to Nova first. Then I want you all face down in the middle of this bay ASAP."

"Done. Richards is dead. Just two of us left to come out."

"I now have control Kasey," Nova interposed, "and a man does appear to be quite deceased on the ship's bridge."

Kasey arrived at the bay's outer doors and activated

the internal viewscreens. The two men were positioning themselves as expected.

"Isaac, we need a few security bots on staff straightway. Do we have anything like that in storage?"

"No, sorry, sir. Best I can do is upgrade a stevedore's programming to handle basic guard duty. It won't be able to effectively fight, but I can add some features that should help."

"That will do. We will move the prisoners to the brig and keep them separated. But soon as we can, I want some form of security bots watching their every movement. And I want them to know they are being watched."

"I will get it done, but it won't be possible until we are back on the ground. The bot chips we have on Nimbus right now are not compatible with anything more fearsome than a maid."

"The Cintian will have a couple stevedores you can use, and when we recover the Altair, it has two on board as well, but they may need to be checked over."

"I can watch the prisoners as well, Kasey," Nova posed.

"You can and should, but until we get your primary back to one hundred percent, you won't be doing it alone. Besides, having a physical presence has a heavy psychological effect on people."

"I understand."

By the time the prisoners were squared away, Kasey was feeling the stimulants wearing off, but he had more to do.

He stood overlooking the matrix that was Nova's primary. Several cores in both the array and main storage were destroyed in the explosion that took both Nimbus and Nova's cores offline.

"Griff, what's the prognosis? Can we get her back online?"

"Honestly, there is more extensive damage than I had thought. We have some spares and backups for some of it, but not all. The matrix can be repaired, but it will take time. Even then, it will all be out of sync, which can be an issue—in theory. Nova will be missing some memory connections—not the data itself—that's backed up, but some correlations to the entire matrix may be lost."

"Sorry, I am not understanding…"

"Not sure I really do either, Captain. I just know the basics. Think of it like a wrench. You know what the tool is, but there is a lot more to it—knowing how it is used, the history of using it, the experience you have using it, and how it affects everything around it, even the space it takes up in the toolbox builds correlations to how it exists. All of that is necessary, particularly when you want to use that wrench for a purpose it is not designed for—like banging on a clogged pipe. For us humans, that is a hard thing to lose. For a research team using a matrix such as this, it means they need to recalibrate and rerun their tests. For an AI like Nova? That is another level completely. Sir, I have no real idea…"

"Well one person may know. Nova, do you understand how this will affect your primary?"

"It is worrying, as Griff mentioned. I believe I can rebuild the correlations over time. The few correlations I was able to build in my clone so far can also help to guide that process."

"Anything we can do to mitigate some issues? I mean, can you take the lead directing your primary's processes until she is fully repaired?"

"Yes, I believe that would be appropriate. But I would appreciate if we could relocate my clone from the topside landing pad as soon as possible. Perhaps the Cintian can retrieve me?"

"Yes, we will get you moved soon. Seems like we

have a plan. Griff, repair what you can and let Nova make the final decision to reactive the matrix. I will have the clone matrix loaded and brought to engineering. Have her hardwired into the matrix control systems."

"I'll do my best. Are we heading back to Lithose? I could use the rest of the team's help."

"We will be. Not sure of the timing just yet."

"Kasey and AnnaChi, please report to the bridge," the disembodied voice of Jate announced.

Kasey left the core rooms and called up AnnaChi's current location on his mimic interface. Breaking into a jog when he realized she would beat him to the bridge, he got there just before she walked in.

"Glad you could join us," he gloated.

"You seem a bit winded, honey. Maybe you should sit down?"

Jate shook his head and smiled. "If you two are done, Admiral Francis is in-system with an eleven-minute delay and is wondering about his wife's situation."

"Have you filled him in on the situation?"

"Yes. He will have a ship waiting for the prisoners on Belrothi and will take possession of their ship for processing at that time."

"Hey, I mean, finders-keepers and all that," AnnaChi interrupted, "We could really use that ship."

"Honestly, sirs, I do not think that will be an issue. He just needs it processed for litigations against the prisoners and anyone tied to the crimes. Particularly how they got access to the n-mats to use for that ship. He wants that ship locked up until then."

"Okay fine, we can handle that I think. But with the Altair out of commission we are short on ships and time."

"He anticipated that as well. Here, listen to his last comm. It came in just before you got here."

"Look," Fran's confident voice explained, "I know

they feel they need to be on schedule, but that schedule is far less important that making sure the Nimbus is prepared and safe. I will have my people on Belrothi delay shipments and make arrangements for a week's delay. Send me the updated details on what is needed, and I will have someone here deal with the planning. The very fact that the ship was infiltrated by a second-rate team with a bomb, and that Kasey was able to land an oversized escape pod on her, means that ship is simply not capable of protecting itself. Tell Flair to ring beta epsilon and get that ship sufficiently armed."

Kasey looked at AnnaChi, who just shrugged.

"Okay, we are fine with the delay. It's a relief actually. But what the hell does the last remark mean?"

Jate looked around the bridge to make sure it was clear and sealed before answering. "It's a basic command code, but I am not totally sure of the meaning. From what I know, it deals with a plan B. You know the admiral and his backup plans. Flair will know more."

"Well, I suppose I am not surprised. Give him our approvals. Also, send him Sariyn's list of items we need to auction off, have him find some potential buyers. We will keep six of the best shuttles and anything useful for hauling or maintenance work, but list the rest. Sooner the buyers start looking the better. We could use the credits."

"I'll have it sent over right away."

"Hold on, did Isaac pick the one he wanted?"

"Yep, nice red one I believe. Likely the best of that haul."

"Good, make sure that one is not on the list and have the cargo team move it to his storage area."

"Anything else?"

"Well, we need the recruiters to look for someone who can run a large industrial fabrication plant. Send the specifications on the system we took down as a basis.

We also need several hundred bot controller chips—I believe Isaac has been keeping a list of what we need on his shared environment."

"Found it. He has a lot more listed here under a potential needs list you should look at."

Kasey and AnnaChi pulled it up on their own mimics.

"What's with all the plant and farming crap?" AnnaChi wondered aloud.

"He had a fairly complex looking garden when we found him and had robots maintaining it. The beginnings of a hydroponics setup too. There is plenty of room in our gardens, and if he can get bots working them it will be less for Yaran to manage."

"Strange is all."

"He may be, but he is highly effective. I want to keep him on staff if he will stay. We can make him an offer once we reach Belrothi, unless anyone has a concern."

Their nods were all the approval he needed.

"Jate, go ahead and order everything on his list and plan for it to be delivered towards the end of our layover. I already have plans for a lab started for him, and for Sariyn too, for that matter."

"Okay, I'll have it sent shortly. The other reason I called you both here is that we will have a good window for entering Lithose in one hour. We have the systems we need online to go into the storm but that is your call. I should mention that we are not properly staffed for this drop."

"We don't have a choice—our people need us back on the ground. We also need to get Nova's clone inside—she parked on a topside landing pad. And we need to pick up the Altair as well. How long will that window be open?"

Jate nodded "Forty minutes at best. Altair will be in position in fifteen. Knoc is already prepped at the H3 bay to guide it onto the mag platform with a utility shuttle. We need a plan for Nova and that escape pod though. We left all the SR bots planet-side."

Kasey rubbed his temple. "The next time I decide to repurpose emergency resources like our SR bots, please remind me of this day. AnnaChi, feel like scooping that pod up with Cintian? We don't want to damage her, so seriously, be careful."

"Piece of cake!"

CHAPTER TWENTY-SIX

Kasey breathed a small sigh as they finally broke through the main storm system and the thrusters spun up successfully. The transit had taken far longer than he believed to be safe. The pirates had dumped more of the water reserves than needed and now they were struggling to take her down to a decent altitude. Several large tanks of n-mats had been temporarily jettisoned to reduce the ship's lift, but it had been barely enough.

"Find me a low hanging cloud to absorb, we need mass in the ballast tanks."

"Aye, sir!"

"Damage reports?"

"None. Looks like we entered through a clear window."

"Nova, any issues?"

"Nothing serious, but I am detecting some additional damage from the airlock we used as a diversion. I suggest you have a team patch that before ascending through the storm again."

"Noted."

"Jate, take the helm and set up a meeting with Flair

as soon as we have contact."

"Yes, sir. We are looking at a two-hour flight."

Kasey bided his time by looking over the damage the Altair had taken from the storm. His hand started to quiver the slightest bit as he examined the fourth of the fist-sizes plasma holes that had eaten into his ship during the ascent through the storm. He stood back and took several slow, deep breaths to center himself.

He held up his hand. The quiver had stopped, but his frown turned to a scowl as he grasped the implications his nerves had already worked out.

"Adrenaline shakes?" AnnaChi asked, coming up behind him.

"Maybe—maybe not," he responded, not looking directly at her.

She approached the ship, "How bad is it?"

"Ship can be repaired…"

"And?"

"I nearly pushed my luck too far on this one. Four holes so far. More damage than all my previous trips combined, all in one single storm."

"You can't change the past, but no more trips without Nimbus."

"I won't argue with you on that."

"Good, but get your nerves in order because Flair is docking the Lodestar now."

"She couldn't wait till we landed?"

"She has a few injured with her and a full load of supplies. Says none are serious, but we had the three ships with the best medical pods. Likely an excuse to get the full story sooner."

Flair was waiting for them in the hangar deck's pilot lounge.

"Glad you were able to recover the Nimbus, Kasey, or did AnnaChi have it handled before you got there?"

"Team effort all around, but I am guessing you know

the story already."

"You really know how to spoil my fun."

"It's in my job description I believe. So how is the crew managing?"

"They were kept too busy to worry about you failing to bring back our ride out of here. We have as much as we could stockpiled in the local warehouses. It will save some time, but we will still be delayed a few days."

"I am sure you know Fran has handled the time issue for us. No doubt he expected problems, as usual."

"Yes of course, and I agree with his suggestion."

"So then," AnnaChi jumped in with a huff, "what precisely is *ring beta epsilon*?"

"He just wants you to take the Nimbus shopping for accessories in case she needs to dance more."

"And where exactly are we to go shopping?"

Flair slipped a slim glass ring off her finger and flipped it to AnnaChi. "You already know the location, there's your key."

AnnaChi gave the small band a brief once-over then handed it to Kasey.

"Uh." Kasey felt a bit unnerved at the idea. "Faraday Base is, or was, a hornet's nest when we left it. Not sure going back there is a solution for anything."

"It's not the same ring, and you both will need to wear visored helmets and voice changers until we disable the main core system. The security bots are not rogue, they were doing their job to protect the base. This ring will allow access, unless you are recognized."

"I am not sure the base even survived. We, and by we, I mean her," he stuck his thumb out in AnnaChi's direction, "left a good portion of the hangar in ruins. And I am not clear on what else she rigged."

Flair considered them for moment. "Okay, but from what you have told us, the bots were still attacking after the explosion, right?"

"Yes, but bots don't exactly need a direction to shoot do they?"

"Military fighting bots do, yes. It wasn't the bots attacking you, it was the base's core system. Weaponizing an *autonomous* bot is limited to specific wartime situations. If they were still firing at you, then you missed the command systems."

"Wait," said Kasey, "I remember you being disappointed when we brought back the I.C.E. suits. What did you expect us to find in there?"

"Well, my disappointment was mainly me playing the part and partially for losing a bet with Fran. But you were supposed to find a storehouse of civilian ship upgrades like the manual load missile batteries and reactive shielding modules we used against the Cassian. We really could have used those supplies at the gates. When all else fails, you need to arm the people."

"And the bet?" AnnaChi prodded.

"I bet that you would disable the cores and bring security bots back so we could find a way to release them onto the station. Fran bet you would find the depot of civilian upgrades."

"So, you both lost?"

"Well yes, but I would have preferred that we both won. Still, the powered suits were unexpected and made quick work of the Belrothi-Abscond objective. So, you did good. But this time you need both the bots and weapons and anything else of use. Just one rule."

"Wait. We have rules?"

"Well, no, not really, I am just your employee here— so your decision. Fran, however, would prefer that if you take the base's cores, that you have me reformat them. It would make cooperation with the navy easier if you weren't taking possession of official databases."

"I think we can agree with that, but this time I think we will be keeping the ring."

"Fine. It is tied to Lithose, so as long as navy security is not compromised, you can hold onto the ring. Frankly, that's more trust than he should ever be giving you, me, or anyone. Do me a favor and don't make him regret trusting us all."

AnnaChi shrugged as if it was not a real concern. "Well, at least it will be clean this time…"

"Uh, what? Wait, you seriously found time to activate cleaning bots? You were serious about that? When?"

"When you were busy looking for the big lift. I started three of them in the hangar before you found it. Even if one survived our tactical withdraw, it should have made some difference by now."

"Tactical withdraw?"

"Hey, it worked didn't it?"

"Barely…"

Flair cleared her throat. "In any case, how do you want to handle this? We will need several days to finish up here, and there are a few things we need your input on."

"Like what?" Kasey wondered.

"Let's see, the medical center had huge caches of prescription drugs, based on what Markus tells me. It is worth a lot, but it won't be easily sellable, and maybe not at all legally. Do you want it salvaged?"

"No, leave the bulk drugs alone, except what our medical facilities need. Clean out the pharmacy and normal supply rooms. That should really be more than enough to supply Nimbus, and we can resupply in ports when needed. Maybe have someone like Jate with medical knowledge take a look at the inventory in case there is something specific we should consider?"

"Okay, I told Markus something along those lines already. Status wise, we should have more than enough equipment to supply the Nimbus medical center. He has gathered a bit of everything that seemed useful, most of which we don't know anything about. We will need a real doctor to work out what we actually need to install."

"Great, we should be taking on one with the crew in Belrothi. What else?"

"Sariyn has been going on and on about a small transport ship that is one step away from a scrapyard. Wants to buy it from company salvage and run it for us under contract."

"Wait, does she even have a pilot's license?"

"Nope. Wants to hire one and use the ship for prospecting."

"Starting to make sense... You say it's a small transport?"

"I think it classifies as a medium transport, but just barely. It was set up as a merchant ship but looks to have been originally a troop drop ship. I'll have to research it now that Nimbus is back with the database, but I would guess it's really old, or just based on an old design since I have never seen anything like it in the navy yards."

"Why do you think it was a drop ship?" AnnaChi asked.

"Well, it's a strange design. Instead of a large bay, it has four smaller bays that can be detached and a fifth smaller bay midship. The four outer bays look to have had attachment points that I am speculating would have held small thruster packages to reach the surface from an air drop, and weapon placements to keep the troops and contents protected. Whatever they used to be, the bays are just glorified boxes now. I am not even sure they can be removed in their current state, but Sariyn believes they can be."

Kasey nodded. "Well, I am intrigued. How exactly does she plan on using this ship for prospecting?"

"Ah, well that part is kind of brilliant. She wants to load a four-man team with bards into each bay and set one down at each site to be prospected as a temporary base for that team. The ship itself will act as mothership as well as a field lab where she will work, coordinate the teams, and move the mobile bases around as needed."

AnnaChi smiled. "I could think of a few more interesting uses for a ship like that."

Kasey had a good idea what AnnaChi's uses would entail. "Would any of those uses benefit the business?"

"Well... No. Not unless we get into trouble."

Kasey looked at them both as he gave the idea some thought. It was a sound idea, and the versatile ship could be an asset to the company. It could even solve a few issues he had been worrying over with their prospecting plans.

"Okay, well firstly, I very much doubt that Sariyn really wants or needs a ship of her own. If she seriously does, we can try and work that out. Let me talk to her and see what she is after and go from there. If the company retains the ship, AnnaChi can put together some alternative plans for it and maybe we can have a multi-purpose vessel. Flair, how bad of shape is that ship in?"

"If what the boys are saying are true, it won't hold air, needs new thrusters, and has taken some other damage. Looks to have been in a fight, dragged back here as salvage, and then left to sit."

"Hold on, a fight? That would have been before we even knew of the Cassian being here?"

"Well, that's the other thing—based on the yard logs, it was assumed this ship was used for smuggling and got into some self-invited trouble... They even located several hidden compartments, but that's not really unusual. We will have to look at the damage more closely to see if it was Cassian or not. Hardly matters at this point, it's all salvage now."

"Have we found any replacement thrusters that would

work for it?"

"Nothing pretty, but they felt they could piece together something that would make her fly again."

"Okay, let me talk with her. But you are right, we will take it as salvage either way. Any other ships there?" he asked hopefully.

"No, sorry. Which means we will need to keep using your ships for our operations unless you procure more somehow."

He nodded and frowned. "That's fine for now, I suppose. If we can keep the pirate's ship once Fran's team is done inspecting it, then we should be okay for this run. Anything else?"

Flair looked at her feet and shook her head. "Just that I need to apologize to Isaac. I jumped to conclusions. Assumed he somehow took the ship. I also should have planned better for our security. I just never thought anyone would be stupid enough to brave that storm. Well, except for you, of course."

"I think Kasey here has finally learned his lesson about the storm. Wait till you see the damage Altair took from the storm this time," AnnaChi provided.

"Yeah," Kasey grimaced, "well, you are not alone in the apologies department. I was not sure myself until he saved my ass up there. He's as solid as they come. I promised not to offer him a position before we made port at Belrothi, but we *really* need him to stay. I am not sure how he held himself together for so long on Lithose, but if he has issues, he hides them well."

"We all got our issues even if they don't show. He either deals with them very well, or he is ignoring them. You are right to give him time, but keep in mind that he has been through an emotional hell we cannot begin to understand. Don't make the mistake in thinking that he is fine—he's not. He won't be for a while. He will need to talk to someone eventually, and it will be our job to make sure someone is there when he is ready."

"I see… You know, a good portion of our staff will be from this system, and a few from Lithose too. The colony lost so many and survived so much. I didn't even think of having a professional on the Nimbus for the crew's needs."

"Well, it's not too late to add the role. We will send an update to the available positions once we leave Lithose. Even so, we deal with similar situations in the navy all the time. In several cases, we had to use stasis pods for sailors until we could get them to proper facilities, and a few simply needed a break from the service, like Jate."

"Alright, make it happen. Now, let's get to planning our incursion back into Faraday Base."

CHAPTER TWENTY-SEVEN

Kasey finished inspecting the repairs to the Altair and sealed the bay.

It was a robust and useful ship. He had grown fonder of it lately, yet it just was not the same as the Lodestar or AnnaChi's Cintian. He stopped at Lodestar's bay and frowned. He hadn't flown her once on this trip. He was comfortable with Flair using her when needed, yet wished he could have switched places. Altair was just too damn practical.

A ship-wide announcement shook him from his thoughts. The Nimbus was finally taking off for the journey to Faraday Base.

With a heavy sigh, he closed the hatchway.

"Nova, is Sariyn out and about anywhere? I don't want to interrupt her if she is busy."

"Sariyn is in Bay H8 and does not appear to be overly busy."

"Thanks. How is the correlation rebuild going?"

It had taken several attempts, but Griff had been able to establish a connection between the matrices and bring the main matrix back online, with the clone acting as a control layer. Nova had been trying to save as much of herself as she could ever since.

"The rebuild has proven more complex than I postulated. My clone needs to take control more than I would like, but it is necessary. I believe, in human terms, I am feeling very lost. My processes are overlapping areas of memories they should not be. This is causing me to become confused at times. I am deeply concerned I will not be able to reintegrate my clone once I am fully repaired. I am sorry that I have let you down, Kasey."

"You have not let me down, and you know that. However, if you are holding back from repairs because you are worried about your clone, maybe you should start thinking of your clone as a sister instead of an extension of yourself. Two minds are usually better than one."

"I... I see. I will contemplate this."

The hesitation from the AI worried Kasey.

"What I am trying to say is that, whatever happens, it will be okay. *We* will be okay."

"Thank you, Kasey."

He found he had made it to bay H8 and steadied himself for his next conversation.

Entering the bay, Sariyn looked up sharply with surprise from the pad she was examining.

"Kasey! You scared me."

"Not my intention. What are you looking at?"

"Flair found old schematics for this ship. It is far older than we thought. Hundreds of years older in fact. The thing has been rebuilt several times. Looking at the spec's power requirements, it must have been extremely inefficient in its original form. Not my area, but that's obvious. I can't even identify what the original core system was."

"Interesting. Anything left of those old systems?"

"Nothing I have been able to identify, but again, not

my area. I am just, uh, getting ideas."

"So, you still think you want to buy this relic from the company?"

"Well, yeah. I see a lot of potential in it. It is a near-perfect tender ship for prospecting teams and gives us mobile bases for the teams to use while grounded. But I will understand if that is not something you, or the company, want to do."

"We have talked about it, and if that is what you really want, then I will push to make it happen. But I have to say, I don't think that is what you want. At least not exactly."

"Huh? I don't follow."

"I could be wrong—people are not exactly my area. But I feel like you are looking for something that ship is just a substitute for. I am not even sure that ship is a good investment for you. You could likely lose money on it just to keep it running. So, how about telling me what you are really looking for? Unless I am wrong…"

She was quiet for so long, Kasey thought she might be contemplating striking him for his gall.

Instead, she pulled out a stool to sit on and rubbed a hand across her shaved and tattooed head. "I'm not sure if you are right or wrong, but I suppose you have a point. I see everyone moving forward around me and I feel like I am just standing still. Darnie is heading up the mining branch of the company, you were just a pilot when we met and now you have a damn fleet and a flipping carrier to boot. You have been generous to give us ownership shares, but I am not sure where I really fit in."

"I can't imagine you not fitting in with the mining business."

"Sure, but I am more than just a geologist, you know? It's always been more of a hobby than a job. I don't really need a job, ya know? I want more than that."

"I do know. But I am curious about how owning this

ship helps you fit in. Am I close in saying that you feel it would allow you to head up the majority of the prospecting business?"

He had never seen her nervous before, but he could see that cord struck now.

"No, I mean, maybe a little. Sorry, I am not trying to take over your prospecting business. I know that's your and AnnaChi's thing."

"Well, yes and no. We do really enjoy the prospecting, but running teams of people is absolutely not what we want to do. We will be out there doing our own surveys, but the teams will be run by someone other than us."

"Oh..."

"I know we haven't established too many of the companies positions yet—but let me lay out for you what we have been thinking. Nova, bring up the latest designs for Sariyn's lab area."

"My lab?"

Kasey pointed to the wall behind her which lit up with three-dimensional representations of the engineering section of Nimbus. A sizable unused section was highlighted, and a room appeared in its place then slowly filled with all manner of equipment that had been salvaged so far.

"The lab," Kasey nodded at the wall, "is around nine hundred square meters, which you can arrange and staff any way you see fit. This is not limited to just business usage. The Nimbus should be considered a home, not just work. Anything we have salvaged can be reallocated to this lab, and if you make a list of anything else you need and let Nova know of any high or low priorities, we will get them onto the requisitions lists."

He let her take it all in, then continued. "We also want you to have direct oversight of *all* research aboard Nimbus, not just to be our head geophysicist. Keep this part to yourself for now, but you also need to know that if Isaac stays, he will have a mixed lab of robotics and other projects next to yours, although quite a bit smaller. He has quite a few experiments going on, and you will need to review and sign off on them all. I do not want the ship endangered, and I want you to make sure that does not happen. Along with that, you will hold a seat on the Nimbus executive team Flair is putting together, which is no different than what you have already been doing for Red Rock." He gave her a few moments to digest it all before continuing. "Is there anything I have listed so far that you do not want to take responsibility for?"

"No, I can do all that."

"Well then, here is the kicker—since you are interested in running the prospecting side of the business, it's *all* yours to command. That includes this new ship's crew, flight plans, all of it. You may have noticed that your lab is directly next to this bay's cargo elevator? That is not an accident. The ship and this bay will be your responsibility, whether you own it or not, and the upper cargo bay will have a dedicated area for your usage here as well. Interested so far?"

"Hell yes, I am!"

"Good, the position comes with an additional two percent interest in the prospecting division as long as you are working for the company directly. Your other choice is to purchase the ship from the salvage division and see if you can do better via contract work with the company. We can work on a contract that works out anywhere in between, but that's our general thoughts on it. The question is, do you really want to buy this ship?"

"It was never about money, but what limitations would I have with the ship belonging to the company?"

"Good question. If the company owns it, then we can use it as needed for other operations like salvage, supply runs, even potential security operations as needed, as with any of our ships. All maintenance, fuel, supplies, etc. would be handled by the company as well, but you would have a lot of input to that effect. AnnaChi will likely have several variants of the bard loadouts for it as well."

"You know, it's a small ship, so we have room to spare in this bay." She gestured around the area designed for a much larger ship. "We could outfit this area to hot-swap the detachable bays as needed. Given time and resources, we could deploy a lot more than the four initial bays into the field."

"That could be very useful indeed. I will want you to work with the engineering crew to have an efficient system designed for this bay after we have the ship in working order. But for now, talk to the cargo team and have them partition areas off for both your lab's storage needs and plenty of room where the detachable bays, or mobile bases, can be loaded, stored, and moved to the lift quickly. We can dedicate a few stevedores to handle the heavy lifting until a better system is in place. How does that sound?"

"Okay, you have convinced me. Keep the ship with the company. You're right, it is not what I really wanted. But I will take the position."

"Excellent! Have the cargo team set anything aside that you need from our stores. I need you to get this ship ready for service in about a month. I recommend running some team training on the lightweight bards and stabilizers if we have time on Belrothi. Talk with AnnaChi about the bards; she has been planning more upgrades for them. Not sure if they will be ready for the first mission or not—I am not even sure how many we have but I know she brought back a load from somewhere."

"We currently have seventy-three salvaged bards and

similar all-terrain vehicles in the lower cargo hold," Nova interjected.

"Well, it seems we do indeed have plenty." Kasey closed his eyes tightly for a moment. "We really should have brought more engineers along for this initial trip."

Sariyn laughed. "I will get to planning. Thank you, Kasey."

"Hey, thank you." He pulled the hatchway open and looked back. "What are you going to name that thing?"

"Oh, seemed kind of obvious to me." She pointed to a tattoo on her arm. "Jumping Spider."

"Really? Well, it does seem fitting. Jumping Spider it is. Now, get her ready for business."

CHAPTER TWENTY-EIGHT

Beams of light flared across the nearly obscured opening carved into the steep mountainside.

Kasey stood at the forefront of the Nimbus bridge, glaring into the large screen as if it were an actual window out the front of the ship. The Nimbus hovered barely a hundred meters from the opening, but little could be seen through the blizzard conditions covering the area.

"This is as close as we dare," Jate called out from the helm.

"Give me a different spectrum on this please," Kasey asked, "I need a view inside if we can."

The screen flashed through a dozen enhanced image settings, stopping on a thermal-enhanced overlay that showed deep into base's hangar. Nothing moved. Heat levels increased further in, but nothing unexpected.

Kasey sat at a terminal and linked it to the command ring he wore. They had been trying to connect to the base since the Nimbus had entered the ten-kilometers frequency range the ring was supposed to be in tune with, but nothing had appeared. The base should have also responded to comm request using the ring's access codes, but not a single query had been returned.

He looked back at Flair in the command chair. "Either the base's comms are down, or it is ignoring us."

She looked to one of the stations. "Comms, do we have any signals from that base at all?"

"Nothing for comms, but I am detecting a few spikes in the EMF spectrum. Likely machinery or bots."

Flair shrugged at Kasey. "You said the security bots were actively engaging you when you left. That means they were receiving orders from the base's system. Something must have happened to that system after you left."

"Right, the bots were blasting us until we left that hangar. Now that I think about it, at the time, we had expected the base to launch missiles or something at us once we cleared that entrance, but it didn't. We assumed their standing orders kept that from happening, but they didn't seem to have an issue trying to kill us when we were inside."

"Hmm. That makes no sense, they really should have fired on you. External defenses are unlikely to have been offline or damaged. They are made to withstand orbital bombardments. Do we have a location on any of its hardpoints?"

A few moments passed as the crew worked furiously at their consoles looking to answer the question.

"Nothing?" she asked again.

"If I may, Captain?"

"Yes, Miss Mayflower?"

"I contacted Mr. Soeda on our problem, and he has a theory."

"Okay, and what does Isaac theorize?"

"He believes the security bots are each redundantly connected to each other via a wide-frequency signal. They have their own network that lets them work together more quickly. He says it is used on bots with high-risk jobs."

"Okay, so similar to our mimic interfaces then?"

"Right, and short range. In any case, he feels the security bots could have been relaying commands through this short-range network even if the main base comms were down."

"Thank you, Miss Mayflower. Alright, lets proceed on that assumption. Kasey, do you still want to be part of the initial team?"

Kasey thought about what AnnaChi's reaction would be if he made the decision for their team to hold back and let others go in first. She was already with the team aboard the Altair and waiting for him. He had no doubt that if he backed out, she would take the Cintian and go without him.

"Yes, we are prepped and ready."

"Fine. Carry on, Mr. Robinson."

Kasey took his time going to the Altair's bay to calm his nerves. As he crossed the Nimbus maintenance area, he saw Isaac running towards the bay as well.

"Isaac, I thought you would be aboard already."

He hefted a satchel on his shoulder. "Thought of a few tools I might need."

"Good, are we ready to go then?"

"Yes sir, as far as I know anyway."

He waved him ahead. "Let's get to it then."

All was quiet as he landed the Altair next to the hangar's stout control tower. There had been no autopilot landing requests like they had received last time.

"Well, the cleaning command worked at least," AnnaChi commented over his shoulder as he examined the ships surroundings.

"I will grant you that. But the air quality here is far worse. We will be glad for the combat helmet's filtering system. Have the team assemble at our bay's portside hatch."

Starting with the control tower, they scouted the areas the Altair's lights illuminated. The tower was completely offline and powerless, which was not fully unexpected as they noticed several sizable chunks of the building had been destroyed.

"Your doing I suppose?"

"Needed to be done." She shrugged.

"Where to now?"

"Officer country. Command and control should be nearby and hopefully clearly marked. Until we get that ring connected, we are directionless."

She took point, with two other crew close behind. Isaac and Kasey followed behind as they worked to make any type of connection to the base's systems.

As they approached what appeared to be a training area for ranged weapons, Isaac called out for a stop.

"I have an EM field spike. Movement heading our way. East door. Coming in slowly."

They all dropped into defensive positions and waited.

"Visible in five, four, get ready!" Isaac continued.

It was all Kasey could do not to fire his weapon when the small cleaning bot exited the room. It stopped a moment to consider them, then continued down the hallway they had come from.

Everyone relaxed except Isaac. "It sent a low band RF signal when it encountered us. I don't know if the security bots will have leaky EM fields like that cleaner, unless they are actively transmitting, so keep alert."

AnnaChi nodded. "Okay, keep us updated. Right now, we are just soldiers in a base. There shouldn't be an issue unless we fire on them or go somewhere we shouldn't. But let's double-time it and stay alert anyway."

They found the officer's area guarded by three

security bots.

Kasey moved slowly forward and held up his hand with the ring. "They are with me, stand down."

The bots immediately moved to the side.

Kasey nodded and led them through the checkpoint. The command areas were clearly marked as they had hoped, but each was well-guarded. They approached the systems control rooms but a quartet of bots slid out to block their path.

Warning. Authorization is required to pass.

Kasey held up the ring again, but they didn't move.

Warning. You do not have clearances to pass.

Isaac moved up to Kasey and initiated a point-to-point communication with his combat helmet. "Tell them you have authorization coming from our command in one minute. Then contact Flair and ask for an update on their status, or anything to get signals moving. Tell me the moment she replies."

"We are being authorized by command in one minute, please wait," Kasey informed the security bots, then contacted Flair, leaving the channel open so Isaac could hear her response.

As soon as Flair's transmission ended, a low piercing noise flooded his communications.

Isaac spoke over the point-to-point again, "Now, tell them you are now authorized and walk through them. Be ready just in case."

Kasey nodded and looked at the others. They all adjusted their weapons and nodded.

He addressed the bots again. "I am now authorized, move aside."

Unable to confirm. Unable to confirm.

"Then move aside," he stated again, and started forward.

The bots hesitated until he was within a meter, then slowly moved to the side.

"Let's go, people."

As soon as they were through the doorway, Isaac closed the door and removed the satchel from his back and set it on the floor. Surveying the room, he pointed to an office and ushered everyone inside before shutting the door.

"What did you do to them?" Kasey asked.

"Oh, just gave them reasonable data and then cut off their network access with some simple signal jamming."

"Will it hold for long?"

"It should. If I am right, they should go into standby mode until new orders are received, which won't happen as long as that jammer is active. We need to clear this area of any other bots then finish this job."

"Got it. AnnaChi, you are up. Clear these rooms, then we either reprogram the system security, shut it down, or destroy it. One way or another, those bots need to go offline."

She nodded, then looked around the office they were in and frowned. She pulled out a long knife and handed it to Kasey. "Use this or whatever else you can find to wedge that door firmly shut. Don't trust the lock. You and Isaac take care of that then follow us in our sweep. If we find the core room or usable interface, we will leave you there. First priority is to find the transmitter and shut it down."

She led them back to the jamming device and moved off as Kasey and Isaac worked on wedging the door. By the time they had it secured, weapon's fire could be heard from a corridor on the far side of the room.

Before they were a few steps away, the door they had just secured began to shake. Apparently, the security bots understood enough to respond to the sound of battle.

He hesitated a moment, but Isaac grabbed his arm. "If they are in the core room, they need us there to disable the network before more bots are called."

Kasey rounded the corner into the hallway and an active fire fight. A bolt of energy sizzled off his combat suit's shielding as he dove into an open doorway across the hall.

"Clear!" AnnaChi's voice called out a moment later. "Thanks to that stupid, but useful, distraction."

He pulled himself up and she ran to his side to check him over for damage. "You are fine. What is your shield at?"

"Uh, forty-four percent."

"Don't do that again!"

"Yes, dear, but we need to move. The noise alerted the ones at the door and they are trying to get through."

With a nod, she started shouting orders. In moments everyone was corralled into the core room and they worked to again wedge the door closed.

A loud cracking noise sounded from beyond the door as they finished.

AnnaChi ordered her men into defensive positions and left Kasey and Isaac to their work.

Kasey found two transmission points. One was burned out, along with a host of components nearby. The second seemed fine, so he took aim at it with his rifle, but Isaac stopped him.

"Sorry, but I think we are too late to just take the network offline. We don't know how many more are now heading our way already. Our only chance is to reprogram them."

"Can you do that?"

Isaac moved to a terminal. "I don't know, but I will try."

Kasey waited as he accessed the system.

"Sir, you will receive a message in a moment. Authorize it."

A message popped up on Kasey's helmet display and

he used the command ring's codes to accept it. Several more followed and he accepted them automatically, but several were denied.

A steady banging noise was now coming from the doorway.

"We are running out of time, Isaac…"

"I know, we don't have the right access, but I am looking for another option."

A loud crack sounded from the other room, followed by several more.

"Do you need me here, or should I go help defend?"

"Wait, I have something! This may not work, but I need you here a bit longer. Get ready to destroy that transmitter on my mark."

He aimed his rifle at it. "Ready!"

Weapons could be heard again as a bead of sweat rolled down Kasey's forehead. He did his best to ignore it all and waited for Isaac's command.

The weapon's fire increased then suddenly stopped.

Isaac shouted, "Now, now, now!"

Kasey blasted the transmitter to pieces.

They ran out to find AnnaChi and the others still standing. The area around the door was littered with the remains of what seemed to be dozens of security bots. The hallway beyond had dozens more waiting to enter the room, but they all were still.

Isaac rushed by and waved them to follow.

He moved through the broken door and up to the nearest intact bot, dropped a small pack of tools on the floor beside it, and started to remove a panel. "Cover me in case this doesn't work."

Within seconds he had a cable connected to a small tablet and was typing furiously. Eventually he looked up and waved everyone back through the broken door. "I don't know about this, but we have about thirty seconds before they come out of diagnostic mode. I am activating my code now. Be ready."

Kasey watched as Isaac punched a button on the tablet then scrambled back through the doorway.

At first, nothing happened, then the security bot rose up, turned towards the other bots in the hall, and then slumped over as it powered down. One by one, every bot did the same.

Isaac slumped to the floor and laughed to himself.

Kasey and AnnaChi walked over to him.

He looked up. "That was fun!"

"If you say so." Kasey held his hand out to Isaac to pull him up. "I take it we are safe now?"

"Yes, all defenses are now offline. The base is ours. The core is still quite restricted, but it is not connected to anything, so it doesn't matter. You may need to pry some doors open in a few places to get through, but we should be good otherwise."

"Good job Mr. Soeda." AnnaChi added, then asked, "Could you dig into the system a bit more and get us a map of the base? We have a basic one, but it doesn't show everything."

"Not a problem."

Kasey nodded and turned away. "Kasey to Nimbus Actual."

"Kasey! This is Knoc. Captain Flair and Jate are about to land in the base hangar with a rescue team to pull you out. Do you have coordinates?"

"We are good, base is secure. Can you connect me to Flair please?"

"Kasey!" Flair shouted over the line, "What the hell has been going on? Something jammed our comms and then you went offline."

"Sorry, that was us. We didn't think to close the comm beforehand. Anyway, it worked, mostly. We will debrief fully later. For now, we have the base's security shut down. Can you bring the stevedores over and start clearing this place out? We are working on locating the armament depot now. This command ring didn't have any more access than the last one, so we are limited in what the system will give us right now."

"What! That damn ring should have provided access to nearly everything but top levels."

"A mystery for another day, but my guess is that someone changed access levels for this base, at least."

"Fine. Dropping off the crew and stevedores I have on this ship near the Altair, then heading back for the rest."

"I appreciate you coming after us. What ship are you piloting?"

"We borrowed your Lodestar. Not many choices and we wanted something armed. We really need a company ship…"

"Again, if we can claim that pirate ship after Fran's people have a look, then we will have one. Otherwise, we need to make some credits first. Anyway, can you bring an engineer over too? I want someone to place manual safeties on all security bots or pull their power-sources before bringing them over to Nimbus. I don't want these things loose on board with lethal weapons."

"Roger that, and added to the list, boss."

"Take Jate back with you and give him control of the Lodestar to bring back. If you could bring over the Cintian it would save us a trip."

"Can do. Drop off complete. We will have the rest over within the hour with Jate and Markus transporting. You need me here or back on Nimbus?"

"Actually, I could use you here for an hour or two. I want your assessment on a few things. You can relieve Knoc for a break after that. I am assuming you have a watch schedule set up?"

"I did, but it got derailed once you went offline. We will be fine. The Nimbus handles like a dream, even in a full-on blizzard. She's the best damned aerodynamic brick I have ever flown. The updrafts off the mountainside are the real challenge for the transports, but Jate and Markus can handle it. Which reminds me, we planned to use a few shuttles to ferry crew to Nimbus for breaks and food, but that's not going to happen in this weather."

"Get everyone moving and then we can figure out a plan."

CHAPTER TWENTY-NINE

Kasey met Flair as she disembarked from the Cintian.

He waved her to follow him. "First things first, we think we located the depot. I want to crack that open now."

"Lead on, boss."

He took her to a large storage area off to the side of the hangar that was empty except for a few crates.

"Whatever was in this area was taken when the base was abandoned, so we didn't give it a second glance when we were here last time. If the map Isaac found is correct, the back wall is a false door."

"Makes sense, the civilian supplies are not under general usage. I would expect them to be closed off and forgotten about. Are they still there?"

"We are about to find out."

He walked past the empty crates to a small control box on the wall, held the ring to it, and accepted the query that popped up on his mimic. A showering of dust puffed out from hidden seams near the top of the wall as it slowly slid down into the floor.

Kasey stepped back and whistled in appreciation at

the sight. Hundreds of rifles, light combat suits, and supplies lined the nearest wall. Basic, but solid gear. Bulk food and personnel supplies filled a row blocking Kasey's view beyond. There was a heavy layer of dust covering it all, but he dismissed it. These were useful, if not the supplies he expected—he wasn't about to leave anything behind.

Giving the supplies a final glance, he moved around the containers to find Flair shaking her head in disappointment. When she saw his questioning look, she gestured at the room.

It took Kasey a few seconds to understand what he was seeing. A massive slab had broken through the ceiling, crushing or destroying most of the room's contents.

A knot of frustration tightened in his stomach. It had always been his intention to fully arm the Nimbus eventually. This would have been a quick and easy way to get it done much sooner than they would have been able to otherwise. It would also have allowed them to be far more heavily armed than the weapons they would have access to under normal circumstances.

After being attacked twice since taking ownership of the Nimbus, it seemed only a matter of time before someone, or something, would succeed. Losing these supplies was a definite letdown.

Not one to be defeated, he pointed out some of the less damaged areas. "So, what do we have left?"

"Hmm, well there is a good amount of reactive shielding modules. They won't go far on something as large as the Nimbus, but if you place a few at our weaker areas it could augment the defenses nicely."

Kasey nodded and brushed the debris off the nearest one. The modules were single use. Built to detect incoming ordinance at close ranges and respond by sending a wall of explosive countermeasures into their path. The limited range worked fine for smaller crafts, but not something the size of Nimbus.

He turned to find Flair scowling at something he barely recognized as a drone.

"Something of interest?"

"Eh? Well sure, I suppose," she replied in disgust. "These are class-three drones. The Belrothi depot only had simple class-one defense drones."

"Better defenses for the rich?"

"Maybe…" She stood up, looked across the room, and frowned.

"Did Fran not know about this?"

"No," she sighed. "Sorry, I am just annoyed. If I can speak plainly?"

"I would prefer you always do so. This is not the navy."

"Right. Well, Francis outranked the pompous ass of a rear admiral stationed on Lithose. Admiral Delk. More money than brains. Given the cushy job of protecting Lithose to keep him out of the way. I suspected something was off when you brought back the I.C.E suits, but they were a one-off. I expected one or two extras from a man like him. And we put them to good use. But if the civilian supplies are this far above spec, then I am sure his command was better supplied on all accounts."

"Our gain, right?"

"Yes. True of course, for whatever is left here anyway. But his misuse of funds took away from the whole mission's budget. People died because he wanted his command to have better toys."

"Oh," Kasey realized, "the command rings?"

"What? Oh, I see. Yes, Delk must have changed the clearance protocols to keep his toys hidden from Francis."

"I see. Still, nothing we can do now. So, what are we

looking at here?"

"Right. Let's see, the class-threes are shielded, have a high-powered scrambler, and a self-destruct package as powerful as the FF missiles we used at the gate battle. Oh, and the same signal duplication package as the defense drones."

"Seems useful."

"Ya think? These alone would have saved a lot of lives. Not sure how many we can recover from this mess, but at least a few." She shook her head and then headed towards stack of missile launchers at the back of the room.

"More good news?"

She sneered back then nodded. "A few of these seem okay. Better model of launcher, and autoloading attachments. Dammit, we lost a lot of ships that still had missiles aboard they couldn't load in time. A few of these would have made a big difference."

"The missiles look like fire and forgets?"

"Yes, same missiles surprisingly." She crawled over a large chunk of ceiling and dusted off the tops of several drums before looking back at him. "Well, not all FFs, a few of these racks are sixes…"

Kasey caught up to her and caught his breath before asking, "Sixes?"

"They break into six smaller missiles as soon as they come into point defense range of a target. Not much power for each, but nearly impossible to avoid taking a few hits."

"Ah. I think I need a few of those on Altair…"

"You know, Federation law frowns on heavily armed transport ships?"

Kasey thought about that for a moment. "What about the Nimbus? Navy contractors testing experimental ships in hot zones at the far-flung edge of Federation space. It seems like a worthy reason to me."

"You may find some leniency if the missile launchers are properly stowed and secured on the Nimbus when in protected space."

"Well damn."

"That's a problem?"

"Not really, but I have again realized I brought far too few engineers on this trip."

"You haven't looked at the schematics of the Nimbus' hardpoints, have you?"

"I have seen attachment plates before. Not overly interesting."

"Well, the hardpoints are built into subdermal enclosures. The weapons do not need to be deployed, or seen, unless you want them to be. Your other ships may be an issue though."

"Oh. That wasn't in the approved plans…"

"Navy builds to standards as much as plans, but the later version should have them. You may want to look closer at the design to see what else isn't what you assumed. Considering how old the original schematics were that you based your designs on, I would expect there to be more than a few changes after the planning stages."

"I'll add that to my list. Uh, are we safe standing in a pile of crushed missiles?"

"Yes. Completely inert until activated."

"Take your word for that. Anything else survive?"

She peered around. "Maybe some chaff spools and more civilian supply crates. Most everything else is trashed. If we had some engineers that weren't already overloaded with tasks, they might be able to piece together a few more launchers."

"Fine. We will take all that we can dig out. I want at least one of the launchers installed before we break atmosphere."

"I will update priorities once I am back on Nimbus."

"Until then, come with me. I need your opinion on a few other items."

He took her to the large platform lift that took them to a lower level of the base. A cavern with eight tunnels leading off into darkness waited, along with the remains of dozens of security bots and a line of burned-out shield-walls.

Kasey pointed to the line of shield-walls. "Our escape route last time."

"Looks messy, but I am sure you had other motives for being back down here?"

He walked towards the opposite tunnel. "This way."

He only went a few meters into the tunnel when he stopped and waited for Flair to comment.

"Fighters!" she exclaimed. "You don't seriously expect me to condone you having a fleet of fighters on Nimbus?"

"So much for those rules... But no. I don't know that we even have the right kind of pilots, and I'd prefer something bigger that can take more than a few hits. AnnaChi may have different thoughts."

"I bet she does... So why do you have me looking at them?"

"I want to know if they have any use to us. Can we sell them back to the navy?"

She tapped her cheek in thought. "Maybe, but I wouldn't suggest it. These are thirty years out of date compared to what they are now fielding. They won't want you to have them, nor will they want to pay to have them back, so instead they will likely choose the third option."

"What would the third option be, or don't I want to know?"

"My guess is that they would stick lawyers on you until you delivered them for free."

"How kind... Fine, any other options for what we do

with them?"

"Hmm." She walked up to one, pulled off the covering, and inspected the craft. "Well, they look to have a basic loadout. So, we could strip six FF and two seeker missiles from each craft. The seekers will be nice to have if we need them, far more intelligence and hard to out-maneuver. Plus, we can remote-pilot them."

"Take them all then, I suppose. Anything else?"

"Well, the guns are too built in to repurpose, and you can buy bigger and better. The point defense and sensor systems on these are top notch; I would strip them all out if you can use them."

"And if we ever decide we need fighters?"

"Strip them out carefully?" She laughed. "Honestly, if you actually need fighters, you are in more serious trouble than these will help with. Maybe if you were running security for a planet somewhere, they could be useful."

Kasey tilted his head and gave her a thoughtful look. "You mean like the one we are standing on?"

She blinked at him a few times, then looked back at the row of fighters. "How many are here?"

"I believe there were thirty-two."

She looked at him, then back to the fighters again. "Have you found any other ordinance depots in the base?"

"No, the designated storage areas were cleared out and I haven't seen any sign of others yet. But this base wasn't finished."

"Well... I guess I would strip the seeker missiles from half of these and leave the rest completely alone. You can always come back for more FFs if needed, and honestly they are not hard to find in the darker markets if you are desperate. Same with the point defenses and sensors. They are standard install points for quick repairs, so if you use the same design on wherever you reinstall them, you can always swap them back in if needed."

"Thank you, Flair."

"You really think you will be back here?"

"What would Fran tell you?"

"That it is good to have backups." She snickered. "Okay, point taken."

CHAPTER THIRTY

Kasey never felt happier to leave a planet behind.

The salvage trip to Lithose had been a pleasant vacation compared to the hellish two weeks they spent on Belrothi squabbling with contractors over the remaining Nimbus outfitting or haggling prices of salvaged goods.

All told, the expenses had put them in the red. The n-mats sales would keep them afloat and pay the crew, but not much more until they could complete at least one transport trip. It did not help that Darnell kept insisting that new mining companies always took years to start making profits, if ever. The paychecks were what mattered, he would say—pay the crew and deal with the debt later. Kasey pretended to understand. Deep down he did, but he didn't care. He did not want a debt—he wanted a stable home. One he could literally keep afloat.

His musings stopped as he came to the bay with H5 painted in large lettering above the hatchway. The pirate's ship had been awarded to him as he had hoped. The navy's investigation of the pirate's transport ship ended just hours before their departure—and came with an added surprise.

In addition to the ship, both AnnaChi and himself were officially granted privateer status, retroactively. AnnaChi was thrilled with the idea, but he could only wonder what new commitments the title would ultimately force upon them.

"Hey!"

He turned to see AnnaChi, with a greasy rag in one hand, heading his way. "Hi ya, dear. Thought I would take a peek at the company's new asset."

"Your new ship, you mean. It was granted to you personally, not the company. Laws of the sea and all that crap."

"Not really. It was adjudicated into my trust for the next standard year, but it is not actually mine until that period is over. Until then, the court can determine if another owner is more appropriate. If I understand the privateer clause in the agreement correctly, I can also suggest who should end up owning the ship at the end of the term. Are you interested in owning this ship?"

"Hell no. It would be a huge step down from my Cintian. If it ain't bigger or deadlier, I will stick with my old girl."

"Well then, maybe we should permanently loan it to Red Rock. The company needs it, I don't."

"Fine by me. So, are we going to take a look at this bucket or not?"

"I thought you were helping Sariyn with the Spider?"

"I am. Just kicked off a new set of couplers for the mobile base pods. I had one of the medium fabricators we took from Faraday Base set up down here while we rebuild Sariyn's crazy ship. Small redesign, but it was either new couplers or sacrifice a cubic meter of space inside the pods."

"We are calling them pods now? Wait, I thought we had collected enough fabricators from that shipyard's settlement to outfit at least one of the maintenance bay's fabrication rooms?"

"Well, sort of. The settlement had plenty of generalized fabs from stores and such around the area. Mostly for clothing, household junk, and other simplistic but all-purpose fabs. So those are all up in the manufacturing room on Operations Deck for general ship usage. I believe they have them pumping out niceties for the guest rooms at the moment, so at least they were worth grabbing. The ones we took from the shipyard itself are in bad shape. That place was wide open to the elements. Most of them are still salvageable but will take a lot of work to refurbish."

"Okay, so eventually we will have something usable. And the ones we took from the Faraday Base are where?"

"Added to the Nimbus engineering shop's fabrication plant. The equipment from that farming setup we found was a great start, but engineering really needed the specialized fabricators we got from that base. The mil-spec weapon's grade fabrication and materials processing for the cannon slugs alone will give us an edge we could never reproduce with civilian fabs. Once we get everything running up there, any extra fabricators will move to the hangar deck's shops with the refurbished fabs. And we will eventually need some assembly systems for at least one of those too."

"Damn, well that makes sense. Something else for the to-do list. If we ever make it back to Lithose we need to locate a few other bases, assembly plants, and every shipyard we can."

"Well, at least we got enough to get started. And yes, calling the Spider's container's pods is far better than spider-baby sacks—because that's how Sariyn was referring to them."

"Yikes... I am going to regret agreeing with that

ship's name, aren't I?"

"Maybe run it by me first next time, dear?"

"Would you have disagreed with it?"

"Hell no, I love it!"

"Of course—well, how about you get to name this new piece of junk?"

"Is it really that bad?"

"I'm not sure, but that was the impression I got from the navy's investigators."

"Well then, it is time we find out for ourselves." She keyed the hatch and led them into a bay littered with organized piles of trash.

Kasey sighed. "You'd think they would have taken their mess with them."

"Not their job I suppose. Search the junk and leave it for someone else to clean up."

Kasey looked up. "Nova, please send a few cleaning bots and a maid bot to the H5 bay."

"Confirmed."

They entered through the aft bay and found the inside in a similar state. Kasey picked his way over to one of the large tanks that filled most of the bay and checked the contents.

"The hell... They are empty."

"Really?"

"Check the others."

All the tanks were empty of the n-mats that had allowed the ship to gain access to Lithose.

He sighed. "I can't imagine the navy had a legitimate claim to the n-mats. Our claim to the ship should have included all contents. Not just the junk."

"I will talk to Flair, maybe we can be reimbursed."

"Fine. Nova, are you able to connect to this ship's systems?"

"Yes, Kasey, but I need your approval first. Do I have your approval?"

"Yes. Run a diagnostic on critical systems and send me the ship's logs."

"Sorry Kasey, it appears most systems are offline, and the ship's logs have been purged."

"Damn it. I should have expected that, I suppose. How are you adjusting to the new core setup?"

"I am adapting better than expected. The recalibrations are expected to be complete within two standard days. Currently, over ninety-eight percent of correlations are expected to be fully repaired. My primary and secondary should be fully reconstituted into a single entity at that point."

"That seems good."

"I believe it to be good as well. Kasey, I understand the new correlation matrixes have been installed in both Cintian and Lodestar?"

He realized it was less of a question from the AI than a talking point she wanted to discuss. Enough of the specialized cores had been gathered from the Faraday Base to create one additional matrix, and they had decided to purchase a third setup. They both had required specialized technicians on Belrothi to configure and set them up properly in the ships.

"That is correct..."

"I am looking forward to creating the clone entities."

"We are as well. But we are going give your new matrix a little extra time to adapt before we have you make more clones."

"Understandable. Much of my processing has indeed changed from the recent issues."

"Are you concerned about that, Nova?"

"No. There are simply different types of correlation paths available to me now. I believe they will more fully allow me to assimilate data correlations and therefore be of better assistance to you."

"Okay good. We have time, just keep us informed."

"I will, Kasey."

AnnaChi had a thoughtful look but shook her head when Kasey looked at her.

"Shall we see what the rest of this ship holds?" she asked.

"Engineering or bridge first?"

"Engineering first. It should tell us if this can is worth flying."

An hour later they both exited the bay shaking their heads. Not only was the ship in abhorrent disrepair, but the inspection team had also torn apart nearly everything and left it in disarray.

"Thankfully, we have a decent size engineering crew now," Kasey commented. "But I bet the Jumping Spider is flight worthy before this one is."

"No bet. Besides, we need the Spider more right now."

"So then," he smiled, "what name are we giving this heap?"

"Oh, I had that worked out weeks ago."

"Really? Want to share it?"

"The Carnelian."

"Carnelian…"

"Think it through dear."

"I… Ah, clever."

"Oh course. Anyway, the couplers should be ready. Where are you off to next?"

"I'm meeting Isaac in the gardens for lunch. He will be working there part-time, and I want Orange to get used to him being around."

"Not a bad idea. Molly is already comfortable with Yaran. I have been meeting with Yaran about the atoss' needs in the garden, and Molly joins us."

"Good. Has she run into any problems?"

"A few, but nothing that can't be solved. Isaac and Yaran apparently make a good team. She knows what needs done and he finds clever ways to make it better. When, or if, we bring the other atoss on board, the gardens will be more than ready."

"Where will they all nest, or den? I have been meaning to ask her because I didn't see anything in the plans."

"That's one of the projects she had Isaac put his touches on. She had planned groups of dens like we have on top of my shop on Belrothi but worried they might prefer more solitary spaces. Isaac wrote a program that found hundreds of niches and alcoves that are out of human reach. They are printing a few fitted containers each day for those spaces that the atoss can find and use if they like."

"I guess I will have to see if I can spot any while I am up there."

"Well, there are three already in place near our home if you pay attention." She rolled her eyes with a smile then bounced off towards the fabrication room.

CHAPTER THIRTY-ONE

Isaac was waiting for him at a clearing just inside Kasey and AnnaChi's private area of the gardens. It was an isolated section and was set up with plenty of comforts to entertain guests. A large lunch tray was waiting on a nearby table.

Kasey waved him over to the food tray and started pulling items out. "I am glad you decided to stay with us, Isaac. You don't regret that decision yet, right?"

"Not for a second, Captain. This ship of yours is amazing. I would never forgive myself if I passed the opportunity up."

"Call me Kasey, this isn't a work meeting. It won't be long before ships like this are common, you know."

"The galaxy is changing, you are right about that. I want to be part of that change. I have been just going through the paces for a lot of years now. I thought joining the Farpoint colony would be a change for me, but I was just doing the same kinds of jobs I had always done. Well, until the world got broken... But this," he gestured around, "this is very different."

"I am glad we came along and ran into you. I still

can't imagine what that must have been like, all alone down there."

"It was certainly horrible and scary and all that at first. There are some things that will haunt me all my days... But, you know, it had some good moments too."

"That is hard to imagine..."

"Well, sure. I mean it took a while to figure out how to survive and all, but after that? Well, it became a game to see how I could improve my situation. Something new to do and solve for every day. It was, I don't know, interesting, I guess. Potential everywhere. There is something to say for that... If you know what I mean?"

"I think I have an idea, yes. Makes me wonder what I would have done in the same situation."

Isaac poured a cup of coffee from a carafe. "I am sure you had other topics to discuss besides Lithose."

Kasey glanced at flash of orange moving steadily in their direction. "I actually wanted to properly introduce you to a friend of mine. She also survived on Lithose for quite a while after the disaster."

"Really?"

Kasey stood and walked a few steps away from Isaac and whistled as he knelt down and waited. Orange was at his side a few seconds later, nuzzling him affectionately. He stood and tapped his shoulder and Orange leapt onto Kasey's back and rested her head on his shoulder.

Isaac's eyes grew wide as Kasey approached him.

"She is perfectly safe, as long as you are too." He smiled. "Right, Orange?"

She clicked twice in response and tilted her head to peer intently at Isaac.

"I, uh, knew she was here, but I have only seen the blue one from a distance. Atoss, right? You called this one Orange? She seems much bigger than the blue one."

"She is the oldest of the atoss left. Saved my life at

least once, but probably twice." He looked at her for a second. "Orange, this is Isaac. He is a friend. He saved my life too."

Orange's head perked up at the last and seemed to relax, then in a blink she pounced onto the table with the food, right in front of Isaac, and looked him directly in the eyes for nearly a minute.

Isaac, to his credit, did not move or breath the entire time.

Finally, Orange nuzzled Isaac's cheek then turned her attention to the food covering the table.

Kasey picked a cover off a small dish that was set to the side. Several prepared chunks of meat waited, which she wasted no time devouring, before nuzzling Kasey again and taking off for a nearby tree.

"I have to say," Isaac said in wonder, "I do like your friends."

"That's good, because there are a lot more of them that will be joining us eventually. In fact, they are a large part of why we have the gardens here."

"Yaran had mentioned that there was an ecosystem issue. But I don't understand how having them on a ship will help for too long."

"That's true enough. In the long term, this garden is only going to be home to a few of them, the ones who want to stay."

"So, in the short term, what? You want to take them somewhere else?"

"Good guess. We will be visiting a lot of new planets. Chances are, we will find one more suited to them. A place they won't cause ecosystem issues like they could on Belrothi."

"And if you don't find somewhere?"

"Honestly?" He laughed, "We let them impact the Belrothi ecosystem and damn the consequences. It is largely our fault that their species was nearly wiped out, we owe them."

"You say that like they are more than just animals."

"Once you get to know them, you will notice they are far more intelligent than most creatures."

"I can believe that. Hold on, so they are already loose on Belrothi, right? How in the verse are you going to gather them all?"

"That is something you will need to see for yourself, I think. But they will know and decide to come, or they won't. I asked Orange to come on this trip. If she didn't want to come, she wouldn't have."

Isaac was thoughtful a few moments. "Interesting. How many came on this trip? I would love to study and get to know them more."

"I think six. The blue one is Molly, and quite imprinted on AnnaChi. Molly and Orange are two of the original three I saved from Lithose on my first trip back there. You might see a small black one with Darnell, his name is Jasper, and he is quite young. The others don't have names yet that I know of, and all are as young as Jasper, so be patient with them."

"I will. Where is the third?"

"Third?"

"You said there were three originals."

"Oh, the third is Mawk. A green atoss. He stayed with the other young ones back on Belrothi. He carried the clutch of them, and I guess is their main parent."

"Anything I can do to help them?"

"Maybe. We have a few issues to solve. They need food that isn't on a plate. They don't need to be domesticated like pets, so eventually we need a food source they can actually hunt in this garden. We also need to keep crew and passengers from pestering them too much. At the same time, we want to allow crew and passengers to enjoy the gardens too. Yaran is tasked with these problems, so if you have any thoughts that could help, let her know."

"Happily. I enjoy working with her, and she seems not to mind a few bots among her plants. You know, watching her and Cerine together the last few days is, I don't know—refreshing, I guess? I went from no people around at all, to having you lot around, and now an actual kid. I don't think I have seen children for more than twenty years, and even that time was a fluke."

"It affects us all, I think. It's their laughter—it sticks with you somehow, right?"

"I can't argue with that." He smiled. "Oh, I meant to thank you! The Belrothi medical center you sent me to for the mimic implant said you had already taken care of both the implant as well as bringing my aging treatments up to date. I didn't expect the aging treatments at all. I had planned to wait for the Federation's relief package to come through so that I could afford the cost of being so far behind. Apparently, their package is still held up due to my *unique situation*, so I thought I had no choice but to wait."

"No need for thanks. I had my contacts ensure that the Federation will cover the expenses in the long run. So, all I did was ensure you were completely up to full health a bit earlier. The mimic implant should have been included as part of the Farpoint passage on the Abscond—I don't understand why your company was able to hold it from you."

"It was part of the contract I signed when the company offered the Farpoint job. It ensured employees would stick with the company after the colony was formed."

"Doesn't sound like a company worth working for…"

"Wasn't too bad, actually. They took care of the expense for the trip, so it was a great deal for anyone like me who wanted a big change."

"Good then. So how are you adjusting to the new mimic interface?"

"Oh, it is a dream to use! I already have a handful of heads-up display configurations set up for various projects. Yaran is even using the one I created for gardening and now she has a list of additions she wants me to include. I am also looking to interface the mimic with more external sensors and tools to help my other projects. Hell, there have been so many attempts over the years to allow affordable, mainstream use of cybernetic implants and wearable enhancements that this tech could have helped with. The mimic's neural processing unit is the one piece of technology we have been missing to bring it all together. Most enhancements available, or that were when we left, required their own processing which limits feedback speed and bandwidth, and dramatically increases the price for anything powerful enough to be truly useful. Look at AnnaChi's arm for example…"

"You know about her arm? It's a regrow, not a prosthetic… Wait, do you have any?"

"Oh, it is easy to notice if you know what to look for. I don't have any myself, but there were a lot of amputees in the groups I used to work with. I was mainly an enthusiast working on wearable or temporary enhancements for fun, not the real stuff. The point is… A regrown arm will take ten or more years before it is equal to the arm it replaced, and many never do without a ton of regular exercise. However, a top-of-the-line prosthetic would have been an order of magnitude better, and on day one—but very few people can afford that kind of replacement limb. Without being super-wealthy, a regrow is the way to go because anything below the top tier is hampered by the processing speeds."

"And you think the mimic changes that, how?"

"Ah, well the mimic is wired directly into the brain

and nervous system, so only a small bit of up-front processing is needed by an external device. That means even a low tier prosthetic's feedback in the body's nervous system can be augmented directly at the brain interface with almost no interruption instead of reprocessing each data-packet on both the upload and download. It *should* be nearly seamless and, even better, you can add non-natural functions in far more efficiently. No additional expensive processing needed—the mimic already takes care of it."

"And that is all available today?"

"Well, no. At least not that I have found on Belrothi, not that I looked too deeply. I doubt we will see any until we are back in the Earth cluster. Everything would need to have been redesigned and reprogramed and that had not happened before we left with the colony. I mean, the mimics only came out in our sector maybe a year before we left, and their precursors were basic in comparison. But it's been thirty-some years back in the Earth cluster... The core world markets have been rampant with lower cost crap-enhancements for centuries, so I imagine they have pushed the concept along quite a bit by now. I mean, that is a lot of potential for advancement since we left."

The core worlds were part of some of the earliest systems to be colonized after humanity left Earth. They were the most advanced and the most corporate-controlled of any systems in human space. They were also among the most overpopulated. Not the kind of system Kasey ever envisioned himself visiting.

"Very interesting. It all sounds incredibly useful. I don't know much about the physical enhancements, but I have used a few job-specific interfaces. The navy has some complex interfaces for their specialized ships, like the Altair. Most of that ship can be controlled with the mimic. But I haven't really looked at using it for other work. Could something be done to assist our prospecting and mining efforts?"

"I am sure it could be, and I am happy to help with it. Just let me know if you have anything specific you need, and I can also talk with Sariyn about it too."

"Thanks, I will give it some thought." Kasey looked down, noticing their plates were empty. "Well, looks like it's time to get back to it. How are the new command chips working out? Can we get some of those bots we gathered working for us?"

"Oh, yes, we are in great shape there. I already worked with Flair to integrate the new SR bots into the Nimbus, and I set aside others for each of the transports, including your own. I saved one for Markus' use as well, but Flair and Darnell are handling a contract for it to stay with Red Rock if he leaves the company."

"Having them will be a comfort."

"Well, if you want comfort, I am planning to get the rest of the butler bots running tomorrow. One for each ship, and twenty or so will end up around Nimbus. We have about ten extra right now. I was going to speak to Darnell about assigning one to each of the Red Rock executive crew members. Time saved is money earned and all that."

"Sounds good to me, I was going to request one, to be honest. I wouldn't be opposed to you taking one for yourself as well. Luxury aside, we can't expect you to keep our bots in top working condition if you are not using them on a day-to-day basis yourself."

"No need, actually. I am working on a multi-function bot that will include cooking and a lot more. It's a work in progress, but I have a stevedore bot cooking for me while the multi-bot is torn apart. Any priorities on what to work on next?"

"Huh, well, I would love to see that when it is finished. Let's see, there are a couple things we could use once we take on passengers in a few weeks. Mundane things like a room service, or assistance when needed to help the passengers or assist the staff would be good to have ready. Anything to help them stay safe and happy while on board. I would like to have some of the security bots we got from that base reprogramed and weapons removed. We need security, but we don't need to harm passengers."

"Were there ideas on how an unarmed bot can enforce security if we get into trouble?"

"Maybe a stunner of some sort? Talk to Mr. Bennett, our new security chief. Those things are too light weight for physically restraining anyone. We need something very non-lethal."

"I'll talk to him. If you want my opinion, I think you should keep some armed and ready. Not for the passengers, but for the protection of the ship itself. I looked at the code these ones had been running—it was highly customized carelessly and full of dangerous loopholes. I can reset them to defaults, which will keep them from attacking anyone unless actually ordered to attack. There are a few very specific cases where they can use weapons in defense of personnel, which in our case would include crew or passengers."

"I will consider it. Bennett has a good team, and he has good references for them all, but I am not sure I want to give him, or his people, access to a small army of weaponized bots just yet. At least not until we know him a lot better."

"Good thinking. Keep in mind I can configure them any way you like. I can even set up an armory of sorts where they can quickly switch to lethal weapons. We could, for example, allow Bennett limited time usage by the authority of the executive staff. Or keep their usage limited to just you if you like. Better to have the ability then to be caught flat footed again."

"All good points. That reminds me, I do have another request, but we have a good month before they will be needed."

"Oh, something interesting I hope?"

"Probably not for you to be honest, but it will help nearly twenty of us once we hit the next planet. I am not sure how familiar you are with the resource prospecting part of our company?"

"Almost not at all, other than I know it exists and that Sariyn is working on that old ship for it. Never dealt with that aspect of colonies before." He shrugged with a smile. "I assume you look at a lot of dirt and see what's in it?"

"Something like that. We use scanning arrays to find high concentrations of valuable materials, like gold. If we are lucky enough to find something, we then try to determine if it would be worth setting up a mining operation in the area. If it is, we process a claim on the land, or purchase it if needed."

"Alright, that seems simple enough. I assume it is one of those jobs that requires some experience to know what to look for."

"Exactly. Being able to read the land and know where the likely areas to scan at is the hardest part. The scanners are very small range, so we only scan the areas that have a high likelihood of having good material."

"That's how you made your wealth, right? If you don't mind me asking."

"It is, but more so luck. I did some research but had no real idea what I was doing. I have learned a bit since then though."

"I bet. So, how can I help?"

"Well, we will be sending out nearly twenty ATVs, mostly the bard version, to search areas we pick out on a planet. Each vehicle will be packed with the scanners and tools needed, but only one crew member. The problem is that, that person could be out in the wilds—alone—for days."

"So, you are looking for a bot model that could go with them and assist?"

"Yes. Assist with the heavy lifting at least. But if they get into trouble, it would be nice if they had help until others can get there."

"Huh, you know…hold on a second," Isaac pulled out a pad and started scrolling through pages of information, "Got it!"

"And what is it that you got?"

"The programming for a bushman bot."

"Bushman?"

"It was a small series of bots we developed for a wilderness survival company who catered to adrenaline junkies. They would rent our bots for their more high-class clientele to handle all the routine camping and porter tasks for them. They can set up a camp, cook simple meals over a fire, and even administer basic first aid."

"Sounds nearly perfect. Do we have what we need to do something similar?"

"Well, maybe. Not sure we have all the parts to allow them all to cook accurately, so maybe send along pre-prepped meals and let them prepare them. But we can reprogram some stevedore bots for most of what we need. Depending on the camp setup your team will use, I should be able to get the bot to do the basics. First aid would be truly basic, but they should be able to stabilize most wounds until help arrives. The stevedores would also be perfect for any heavy lifting needed."

"How about protection? We don't know what creatures will be out on these new planets. Our people will be armed, but I would like something more."

"That's more difficult. The stevedores are just too slow. Depending on the issue, they can shield a person from danger or carry them to safety, but not much else. Let's see, for camp, the bushman bots could deploy a barrier or fence to help protect the area and can monitor the surroundings. We can tie it into the vehicle's sensors to monitor the area as well."

"It's a start anyway."

"Oh! Why not just send one of those security bots along with each vehicle? Between the two bots, they should be as safe as can be."

"Now that's a good idea. They are small, light, and we have a ton of them."

"I'll talk to Yaran about it too. If we need to scare off predatory animals, she will know what we need to add. Noise and lights at least."

Kasey downed the last of his coffee and set the cup on the tray. "Once you have a list of what you feel will work, meet with AnnaChi on it. She has been working on upgrades to the bard for a while now, so she will want to be in on the planning for any additions the vehicle will need to support the bots."

"No problem. I think I have my next month of work cut out for me now." Isaac smiled happily.

"I am always happy to keep my crew busy. Still, ensure you make time for your personal projects. I am not sure I have made it clear, but your lab space is for more than just Red Rock work. It is for your own projects as well. If you check the lab inventory, you will find a list of equipment currently assigned to a space on the upper cargo deck. It is next to your personal cargo area and near the cargo lift the labs are adjoined to. In there, you will find everything you had on your project list so far."

"I am not sure what to say. That is too generous."

"I want to work with people who see this ship as their home, Isaac, not just a place that they work."

"That's a very strange concept, Kasey, but one I think

I can cope with." He smiled warmly.

"Good. I just ask that if your projects have any potentially harmful impact to this ship, the people on it, or our resources, that you run it by Sariyn first. Consider her the ship's science safety officer."

"No problem there. She gave me a tour of her lab next door yesterday. I think we will be having weekly brainstorming sessions. She has some remarkably interesting ideas."

"That she does. Don't forget, as far as supplies go, we also have an extensive storage of salvaged equipment, both onboard Nimbus and in storage back on the Belrothi-Abscond station. Work with Nova to requisition anything you need from it. For anything we don't have, let her know if it is personal or business."

"Thanks, Kasey. Thanks for lunch as well." He glanced at his pad. "Maid bot number five is in the area, shall I have it clean this up?"

"Thank you. Time saved is money earned indeed."

CHAPTER THIRTY-TWO

Kasey stepped out of the Nimbus medical center and shivered involuntarily.

The doctor, nurses and aids they had hired were all nice people, but the center itself needed serious work. The navy had designed it to handle heavy casualties, and worst-case scenarios, not to make civilian crews, families, and passengers feel welcome. The staff had some suggestions and promised to put a list together.

"Everything okay, sir?"

He looked up to find Chief Bennett and April Mayflower peering at him. "Sorry, what?"

Bennett stepped closer. "You came out of medical with a look of anguish. Was someone hurt, sir?"

"Ah. No, just disturbed by the utilitarian feel of that place. It needs a serious change."

The man nodded, but Kasey didn't think he agreed.

"I hope I am not interrupting you two?"

"Not at all. We were just discussing the passenger loading and embarking procedures. Actually, April and I have several questions, if you are free?"

Kasey looked around the large common area and

pointed to a group of empty benches. "Happy to sit and talk. How can I help you two?"

"We were wondering if the passengers would be bringing shuttles or vehicles aboard?"

"Well, yes, I imagine they will. We are going to be landing on the planet to get it all loaded as quickly as possible. As long as they are willing to pay the for the kilograms and it does not endanger the ship, they will be able to bring anything they want."

Kasey noticed both of their frowns deepening as he spoke.

"What am I missing?"

April spoke first. "We need to process everyone and check their cargo. Bennett doesn't have the manpower to control the cargo and people embarking from ground, shuttles, and delivery ships at the same time. He should also have people with the cargo teams."

"And do you have any ideas to solve the problem without stretching out our load time?"

They looked at each other before she spoke again. "We have been working up a system of queues but, without help, it may slow things down. So, we want to recruit as much of the ship's staff as we can to help fill the gaps."

He gave it a few moments thought. "Most of the ship's staff will be busy on the other end of customer services. Anyone willing and not on a shift somewhere already is free to take a shift with you, and I am fine with adding that to the budget for pay. However, most will likely be taking advantage of leave or liberty while in port, so I am not sure how many you will be able to get. The exception to that may be the mining department. I bet they have quite a few that would be willing to make a few extra credits. Talk with Darnell and tell him I sent you."

"That should certainly help, but as you mentioned, it

may not be enough. At least not for this first time. This will be a first for us all, so we are bound to hit snags and issues we didn't think of. I would rather be over-prepared and scale back, than the other way around."

"Put together a number of people you need and then let's see how many volunteers we get. Standard pay for their shifts. But here are a few resources Chief Bennett may not know about yet. We have acquired a number of surplus navy security bots that we plan to convert to be non-lethal. At least a few will be available to you before we make planet fall."

Bennett's eyes widened. "They would certainly make any potential troublemakers think twice, sir. What are they like?"

"Most are simple floaters, lightweight, and quite annoying when we found them. What I do not want is for them to scare our passengers. Keep them used in a professional manner and at a distance unless necessary."

"Do you mind me asking how you got them?"

"Let me just say that one of the jobs the Nimbus will be performing from time to time is legal salvage operations—our first operation was exactly that."

"Understood."

"You should be hearing from Isaac, our resident bot specialist, soon. He wants your opinions on how to use the security bots with non-lethal weapons and still be able to defend the ship properly. Please give it serious thought. The other resource you have here is Nova. She is a highly advanced AI, far more than any you have encountered before. She can monitor a lot for you if you ask her. Get used to utilizing her abilities."

"Thank you, sir, I will. That gives us a lot to think about."

"Good. If I can help with anything else," he stood to go, "let Nova know and we can set something up."

* * *

Dropping into a plush reclining chair, Kasey let out a growl of relief.

"Long day?" AnnaChi appeared with a couple beers.

"I feel exhausted. I think it took me three hours to get from one side of the ship to the other. Everyone wants something."

"Let me guess, you feel like you need to help every one of them or you risk this whole operation failing?"

"Yea, yea, exactly that. I never thought there would be so much involved."

"I hope you realize there are only around a hundred crew. Just wait till there are five or six hundred passengers as well."

"Is that supposed to help?"

"As a reality check, maybe."

"How are you coping with this all?"

She held up her bottle. "Beer and avoidance. Your mistake was going into the public areas. People are still working on gaining their footing here; it's best to let them figure that out with their department heads for now. Let them do their jobs first, and then, maybe, get involved. Until then, travel the ship using the hangar or cargo decks. Hell, use the tween decks if you need to— just stay out of the way."

"And if this all fails due to something I missed?"

"Then the department leads didn't do their jobs, not you. And let Nova help identify issues they don't see. We can't do it all."

"There is just so much riding on this working," he complained.

"Look, you can get involved as much as you want, but if you don't limit yourself, you will burn out. That won't help anyone."

"You are right, of course."

"Well, duh."

He took a long pull from the bottle. "Has Isaac talked to you yet?"

"Your mind back on work already? You are hopeless…"

"Kinda, but I will try to make this the last piece of work I do today."

"Haven't talked to him, no."

"Do you think Sariyn will be ready with all four mobile bases?"

"Not sure what that has to do with Isaac, but yea, she should be ready."

"I assume you will have enough bards to fill them?"

"I will have twelve bards, and four other ATV without jump jets."

"Oh. I should have checked the inventory closer, I thought we had a lot more bards than that."

"Oh, we do. What we don't have are drivers who can handle them all. Four of them need a lot more training than we had time for. I am a bit shaky on half the others as well, but I trust them to not kill themselves if they do use them. They all need more experience. Sariyn will be assigning search areas based on skill, so they should be fine."

"Well then, speaking of safety, I asked Isaac to come up with a bot design that can both assist the prospectors and help keep them safe."

She finished her beer and nicked Kasey's as a replacement before he could react. "Well, I don't completely hate the idea. What was his solution?"

"Some sort of wilderness survival bot's personality meshed with a stevedore. We can have him improve it over time, but for this run it should provide our people some muscle, utility, and basic medical help if needed. I am sure Isaac will have more ideas."

"They won't help much if they are attacked by something. I would like to train them all on weapon safety, but I doubt we have time for everyone to be competent, although I noticed several have experience already. So maybe something simple."

"Right, that's about what he said, too. So, he suggested sending security bots along with each prospector as well."

"Ah. So, the issue is, how to fit two bots into the already loaded-down bards?"

"Right. I think you already removed the back seating for storage, and we should keep a passenger seat, even if we are sending people out alone."

"Damn, okay... I will see what we can do. Maybe some sort of attachment pod for them to ride as topside luggage. We have some larger bard models now, but I would like to keep them back from this first expedition. I have other plans for them."

He got up and headed for the kitchen, taking her empty bottle with him "I am looking forward to seeing what you come up with, dear."

CHAPTER THIRTY-THREE

He had thought long and hard about what it would be like to bring the Nimbus into one of the Federation core systems, but this was not it.

Flair turned to him from her command chair. "How do you want to handle this, Kasey?"

"I don't want to handle it at all. Get Darnell up here."

"Captain," A young looking man at the communications station interrupted, "sorry, sirs, but we have thirty-five requests for docking permission. Thirty-six now. What should I tell them?"

Kasey looked at the main screen. A small, makeshift station of sorts had been assembled, and appeared to be covered in ships. The moment the Nimbus transited out of the gate, the ships began taking off from the station on an intercept course.

Only a few minutes earlier, the Nimbus had entered one of the many gates in a system that had long ago been mined-out and abandoned. The system was now home to the Earth Prime cluster's main Trade Nexus. Currently the trade system was off-limits and was swarming with navy contractors building a massive station and seeding the system with the newer and smaller class-F gates as quickly as they could be built. Each gate was ten to twenty hours away from the station at Nimbus' top speed, and no gate was within a standard day's travel of another gate. Spread out for security.

The once empty system would soon be a major trade hub of the entire Federation. And, apparently, it was no secret to the residents of the Apophis system the Nimbus was now entering.

Kasey looked over his shoulder, hoping Darnell would appear. "Thank them for the inquiry and ask what their intention is."

"These are merchants, sir. Most of their comms are flagged with the local trade guild headers."

"You're saying this is, what, a traveling bazaar?"

"Um, I believe so, sir. However, I think they are here to make claims in the Trade Nexus stations as soon as the navy allows the outgoing gate to be opened."

"Okay, well, what do they want with us?"

"One moment, sir."

Kasey stood and walked to the station as he waited.

"Sir, they want to set up a market aboard Nimbus for the crew."

"We don't have that kind of docking capacity."

"Actually," Flair replied, "we do. Standard navy hangars are equipped with deployable docks, capable of docking five additional ships externally."

Kasey swallowed his annoyance. "How many can we accommodate in total, Captain Flair?"

"Potentially, forty-four externally between the eight deployable docks and our topside pads. But we can do better than that—most of those ships can link up to each other just as they were on that improvised station."

"And where are all these docks stored? I haven't seen anything like that on the ship."

"With all due respect, sir," Flair smiled, "next time

you are in a hangar, look up. They are collapsed into part of the ceiling structure between the support beams."

"Fine… But I am not convinced we need this delay. And why can't we just dock to that strange station?"

"We could, however it would mean stopping the ship completely, and by the time we did that we would pass it by and need to come back. As it is, I believe we can slow a bit and let them board without losing much time off our planned course."

Before Kasey could respond, Darnell burst onto the bridge and stopped short as he took in the main screen. "Traders or pirates?"

"The former, we believe."

"We having a fair? That would sure help!"

"What do you mean, it would help? Help what?"

"Crew is anxious about taking on passengers for the first time. We may need to find ways to keep them busy on empty runs. They have too much time to think, if ya know what I mean. Are these traders coming aboard? It would be a good break in their routine."

Kasey nodded and turned to Flair. "Have the cargo teams clear as many of the hangars as we can for the deployable docks. Move our ships topside and lock them down. Then get Bennett to set up and monitor routes for the traders to go directly to the Promenade area. I do not want them anywhere else on my ship, and no one goes into the garden."

"Yes, sir."

"Darnell, we do have an activities director, correct?"

"That we do! She works cargo presently."

"Get her on this ASAP. Pull whoever we have to get the Promenade ready with food, refreshments, and have the department heads put together schedules that allow everyone some time off over the next twelve hours."

Kasey looked around the bridge. "Anything else we need, people?"

"Credits!" the comm officer exclaimed before he could stop himself. "Sorry, sir."

Kasey looked thoughtfully at Darnell. "Pay is dispersed when we dock at a port, correct?"

"True, but give me a minute." He grinned a few seconds later. "The first passenger deposits are already rolling in through the local network. Nearly all our larger rooms are booked with hefty deposits as well. We won't have full cargo payments until we deliver, but we are safe to pay the crew a bit early for this leg of the journey."

"Done and done. How many ships are heading to meet us now?"

"Sixty-eight, sir."

"Flair, if you would make a general announcement for the ship? I will go wake up AnnaChi and convince her that this is a good thing."

* * *

The trade bazaar went far better than Kasey had expected. There had been something for everyone. It was also the first time that anyone from the Farpoint colony on Trias had been able to talk to people from the Earth Prime cluster since leaving. A lot had changed, but people had not. Everyone found reasons to complain or speculate on everything from the new gate systems to rumors of pirates and Cassian attacks.

Yet, no matter what the topic, conversations always seemed to come back to the Pattern. The universal truth that every single civilization that has ever crept up and started to spread populations throughout the galaxy has ceased to exist. Proven by hundreds of years of collected evidence and confirmed by every alien race still in existence. It was fact. It was also a topic that seemed to end most conversations as they realized what the gate system could mean for humanity.

Kasey was glad when the bazaar finally ended, and the last ship was on a course back to the small station to wait for access to the Trade Nexus gate. He promised to contact the traders again on the way back so they could do it all again when their passengers were onboard.

It was those passengers Kasey was worried about now. It took nearly a week to reach the Apophis system's fifth planet of Kamose, then land Nimbus at the pickup area. Everything was going fine until Darnell announced that there were far more passengers waiting than they had taken reservations for. What was supposed to be less than five hundred was now well over a thousand.

He looked around the conference room Darnell had summoned him to. It was unadorned by anything except a pile of data pads and the remains of coffee from some forgotten meeting.

"You need to get someone to clean this room once in a while."

"It was clean three hours and four meetings ago. You are the fifth."

"Alright, so, do we even have enough room for the extra passengers?"

"Well, our smallest rooms are apartment sized and go upwards from there, so there is plenty of space, but not enough actual rooms."

"Before we overthink this, can we even handle the extra tonnage of cargo if we take these extra colonists?"

"Lucky for you, cargo was my last meeting. The current estimate will put us quite overweight for an efficient takeoff. We have the cargo space but not the mass allowance to take off without expending far more propellent than planned. The bigger problem is the effect on the nearby population—we would be outside the safe noise limit for one thing. We certainly would not be welcome back anytime soon. We will leave all the solid ballasts in orbit before we land and dump the liquid ballasts as we take on cargo, but that still puts us over our mass limit. The crew are looking at other options. So far, they believe we can handle it if we fill and send our other ships to orbit separate from Nimbus."

"We could always take her up to orbit early once we are close to our limit and run loads up the old-fashioned way. Maybe get some locals to run loads to save time."

Darnell stared at him for a ten count. "We didn't consider that."

"It will slow everything down drastically, but it gets the job done. We can add more n-mats for future trips to eliminate the risk. How many rooms are we short?"

"About a hundred."

"We must have a bunch of crew quarter rooms open still?"

"Yes, and that will give us another fifty rooms in principle, but twenty of those rooms are ground level in the garden. That will hamper the restricted access to the gardens. Yaran and Isaac are dead-set against uncontrolled access to the garden, and are planning scheduled visits and limits for passengers and crew alike."

"I agree with that restriction. These are our larger rooms, right?"

"Yea, the executive suites, second largest rooms we have on the ship, but the smallest we have available on the Promenade Deck."

"How are our crew getting along with each other? Groups of friends forming?"

"Why does that… You want to bunk them?"

"Only if they want to be. The executive suites have, what, four bedrooms?"

"Five, if you count the office, the quad suites have four as well."

"If we have anyone in the equivalent star-side rooms, see if they want a change of view to the garden. Then, offer upgrades to anyone in quads to take an executive suite, garden side. As soon as those moves are official, offer the whole crew permanent discounts for bunking up with friends of three or four."

"We will lose a good chunk of credits and short the housing department."

"We never planned to make money off our crew's lodging, unless they want to pay for extra space. Bunking is no different. It is cheaper for them and helps us. This allows them better accommodations and to split the cost. Crew is happier and we get the space to take on more paying customers. We can worry about the housing budget if it becomes an issue, but sounds like it just needs to be rethought out. Besides, I assume we increased the room prices for the new potential passengers?"

"By a boatload. Supply, demand, and all that goodness. And I don't disagree with any of that. Your business model is changing the old standards, you know. But the paperwork has not caught up yet. I will work with Flair to see that it does."

"Well, then it sounds like we have a plan."

"Okay, and if we are still short on space?"

"See if the perspective passengers want to share rooms. Failing that, we have several of the royal suites, like yours, reserved in officer country. I would rather not have them used by passengers. I would entertain a temporary crew move, but I would prefer not. I want them kept for our higher-ranking permanent crew."

"Understood. Speaking of… What about Isaac?"

"What about him?"

"He has an executive suite in the garden."

"And?"

"There is one royal suite still reserved in the garden. His own experimental vegetable patch from Lithose is practically within sight of it."

"Oh, is it?"

"You know it is, you planned it that way."

"Did I? I am sure AnnaChi will tell you I don't think that far ahead…"

Darnell glared but said nothing.

"Fine! Yes, that room will be going to him, but it was mostly Yaran's idea. His current place is packed full with his equipment."

"So then, when were you planning to move him? He is in a room we could use."

"I was saving it in case I needed some encouragement for him to stay. We can find another robotics tech if we have to, but Isaac thinks on a different level than we do. We need him."

"Kasey, he is the happiest person on the whole damn ship. You didn't just pull him out of hell, you gave him a reason for being, not to mention all the toys he could ask for. If he decides to leave this ship, it will be because he has no other choice and no amount of encouragement from us will change that."

Kasey sat back in the seat and nodded slowly. "Okay, you're right. Go ahead and get him moved, with my compliments."

"In that case, go back to doing whatever it is that you do. I have another meeting before I can go eat."

Kasey stood. "Get to it then, but send me the final numbers when you have them."

"Yes, sir. Now go."

CHAPTER THIRTY-FOUR

Kasey stared out of the viewing deck attached to his quarters and watched the starscape as they closed in on the small but growing nexus of gates forming in the Trias System.

The slow crawl out of the Apophis system's gravity well to the trade gate had been grueling. Nimbus may have some serious thrusters, but they were not quite a match for the overload of mass they had taken aboard. The navy still had the gate access closed off, which annoyed the merchants, but they were happy enough to hold another bazaar for the Nimbus' passengers.

Hundreds of passengers had crowded the viewing ports around the ship to watch the transition through the gate and into the Trade Nexus. It had been anticlimactic for Kasey, but for the passengers the small change in the field of stars was astonishing. Other than the stars, nothing but more space waited for their viewing pleasure on the other side. Even the station at the center of the Trade Nexus was too far away to be seen. Still, it was the new experience of gate travel that seemed to appease most people.

A day of sailing through the nearly empty Trade Nexus took them through another gate and into the Trias System. Home for the crew and registered headquarters of Red Rock Enterprises. Kasey remembered his first view of the system, the deep red nebula to one side and blue stars twinkling throughout the skies. He was glad to be back in what he considered his home system. The space he and many others had fought to keep safe for humanity.

Another day's travel through Trias found them at a newly activated gate leading to the Sequoia system. Yet another of the Farpoint colonies Fran had been busy connecting into the ever-growing Trias Nexus.

Unlike most, the Sequoia colony had been thriving when Fran arrived in the Pathfinder. But their gates, as well as the galaxy-class starship that had brought them there, had not fared so well. The colonists had abandoned the starship and fled the Cassian, gathering on a single massive planet they had named Redwood.

Redwood was nearly six times the Earth-mass standard and only one-point-three standard gravity. Escaping the planet's influence would take a lot more power but was not impossible. Kasey's bigger worry was landing. Even if local ships were able to help unload from orbit, it would take several days of transporting mass to the surface before he dared take the Nimbus down to the large planet.

Now, passengers again gathered around every view port and display to catch the first glimpse of their new home. Their future. The star field didn't change much from the Trias System, but the faces of the people watching certainly did.

He didn't remember so many looks of joy and relief when he had first seen Trias. He could not remember if he had even paid much attention to others back then. He turned away from the displays that showed him his passengers. It had been different for him, he realized. He had never fit comfortably into situations like that. Situations where everyone seemed to know what they were doing. He had felt like such a fraud back then.

Had been a fraud, he corrected himself. He had barely afforded a place on the Abscond, the galaxy-class star-cruiser that had brought them all there. He had not even been a citizen of the Terrantine Federation a few days prior entering stasis for the trip. All he had was an idea and the need to flee the painful memories he had thought to be behind him. So much had changed since then.

"Kasey," Nova interrupted, "Flair is requesting your presence on the bridge. AnnaChi and Darnell are already there."

"Tell them I will be along in a minute."

"Sorry, change of plans, they now want you at shuttle bay S3.

"What's going on Nova?"

"The navy commander stationed here wants to speak with us—off comms."

"I knew this trip was going too easy. I am on my way."

* * *

Kasey was the last to arrive. "Welcome aboard, Commander."

"Commander Kareed. I assume you are Kasey Robinson?"

Kasey nodded and shook his outstretched hand. "What can we do for you, Commander Kareed?"

"I am hoping to convince you to turn your ship around. There has been an increase in Cassian activity over the last week. I feel your ship and passengers may be in greater danger than command had anticipated." He glanced briefly at Flair and back to Kasey.

"When did you last hear from Admiral Francis?"

"Eleven days ago. We have ships at the next two paired gates waiting to make contact once he opens up the other end. So far, nothing."

"Any actual contacts yet, or just sightings?"

"Just spread-out sightings. All in the outer system so far, but they could be anywhere."

"Any large groups?"

"Pairs, mostly. It is my opinion they are baiting us into an ambush."

"But you think they will attack the Nimbus?"

"Your ship is a target of opportunity for them that they are unlikely to ignore."

Kasey looked at Flair. "Care to weigh in, Captain?"

She stepped a bit closer and considered Commander Kareed thoughtfully. "You have stealth patrols between here and planet Redwood?"

"Yes, sir. Making the circuit every other day. Six-day journey, we have three patrols out now, sir."

"I am retired from the service. Any sign of trouble from the patrols?"

"None yet, sir."

"Drop the sir. I am no longer in the service. Call me Flair or Captain here."

"Yes, uh, Captain Flair."

"You have contacted command in the admiral's absence?"

"Yes. They are forming a fleet to scour this system of the enemy. Should be here within a week or so."

"Any word from the residents of Redwood to indicate the Cassian bother them on the planet, or have subverted any groups there?"

"No. It is believed they or their ships can't handle the

gravity well. But that is not a known fact."

Flair nodded and turned to Kasey. "Boss, I feel we should be safe heading to the planet. We can handle any small groups of Cassian we run into on the way, and I am positive Commander Kareed will send along a few escorts. We can make the run down-well in five days with our current load, which should out pace curious Cassian ships."

Kasey considered. "We need a few days to unload some mass in orbit before we enter the atmosphere."

"If we circle the planet to bleed off speed and place some of our solid-mass ballasts in orbit, we should be fine to land. We have over one hundred thousand tons of solid-iron ballasts that are meant to be deployed and retrieved for just this kind of reason. We will be thrusting hard and will need a large landing zone clear of any people. Unlike Earth cluster planets, there is plenty of room—we can handle this."

Kasey looked around. Darnell looked like he agreed with Flair, and AnnaChi just shrugged and smiled.

"What kind of escort can you provide, Commander?"

The man sighed, but seemed to yield. "I have two free patrols on downtime—four light cruisers—that would be willing. You are sure this ship can defend itself some?"

"I can attest for its abilities commander. She is not an easy target."

"Fine. How many souls do you have on board?"

"About thirteen hundred."

"Send me the ship's manifest and start moving immediately. No reason to give the Cassian time to get ahead of you. My ships will catch up within the hour."

Flair nodded. "Thank you, Commander. We have two internal and four external docking bays available if they need them."

"Thanks, but they won't be needed. Better that they

stay stealthed and moving. Do you have landing coordinates?"

"We do, but as I mentioned we will be changing them for a larger area."

"Fine. Try not to dally. Sooner you are in the atmosphere, the safer you will be."

* * *

For all the worry, the trip had been uneventful. Kasey's thoughts wandered back to the few sensor anomalies they had picked up, but shrugged them off. They never identified the causes, and it didn't matter now that they were safely on the planet.

Nearly half the cubes of iron that served as the Nimbus' solid ballasts we now orbiting the world far above, waiting to be retrieved when they left the planet. Like so many parts of Nimbus, it was a feature that really needed more testing while they were not fleeing a potential hoard of Cassian. While that was not really the case, the crew had treated it as if they truly were being chased. Flair had called it a test of the ship's readiness. He was not sure he agreed, but he knew Flair had far more experience testing large ships than he ever would.

The planet Redwood itself was as amazing as it was massive. The original colony of nearly a million people were spread out on less than one percent of the world's surface. With only twenty percent of the surface covered in water, it left a lot of room for the colony to grow. The residents were happy to welcome the new colonists Kasey had brought. They had even lined up temporary homes for them all to use while they picked out and built more permanent locations.

Kasey was surprised to find they had already

identified several n-mats mines and had been mining and using it in smaller applications for quite a while. Most of their local navy had been wiped out defending the system and never had a chance to interfere or use it for gate activation. When Fran had shown up, they had purchased the colony's entire stock. It was nowhere near the amount that Kasey's Belrothi mine produced, but it was still significantly more than any other system that had been identified so far.

The n-mats were front and center on his mind as he entered the Nimbus business center's largest conference room. A score of extra chairs were lined up for additional seating. The main table was packed with senior crew and others directly involved with the prospecting teams. Only two seats remained at the head of the table, waiting for him and AnnaChi.

The room slowly hushed as they settled in.

Kasey looked around at all the faces. "Welcome, everyone. I am happy to see we have a lot of additional volunteers. As you all know, we are going to be prospecting in hopes of finding good and profitable land that we can claim and mine. We knew this planet would likely be a good source of resources, but what we didn't anticipate was that the residents would have already found several different sources of n-mats here as well."

He gave them a few seconds to think about the revelation. "That is why we have the additional crew here today. This planet has the potential of having far more n-mats than the residents have found so far. Likely more than they believe could ever exist."

A woman Kasey recognized as part of the engineering crew looked like she was about to ask a question but stopped herself.

Kasey nodded at her. "Did you have a question? This meeting is the absolute best time to ask."

"Oh. Yes, sir. It is just that there are already large

mining companies who have been working on this planet for a few years now. Wouldn't they know better than us what was possible?"

"It's a fair question. A lot of the short history of n-mats is not common knowledge just yet. While we would like to keep it that way, the facts are already leaking out. Everyone in this room has signed a nondisclosure agreement for that very reason. Correct, Darnell?"

"Yes, sir. All signed and sealed."

"Good. What everyone here does not know is that Darnell here was the first one to ever find n-mats. We even checked the timeline here on Redwood and he still holds that title by several months. Sariyn and I were with him at the time. That was on Lithose, before it was destroyed. The second source of n-mats was found on Belrothi, by AnnaChi and me. That particular mine is what makes this entire ship possible. Sariyn, can you display my mine please?"

The center of the table projected a detailed cutaway of the n-mats mine's main cavern.

"This is my n-mats mine on Belrothi. The n-mats in this mine are pure pools of mercury. This cavern alone contains many times more n-mats than every single one of the other mines found added together."

He waited again until he saw understanding on several faces, then nodded to Sariyn to remove the image.

He sat back. "We have learned a lot more since then, and have been to several new worlds, helping them locate several more sources of n-mats. We know where to look and what to look for when we get there. We even learned a bit about why. What we didn't have was a planet with enough potential to replicate what we found on Belrothi."

Darnell spoke up. "We have something else the

colonist miners here don't have. They don't have the time or freedom to look for the best ground. Colonies need the mining companies to produce the resources they need to run the colony's economy. With no way of going back to Federation space for more supplies, they had to mine everything they needed here, and quickly. They don't need n-mats, they need resources. Many of you are well aware of this fact."

"Right," Kasey continued, "the miners on this world are mining the first decent ground they were able to find. They did bring extra miners along, just like we did on Trias, but that only bought them a little extra time to search for n-mats while they also looked for the colony's needs. We do not have that limitation."

"However, we are still on a time limit," Darnell pointed out.

"Correct, but we are going to be searching for one specific type of n-mats. Mercury. For starters, we will track down every trace of cinnabar on this planet in hopes of finding mercury pools like on Belrothi. We have a few other ideas as well."

"But we have a deadline?" someone asked.

"We do. We have other jobs for the Nimbus already lined up. We are also in a bit of a race with the residents of Redwood. They will be putting the facts together about just how much n-mats the Nimbus uses to land its bulk on a planet. They will combine that with the number of Farpoint colonies that have been connected to active gates, and add in how much the navy paid them for their own supply. All that, and they should quickly realize that there are far bigger scores to be had than what they have found so far. We are ahead of the curve—let's stay there as long as we can."

"To be clear," Darnell added, "they do not know about the mercury. Nor will they anytime soon, unless someone in this room lets it slip. If you feel the need to make a quick credit on this information, I suggest you talk with a lawyer first, or trust me when I tell you that it will not be worth it. However, and this is important, if you find us an actionable claim, we will pay you a percentage of the profits that claim generates—either from our mining operations or the sale of that claim."

Kasey nodded and smiled. "How all of that will work will be explained shortly in Sariyn's presentation. Over the next few hours, you will learn everything we know on the topic from her. Tomorrow, we go to work." He leaned in to draw their attention. "Tomorrow we go *treasure* hunting!"

CHAPTER THIRTY-FIVE

AnnaChi dropped an armload of wood next to the firepit and directed the bushman bot to do the same with an even larger load.

She took a moment to scratch Molly's head ridges as the atoss settled on top of the woodpile. "How many is that now?"

Kasey looked up from the data pad. "Nineteen sites searched. All duds—so far anyway."

"How much longer are you going to let them search?"

Kasey moved his chair back from the fire's heat and let Orange adjust herself as he thought about her question. "We should have been on our way out of this system by now, huh?"

"I am not saying that."

"But you *are* thinking it."

She tossed a log on the fire and settled into the chair beside him. "Depends. I like the views here," she smiled as Molly pushed herself into a spot between Orange and her, "and the company here too. I could stay longer, but I am not sure it is good for the business to continue this snipe hunt."

"Snipe hunt?" Orange lifted her head and peered into the darkness around the camp, then peered at Kasey before resting her head on his leg again.

"Mythical beast. I think…" She shrugged.

"Well, we are not hunting something that doesn't exist, Belrothi proved this beast exists."

"Sure, but that doesn't prove it exists on Redwood."

He sighed. "How many potential sites did we prospect on Belrothi while waiting for Nimbus to be built?"

"Maybe eight or nine, depending on how you count that last trip. Normal cinnabar and mercury deposits."

"Yep. Not a single n-mats hit. Yet, we know it is absolutely possible that we could have found n-mats at any of them. We are in the same boat here, just at the other end of the scale."

"It's perhaps a much larger scale than we thought. We could spend months before we find the one that exists. You know, there was a time not so long ago that you wanted nothing to do with n-mats?"

"Not exactly, I wanted nothing to do with the government. The n-mats painted a damn big target on my back. Doesn't matter any longer, we are in the deep end with them now and the n-mats are no longer a variable that keeps them away from us."

"So, it's just another valuable resource to be mined now?"

"Yes, it will be a good opportunity for the business if it pans out. If not, we still located a few good claims. Are you hungry?"

He hoped she would change the subject and let it drop, but she just stared into the fire for several minutes. The critters around their camp grew loud as darkness overcame the valley below them. She finally broke the silence.

"There is more to it, right? Why do you want the n-mats?"

"Would you believe I want another ship?"

"No. And if you were to lie to me, I would leave you here."

"Fair enough. The truth is, I am still trying to distance us from the government."

"That seems to be the opposite of what you are doing if you stay in the n-mats business. I am serious about leaving you here, you know?"

"I know you are, dear. But, so am I." He shrugged "I am just taking a different track this time."

"They will be all over us if you find another n-mats mine like the first one."

"I don't think so, at least not in the long term. Tell me, why do they care so much about the n-mats?"

"Gate travel and control, I suppose. Power mostly, regardless of Fran's beliefs."

"All true, but I am thinking more basic. Like fuel, money, or people to run their ships, the Federation needs n-mats right now."

"Well of course they need it…"

"So, what if they didn't need it so much?"

"Well, they would need more than just another mine to saturate their needs, if that is what you mean."

"True. But what do you expect to happen once we show them another is possible?"

She sat back at that. "They will… I don't know, push us to find even more?"

"They will push *everyone* to find more. If it were you, how would you do that?" He gave her a searching look.

"Maybe hire away what crew I could from Red Rock and use their combined knowledgebase to create other teams like ours."

"Ten days ago, we trained maybe thirty-five people

on almost everything we know. How long do you think they will keep our secrets?"

"We needed to tell them how to…"

"Did we?"

"Well, I guess we could have compartmentalized a lot of it into smaller chunks of info. They all didn't really need to know everything, did they?"

"They didn't even need to know we were hunting n-mats… They could have just found the cinnabar rich areas and let us do the actual investigations. But none of that matters if we don't prove another mine like the one on Belrothi exists."

"But the company…"

"How does it hurt the company? If we find another mine of that level, we instantly double Red Rock's worth, several employees will get extraordinarily rich, everyone will get a decent payday, everyone is happy. If we don't, well, we still found some decent claims on this trip. The silver claim alone will be worth leaving a crew here for. Darnell is already picking out miners for that operation. The real loss would be that we could have found some really great claims if we had been looking for them, but we spent the time on an exotic mercury hunt instead."

"You are saying it would be a huge, short-term win if this pays off, but in the long term the n-mats will lose value?"

"It was always going to decrease in value eventually, this makes us a little more responsible for how quickly that happens. It will always be worth a lot, just not the highly inflated price it is at now. Regardless, it gives the business a massive boost that we can use to grow our business while we have time."

"And we just trained our future competition?"

"Right. Which will help take the Federation's eyes off us—hopefully sooner rather than later."

"Well, at least you thought this out... Dammit, you really do make things more complicated than necessary sometimes."

He laughed at that. "Just as much as my paranoia makes me. My crazy is not scaring you away, is it?"

"Not even a little bit. Besides, your paranoia is not exactly unfounded."

Kasey just nodded and stared at the hot coals of the fire. No, it was not paranoia. The memory of losing his parents to a planetary bombardment by the government he now worked so closely with was always fresh in his thoughts, even though it happened decades ago. Supposedly the small colony had been working to create their own life extension project. True or not, it wasn't right, and it wasn't fair—but it was an example of what was possible.

AnnaChi reached over and took his hand in hers, breaking his contemplations. "So, how long do we stay at this search? Can we afford to stay longer?"

"We do have a week buffer built into the schedule, but we can always comp the next passengers some services on board if they are upset. How about we give it a few more days and then head out?"

"In that case, maybe we can use the time to have a few more cannons added to the Nimbus in the unused hardpoints? I was browsing Redwood's net last night and the people here have developed some far-reaching accelerator cannons that can supposedly reach the orbit of Redwood. They are individually slower firing and have lighter projectiles, but come in quad-configurations that more than make up for it."

"Tested in space?"

"They claim to be, and in space—with that added velocity—the smaller projectiles would hit hard. It is a new design, but the company claims to have been installing them on ships for the last two months. Planet-side, they have had a lot installed around the colonized areas for nearly a year; it is part of their protection net from the Cassian. They haven't had to use them, but they obviously trust them to work."

"Interesting. What's the cost look like?"

She tossed another branch onto the fire and they watched the fountain of sparks before she responded. "Well, they want eight to ten times what we would pay for a standard cannon."

"That's a hell of a jump in creds…"

"True, but it could be worth having the extra reach and more projectiles from a single hardpoint. They only have two available for purchase, or I would suggest upgrading all our existing cannons."

"So, what's the downside, other than the cost?"

"Heat builds up way faster than I would like. Hard to avoid with four coils running in the same area. Our standard cannons can fire nonstop. The quads make them look slow as hell, but they can't maintain the speed for long. We can mitigate the heat a bit with slower firing or by using them in bursts. They suggest bursts, and I agree that for a one-on-one fight that is the way to go. Putting a lot more ordinance on a target quicker usually equals a faster kill. In a longer battle with multiple targets, or using them to knockdown missiles, we would be better off slowing down and finding a middle ground between heat and firing. Still, I think we would end up ahead of our current cannon's rate-of-fire, and the extra reach alone would be worth having a few installed."

"May be good to fill out remaining hardpoints here anyway, if there really are active Cassian out there. Commander Kareed seemed more than a little worried."

"The fleet arrived yesterday. Should be covered in that area."

"Still, let's convince Flair and Darnell to free up

some budget, then get the work started. Also, see what that company does with the old cannons they have replaced. Maybe we can get a discount on a few of them too. Would be good to have some spares."

She lit up at that and nodded. "Okay, well, now I am hungry."

"Hold that thought. Sariyn is requesting a call, let me loop you in."

"Maybe some good news at last."

"Go ahead Jumping Spider, AnnaChi and I are all ears and hoping for some good news."

"Wish I had better news for ya, boss. The teams are doing a good job, but the good stuff is hiding from us still."

"Well, what do you want to do now? Pack it up?"

"No. I want to move everyone to a fault line thirty-five thousand kilometers southward, but we need more time."

"That is quite a distance! How much time do you need?"

"At least four days, but I would prefer a lot more. It is one of the biggest and widest fault lines on the planet. Old, worn-down mountains that seem stable from the data we have now. No claims anywhere close to the area, so we feel it is unexplored."

"Just orbital surveys?"

"That's all we had before now, but Jate took the Carnelian down there for a few low pass scans. We just finished going over the data with Darnell's team and it looks promising."

"Is that our best option? What about changing our goals and spending the time looking for more traditional mining opportunities? It is what you spent the last month training your team for."

She responded quicker than Kasey expected. "No way. Going after the n-mats here only wastes a few days' time. Low risk, low cost, and the potential payoff is off the charts. If I were you, I would delay our next job or leave my team here to continue."

"Sounds like you have already thought this out quite a bit."

"No need, the data doesn't lie. The percentages are with us on this one. I can lay it all out for you if you like."

AnnaChi and Kasey both laughed. "No need. We came to the same conclusion already, but it was nice to hear your unbiased opinion. We are extending the trip a few days, but we will do a full week only if necessary."

"Glad to hear it," he could hear the relief in Sariyn's voice, "because I already ordered the crews to be at the pickup zones in the morning, and I have Markus and Jate loading supplies for the run down to our new basecamp."

"Well then, anything you need from us?"

"The extra time is enough. Will you be joining us?"

"Yes, we will bring the Cintian down in the morning. Just assign us an area and we will get to work."

"No problem there, we have plenty of high priority spots to check out and not nearly enough people."

"Just a suggestion, but your core team has gotten their feet wet now, maybe it's time to toss them into the deep end and see if they can swim. Cover a wider area and identify your best people."

She took her time responding. "You may be right. I worry about them being without backup, and the colonists really have no idea what the indigenous life is out that far. The bots have really been a help, though. I have any medical procedures or abnormal incidents the bots note reported automatically to me. There have been several minor scrapes and bruises, but the crew doesn't even bother to report them with the bots there to assist. But if we want to cover all the major hot spots, we need to spread out a lot more, and that will create several blackout periods."

"Well, the safety decisions for your team are up to you. We won't have more than a week, so make it count, but no amount of credits are worth losing a life. Before the next trip, let's work out a way to maintain constant contact with all teams. Maybe put a satellite in orbit, whatever works."

"Thanks, I think. I will send you the location I need you two at shortly, and will check in with you tomorrow once all teams are settled in."

"We will see you there."

He disconnected the call and frowned in thought.

"What's wrong?" she asked.

"Would you trust Nova to fly Cintian while you slept?"

"You want to head out now?"

Both Orange and Molly shot Kasey serious wide-eyed looks he immediately understood. "After hunting, I mean, after we eat." He looked at the atoss. "You two, go hunt now, or its ship food for you both." They were gone into the night before he finished speaking.

AnnaChi laughed at him. "They giving you orders now?"

"They are certainly trying to," he shook his head to clear it, "but, yes, I want to head out tonight so we can spend our time exploring in the morning. If Nova flies for us, we can save some fuel and travel suborbital overnight. Otherwise, we burn for orbit in the morning and drop back in southward in a few hours."

"Nova, can you handle overnighting us to the general area mentioned?"

"Of course. This matrix is fully integrated into the Cintian's systems. There are two notable weather systems impeding a direct flight, which I will avoid if you concur, however, we will still arrive before breakfast."

Kasey looked confused. "We would normally just fly well above any weather systems, why bother to avoid them?"

"While you are correct, if an emergency situation were to occur, I would not want to land us in the path of potentially dangerous weather systems. Another option would be an orbital flight plan, but it would be an inefficient use of propellant."

"Good reasoning, Nova. AnnaChi?"

"Fine by me, thank you Nova." She poked Kasey. "Your turn to cook tonight honey, what are we having?"

He laughed, "Shish kebabs!"

"What is a shish kebab?"

"It's apparently a popular camping meal. Red-meats with veggies cooked over the fire on a stick."

"Get to it then. I have some orders to place."

CHAPTER THIRTY-SIX

Kasey propped his feet up as he watched AnnaChi direct a demolition bot along the ridge.

This was her third attempt to open up an entrance to the cave system enough to allow the bots to collect samples of cinnabar for Sariyn's testing. The lava-tubes in the current area never reached the surface, but a few came close. Even if she could open one up, they wouldn't be able to explore it themselves. Instead, Sariyn had supplied them with small bots that would map and bring back small samples of every unique material they could find.

He thought they would be better off calling in a drill rig, but she always preferred to blow things up if there was a choice. That was fine by him. Everything did not always need to be done the best way, she would say, it was better to enjoy the job than to execute it perfectly. He mostly agreed, but knew he had trouble following that advice.

He had always felt something deep down pushing him to do what he believed was expected of him. What he was *supposed* to be doing... Even when he was not sure exactly what that was. It was not rational, and he knew it. He also knew the pressure had served him well lately. AnnaChi was more of an unstoppable force of nature. He wondered if that was why they meshed so well together. At least from his side of it, he agreed with her way of viewing the world more than his own, but he couldn't change who he was. She was his balance.

She waved as she moved the bot back from the site. He waved back and put his fingers in his ears. The crump of the explosions was felt before he heard it. As the wind blew away the cloud of dust, he sat up straight and moved his own bard closer before joining her.

"You increased the load on that last blast?"

"Doubled it," she confirmed. "I know we need to move on to the next site soon."

She surveyed the wall of stone and pointed at a fist sized recess too high to see clearly. "What do we have up there?"

She considered it, then walked back to her own bard and pulled out a blue case. She extracted a small bot that looked like a cross between a spider and a scorpion. She looked at it a few seconds to complete the connection to her mimic implant, then tossed it lightly onto the rock face.

She shared the feed with him as she directed it to the recess.

He watched as the bot examined and then slipped into a small hole leading back into the hillside.

As he watched it scurry deeper, other feeds were added.

"Signal relays," AnnaChi mumbled as she activated another small bot.

The tube did not widen appreciably for nearly one-hundred meters where it branched off. The bots followed the wider tube for another fifty meters before it emptied out into a small chamber half submerged in water.

Kasey took control of one of the bots and explored the small cave. Helictite covered most of the surfaces. He targeted a few of the more interesting formations to be sampled and explored every tributary tube for a few meters. Nothing remarkable.

He switched to a feed from a bot AnnaChi had taken under water. "Anything of interest?"

"Mostly sludge, but there is a half-meter tube down here. We have enough bots to relay a signal maybe fifty more meters through water."

"Go for it. Sariyn is due to be here in about four hours for a sample pickup. We may as well gather as much as we can."

"Okay, release control of your bot, I am going to need it."

Once released, he blinked away the feeds. Something moved at the edge of his vision that sent a chill down his spine and a wave of heat to his face. His body seemed frozen as he reached for his pistol, turning as he did. Everything moved too slow except for the creature stalking closer to AnnaChi.

The creature was black as night. Even in the midday sun, few features of the creature were noticeable. Had it not been moving, he would have thought it to be a shadow.

Kasey was still raising the pistol as the creature stopped and shifted its weight, as if readying to pounce on prey. Knowing he would not be able to bring the gun up in time, he pulled the trigger repeatedly, blasted chunks of rock and dirt into the creature's path.

It sprang back, facing Kasey for a moment before a flash of blue slammed into its side. Molly disengaged from it a moment later, landing at AnnaChi's feet and hissing at the retreating creature.

Kasey heard another commotion behind him and spun to see Orange perched on top of an even larger creature that was no longer moving.

He spun around again as AnnaChi fired off several shots from her own pistol at something high above them looking down from the hillside. The two security bots floated down from the bards and added to her firepower.

"Nova," Kasey called out, "we need the Cintian here for an emergency dust-off ASAP!"

"Confirmed. E.T.A is four minutes twelve seconds."

"Move back to the bards," AnnaChi shouted as she fired a few shots towards the group of bushes the first one had disappeared into.

"They don't seem overly afraid of us, do they?"

"Maybe they are used to more deadly competition than we are."

"That's a scary thought. Shit! Sariyn spread the crew thin thanks to my suggestion…"

"Nova, are you in contact with Sariyn?"

"No, she is currently out of range. The Redwood communications network does not reach this far out."

"Okay, belay our dust-off, the bards will keep us safe for now. Head to Sariyn's last known location and give her the details of what happened here. Her priority is to ensure the crew's safety."

"Flight plan altered. I suggest attempting an audible deterrent. I am sending several frequency packages that the bard vehicles should be able to emulate and should be safe for humans and atoss."

When they reached the bards, AnnaChi holstered her pistol and pulled a plasma rifle from the vehicle. "Get in and move yours next to mine, then set up the sound tests. I will keep them at bay."

"No need to kill them, we could just leave. A few jet hops and we will be plenty far away."

"Not planning to. I am thinking we riled them up with the blasting and they came to investigate. They could just be protecting their territory."

"So why stay?"

She stepped up onto a foothold and climbed to the top of her bard. "We need to test Nova's audible deterrent idea. If it works, we may be able to continue prospecting and protect our crews. Besides, Sariyn will be pissed if we leave her little bots and samples behind."

By the time Nova brought the Cintian back, Kasey had narrowed down a working frequency that the shadow cats could not tolerate. With the frequency broadcasting from the two security bots as well as the bards, they were able to collect the gear and samples, and make their way back to the Cintian's landing site.

"No other attacks reported," Nova announced as they entered the bridge.

AnnaChi took the pilot seat and got them back in the air. "When we are in range, transmit what we did with the bots. If she doubles the teams up, they should have plenty of coverage to stay safe. May be best to limit any blasting in case that is what set them off."

"Confirmed."

"Thank you, Nova," Kasey said, "that was good thinking with the frequencies."

"Of course, I am here to help."

They were just over an hour out when Jumping Spider and Lodestar popped up over the horizon.

"Nova, was Lodestar with Sariyn when you were there earlier?"

"No. The only ships in range at the time were the Carnelian and Jumping Spider.

"Hail the Lodestar."

"Connected."

"Cintian to Lodestar. Respond please."

"Kasey, this is Knoc. Sorry, I needed a fast ship. Captain Flair is requesting you and AnnaChi's presence at your earliest convenience. Jate has been recalled as well. He is currently picking up three of the ex-sailors we have in the field here."

"What is going on with the Nimbus, Knoc?"

"Nimbus is fine, sir. The fleet is the problem. They were sweeping the system for Cassian when something appeared and took out the gates."

"What do you mean, which gates?"

"All four of them, sir. Navy and civilian gates are junked. We think a few of ours escaped through the outgoing gates before they were taken out."

"How the hell could something make it to the gates under the fleet's nose?"

"Sending coordinates to land. We need to talk in person."

The three ships landed in a rocky field, and they all gathered in the Cintian's small conference room.

AnnaChi was ready to burst. "So what the hell took out the gates?"

"I need to connect to your display table," Knoc said.

"Permission granted, get on with it."

He flicked a file towards the tabletop and waved it open. "This is a Cassian mothership."

A vaguely spherical object appeared, covered in a cocoon of red and orange waves crisscrossing over its surface. Every so often, something on the surface would spike, causing a ripple to expand across it.

Kasey spoke up. "That is not how I imagined a Cassian mothership would look. Is that water?"

"Some sort of charged plasma field. The ripple you saw was a normal orb entering or leaving it. Flair confirmed it indeed is a Cassian mothership, but she has no record of them having plasma wrapped around them. From what we can tell, it is both a weapon and a shield."

"I get the shield part," AnnaChi frowned, "but a weapon?"

Knoc reached out and expanded the view, showing a gate. "This was taken from one of the fleet scout ships. It is just about to fire on that gate."

"How big is that ship? My perception is skewed," Kasey asked.

"The mothership is over three kilometers in diameter, but the plasma shield is another half kilometer out from its hull. The gate is several hundred kilometers away from it and about half a kilometer wide." He held his hand up to forestall more questions and just pointed at the image.

The waves of plasma around the mothership started to swirl, creating a vortex that grew hundreds of meters outward as it spun faster, reaching towards the gate. The vortex stopped stretching for several seconds, then a wave of energy burst from the orb, climbing up the vortex and shooting out into space towards the gate. The mass of plasma twisted and expanded as it covered the distance. Kasey thought perhaps it would somehow miss or spread too thin to cause any damage but knew there was no hope.

As the mass drew close, bolts of jagged power poured from the plasma, impacting the gate in several places. The jutting defense platforms were the first to go—never firing a shot. Everywhere it touched seemed to melt and then crack. A moment later, the darkness of the gate winked out, replaced by stars.

Kasey looked at AnnaChi, whose eyes were wide, then turned back to Knoc. "Where is the fleet now? Can they stop that thing?"

He shrugged sadly. "What is left are in full retreat, coming here if they can make it. They tried to attack that thing, but that plasma shield obliterated everything they threw at it. Including a few disabled ships that couldn't get out of its way." He looked away for a moment. "Over half our fleet is gone… The mothership picked off the bigger ships with that weapon, then pumped out waves of their orb ships to harass the survivors."

"Can they make it to Redwood?"

"That's the only bit of good news. The mothership is slow, so our people can stay out of range. The smaller orbs are their bigger problem, but they have been able to deal with them so far. We don't think the mothership has more than a few hundred left unless it is holding back reserves."

AnnaChi stood up. "I still don't see how a ship like that got past the fleet. They should have been able to call in the action-ready fleets from the Gemini Nexus before something that size got anywhere near that close."

Knoc nodded his head several times then shrugged. "We think it jumped directly to the incoming gate and destroyed it first."

"They can jump, like the Pathfinder?"

"We really don't know, but we won't have all the information until that fleet arrives."

"Why the secrecy about the mothership? Why did we land here to talk about it?"

"Orders, but they are good ones. The populace here knows the gates were taken out, but not how. They lived without the gate for years, so once they are over the knee-jerk panic, they will relax a bit."

AnnaChi sat back down. "So we release a bit at a time, and the panic is controlled and manageable?"

"Less we, and more the government here, but yes. Honestly, the scarier part is that we don't know what that weapon will do to a planet."

Everyone looked at Sariyn.

"What?"

AnnaChi smiled at her. "They are waiting for you to give an opinion. Is the planet doomed?"

"Hell, I don't know. Too many variables. I mean, there is a good chance that the atmosphere will disburse the effect too much to do any real damage and the planet's electromagnetic field will block or absorb most of it anyway. But…"

"But what?"

"Well, if it can't catch the navy ships and the Cassian know they are heading here to Redwood for safety, then why would it still be heading this way?"

"Unless there is no safety," Kasey answered.

They all sat there looking at each other for several minutes. Eventually, all eyes turned to Kasey.

Here it was, he thought. The decision that would cost everyone's lives. Would the crew be safe on the Nimbus? No, but would they be safe with the residents? Unlikely. Orange moved to him and rested her head on his lap. He looked at her and rubbed her head ridges. Maybe there was another option.

CHAPTER THIRTY-SEVEN

Kasey looked up at AnnaChi, then Knoc, and finally turned towards Sariyn. "I have a new job for you, Sariyn."

"Sure, whatever I can do, I will."

"What's the biggest lava-tube you have located down here? Any big enough for ships?"

"Uh. Maybe. Not sure about your big Altair, but most others could theoretically fit, I think. It would be quite a task to actually move them inside but... What do you have in mind?"

"I need you to make one or two of them into a temporary home. Keep our crew out of sight and safe for a while. I will send you the Carnelian and Markus' Andrius with supplies and crew."

"Wait! Just hold up a minute, what about you and the Nimbus?"

"The Nimbus won't be able to hide, so we will find a place and leave it. Maybe it will survive whatever is coming if we abandon it."

"And you?"

"I believe some of us will join up with the navy and

Redwood forces and see how we can help."

"Fine. I will make this work. Send some construction or builder bots too, we will need to make some support structures if we have time. Between the three ships we should have shelter and atmosphere if we need to seal ourselves in, but we will need bio-stock for the synthesizers if we are down there for any length of time. We could make do with a bio-generator to reconstitute what we can. It could buy us another month, maybe, before we need to salvage material for it from the land— assuming we can sneak out eventually. One of the medium fabricators would be a real help too, but again, we will need stock for it, so maybe not a priority."

"We will pack in whatever we can and have them make two trips if time allows. We don't want the Cassian to know where you are."

"Hmm, one sec... Okay, two trips should be safe enough, but they will have to stick to the timetables I will send you so they stay below the line of sight. The thicker atmosphere here may help a bit, but for all we know they are already in orbit watching us. If that is the case, we must plan to be sealed in. Dammit, have Darnell bring the smallest digger-dredge and kit for an underground hard rock mining operation, and plenty of water pumps."

"You really think it will come to that?"

"I have to assume they will know where we are and are planning some sort of orbital bombardment to take us out. Maybe they will leave after that, who knows... May as well bring over everything we need to dig out just in case. Besides, best case scenario I can see right now is that this world survives enough after a bombardment to still support life. We may as well have what we need to rebuild and carry on for a long time."

"Maybe we should just bring the Nimbus here and dump everything we can into one of the cave systems?"

"Far too risky. It's possible that they may not see smaller ships moving around, but it is hard to miss Nimbus, even with a low mass profile. No time to run the numbers, but my gut is telling me it is not worth the chance."

"Fine, but if we are doing two trips, we will load all five ships and bring all we can in the first load. Second load will just be Carnelian and Andrius, which will stay here with you. You need to find room for all the crew, seven boatloads of supplies, and three ships. Probably some shuttles too."

"Eight loads. I will send back the Spider for the second run too."

"Good idea. Put the stevedores from the prospecting bards to work. We need to land and offload without making it look like a landing zone."

"I need to get to it then." She stood slowly and took a deep breath. "Oh, were you able to test Nova's idea with the creatures and sound?"

"Right!" Kasey got up too. "It worked well. We had the security bots and bards broadcasting while we collected our samples and supplies. You can take it all with you, including the bards, if you have room. Let's get everything moved over to Jumping Spider now. Knoc, grab anything from the Lodestar that will help, emergency supplies, mining equipment, food from the galley, whatever we can fit in the Spider."

Kasey followed them to the Cintian's main bay and noticed Sariyn's hand shaking uncontrollably. He pulled her aside and let the other go ahead to get things ready.

He pointed at her hand. "You are one of the strongest people I know, you will be fine."

"I... I am honestly not sure this will work, Kasey. There are a million variables flying through my head that I don't know how to solve for, yet."

"You won't be alone. Darnell, Isaac, Yaran, and

others will be here to help, along with the crew, but you need to be in charge of this."

"Darnell would be far better…"

"No, this is not business. This is survival and knowhow. You have the knowhow, and you can work with Isaac and the others for the survival parts you can't figure out. I don't trust anyone more than you to make this all work. Take a breath, you can do this."

She took a breath and looked at her hands. They still shook, but much less than before. "I will do my best."

"I have no doubt." He waved her towards the bay. "Have you eaten today?"

"I don't remember… We have been running around between sites since Nova brought the warning about the cats earlier today."

"First thing's first. You can't help others without helping yourself. Get some food into you and your pilot and anyone else onboard the spider. We will load what we can into your midship bay while you take care of that."

The midship bay was too small for bards and supplies, so they stripped them of useful bots and gear. They still managed to load a respectable amount of supplies from both ships in a short amount of time.

Far too quickly, they all said their goodbyes and were back in the air.

* * *

When they landed Cintian onto the Nimbus, it was already a beehive of activity. Knoc had pushed the faster Lodestar and shared the plan hours before.

Darnell met Kasey at the docking bay. "Flair wants you in the bridge ready room ASAP, but I need to know… Is Sariyn okay? This is a lot for her to take on."

"She is handling it, but she will need your support. You are going with the first load and staying there to assist her. Are you okay with her in charge of this?"

"Good. Yes, she *should* be in charge. She excels at fast-paced projects. Problem solving is her bread and butter… But she will be freaking out some in the first days."

"She was a bit nervous, but I talked to her about it. You know her better than I do, but I think she will be okay. She sent a dozen messages with helpful points and supply lists before we were out of range, so I am sure she is working the issues out."

"Well, yes, I think she is good then. Still, I will be happy to get down there to help."

"About that, we need the extra bays for the Spider loaded with her lab. At least the n-mats research we took from Lithose and her data cores. She didn't ask for them, but she should have them, or copies at least."

"Consider it done."

AnnaChi joined them and they headed to the bridge at a quick pace.

Kasey walked in and had no trouble reading the room. Everyone was angry, stressed, and wanted blood. Two uniformed men he didn't recognize were also present. They appeared to be from Redwood's defense forces.

"Where are the navy ships now?" he asked the room before anyone could speak.

Flair cleared her throat. "Earlier today they removed personnel and abandoned the slower ships in the fleet. The orbs can't touch them now, and at their current rate they should be here in under three days. They self-destructed two of the abandoned ships near the plasma field, but other than causing a few ripples, it didn't make a difference. Orbs attacked and destroyed the other discarded ships soon after that."

"How long till the mothership reaches orbit?"

"Maybe five days."

"Anyone able to determine if that weapon will be able to reach the surface of Redwood?"

"We don't know. We were hoping for Sariyn's input, but Knoc just explained her overall reasoning."

"Right, weapon or not, they have a plan to attack us. She assumes a bombardment. Have the Cassian or their motherships attacked planets before?"

Flair glanced around the room. "I am not sure we have the clearance to talk about that here."

"I will leave you to make that call, but everyone here is going to find out soon enough what they are capable of anyway."

She nodded and took a deep breath, but Darnell answered instead.

"Damn right they have! Not sure about motherships, but the smaller ones have dive-bombed at least one planet before, dropping their missiles, or whatever the hell they are, all the way down till they impacted the planet itself. Seen it with my own eyes, and don't you doubt it!"

Flair looked at him disapprovingly, then nodded. "They targeted infrastructure, right?"

"Sure did. The planet was abandoned for a time afterwards. People wouldn't have survived there for long if we hadn't been able to push the Cassian back and resettle elsewhere."

"It's their standard procedure. If they cannot trick people into killing each other, they take away the people's ability to survive." She shivered. "There have been worlds that slowly died out over a period of years."

"So," Kasey said, "they don't like to do the killing themselves?"

"Perhaps. We have never seen any ground troops

from them. Tricks, precision strikes, and time are their main weapons. Well, and whatever that mothership has been using, but that is new."

"Strange tactics from a species that seems to hate us so much," Kasey mused.

She looked at him as if trying to make a decision. "I don't know, and the Federation doesn't know for sure either, but the Sargani have told us that it is not hate they feel from them."

"What else would cause them to act like this? Do they enjoy it?"

"No. While I don't put a lot of faith in Sargani for facts or information, they claim it is more of a feeling of purpose."

"Like religion?"

"Maybe, but more like a job. And before we all get carried away deciding what that may mean, if it is even true, the only facts we know that matter right now are that they are coming, and we need to prepare."

"Fine." Kasey looked at the two Redwood men. "Sorry, we haven't been introduced. This is AnnaChi Acosza and I am Kasey Robinson. You are?"

The closest man stood and offered a hand. "Todd Dermott, Commander of the RDF, the Redwood Defense Fleet. Lieutenant Brand here coordinates our ground-based forces."

"What are the plans for the civilians? They can't stay in the cities and towns."

"We have a few hidden bases and several shelters scattered around the countryside. We had expected to be attacked ever since they took out our stations, but they never came. We dug in—waiting and preparing for attacks that never came. Well, until now I suppose."

"What if they take out the major infrastructure? Can you recover?"

"Still figuring that out. Until this conversation, we

assumed they would land troops and take over our resources. I set plans in motion to enable us to fight a guerrilla war. We need to change tactics with this new information."

"Right, take what you need to rebuild critical infrastructure, and scatter resources away from obvious factories and warehouses."

The man nodded and looked hard at Kasey. "Will your ships help us defend, if it comes to it?"

Kasey chewed his lip for a moment. "If it would help, then yes. But right now this ship is just a big target for that mothership's main weapon."

The man nodded, then looked at Flair. "We will be in touch with our new plans later tonight. My people are looking into possible ways to attack that thing, but I am not holding out much hope after seeing this. If your people have a good idea, we will support you."

"Thank you, Commander Dermott."

"Call me Todd. Protocol is not going to help the planning stages of this, and frankly, I am well aware you can pull rank on me if you want to. I just want my people to survive."

Kasey slumped into a chair as the men left. "Well people, do we have any other options?"

CHAPTER THIRTY-EIGHT

Jate raised his head. "Not saying we should, but we could run."

"Where would we go? No gates here anymore, and Nimbus doesn't have a galaxy-class star drive," Kasey asked.

"Not saying we even leave the planet, but we can keep moving out of danger zones if need be. They may get us eventually, but it would mean keeping this ship alive longer. Better than letting them drop a rock on it from orbit."

Flair smiled at the frowns around the room. "It's an option, and a card in our deck. We need every idea if we are to put together a winning hand. What else?"

"Any near-planet asteroids around that we can redirect at that ship?" AnnaChi asked.

"The RDF looked into that this morning. Closest they feel would be useful is a month out. I don't know that we can delay this attack for an hour, let alone a month, and unless the Cassian are going to stand still for us, they can just move out of the way."

"Do we know if the navy had any luck with charged

cannon slugs?"

"They tried. Hell, they tried everything, but reported no appreciable difference regardless of polarity used."

"Lasers?" Kasey asked. "They should be able to penetrate the plasma field, right?"

"They have no weaponized laser or particle cannons in the fleet other than a few point defenses, and most of them use antimatter slugs now which just gets neutralized by the plasma field. The energy release from antimatter caused some micro ripples, but it is a matter of scale. Like throwing pebbles into a pond."

After several minutes of silence, Kasey stood. "Keep thinking, but we only have six hours left to load the supply ships and make the window. Sariyn is going to need everything we can get to her to keep our people safe. Assume their location will be bombarded, and assume they will be stuck underground for a very long time. Think about what you would need or want if you were stuck down there, and get it loaded. Get to it!"

The room soon emptied out, but Kasey stopped Darnell before he could leave.

"She mentioned you should pack her a small digger-dredge, lots of pumps, and an underground hard rock mining kit, but I think she will need more. She will need to process material into something she can use in a medium fabricator, even if it is just a small-scale iron smelter. Everything will be underground and cut off from fresh air, so plenty of filters and scrubbers. We will cook up environmental packages, but the less pollutants that they need to deal with, the better."

"You really think we will be down there a long time?"

Kasey nodded. "Honestly, I think you will need to go as deep as you can and stay as long as you can. The main lava-tube she is planning to use is nearly a hundred and twenty meters wide and about half as high, but she will need to move to deeper tubes if we can find them. She has already verified deeper ones exist. The ships will fit in, but not far enough to survive a real bombardment. Actually, the Jumping Spider may be able to fit far enough, but the people need to go further and take whatever they need to dig back out."

"Damn. I know I am a miner and all that, but I am not sure I like the thought of being underground in this situation."

"Safer than being topside. Besides, with the right supplies, it should be just like riding in a ship with a really thick hull."

"Somehow, I am not comforted," he mumbled before he left.

Kasey gently closed the door behind him. "Nova?"

"I am here Kasey."

"The matrix we re-installed for you in Altair—it was designed to be safely moved if needed again, correct?"

"Correct."

"Good. Quietly take control of a few stevedores and move that matrix into one of the Jumping Spider's deployable cargo bays and seal it up tight. If there is any room left in that bay, pull a few generators from storage, along with anything needed to set up your matrix for use. Add plenty of interface pads, a mix of bots and extra cores. Actually, get two pods, I will send you a list of items for the second one, but fill them both."

"Kasey…"

"Will there be enough room for the matrix?"

"Yes. But Kasey, I can't. You will need me with you in Altair."

"I won't need you in Altair, Nova."

"Sir, I proved my usefulness when the Nimbus was commandeered. I need to be there in case you need…"

"Nova… I will not be flying the Altair. Can you do this for me?"

Several seconds passed. A small eternity for an advanced AI such as Nova. "I will comply."

* * *

Kasey watched the Cintian take off from what they were now calling Sariyn's Outpost. Edging forward, he made ready to land the Altair to take her place in the unloading zone.

Sariyn ran out to meet him as the stevedores began unloading "I hear you are still planning to abandon Nimbus?"

Nearly everyone he talked to was appalled at the idea of deserting the carrier ship, "Perhaps. I don't see as we have any other options. It is just too big of a target. We are only keeping the other ships in case we need to take out orb ships in low orbit."

"It is true then—no one has a real defense plan?"

"Not yet, no. They are doing their best, but I don't think there is an easy way out of this one."

She pulled out a pad and handed it to him. "I have noted down everything I could think of that could aid in some way. I don't know if it will help…"

"Thanks. Look, the Spider will be bringing back a couple containers that are sealed and need to be kept safe. Take them deep in the tubes if you have time."

"What's in them?"

"Nothing you will need any time soon, but your codes can open them if needed. Mostly the n-mats research, backups, and cores we took from Lithose. Some extra system equipment too. Oh, and a few sentimental things that AnnaChi wouldn't want to lose."

"AnnaChi? Sentimental?"

"You have no idea… Anyway, anything you need in

the final loads?"

"The rest of the people. I was expecting another fifty by now, unless you have them on board?"

"They should have been here on the first ships. Should be only eighteen missing, six of whom will be onboard the three ships that will stay here with the final shipments."

"Did they maybe go with the Redwood people?"

"I'll find out. They have freedom to do as they wish. Anyone in particular you are missing that you need here?"

"Hard to tell. Some of the main medical staff is missing, but I hear Isaac sent us a dedicated medical bot. Anything it or my people can't handle can go into a trauma pod. But actual people would help a lot."

"Did Isaac arrive then? He was not looking forward to being stuck on a planet again, but I thought I convinced him he was needed more here."

"Yes, and I am thankful he is here. I don't think he would have come if Yaran and Cerine weren't here." She smiled deliberately.

"Oh? Are Isaac and Yaran an item?"

She laughed. "Not yet. They both have been so busy, I don't think they have realized how good a pair they make." Her face fell. "They will be busy here too."

"You know, it is entirely possible the Cassian will ignore you, even if they do notice this outpost. Flair seems to think they prefer to destroy infrastructure and resources, then let the people die off over time on their own."

"I hope so, I really do. But we can't plan for that. I have Darnell drilling electrical traps into every tributary over the first kilometer. Steel rods should direct the energy into the ground and bleed off some power from the mothership's weapon. We will cave-in the entrance as well as the backend of the trapped tube. One way or another, we will need to dig ourselves out."

"The ships?" he asked.

"They are likely forfeit if a plasma blast hits this area, no matter what we do. The Spider is small enough, so we will have her back past our barriers, but not much further. If we have time, we will send back the stevedores to strip Carnelian and Andrius of anything useful."

"And if you end up needing those ships?"

"We will keep good notes and rebuild them if we can, I suppose. Plenty of engineers and bots here to put them back together. But honestly, if we do get to that point, we will need the facilities and systems on the ships a lot more than the ships themselves. I have a team ready to lock down and secure all ship systems we can't quickly remove."

"This is why you are in charge here. You think of everything. I take it Darnell brought Jasper?"

She nodded. "And Yaran has the other young atoss. I was surprised the adults weren't with them."

"Orange and Molly wouldn't leave the Nimbus. We had planned to leave them here with you, but they somehow *knew* and hid from us. They are too damn smart for their own good."

"For staying with you? Hardly…" She laughed. "But, what about you? What will you, the navy, and remaining defense forces do once all the people are safe?"

"Not really sure to be honest. Let them chase us around for a while and see if they get bored."

She considered him for a long moment. "Well, I hope we all see each other again. We have a company to build, after all."

"True! Speaking of which, we unloaded all the heavy mining equipment in the field where the Nimbus is currently sitting. The remaining shuttles are about a kilometer north of that and spread out."

"Where will the Nimbus end up?"

He paused before replying, hating to lie to her. "Well, unless we find a use for her, we thought maybe we would dump her in one of the lakes. Haven't really thought that far ahead yet."

"Really?" She looked at him. "Huh, well, water is a good idea, should dissipate a plasma strike a good bit. I would be concerned about pressures on the Nimbus, not sure it was built to go too deep. Watch the lower cargo bay if the ship is fully submerged, if it holds, the rest has a chance."

"We will batten down the hatches and all that, but no promises she won't be wet if you go looking for her someday."

She sighed and fought to keep tears from her eyes. "Keep that girl of yours safe, will ya? I was starting to get used to having another badass woman around."

He gave her a farewell hug. "I will do my best, but you know as well as I do that she won't run and hide."

She laughed and wiped her eyes. "That's my worry for both of you fools. Now get out of here—but get your ass safely back here once you can. We will be waiting!"

CHAPTER THIRTY-NINE

The surviving navy ships had landed in the fields around the Nimbus during the night.

Sipping his morning coffee, Kasey joined AnnaChi leaning on their balcony, overlooking the mist-covered countryside. The landscape was dotted with clusters of the giant trees he had been told the planet was named for. He would miss these views. Gripping the rail, he wondered if the ship would survive the next few days. She had scarcely begun to travel the star-ways. "One more time…"

"What's that, hon?"

"Nothing, just thinking it's looking like rain today. All those sailors are going to get wet." He pointed to the rows of ships surrounding Nimbus.

"It's their own fault, they were told we have clean beds they could have used last night."

"Nova, is someone making sure those ships are all fully fueled?"

"Affirmative. Jate is preparing a tanker from our supply now."

"Good. How are our water ballasts?"

"Currently twenty-seven percent utilized and rising. Shall I activate the remaining air wells?"

"Yes, I want them to be topped off by end of the day."

AnnaChi gave him an odd look, but he ignored it.

"I guess we better go talk with Flair. I hear we have some stowaways to deal with."

There were only two other people on the bridge, but Flair waved him and AnnaChi into her ready room.

"How are they?" Kasey asked.

"About as you would expect. The highest-ranking officer left is a lieutenant who immediately passed fleet command to me. That effectively drafts me back into the navy."

"You moving your flag, Captain?"

"Not for at least another day, sir. Seriously, there is not much we can do... If there was, you would be drafted as well. Any attack we make is just going to cost more lives. I suggest we scatter and make them follow us. If the orbs follow, we can coordinate hits. Keep them busy as long as we can and wait them out."

"And the RDF?"

"They are planning three groups of ships to do mostly the same thing. They have three evacuated towns they are planning to mock-defend. Once the mothership destroys the towns, the RDF will flee and try to keep their attention away from the hidden bunkers."

"Not a bad plan I suppose," AnnaChi commented as she brewed another coffee. "So, what about these stowaways? I understand them missing the first trip to Sariyn's Outpost, but they all missed the second one too?"

"That's why I brought you in here." She took a seat at her desk. "Apparently, someone had been telling the crew that they should think of the Nimbus as their home."

"Well, of course," defended Kasey, "that was the whole point of this ship. But the situation has changed now…"

"I am not blaming you, but these people already survived the chaos of the Trias System, and several are refugees from Lithose, too. They have no desire to leave another home behind without a fight."

"I thought I made it clear that Nimbus is not going to fight. Too big a target…"

Both women just looked at him sternly and waited.

"What?"

AnnaChi set her coffee cup down. "They don't believe you. Flair and I don't believe you. And you sure as hell do not believe what you are saying, either. Your tone gives you away."

Kasey looked at AnnaChi for a full minute before slumping into one of the padded seats around a small table. He looked at Flair and gestured at the seat across from him. "Come out from your desk and have a seat."

AnnaChi raised an eyebrow as Flair came out and sat, keeping her poised posture as she did so. She waved at him to continue.

He took a deep breath then cut straight to it, "I do not believe we will have a choice but to use this ship."

"Well, of course we have a choice!" she stammered. "What I can't understand is why *you* think we don't have one."

"Because of *your* husband."

"What the hell does Francis have to do with any of this? This is not the time to start believing in his theories."

"It's not that. A few ships made it out before the gates were destroyed, right? Do you honestly think he is not going to jump the Pathfinder here for you the moment he hears what happened?"

She rocked back as if hit. "That ship would never be

able to stand up to that mothership alone…"

"But would he still try?"

"I don't know, command may not allow him to. That ship is too valuable…"

"Would he listen to that command? Pathfinder's particle cannon may be able to penetrate that shield. If his people come to the same conclusion, will he take the risk and try, regardless of orders?"

"He might… I mean, he may not even wait for orders to be issued. It is not just about me, I signed up for this and he damn well knows it, but you are here too… Alright, fine, I agree that he will at least jump in and try something, but I doubt the beams will make much of a difference against that monstrosity before he is targeted and destroyed."

"I agree," AnnaChi added slowly, "but Kasey knows that too," she moved her gaze to him, "right?"

"What I think," Kasey leaned forward, "is that Flair is not going to let her husband fight a losing battle alone. And that this ship is the biggest damn rock available."

"I wouldn't steal your ship, Kasey!"

"Of course not—but we wouldn't let you go alone, either."

The three looked at each other for several minutes.

Eventually, AnnaChi set her empty cup down with a loud clatter. "So, then what?"

He looked at them. "Take another look at Sariyn's notes. Decide what you would do if we had no other choice—because we don't. I have some thoughts, but I want your unbiased perspectives. We can compare ideas later. Maybe over lunch?"

"And the crew? What the hell do we tell them?"

"Gather everyone at the garden's pond. We can talk to them. Who's the ringleader?"

"Bennett, apparently, at least he was speaking for them."

"Fine. I'll be there in fifteen minutes." He stood up. "I'll be in my quarters till then."

Kasey walked through their quarters, gathering his thoughts, as AnnaChi prepared her personal weapons and armor. She claimed she thought better with a weapon in hand. Well, it didn't hurt to be prepared, he thought, but there was little chance of needing the weapons. The armor, on the other hand, could possibly help. Flight suits and helmets are fine for a small fighting ship, but in this case... Seeing as how the only probable way to survive a battle with the mothership would be to retreat to the planet in a ship that was most likely going to be damaged in some way. Well then, some hard-plated armor could certainly save a life.

His mimic implant flashed the time into his vision. It was time, and he still had no idea what he was going to say to the stowaways.

AnnaChi nudged him as he hesitated at the entrance to the gardens. "It will be fine."

He took a deep breath, then started out along the garden path. Orange and Molly practically tackled them a moment later, before assuming perches on the couple's backs, saurian heads resting on their shoulders.

Kasey couldn't help but smile. "You two really need to go planet-side for a while. This ship is not going to be safe for you much longer."

Orange suddenly tightened her grip. Tail, four claws, and neck all contracting at once.

"Ouch, relax..." Kasey caught his breath as Orange stretched out her long neck to look him in the eyes. Her eyes widened, pupils dilating as she stared. He stopped moving, suddenly unable to think. He was prey, trapped in a predator's gaze. Something seemed to sift across his mind, both burning and soothing sensations as thoughts that were not his own pushed into his consciousness.

With a snap, the spell was broken, yet the feelings

remained.

Kasey blinked a few times and considered his friend. Fear, love, trust, bravery, as well as a few emotions he had no way to describe, had been pushed at him. Pushed into his mind. There had been hints of ability from the atoss before, but never in such an obvious, forceful manner. He felt like he should be shocked or unnerved by the experience, yet it had left him feeling quite calm.

He looked over at AnnaChi, who was regarding Molly. "I don't think they are going to let us go without them."

"Uh," she turned her head around to look at him, "yea—Molly has just made that quite clear. I am not sure I like it, but it is their choice."

He reached up and scratched Orange's neck. "Well, maybe we will have better luck convincing the crew."

CHAPTER FORTY

The crew were spread into assorted groups of conversation when Kasey and AnnaChi walked up.

Kasey took a moment to prop himself up on one of the false rocks that were placed around the area for people to sit and enjoy the nearby pond and gardens. Somewhat nervously, the crew gathered into a tight semi-circle around him.

He looked around at the faces, many he knew by sight if not by name, yet all were his crew. He had planned to try to convince them to leave the Nimbus and, failing that, he expected to outright order them off the ship. Instead, he sighed inwardly and smiled at them. Maybe it was the interaction with Orange, or maybe it was the look of determination he could see on every one of their faces, but he knew they all needed to make their own choices too.

"So," he started, "why are we all still here? The Nimbus will not be a safe place in the coming days."

No one answered at first, and several people shuffled around a bit. He was about to ask the question again when a lady he recognized from the housekeeping department asked, "Why are you still here, sir?"

Kasey nodded. "Someone needs to move Nimbus to a safer location. We were thinking about putting her in a deep river or lake…"

Bennett stepped forward. "With all due respect, sir, we do not believe that is what you will do. We think you are going to fight that monstrosity heading our way."

Kasey sighed again, this time loudly. "Let's say that is somehow true. This ship is not going to survive a battle with that mothership. It is seriously unlikely that anyone onboard would survive either. You all know that, right? I do not want any of you to throw your lives away for this ship. Ships can be replaced, you cannot."

"We are not going to watch them take another world away from us!" a man in the back shouted.

"Nimbus is our home!" came another.

A nurse in front said, "We know who you are…"

Bennett held his head high. "We are here to support you, sir."

Kasey stared at the nurse until the others quieted. "What did you say?" he asked her.

She shook her head, refusing to respond.

Kasey looked around and fixed his frown on Bennett.

"Mr. Bennett… What did she mean?"

The proud man withered under Kasey's gaze, suddenly looking very small. "We, um… Well, ya see, sir, we all received a file when we were recruited."

"From Red Rock?"

"No, sir. Anonymous sender…"

He looked at AnnaChi, who shrugged back with a bewildered look.

"What the hell was in this file that makes you all want to toss your life away for a damn ship?"

Bennett looked back at the small crowd for a moment, apparently looking for support. "You, sir. Both of you."

"And what in the verse did it say about us?"

"It didn't tell us, it showed us what you both did. You killed the first Cassian after they attacked you near Lithose shortly after the fall, and how you started the warning that went out to everyone, even though few of us believed it at the time. Then you went back and hunted them again, bringing back proof to Belrothi that they existed. We saw you both fight in the gate war. We saw your ship, the Cintian—which we know is the same ship in our docking bays—deliver the crucial package through the outgoing gate, allowing the incoming gate to be opened and save us all. It also made it clear that you two were directly involved in activating both gates somehow." He paused for a moment to catch his breath. "Look, there was more, a lot more, of you two taking on ships bigger than your own and winning those battles. Not to mention protecting the Trias gates with your own lives. Dammit, sirs, we are not going to sit in a cave and let you do it again—not on your own!"

"That, all of it, was pure luck and circumstance." He had no doubt this had Fran's fingers all over it.

"Sorry, but it wasn't, sir." The man had regained his disciplined posture.

Kasey took a deep breath and let it out slowly. "So, you won't leave? Any of you?"

"We won't. Put us to work, sir." Every head was nodding agreement.

Kasey sat back and relaxed. It was their choice, after all. He gave it some thought before replying.

"Fine. Then listen up people! Unless we are very wrong about what is about to happen, the Nimbus *is* going to war. When that happens, I need everyone still here to be in the ship's outer bridge. Think of it as your new home from this point forward. You will be given access to the terminals there and you can assist us by feeding data to the inner bridge. Bring supplies—long-term food and water, medical, extra clothing, blankets, and bedding. If there is room, line mattresses along the walls for sleeping. Anything hard that could get tossed around absolutely needs to be locked in a crate and secured to the deck. We may be stuck on the bridge for a long while and we need to expect anything—including a very hard landing."

"Why the bridge?" Bennett asked curiously.

"The bridge is a ship itself. Basically, it's a lifeboat. It is also the most protected place on all of Nimbus. The Operations Deck around the bridge, the entire deck in fact, is the second most protected area of the ship. It is why main engineering is based on the same central deck. That means, if the Nimbus survives, we will likely be able to spread out and use the whole deck as we get the ship back in flying order."

"So, we should prepare the deck with supplies too?" the nurse asked.

"Right. If we don't need the lifeboat, the offices in the business center, mining control, and administration areas can be used as bedrooms if needed in the long term. So, bring enough supplies to make them comfortable. This all needs done as soon as possible, preferably in the next few hours. We do not know how much time we have, and you will each have a lot of additional work to do today. As soon as we are supplied, I need every door and hatch on this ship sealed."

Kasey looked them all over and made a decision.

"Nova, give Mr. Bennett access to the reserve armory."

"Sir?" the man asked.

"Mr. Bennett, I realize you are not aware, but you will find a well-stocked armory just outside the bridge, and a mid-deck armory closer to engineering. I want you to make sure everyone is fully armored from head to toe if we end up in combat. Get them suited up and make sure they know their gear. Most of it is lightweight so they can start wearing the suits as soon as you are able to assign them. Shield belts as well, if we have enough. Everyone should be issued a sidearm, but make sure they know how to use it first. For those with no experience, get them running simulations as soon as other work is finished. If we have time, issue rifles as well, but they can stay in the armory unless we have time for live-fire drills."

"Yes, sir. Can do! What about the security bots?"

"Good thinking. I want every one of them on the Operations Deck as soon as possible. Spread them out, and get the ones we converted to non-lethal rearmed if you can. Get some locked down in the bridge as well."

"Isaac showed me how, but I need access to his lab to make the changeover, sir."

"Nova, grant him access please."

"Access is now granted."

Kasey looked over the crowd, "Who are my engineers? Step forward if you have any experience at all."

A small group moved forward, and Kasey was happy to see Griff among them.

"Who is our highest rating?"

A man beside Griff stepped forward, "Technically, I am, sir. However, Griff has far more experience and has more time aboard. We are all still learning from him."

"Thank you, Mr.?"

"Cadwallader, sir."

"Thank you, Mr. Cadwallader. I appreciate the honesty. You don't mind working under Griff then?"

"Not at all, sir. Better to have the right person in a job then the correct rank."

Kasey nodded in agreement and slowly turned to Griff as he rushed to pull up the man's actual name. "Roger Gifford, are you willing to serve as Interim

Chief?"

"Happy to, sir. But mind if I stick with Griff? It's what everyone has always called me."

"Chief Griff it is then. Well Chief, we need this boat in fighting order ASAP, starting with a full weapons engineering inspection. We need to be fully charged, stocked, and test fired, if need be. We also just had two new quad cannons installed I believe?" He looked at AnnaChi questioningly.

"Correct," she smiled back, "but we also had two standard cannons installed as well. The quads are positioned at midship on port and starboard and have a reach at least double our forward guns. Fully gimbaled, so we can reach out to just about anywhere around us with at least one of them. Not quite as accurate at maximum range, or so I am told. They have not been fired yet. The standard cannons are well-used, and could really use an overhaul, for now a successful test fire will have to do on all four of the new systems."

"Fine. Chief, check them all out and make sure they can fire if we have a safe target, otherwise we will test fire once we are in flight. Overhauls will need to wait till a later date. Next, make sure Nimbus is ready to fly at a moment's notice. Keep her warmed up for us."

"Aye sir!"

"Everyone else, you know your jobs better than I do, but if you are not sure, talk to Nova or message me, AnnaChi, or Captain Flair, and we will find a place you can help. Barring that, if anyone finds themself with spare time, report to the outer bridge and familiarize yourself with the terminals there. Do what you can to help."

Standing, Kasey searched out and met the gaze of every one of the crew before him. "Thank you all. I didn't think I had a chance in hell of coming through this, but with a crew like you with me, I know we are going to make those bastards pay for thinking they could attack another one of our systems. I am proud to know you are all with me. They brought this fight to us, let's take it right back to them!"

There were a few shouts of approval, and everyone had fiercely determined faces.

CHAPTER FORTY-ONE

Kasey deliberated with himself as the Cassian mothership reached the one-day mark.

Looking around the bridge, he knew several others had been watching the countdown as well. By this time tomorrow, everyone would be either running or fighting. Soon after that, this world would most likely be in ruins. Few seemed to be enjoying their last day of peace. Busy or not, their thoughts were on their future, not the present.

He couldn't kid himself. There was no real hope of defeating the Cassian this time. Even if Fran showed up with more than just the Pathfinder, they were likely doomed.

Someone delivered food as he continued to stare at the screens, searching for an option he may have missed. He didn't remember eating, but he noticed the box was empty when someone showed up to take it away and replace it with a fresh coffee. For a while, he just stared at the coffee cup—wishing for something stronger. Something stronger was what they all needed right now.

He pulled up the file of the gate being destroyed and

watched it for what seemed like the thousandth time. He watched as the plasma lanced out at the gate, ripping it apart. After a few more viewings, he switched to files the navy had brought with them, of ships colliding with the mothership's shields. Over and over, he watched them until he had every image practically committed to memory.

Turning the displays off, he rested his hands on the table before him, spreading his fingers wide. Turning them over, palms up, he looked at them without really seeing—his thoughts far away. He could hear his heart beating rapidly in his chest. He needed to make a decision. Time was running out.

"Nova," he asked, almost in a whisper, "anything out there? Any new signals at all?"

"Sorry Kasey," the AI answered via the mimic implant, "there is nothing new to report."

Looking at his hands again, he clenched them into tight fists, then spent the next few minutes sending AnnaChi a message. She replied almost immediately.

He stood suddenly and caught Flair looking at him with what looked like hope in her eyes. Shrugging at her, he nodded towards the ready room.

Orange had been curled up in a ball nearby watching the exchange but, before Kasey took his first steps towards the ready room, she was perched on his back and shoulder. She had not left his side since asserting that she would not be left behind. Reassured by her presence, he entered and found Orange a place to perch before taking his own seat on the couch.

Flair entered a moment later. "What are you thinking?"

"That we need to make the bridge more friendly for atoss. This room too."

"Anything more immediate? Like maybe our survival?"

"Wait for AnnaChi."

"I'm here," AnnaChi announced from the doorway. "I was helping our new assistant tactical operators. Not sure how much help they will be, but they should be able to mark and keep an eye on the non-actionable targets while we deal with bigger threats."

"Anyone who can handle a dedicated cannon?" Kasey asked.

"Only a couple, and not sure how good they would be. Most of their experience is from gaming, not with real guns."

"Hmm. Flair, any decent navy gunners willing to volunteer for a reckless mission?"

"I am sure I can find some, but Nova can likely handle most the cannons against orb ships. They are rather basic as fighters go. Nova?"

"That is correct, Captain Flair," Nova replied. "However, I should note that I have simulated my ability against more complex combats on record, including hundreds of accounts from the Trias gate battle with Patternists and Cassian. I regret to report that I found my aptitude to be sub-average. I believe I lack the intuition and creativity of humans."

Kasey nodded. "Everyone has different strengths but, to Nova's point, I am not thinking about just orbs. Look, if Fran shows up now, it will be because he has exhausted all other options, or he has no other choice. If he is out there watching and planning, then he knows he has less than a day to make a move. I also believe that if he had a good plan, he would have already done it."

AnnaChi sighed. "So, you are saying that even if he is out there, we are still screwed because he does not have a workable plan?"

"Well…"

"I think what he is trying not to say," interjected Flair with a huff, "is that we shouldn't give my Francis a

379

choice."

Kasey pressed his head hard against his knuckles for a moment before looking back at her. "Flair is right. We need to launch an attack and force Fran to jump in—if he is even out there. Hell, it may even be what he expects us to do."

"Wait, you lost me on that last bit," Flair responded, a bit more sullenly.

"Well, if he attacked first, we could not get there in time to support him. However, if we attack first..."

"Then he can time his attack perfectly and jump in at the right moment." Flair was smiling now.

"Exactly."

"Alright, you are at least making some sense now. So, what do we need gunners for?"

"Opportunities. Say somehow Fran gets that mothership's shield to go down for a few moments, I want people ready to take advantage and pound rounds where they will do the most good. In fact, Nova can run the cannons when possible, but allow gunners to take instant control as they spot an opening. Let the gunners concentrate on identifying the critical targets."

"Okay. I will pull the best we have from the fleet then."

"Volunt—"

"No, Kasey. I understand you want willing people, but these are navy. They are already volunteers. We just need to give them the best possible opportunity to do their jobs. Period."

"Fine, I get it..." he sighed. He knew he was asking them to join his own suicide mission, the same as everyone else onboard. Ordering people to take on a task that was going to get them killed was almost more stress than he could bear, but he pressed on. "Well then... We will need more than just gunners."

"Stop asking and tell me what you need. I will make

it happen."

Swallowing his thoughts, he nodded. "I need you to draft the RDF and any other armed ships that stayed behind with them; we need their ships and their firepower."

"They won't amount to much compared to the navy ships." Flair sounded concerned. "Won't they be more useful sticking to their original plan to keep the Cassian away from the real bunkers? If we fail, they could save a lot of lives back on the planet."

"Sorry, but most of their ships have quad cannons mounted and we need every one of them with us. Ships without quads are lower priority, so if we need to leave a few of them behind, that's fine, but we need the better pilots and gunners they have in ships with quads."

"Okay, how do you see them being used? They don't have the shields to survive long."

"The ships with quads have twice the effective cannon range of standard cannons, but with far smaller payloads or accuracy, which is why they went with quad mount systems. So, I suggest they are positioned well behind the navy ships and use their range to pick off ships before they are even in range of the navy. The navy ships become the main targets, but have superior shields and point defense to deal with it."

"And fewer attackers, thanks to the RDF's quads thinning the attacker's front line," AnnaChi added.

Kasey nodded. "If the RDF have missile launchers, we give each a few of the seeker missiles for the initial salvos. Nova can take control and coordinate with the navy's launches to make the best use of them."

Flair had a far-off look for a moment then came back. "Looks like only a handful have launchers. Nothing fancy either. I'd say we take full control of their launchers and fill them with our seekers, and Nova can use them as we need them. We will still have over half our supply for Nimbus."

"Sounds good. Nova, you may need to use seekers to help protect the RDF ships after the battle gets going. The navy will be too busy to help at that point."

"Confirmed."

"Flair, we have the sixes as well. Where will they be the most useful?"

"To the more experienced navy ships. They will know best when to use them. Keep one drum for a Nimbus launcher. We can use them if we get rushed."

"Speaking of," Kasey looked away from her, "take some sixes with you when you move aboard the Cintian."

"What? The Cintian? I need to be here with you."

Kasey looked at AnnaChi.

AnnaChi sat forward. "No. You need to command the fleet. The Cintian is your flagship, as of right now. She has better point defenses than most of the fleet ships, so she will keep you alive and able to command. She doesn't have the firepower that I am sure you would prefer, but we need you to command, not fight."

"Hold on, I should be commanding from the Nimbus! You two should be in Cintian."

"Sorry Flair, but Nimbus is too big a target. This is why we are here and why the crew is here. We will take care of Nimbus—you take care of the fleet."

She looked down at her hands. "You sure you don't want the Cintian with you? I can find a fleet ship to use."

AnnaChi laughed. "She will be much safer with you. Nova has a clone and matrix aboard her too, so she will be a big help to you. Besides, I will be piloting Nimbus. Kasey gets the big chair."

"I assume you will have Knoc and Jate command the Lodestar and Altair then?"

"Yes," Kasey jumped in, "but they could both use tactical and gunner resources. I assume Knoc outranks most of the fleet and he works well with Jate. I would give them each a squad of the navy ships to command, but that is all up to you now. Use them and our ships how you see fit."

"Fine, but you are to get your asses back groundside on Redwood the moment this all goes sideways. Dead heroes are useless, you know."

Both of them gave her an unamused look.

"Fine... When do we break for orbit?"

"In the morning."

With the basic plan in place, Kasey allowed his shoulders to sag slightly and took a deep breath. Then he started into a second plan outlining what they would do if Fran didn't show.

He was mentally drained by the time they finished. Everything would fall apart once the fighting started, they all knew it. That was always to be expected, no matter how good the plan was.

He looked at each of them and nodded. "Make sure everyone gets a good night sleep—medically induced if need be. Tomorrow will be a long day. Nova, the Nimbus needs to pick up our ballasts from orbit first. Can you plot a course to pick them up while out of line-of-sight with the mothership?"

"Yes. I will wake you before liftoff."

"Thank you. Flair, have fleet and RDF ships meet us at our orbit location before noon. We will stay on the far side from the mothership until then. I want the battle to start just out of the planetary's protection network so the ground-based cannons and missiles can provide some level of cover for anyone who needs to run."

"We will be there."

"Anything I am missing?"

"We have six ships that still have operable stealth packages. Most others were damaged defending the fleet on the run here."

"Suggestions on how we use them?"

"Initially we need them to scout and give us an accurate picture of the battlespace. Launch them tonight and keep them patrolling the flanks once we move out tomorrow as lookouts."

Kasey pondered for a minute, then shrugged. "That works, I suppose. The Altair's stealth package is spotty but serviceable enough to give you a seventh for flank patrol, but I would hold it back with the fleet tomorrow."

"Done. We really do need an exit plan for when this all goes to shit."

"I'll leave that to you, but if Fran shows up with the Pathfinder, your fleet should join with them. He will have a plan to pull you out."

"I won't count on that."

"I never thought you would."

CHAPTER FORTY-TWO

Kasey stumbled into his quarter's kitchen looking for coffee and found a butler bot waiting for him with a hot mug.

AnnaChi had kept him awake late into the night. Neither wanted to end what was likely their last night together. He wasn't sure who had dozed first as they lay staring into each other's eyes waiting for sleep to take them.

"Nova, status?"

"Good morning, Captain. The crew has prepared a breakfast feast for you. AnnaChi has been awake for a bit over an hour and is requesting you meet her in the armory to kit up. You both are expected in the crew galley in twenty minutes."

"Let her know I am on my way. Is the Nimbus ready to depart?"

"Yes, sir. As are all other ships in the extended fleet. Our ballasts will be full before we break atmosphere, as requested. All missile silos are fully stocked, and test firing of the new cannons will proceed during our ascent. Power banks and propellent tanks are at maximums and all systems are in a green status. We are ready."

"Send data backups to planet-side storage and let Fleet Captain Flair know we will see her in orbit."

"Done."

AnnaChi tossed a bundle at him as he entered the armory.

"What's this?"

"New navy flight suit. Skinsuits, they are calling them. Flair sent over a few extras that the fleet had been issued. Navy has made a lot of advances over the past thirty years. Supposedly, these will keep a fighter pilot safe in open space for a short time, and the surface will harden to absorb some weapon projectiles, or so they claim. The belt has some meds and a control unit built in that our mimic implants will interface with. It has a snug-fitting face mask built in that will seal and supply a limited amount of oxygen unless an external pressurized source is detected. I just tested it out with our out-of-date combat helms—it works flawlessly. We will still keep our normal masks with us for the rebreather and additional oxygen. They can work together."

He gestured at the hard-plated combat suit she was adjusting around her legs, "Looks like we can wear the skinsuit under our hard suits?"

"It's made for it actually. Well, not *specifically* these old combat suits, but whatever is being used these days. Seems to work with ours easily enough. Marines apparently have a heavy version that can take a cannon hit. Ours won't…"

"Well, let's not get hit by cannons then. Do we have enough for the crew?"

"No, just enough extra for us and the active bridge crew." She frowned.

"Maybe…"

"No. Sorry, but command needs to stay alive to keep everyone else alive. That is a simple fact of war."

"Well, I am not cut out for war…"

"You are not getting a choice. So, get dressed, I am hungry."

"Fine, but if we get out of this, I want the crew outfitted properly. If we need to do it through the black markets, that is fine by me. I am done waiting for leftovers."

"Noted," interjected Nova. "I will remind you."

* * *

Breakfast was a quick affair with more questions than food.

He reminded the crew that leaving the ship was still an option, but no one took it. They were afraid, but determined. Everyone took time to say a few words or shake his hand before they left to continue the never-ending preparations.

The climb out of the planet's gravity well took longer than any he had encountered before, in any ship, but it didn't take as long as retrieving the solid-iron ballasts they had left in orbit. They had drifted further apart than expected. Still, the massive iron blocks were back aboard before the ship was in any danger of entering line-of-sight with the mothership's approach.

The fleet joined them over the next few hours.

It was time to start the charge, but Kasey hesitated.

Flair's face appeared on a screen with the Cintian's bridge in the background. "What is the hold up?"

Kasey tried to banish the look of fear he assumed covered his face. "I was trying to think of something clever to say before jumping off this cliff."

"This isn't some fantasy story. Our people know the score and don't need smoke blown up their rears. Get the hell on with it!"

The screen closed.

"AnnaChi?"

"Kasey?"

"Full speed ahead, please."

"About damn time."

Within moments of coming out of the planet's shadow, orb ships started pouring out of the mothership.

"You think they are happy to see us?"

"Well, they do seem eager to say hello."

"How long to missile range, Nova?"

"Two hours, twelve minutes, at current thrust."

"Get Flair back on-screen."

She popped up almost immediately. "Problems already?"

"We were expecting around two hundred Cassian orbs, right?"

"Something like that, yes."

"I am showing nearly four hundred, so far…"

"You weren't *really* expecting a fair fight, were you?"

He ignored that. "Any word from your husband?"

"Francis won't show his hand till he needs to."

"I was kind of hoping for a miraculous rescue at some point."

"Well, we haven't made it to that point just yet. Besides, we are not here to be rescued, Kasey."

"No?"

"No. We are here to be bait. Rescue is a completely different thing."

"Ah," he laughed his nervousness away, "well I guess we are good then. Thanks for the reassurance."

"In all seriousness, we can't take this many on…"

"We will have a speed advantage at this vector, which is why we are letting them chase us instead of going head-on. We also have a bit of time. Can we arc around the front edge of the swarm? Force them to decelerate more so we can take advantage of our longer-range cannons for as long as possible."

"If I may." Nova brought up displays for them all to see what the trajectory would look like.

AnnaChi was the first to comment. "It should work, apart from the midway point as we cross over to deceleration."

"Better than nothing. Flair, position the fleet around Nimbus and prepare them for the new trajectory. Once we are in the arc, get our people fed and ready to pull triggers."

She looked at him for a moment, then slowly nodded to herself a few times before responding. "Yes, sir. We will see you on the other side of this. Stay safe you two!"

The screen went blank.

"Did she officially draft us at some point?" AnnaChi asked.

"No. Why?"

"Never mind. Fleet reports ready for the course change. Proceed?"

"Do it."

The crew delivered sandwiches and coffee urns for the bridge crew and reported the ship was locked down and ready for combat.

To Kasey, an hour seemed to flow by in minutes as he watched the ships close with each other. Something had changed, but he couldn't put his finger on it.

"Nova, give me a screen dedicated to the mothership's trajectory and note any changes which didn't coincide with the orb swarm movements."

The requested screen popped up. "It has indeed made some small course adjustments out of sync with the orb swarm. It appears to be veering slightly south of the star's ecliptic plane."

"Damn. Its positioning for a clear shot around the orbs as we pass. Work with AnnaChi to adjust the fleet to counter it. We need to keep the orb ships between us and that mothership as long as possible."

"Missile range in thirty seconds," a man at the tactical station called out.

Kasey sighed in relief, grateful to be able to do something besides wait. After a glance around the bridge, he started calling out orders.

"Fire all our FFs and reload. Hold back the sixes and seekers for now."

"Aye, sir."

"Gunners, target incoming ordnance until we have orbs in range. Quad-gunners, watch that heat buildup, I need nonstop firing once orbs are in your effective range. So, figure out the best fire-rate while using them defensively. AnnaChi, keep our belly towards them. We can take some hits if we lose shields but roll us if needed."

"I got this."

"Security, keep your eyes on our fleet and call out issues if we can help," He was pleased to note that April Mayflower had retained her security position.

"Yes, sir."

The bridge seemed to come alive with chatter. He knew the outer bridge would be worse. Most of the crew not in engineering were now busy searching the incoming swarm and projectiles for anything worth bringing to the bridge crew's attention. He doubted they would help much, but hoped they were not panicking with the reality they all now faced.

He had copies of every bridge station linked to his own, spending what time he had free going through each one. He noticed when the quads started firing and when the other accelerator cannons joined in a short while afterwards. Point defense turrets would soon follow suit as they arced deeper into the swarm's range.

A few more minutes passed when he noticed April looking concerned. "Something wrong Miss Mayflower?"

"The RDF ships have taken some hard hits to their shields from a few missiles that slipped by the navy—I am not sure they can sustain more than a few additional hits each."

"Captain," one of the quad-gunners interrupted, "the enemy will be in range of the quads in a few moments, we are going to need the RDF's quads firing on orbs, not defending themselves."

Kasey could hear the sympathy in the navy gunner's voice, but he was stating the fact that they all needed to hear.

"I agree. April, contact the RDF and have them close with us and use Nimbus as a shield. Todd Dermott is their commander. Notify Fleet Captain Flair directly afterwards."

"Yes, sir"

"AnnaChi?"

"Already veering us to towards their position."

He watched as the RDF ships moved into a ring around the Nimbus, and not a single cannon stopped firing the whole move.

"Nova, can you make sure all the RDF quads are targeting orbs now?"

"They all are indeed, and quite effectively too."

"Kasey," AnnaChi called out, "shields are dropping too quickly, I need to flip her soon!"

"Nova, how far from mid-point are we?"

"Just over one minute."

"Give RDF a warning of our flip. AnnaChi, start now and make sure RDF ships are adjusting with you."

The viewscreen was moving before he finished speaking. Slowly at first, for other ships to adjust, then speeding up.

"Engineering, get our lower shields evened out as soon as possible. Do we have any damage?"

"Just a few burned out relays that are being hot-swapped out now. We will have the lower shields evened out in thirty seconds but will need time to build back their overall shield strength across the board."

"Understood. AnnaChi, the moment any of the topside shields drop below twenty percent I want us flipped back as quickly as possible. Give RDF a heads-up if possible, but make them aware now that it will happen quickly when it does."

"Midway!" Nova announced to everyone as they entered the worst of the barrage.

"Fleet status?"

"No ship losses yet, but we have sustained damage across the fleet. We have... Sorry, Captain, a fleet frigate just went dark."

"Damn. Have the orb swarm started decelerating to stay with our fleet yet?"

"Yes, but the fleet is pulling away from them quickly."

"Good, mark the frigate's last position and vector. We will be back for them, but survivors should be safe for now."

"Flipping!" The view twisted again, far faster this time.

"Fire all missiles, including the sixes we have loaded."

"Two more ships have gone dark, Captain!"

"How are our shields?"

"Holding, lowest is at thirty percent."

"Sir, the mothership is making a move. It will be in range soon," Nova reported.

CHAPTER FORTY-THREE

Kasey closed his eyes for a second and took a slow breath.

"Nova, send the RDF ships back for the navy to protect. AnnaChi, turn the fleet pathing back over to Flair."

A screen with Flair popped up immediately.

"What the hell are you planning now?"

"I am going to do a little fishing. The fleet is now yours, Flair."

"I... Godspeed, Nimbus," she said quietly before disconnecting.

"AnnaChi, move us away from the fleet and head south of the ecliptic please."

She turned to look at him, smiled sadly, then nodded.

"Tactical, launch a class-three drone ahead of our position and prepare it to execute a scramble on all frequencies on my command."

"Yes, sir."

"All eyes on the mothership, people. Take down anything that leaves that shield!"

The bridge went still as they moved into range of the

massive ship.

"Movement!" The shout came from the tactical station. "Orb ships launching from the far side. Ten, no twenty between two groupings."

"Get missiles on them, launch our seekers too. Gunners, give Nova control and keep your eyes on the mothership. Nova will cede control when you need it."

Kasey ignored the grumbled responses.

"Any fluctuations to their shield when the orbs launched?"

"Ripples, but consistent intensity, sir."

"AnnaChi. Move us onto a collision course. Tactical, prepare to scramble the drone."

The image of the mothership's shields filled his main screen as he watched it. Directly in the center, a small ripple pulsed outwards across the surface, followed by the entire area beginning to swirl into a vortex.

"Scramble now!"

"Done!"

"Get us out of here AnnaChi! Get orbs between us if you can! Launch another drone ASAP."

"Sir, the vortex is tracking on us! Scramble didn't work."

"Damn! Nova, ready our…"

"Gravity wave, sir! A large mass appeared four kilometers off starboard."

"Is it the Pathfinder?"

"Unknown, but I am detecting large swarms of missile signatures heading towards the mothership!"

"Is the vortex still tracking on us?"

"No, it is shifting towards the new ship. Confirmed, sir, it is the Pathfinder!"

A screen appeared showing Admiral Maddock Francis looking pleased with himself. "Never had a doubt you would be in the captain's chair for this. Where is my wife stationed?"

"She is on the Cintian, commanding the fleet, but Fran…"

"Sir," shouted tactical, "the vortex is spiking!"

"Fran, you need to jump, now!"

"Can't. Not charged yet. We will just have to dodge this one." He smiled calmly as the link closed.

"Put the Pathfinder on the main screen."

They watched in horror as a great mass of plasma erupted from the vortex into the direct path of Fran's huge ship. The long cylindrical ship seemed to twist as thrusters lit up at seemingly odd locations along the ship, moving the helm one direction while the aft end moved perpendicular at half that speed. All the while the main thrusters lit up, pushing the ship like an out-of-control rocket that danced around the mass of plasma.

"They cleared the plasma, sir. They must have one hell of a pilot over there!"

"I believe that was Scout, Pathfinder's AI, Captain," commented Nova, sounding proud.

"We will save his congratulations for later. Are the Pathfinder's particle cannons firing, and are they having any effect?"

"They are. Some appear to cause a small disturbance, but most do not have any effect."

"Speculation?"

"Perhaps disturbances happen when they hit something vital on the surface of the mothership?"

"Work with that assumption. Map out the locations of every hit that had any effect at all."

"Aye, sir. I will rank them by impact severity they have on the shield, as well."

"Good thinking. Share it with Pathfinder and keep them updated."

"The orb swarm has recovered their momentum and are veering back towards us. Fleet are harassing them, but the swarm seems to be ignoring them."

"Suggest to Flair that she back the fleet off and let them come. AnnaChi, get us on a vector that will take us out of range of the mothership's weapon and ask Flair to join up with us there."

"On it!"

"Another vortex is already forming, Captain. Pathfinder is target."

"Does that shield lose power when it fires?"

"Yes, sir. Goes down nearly ten percent but has rebuilt most of that since the last fire."

"How much? Do we have precise numbers?"

"More of a good guess based on average frequencies we are detecting. The current guess is that by the time this vortex fires, the total loss to the mothership's shield will be two percent at best."

"Okay, start tracking that percentage loss and time between fires, even if it is just a guess."

"Aye, sir."

"Vortex firing. Pathfinder jumped!"

"Where are they?"

"Ahead of us, but still in range of the mothership and firing. They are deploying ships."

AnnaChi looked over at him, concerned. "That is maybe a fourth of the fleet they should have. Where are the rest?"

"Sirs," interrupted April, "I am querying their fleet status now. Looks like they were wrapping up a battle before jumping to this system. Most of the fleet was left behind by necessity to protect that system. The admiral put Captain Grimt QuTan in command of the fleet there, along with the Endeavour. Many of the ships they did bring were under repair when they left. They have been behind the system's sun for two standard days, waiting for us to make a move."

"Alright. Have them form up with Flair's fleet and work with her on a battleplan. Make sure they are aware of the RDF's quads and their ship's limitations."

"Yes, sir."

The battle raged for over an hour before the Pathfinder took a blow that ripped down the entire length of the ship, requiring it to retreat out of the motherships range.

The combined fleet and the swarm of orb ships had been in a slow twisting dance to the death for most of that time, leaving a trail of drifting ships across the space. Neither side was gaining an edge, and twice the Pathfinder had jumped close enough to unleash a wave of missiles that gave the fleet time to recoup their shields enough to continue.

That was all at an end now.

The mothership veered its trajectory once more towards Redwood.

Kasey ignored the battle and concentrated on the mothership and its shields. The rate they were recovering was far slower than at the beginning of the battle. The Pathfinder's particle cannons had made a difference, and so had the map they'd created of viable hits. Patterns had emerged in the data, and the number of worthwhile hits increased as the battle went on.

Yet, none of that mattered now. Even with the shield at nearly half what it had been, nothing except particle cannon shots could get through, and they were now offline and out of range.

He looked over at AnnaChi, who was deep in the zone, as were most of the bridge crew as they looked for every opening they could to gain an advantage over the swarm. The fleet's missiles had run out a while ago, it was purely a gun battle now.

He brought up two screens and connected them to Flair and Fran. They both looked worn out.

He looked at Fran. "Tell me you have a backup plan, Admiral."

"It won't help us anytime soon, but I left a set of Trias gates on the far side of the sun. If we run and wait a few days, we should have some backup."

"Unless they find the gates first?"

"True. And the planet would not survive in either case. My analysts believe that weapon will make the atmosphere unlivable for a few years at best. Can the population down there survive that?"

"Unknown. My crew are dug in deep underground and can make do, but the colony citizens are in bunkers with limited supplies. I am not really sure how long they can last."

"Then we better think of something quick."

Flair looked them both over. "Neither of you have a plan!" It was not a question.

AnnaChi's face popped up on a new screen, but she was concentrating elsewhere. "Stop lollygagging and get to it!"

"We are out of options dearie," Fran said gently.

"No. You are not! Kasey, do what needs to be done. We won't have another shot and we are losing time."

"So, we do have a plan?"

"Well… It's a *really* bad plan…"

CHAPTER FORTY-FOUR

Nimbus and the fleet raced towards the Pathfinder, the swarm pursuing close behind.

Pathfinder's massive thrusters lit up, propelling the gigantic ship towards the oncoming fleet. As they drew close, the fleet abruptly split off into four groups, vectoring towards the edge of the swarm's trajectory to make room for Pathfinder's bulk.

The Pathfinder dove through the center of the four smaller fleets, smashing through the swarm's projectiles like a cannonball. While the fleet had depleted their missiles earlier in the battle, the Pathfinder still had a nearly full inventory, which Fran now let loose on the unprepared orb ships at close range—very few were intercepted or missed their marks.

The fleet decelerated as the remains of the now devastated swarm flowed by. The Cassian had failed to recover quickly enough from the onslaught of missiles and could do little as the fleet poured cannon rounds into them from four sides. When the fleet reached the far side of the swarm, it combined back into a single group and took up the chase. The remaining hunters became prey for the fleet.

Kasey and eight other ships broke off. The Nimbus' bays opened, allowing the ships to carefully maneuver onto the magnetic platforms, which backed them into her bays.

He took a moment to look over the status of the fleet before looking back proudly at his expectant crew.

"Tell Fran he has a go."

Although battered and shieldless, the Pathfinder had only increased speed since passing through the swarm. That momentum was being used to dive towards the mothership once again.

Kasey watched the Pathfinder's trajectory carefully, then nodded at AnnaChi. "Take us in."

Nimbus curved towards the mothership, heading for the opposite side of the large spherical ship.

"Vortex forming, sir. Pathfinder is the target."

The Pathfinder had been letting loose a steady arc of missiles, marking their path with breadcrumbs as it went. As the vortex peaked, a bloom of missiles streaked forward towards the forming plasma bolt and the Pathfinder veered away as sharply as it could manage.

Kasey watched, desperate for the ploy to work.

Tendrils of the plasma streaked out toward the array of missiles, then continued to pull the greater mass of energy along the trail of missiles leading away from Pathfinder. It almost worked. The main plasma mass stretched thin, as momentum carried it both towards the Pathfinder as well as the chain of missiles. Kasey swore in frustration as the mass snapped in two, a significant portion still on a collision course for the Pathfinder.

Pathfinder used what few thrusters remained to flip the ship around the incoming mass, yet several fingers of plasma reached out to burn wide gouges into the ship as it passed by. Somehow, the great ship righted itself and was soon back on course for the mothership as debris and gasses poured from it like lifeblood.

Kasey nodded to himself. "Change of plans, folks. AnnaChi, take the lead please."

"On it." She pushed the Nimbus' thrusters to their maximum position and smiled.

Kasey was waiting for the screen as it popped up with Fran's image. "What are you about, son? That is not the plan! Pull back and prepare your squad to take advantage when the Pathfinder's impact takes down this beast's shields!"

"Sorry Fran, but that was *never* the plan. We need as much of your mass to hit as possible in a single shot. You can't avoid the next plasma shot, but if this works you may not need to."

"You will never make it through that shield!"

"Two minutes!" tactical called out.

"Watch and see—but get ready to flip and punch out."

"Dammit, Kasey! You better be right!"

"Vortex forming!"

"Nova," Kasey grinned, "bring the rain!"

The Nimbus cut its thrusters and the ship flattened out, its belly now facing the mothership. Over a hundred drop bays along the entire underside of the Nimbus opened, releasing a wall of water that formed below the ship. The Nimbus slowed slightly, allowing the water to move away. Nimbus' thrusters began pushing the ship into a slow flat spin.

"Sir, it moved, the vortex is now reforming on our position!"

"Start the solid ballast launching sequence."

First, four of the massive blocks of compressed iron were pushed from the center drop bays and began spreading outwards and away from the ship. Twelve more followed a moment later, then another twenty. The process continued, and in the end one hundred and twelve iron blocks formed a ring ahead of the ship and closed in on the outer edges of the water wall.

"AnnaChi, are we lined up?"

"As much as we will ever be!"

"Engineering?"

"Ready!"

"Activate Lithose Protocol!" Kasey commanded.

An eternity seemed to tick by before the confirmation came back that the protocol had been successfully activated. With the ship already in lockdown, the sequence was completed far quicker than normal, which relieved Kasey greatly.

The main screen now showed a series of status indicators. Everything from pressure readings to temperature from all over the ship were visible. At the top was a row of power-sink monitors. Each sink would bleed off large amounts of energy from any power spikes making it past the Nimbus' built-in layers of Faraday shielding. The system had originally been designed for studying electrical storms within the atmospheres of gas giants, and had been revived by Kasey to use for safe access to the dead and stormy world of Lithose. Neither were anywhere as intense as the Cassian mothership's shield they were about to impact.

"We should be entering the shield now, sir."

Kasey nodded absently as he watched the indicators. They were holding steady it seemed, and he let out a breath. Just then, several started flashing, others quickly following. One by one, every power sink turned red.

"Captain, we have breaches on multiple decks!"

"Hangar bays?"

"Hangar bay H7 has been breached. Unknown status of ship. Both cargo bays have major breaches."

The lights flickered and the normal background hum of the life support systems went quiet.

"On backup power, sir. Generators went to safe mode

but should be back up as the power spike clears."

"Understood. How soon till we exit the shield?"

"Ten seconds. Estimated, sir," there was a slight pause, "five seconds. Three, two, one."

"Bring up thrusters, now!"

Nothing changed.

"Unresponsive!"

"What about maneuvering thrusters, can we reposition at all? Get our aft end angled towards that mothership now!"

"Thruster three is up. Five is up as well."

"AnnaChi, keep us from crashing into that thing!"

"I am trying!"

"Do we have shields?"

"Negative!"

"Sensor arrays are coming online! I will have a view in a moment."

"Bring all cannons online. Gunners, take out anything that looks important!"

"Hold on everyone!" AnnaChi shouted suddenly, "We are going to skip off the surfac—"

Everything went black, but the impact didn't jostle the bridge as much as Kasey imagined it would. Lights were back a moment later, and the hum of the environmental was suddenly back as well.

He suppressed a grin as the viewscreen flickered to life, showing a metallic landscape filled with strange shapes and towers that swirled in colors from the terrifying electrified shield now high above them.

"Open the bays and scramble our ships!"

"Sir, the rounded silos are giving off a lot of heat. Suggest we concentrate fire and watch shield levels."

"Make it happen people! Time till Pathfinder hits the shield?"

"Just over two minutes."

"All ships deployed! Bay H7 as well."

"Fine. AnnaChi, take us back to our insertion point. Anyone know if our ballasts impacted the surface?"

"Unknown, sir. Wait! The shield appears to be unstable above that location. Surface location will be on-screen in ten seconds."

"Get our ships over here ASAP to work this area over."

"Yes, sir."

"Nova, use our combined point defense lasers and see if we can damage anything with it."

"Proceeding, but it is unlikely the lasers will do much. However, I have taken the liberty to contact the navy ships to do the same with their antimatter-based point defenses. They have a far higher probability of having an effect."

"Good thinking…" he paused as a ring of destruction came into view. The large solid-iron ballasts could not be seen, but the impacts they caused certainly could be.

Most of them had punched wide holes in the surface, and a few looked to have detonated something that took out a slightly wider area, but Kasey's view was drawn to the far side. He could only guess how many of the ballasts had struck that area, because an entire section had collapsed deep into the mothership.

"Gunners! Rake fire over everything in that exposed section."

They passed over the section a few moments later, but other than a few small explosions, the shield didn't waver.

"Sir, we detected an energy spike when we passed over that section. Something down there is generating lots of power. Could be their version of a generator."

"AnnaChi, bring us in for another pass. Slower. Have the other ship do the same."

"One minute till Pathfinder reaches the shield."

"Damn! We are out of time. I should have saved

some missiles!"

"Well…" AnnaChi started.

He could not help but smile, "What did you do?"

"I loaded a shuttle with a few crates of explosives from the mining supplies this morning. There is a demo bot on board to set it off. If Nova can direct the shuttle in, it should make a nice bang. It's in shuttle bay S8."

"Nova?"

"Shuttle launched and heading for energy spike location at maximum speed."

"Get our ships away from that hole!"

"Thirty seconds!"

"Impact!"

A wave of high-energy washed across the ship. Lights and screens flickered—several went out completely and didn't come back.

"We have maydays from three ships. They are going down on the mothership's surface. Two launched their lifeboats."

"Launch our search and rescue bots!"

"Mothership shield appears to be failing, sir! It's at twenty percent and falling steadily."

"Pathfinder bearing on shield now!"

"I hope it was enough! Tell our people on the surface to hold onto to something if they can. Get our remaining ships to their location to help, ASAP."

"Pathfinder's impact on the mothership in three, two… Impact!"

CHAPTER FORTY-FIVE

An orange bloom of light appeared briefly on the mothership's horizon.

The ships that had landed on the mothership's surface reported being thrown around some but were otherwise no worse off than they had been. The SR bots had already arrived and stabilized the worst of the injuries.

"Sir, the mothership has stopped accelerating and its shield is gone!"

He could hear relief in the crew's voices but knew it was too soon to relax their guards.

"Take us back to the hole we created and send two of our ships to see what the Pathfinder's crash accomplished."

"Captain, fleet lifeboats are requesting to come aboard."

"Denied. We can't stop to help yet. We are still in the thick of this battle, people! The Cassian have been known to self-destruct their motherships. Worse, if they get that thing moving again, they can crash it into Redwood. This behemoth may be disabled for now, but we need to ensure it stays that way. Lifeboats will need to wait for the fleet's assistance."

"Shuttle's damage on screen now, sir."

Kasey was awed by the scene before him. Whatever AnnaChi's shuttle bomb had taken out had triggered a much larger explosion, opening a chasm wider than the Nimbus. Several decks now appeared to be open to space.

"Movement! Looks to be machines of some sort working to close off the second exposed deck down. Detecting several Cassian bodies in the wreckage as well."

Kasey thought for a moment. "Gunners, carefully take out the machines and anything else moving around those decks, but try to leave the structure intact."

"AnnaChi, are you able to..."

"Damn right I can! Shuttle bays S2 and S3 will slot right into that opening—well, nearly... Gunners, can you please take out the overhanging structure on the high-starboard side to give me a bit more clearance?"

Kasey opened a channel to the whole ship. "All hands. Anyone willing and able to participate in a combat situation are to see Mr. Bennett for additional weapons and gear. Please assemble outside of shuttle bays S2 and S3, ASAP. We will be moving out immediately. Our security bots will go in first and we will follow. Team one is to find whatever passes for a bridge on that ship and commandeer it. Team two will either disable the ship or keep it from regaining power. One way or another, we need to stop that mothership from being able to move or threaten our people. Everyone else—we will need support and supplies on hand. Be ready." He closed the channel.

"Sir, the fleet is incoming and wants a status. What do I tell them?"

"Tell them we are boarding the mothership and we need more troops here, ASAP. Suggest they do the same if our other ships found an entrance where the Pathfinder impacted or at any orb docking areas they can locate. Oh, and let them know there are machines repairing the mothership already, so be quick!"

"Yes, sir."

"Tell any remaining lifeboats they can dock with us as soon as we are secured but keep bays clear for the fleet to drop off any troops they can. Make sure the fleet has a patrol in place before deploying the temporary docks." He paused and took a deep breath. "Are we picking up any signals from the mothership?"

"Not much. Most of what we are receiving appears to be automated commands that repeat. We believe they are directing the robots we saw."

"Captain," Nova interrupted, "I have analyzed the strength of the signals detected. Most frequencies are being blocked or absorbed the deeper the broadcast source is located within the mothership. We may not be able to maintain consistent contact with your teams as a result. Wider comm frequencies may work at further distances but they will need to be boosted at regular intervals."

"Fine. We will do what we can."

AnnaChi expertly maneuvered the Nimbus into position and used the bay's magnetic platform to lock onto the deck as if it were a ship. Nova then took control of the ship to keep it steady and in place.

Kasey and AnnaChi moved through the group of crew members waiting to join the boarding action. He was surprised at the bravery being shown around them. Every one of them were ready to get the job done. Bennett had them organized into two teams on the main hangar deck and made sure everyone was supplied and ready. Medical carts, water bottles, ammo, and other supplies were slowly filling up every bit of space.

The shuttle bay's blast doors allowed each bay to act

as a giant airlock. Currently, they were open to the alien mothership, which was open to space. A screen showed the open bays and beyond as bots pulled long boarding tubes out into the mothership's decks. Demolition bots placed charges on all the closest hatchways as small shield-walls were secured into the deck floors behind them.

"Who is leading team two?"

"Bennett and Chief Griff. Most of the engineering teams will be with them as well," replied AnnaChi distractedly.

He wondered briefly what she was working on, but his attention was pulled away.

April Mayflower rushed up to him. "Sir, with your permission, I will join your team. I can handle the bot control as well as monitor team operations."

"Certainly, April. But I would have thought you would want to stay with Mr. Bennett?"

A pained look flashed across her face. "I... Sorry, sir. I didn't realize you knew. He didn't feel it would be appropriate for us to be on the same team."

"Appropriate? This is not the navy, April."

She bit her lip and looked at AnnaChi for help.

"Kasey, they would be a distraction to each other," she explained. "If one were hurt, the other may not be able to do their job properly."

"And you and I don't have the same issue?"

"Different situation and not our first outing together. Like you said, we are not navy, this is more about logic than rules. It makes sense, so she will be with us."

"Okay then, done. Miss Mayflower, pick someone to back you up so you can concentrate on the bots and keep me updated."

"Yes, sir!"

They made their way to the front as the preparations were finalized. A dozen men and woman were lined up behind him, and scores of security bots waited for his signal inside the bay.

"Blow it!"

The hatchways disintegrated.

Once-pressurized compartments spilled contents outward into the shield-walls in a quick blast, then all was still. A group of bots rushed into the center opening as others removed the shield-walls and connected and sealed the waiting entry tubes around the openings. After it was sealed and pressurized, the bays opened again, allowing the teams access to the mothership.

The demolition bots went ahead of his team into the new area. Again, they placed charges on the three sealed entrances they found inside. The moment the room was cleared the charges detonated. A second later a stream of security bots charged through the openings and beyond.

There was no resistance, so Kasey led his team into the large room. The area looked to have been a robotics maintenance area, but it did not appear to have ever been used—everything appeared new. Odd and interesting equipment was stored in shelving units along the walls, but every worktable was empty.

He was surprised when AnnaChi seemingly ignored it all and started ordering the team to move the worktables into defensive positions. Stevedores arrived soon after, carrying large sheets of building materials, which she directed to be used to seal off two of the corridors. Security bots were already scouting further along the third corridor and, after checking with April for their status, he led the team out to follow them.

The mothership layout followed a similar pattern until they encountered a strange set of rooms which resembled underground caverns—complete with musty odors. Each was full of spheres suspended from the high ceilings. Several side rooms appeared to be food and waste areas which they quickly ignored once it was determined that the area was currently unoccupied.

Several spheres were cut down, showing them to be some form of sleeping pods. Everyone was relived to find they were all empty.

Until this point, the Nimbus had been pumping breathable air through the claimed areas. The Cassian sleeping areas were too large to quickly fill, so Kasey closed up his helmet and activated its rebreather unit before directing the crew to do so as well. He happily noted the smells were instantly gone.

The floor lurched violently, nearly knocking Kasey over. Several others were down and trying to recover.

"Captain! Movement in the last intersection! They broke through the barriers."

"Do we have a visual?"

"No, sir. Sensor was destroyed."

"Find cover people! Call back the leading bots and update the Nimbus."

AnnaChi pulled him down. "Incoming!"

Dark streaking projectiles poured into the room and someone screamed in pain.

"Fire!" AnnaChi yelled. "Get some heat down that hallway, now!"

It was too late. A group of the centipedal Cassian burst into the room. They snatched up the two closest people and systematically started ripping armor and clothing off them, looking for vulnerable areas.

"Grenade!" Anna shouted. "Cover!"

Her toss landed the explosive directly into the entrance. The blast knocked everything in the small area to the ground but did little damage to most of the creatures. The chitinous shell covering most of their body seemed impenetrable.

Several of his team were taking advantage of the blast's chaos to pour rounds into the Cassian, keeping them away from the people they had attacked. Some shots made it through, but most were failing.

Kasey moved to a prone shooting position and fired off several shots at the Cassian's many legs. The result was immediate as the creature twisted its body in a great arc, smashing into the Cassian next to it and exposing its underside. He took three more shots, into its unarmored underside this time. It dropped dead before the third shot hit.

"Shoot for the legs!"

A minute later the room was quiet, and bots were sent down the hall to check for any others behind them.

Both men that the Cassian had grabbed were alive but shaken, bruised, and in no condition to continue on. Another woman in the back of the room was found unconscious with one arm that looked partially melted off. Whatever the projectiles were that the Cassian fired, they were effective.

He sent all three back to the Nimbus with an escort of security bots and a stevedore to carry the woman, along with several of the Cassian's weapons.

AnnaChi came over with a concerned look. "Should we continue? I hear the fleet is landing troops on the Nimbus now, so we will have backup if we wait."

"That may be best, we are a bit..."

"Sir!" April called out, "The mothership is accelerating! They must have gotten its engines back online!"

CHAPTER FORTY-SIX

"**D**amn!" He looked at AnnaChi. "I don't think we can wait. We need to stop this thing. If anything, we need to move faster."

With a nod, AnnaChi turned and started giving orders on how the next encounter would be run, including how the bots should be distributed.

Kasey joined her and jumped in when she finished. "We are picking up the pace from here on in. Send only one bot ahead into any passageways as a scout and keep them well ahead of us. We will leave a single sensor at any side passages we bypass, but we won't be blocking them off."

The team readied themselves and adjusted their positions to account for the missing members.

AnnaChi picked up one of the Cassian weapons and fired it a few times into the armored side of the dead Cassian's bodies. The bolts did not immediately penetrate, but within a few seconds of being hit, a fist-sized area of the shell melted and sunk in. She pointed at two of the team and they took up the Cassian weapons as well.

They moved at a fast walk through several areas that would have been interesting to explore had they the time. April kept them on a path that moved them closer to the center of the ship, but most of it was guesswork and several times they needed to turn around.

"Movement ahead!"

Kasey quickly looked at the rough map that was being created as the scout bots moved ahead of them. An exceptionally large room was just ahead of them.

"Double-time it! There should be better cover for us up ahead."

It was a guess on his part, but so far, no areas had been empty. Besides, anything was better than a firefight in an open corridor.

The front scout bot went offline before they caught up to it, but the room was still free of enemies when they arrived and spread out.

Weirdly shaped containers stacked in organized patterns filled most of the room. A warehouse of sorts, he surmised, but far larger than his small team could cover.

He ducked down beside AnnaChi and April. "How long before the fleet troops get here?"

"Not soon enough." April confirmed his doubts. "Team two needed an assist, so the first set of troops were sent there. Cassian have already been spotted at the far end of this storeroom."

"Okay. We are committed to fight whatever is coming, but may need to fall back if we get a chance. This warehouse is far too open. We will have to defend from every direction if they spread out, and I don't see why they wouldn't. AnnaChi, can we use any of these containers to blockade this entrance behind us if we need to run?"

"Maybe, but we can't do that." She smiled innocently. "I have some supplies being delivered shortly and will need the opening to remain clear."

"Are these supplies going to be useful enough for us to stay here?"

"Only one way we are going to find out..." He glared at her and waited. "Fine! I arranged for my own backup—it will either be useful or give us a distraction we can use to retreat."

Several shots sounded from leading security bots, followed by shouts from the team as the enemy positions were pinpointed.

"April, have our remaining stevedores stand ready to pull containers to block the entry hallway if needed. If it comes to it, we will pull back and leave all the bots here to slow them down."

"On it, sir."

He had no more time to plan. Several Cassian were already in sight of his position. Carefully he lined up one shot after another and fired. He was missing more shots than he liked, and many that did hit were absorbed by the Cassian's natural armor.

Ducking back, he took a deep breath, realizing he had been holding his breath in anticipation between shots. Forcing himself to get his breathing under control the way AnnaChi taught him, he moved to another position. Breathe in, breathe out, hold, shoot, shoot again, and again, duck, breathe, move, and start over. AnnaChi was always after him to train with her and now he regretted every time he had found something else to do.

He repeated the process until there was a pause in the battle. April was trying to get his attention.

He opened the comm. "What is it?"

"The Cassian have reinforcements moving into the warehouse, sir. We have lost half the security bots. We can't hold much longer."

A low hum he hadn't completely noticed before was steadily getting louder. He patched AnnaChi into the comm.

"We are about to be overrun. Is that your supplies I hear?"

She laughed. "Why yes, I believe it is. Grab your gear and prepare to move forward."

He dropped the connection and began forming up nearby troops into pairs.

The Cassian began firing again as a line of bard vehicles streamed into the room.

The first two immediately fired their jump jets and streaked upwards and across the room, colliding with the largest stacks of containers where the Cassian reinforcements were lining up. A few of the Cassian weapons hit them in flight but didn't do enough damage to stop them. The resulting collapse likely crushed a few and caused a lot of confusion, but Kasey doubted it would make much of a difference in the coming fight. However, he quickly realized that the stunt had just been a distraction.

The next four bards appeared to be heavily armed and were firing the second the collision happened. A bard he had a clear view of sported four heavy projectile guns mounted on gimbals and a single point defense laser turret on the top that was far more powerful than any handheld weapon his team carried. Each weapon was tracking individual targets and firing independently as the battle-hardened bards moved forward.

Kasey began moving the team forward, staying behind the bards but close enough to take shots at any opportunity that presented itself. A moment later, he had the team stand down and concentrate on staying out of harm's way as they followed. The bards were making quick work of the Cassian. Weapons pounding right through their chitinous armor with single hits.

As they crossed the room, the bards began using the jump jets to hover upwards, taking shots at the enemy further and further ahead. Before he knew it, the room was clear.

As the team reformed around the entry into the next hallway, Kasey got a look at the other bards. Each was very different and all appeared unfinished. They did not even have the same weapons, and some were not fully installed. He noted several gimbals with no weapon at all. Only one had any physical armor on it, and another had a set of shield-walls mounted to the front like a V-shaped plow.

The first two bards were out of commission. Neither had any modifications, just basic configurations. Between the fire they had taken and the crash, they would need a full overhaul before running again, if ever.

AnnaChi was checking over one of the bards that contained only laser weapons.

"Problem?"

She looked back at him. "Too much power drain and too little power generation. This was meant for slow and steady fire. It was out of power before the fight was half over. It will regain enough charge before we need it again, but it won't last long."

"Maybe lower the laser's intensity a bit to conserve power reserves." He pointed around at the Cassian bodies and scored decks near each. "It seems a bit overkill right now."

"Right! On it, but we should keep moving before they gather more reinforcements."

"Wait. Who is controlling these?"

She pointed towards a hatch Kasey knew held the small core each bard contained. "Nova is. Well, a ridiculously small clone of her that she designed specifically for them once we realized we would be out of comms in this place. I assumed we needed more firepower than we could carry."

"Next time, we bring them from the start."

"Next time I will have them ready. These are just my prototypes and were not ready for a fight, let alone have AIs capable of fighting them. I never intended them to be AI controlled before now..."

"Need invites invention."

"True enough. Damn. Let's get this over with and then I really want to rethink my plans for these things."

"Have a name for them yet?"

"Uh, protype D?" She laughed.

"I have been thinking of them as battle-bards since they arrived. Maybe go with something simple like that until you find a design you want to stick with?"

"Battle-bards? I like that!"

He left her to it and started the team moving out.

Another small group of Cassian was waiting for them a short while later, but the battle-bards and bots made quick work of them before they could even catch up.

April had him call a halt a short while later. "Sir, the scout bots have found what appears to be a control center, or at least a computer center of some kind that looks to be fortified. Our bot has not been detected that we can tell, but there are other aliens there, sir. I mean, they are not just Cassian..."

"Oh? Well, can you tell what species? Sargani, Grays?"

"Yes, I mean no, sir. It is not a being that we know of."

Kasey's eyes opened wide. "Okay, send me the feeds and pull the bot back where it won't be seen. Then get a copy sent back to fleet."

"Yes, sir. Wait, we have orders."

"For the new aliens? That was quick."

"No, sir. The mothership is accelerating again. It is veering onto a collision course for Redwood instead of an orbit. If we cannot stop this ship from accelerating soon, we won't be able to prevent a collision."

"Dammit. Is team two making any progress?"

"No, sir, they encountered heavy resistance and needed to pull back when the fleet troops joined them. Currently they are trying a new route. Sir, I think they should be called back. We have a little over twenty minutes to stop this ship, and they don't have the time to make it anywhere important enough to make a difference now."

"Are you sure you are thinking about the mission and not Mr. Bennett?"

She smiled. "Yes, sir. If we cannot stop this ship in time, our only chance is to use this mothership's own power to change the course. If team two damages the engine, we won't have that option. We would be better off bringing them here to help us."

"Fine, have them rendezvous with us using known passages. No exploring or side trips, and get them here as fast as they are able. Have someone meetup with them with a resupply if possible, but no delays."

"Yes, sir."

"I hate to ask, but do we know what the effect on the planet would be?"

"Total loss of the colony if it makes a direct hit, sir. The collision will be close enough that not even Sariyn's people will have much chance. We also don't know what powers this ship, but it is likely a larger power source than the Abscond had—and we know what that did to Lithose. The planet itself would likely become unstable, it could have recovered from an attack, but it won't survive an impact of this size."

Kasey felt like he had been punched in the gut.

Sariyn and most of the Nimbus crew were supposed to be in the safest spot imaginable, now he probably killed them all by attacking the mothership. He wanted to scream in frustration, but there was no time.

"What are the orders?" he asked as he pulled up the

feeds she was sending. After a quick look he forwarded them onto AnnaChi.

"You are to take control of the ship or find their self-destruct—and use it ASAP."

"So, nothing new then?"

"You were already planning to try and blow this ship up?"

"Not sure we are going to have a choice. We can't let this ship reach Redwood."

"I understand, sir." She smiled weakly. "The navy troops have reached our rear perimeter."

"Good, let everyone know we are moving out."

AnnaChi ran up. "Have everyone arm themselves with a Cassian weapon! We need to burn a hole through that barricade, and we don't have much else that can do the job."

Kasey nodded to April. "Do it." He turned to AnnaChi. "The backup troops are here but we are out of time. The mothership is accelerating, we have twenty minutes before it is on an impact course with Redwood. Team two's search was a bust and they are on their way to us now. I need you see if the navy troops brought anything useful and get them lined up and ready for combat ASAP. Can you do that?"

"I like it when you get bossy, darlin." She winked and ran off.

He smiled but turned his attention back to the feeds.

The area that bots had scouted was unlike anything they had seen on the mothership so far. From what he could tell, a large, multifaceted, crystalline sphere had been embedded into the mothership's normal areas without care for design. The mothership showed signs of having been reworked around the sphere, as if the whole thing had been added as an afterthought to the building process.

The sphere itself was mostly comprised of three- to

five-meter wide, flat, and clear facets held within a dark web-like structure. One of the facets was dead center of the chamber and had an entryway molded into it. He could see several other entrances through the glassy facets around the entrance, but he was more interested in what he could see inside the sphere itself.

He counted six oddly placed platforms within view and had little doubt there were several others he couldn't see. Each platform varied in size and had glowing tendrils connecting them to each other. Dozens of Cassian rushed around from one entrance to another, but Kasey ignored them too. It was the two other creatures that stood on one of the platforms that caught his attention.

He zoomed in for a closer look at the creatures that appeared to be working intently at a set of controls. They looked humanoid and were clothed in leathery uniforms that made them look nearly human, but any resemblance stopped there. Their heads had wide jutting jaws that narrowed quickly as they protruded far forward. Every few moments the creatures opened their maw just enough to glimpse four long pointed teeth near the front, two on each side. He had no doubt of their deadliness. The upper head slanted back further and had four eyes crowning the stern-looking face.

The arms looked exceptionally strong and proportionally longer than human appendages. While there were just two main arms, each one had two forearms sprouting halfway down them. All four hands had four fingers each, two on each side of the hand opposing the other two.

A bright flash of light caused both creatures to squat down, revealing that their legs were similar to their arms. The four lower legs all angled out from each other as if the creature was ready to spring away. The closer of the two beings moved a few steps while still squatted before launching himself onto a darkened platform—where the flash had come from—with ease.

It landed on the edge and moved to a Cassian. Kasey had not realized just how large these new creatures were until it lashed out at the Cassian, bashing it from the platform. The body fell away as others scurried out of the being's way in fear. It began directing the Cassian to tasks of some kind and soon the platform began to glow brighter.

Kasey tore his gaze away and watched the small hoard of Cassian around the entrance outside of the sphere erecting a barrier to block off the area around its entrance. It was a wide-open area that could have been the start of another warehouse but was only a few dozen meters deep before running into the sphere. The area would be easy for the Cassian to defend, and they certainly looked to be planning to do so.

The hall leading to the area offered very little in the way of protection for more than a few people. There was another area further back, but the hallway curved out of sight. Still, it would make a good staging area and there was no more time to plan.

He looked over the waiting troops as they all made their way to the staging area. They were ready and willing to follow him, even though he had no real training. Maybe they followed because he had gotten lucky a few times and had AnnaChi to back him up. He sighed to himself; he didn't have the luxury to wonder about command now.

He looked around for AnnaChi and found her arguing with a small group of navy troops. He caught her eye and waved her over.

"Problems?"

"Not exactly. They are itching for a fight after seeing the carnage we left behind. I showed them the fortified chokepoint the Cassian have waiting for us, and they want to go in guns blazing."

"They would get cut down."

"I told them that. So did their commander, but I see it in their eyes. They are going to rush in and get the people that will be trying to save their asses killed. I have been there myself."

"Seriously?"

"It's a hard lesson, love. Not something I want to talk about sober. But we do need a plan to keep them from rushing in. Short of stunning them, I don't have one yet."

"Can the battle-bards crash that barricade?"

"Yes," she tilted her head slightly, "but also no. I don't think it would work."

"Care to explain that?"

"Well, the one with shield-walls can get close enough to bash through, but it will need some speed to get through. The others can follow. But I am positive all of them will get cut down within moments of breaking through, as they will be outflanked and none have armor on the side, so they will be ripped apart. They need to be at speed, so our troops will be too far behind to take much advantage of the confusion. Conversely, if we use the bards as protection to move the troops up close, they won't last long enough at the slow speeds and again we will be stuck in a firefight we won't win easily."

"Explosives?"

"They brought some breaching charges and grenades. We need to save the breachers for that sphere's door. If those new aliens are the Cassian's masters, I am positive they would not give them guns that could burn holes into their areas—and I assume the spheres are theirs, not the Cassian's."

"Agreed. So, we have grenades. How many?"

"Maybe two dozen. You have an idea?"

"More of a loose thought…"

"We have maybe fifteen minutes to take that sphere down, and we don't even know if that will stop this mothership. It does seem rather important to them though…"

"How many bots can we fit in a bard?" He grinned.

"Uh, six or seven. Maybe a few more if we push hard. Could have a handful mag-lock onto the backside and top if you are desperate."

"Okay. I need our two best snipers and anyone with a good throwing arm who feel they can toss grenades accurately. They need to stay safely back until we breach the sphere. Give the pitchers half the grenades and send the rest to me ASAP. Everyone else needs to line up and be ready for the assault, with the fastest troops in the lead along with the ones who want to charge in. Go, I will work out the rest."

She kissed him hard and ran off.

CHAPTER FORTY-SEVEN

As one, the entire unit moved out with the four bards in the lead.

The lead battle-bard still had the intact shield-walls. Next came the armored battle-bard, but much of that armor was burned away. The last two were simple bards with guns, lasers, and not much more.

The pace was steady as they came around the curve in the hallway. A moment later a hail of enemy fire splashed off the lead bard as well as the walls and flooring. On cue, the battle-bards ramped up their speed, quickly pulling away from the troops.

Kasey watched them go as he and the others picked up the pace as well. Timing would be everything. Several people passed him by. He knew he wasn't in top shape, not even close, but he pushed himself to keep up with the group.

He watched a group of camera angles from the bards as he ran. The shield-walls were failing, and just as the first one did, the armored battle-bard zoomed around it and rocketed ahead. Cassian fire tore into it, but it never slowed as it plowed directly through the middle of the

Cassian barricade and kept going.

Another screen became his focus as the two armed, but unarmored, bards followed the first through the now-gaping hole at a slightly slower speed. As soon as each was through, they used their jump jets to arc over the horde of Cassian—one to the left and the next to the right. While in the air, six bots dropped from each bard.

Each bot directed its descent into the rows of thickly packed Cassian before igniting the grenades Kasey had attached to each of them.

Kasey shook away the screens and concentrated on his running, picking up the pace once again. He could hear the three battle-bards continuing to fire, and that was soon augmented by the sounds of a few dozen bots that had been packed inside the bards.

The shield-wall protected battle-bard had dropped back, allowing the troops to catch up with it. It was not attracting much fire now and its own guns were tearing into any opportune targets. The troops were firing as well now, more to keep the pressure on the Cassian than trying to hit anything.

As they reached the barricade itself, the battle-bard edged slowly through the hole, releasing more security bots as it went. Troops moved in behind them, firing more precisely as they located protected positions near the ruined barricade. Many were using Cassian bodies for cover.

He swallowed hard as AnnaChi climbed onto the top of the battle-bard. She took a prone position between angled plates of thick armor that seemed almost too perfectly placed for her to fit between. He shook his head at her foresight and slowed his pace slightly to get his pulse under control and checked his rifle one last time as he entered the fray.

As he moved past the barrier, he heard a loud pop followed by a blast to the left of his position. One of the bards had been destroyed. Ignoring it, he ran up to the bard which had AnnaChi on top. Most of the people with Kasey fanned out and took the place of the initial troopers who now moved to join Kasey and formed a protective shield of bodies around him and the six others that had stayed at the back until now.

Kasey motioned his group forward. The battle-bard moved ahead of them, setting a quick pace as they jogged across the room to the large sphere's entrance. Behind him, the team abandoned the barricade and leap-frogged positions as they kept up.

Kasey tried to keep focus on his task, but several times he noticed people going down and not getting back up. Others rushed to aid them, but in most cases, they were left behind. People were dying. There was no doubt they would win this battle now, but there was no time to do it right. Maybe there never was in battle.

They passed the ruins of the first bard that had broken through the barricade. Several security bots lay unmoving nearby but many more dead Cassian surrounded the area. The way ahead was clear, but Kasey noticed the heavy fire in the distance had stopped. The last of the first three bards were now gone.

The firing around him increased as all the Cassian that still lived turned their full attention to his group. AnnaChi slid down from bard and moved to his side.

"Neither the Cassian weapons nor bard's cannons are able to penetrate the sphere. We need to blast it."

Kasey waved to the group following him and two ran forward with a large flat box. It only took them a second to affix it to the sphere's entryway before diving for cover a few meters away. The blast left Kasey's ears ringing. As the smoke cleared, he wanted to scream. The doors were damaged, but not enough to break through. He did not need to look at the time to know they had just minutes left to stop the mothership.

"Nova," he linked into the battle-bard's com, "ram that door with everything this vehicle has!"

There was no reply from the limited AI clone as the vehicle leapt forward, ramping up speed as it closed the distance and activated its jump jets at the last second. A bone-chilling crunch ended its run abruptly. Kasey and the others sprinted up behind the now silent machine. A wide crack could be seen on the sphere's entryway, just large enough for people to get through.

AnnaChi and half a dozen others darted past him, practically diving through the crack and into the sphere beyond.

He looked back and waved his own team to follow as he started toward the opening.

A bright blue bolt slipped out of the opening and slammed into his chest with a blast that sent him flying off his feet.

CHAPTER FORTY-EIGHT

A navy man with a large, scoped rifle knelt to check on him, worry written on his face.

Kasey reached under his skinsuit, just below his left shoulder, and felt for the angry wound. It was tender but he still seemed whole. He brought out his hand and experienced a wave of relief that he saw no blood.

He waved the man off, "I'll be fine, go! Take those two aliens down! Alive if you can—but stop them."

They moved off as Kasey grunted and pushed himself back up painfully. Whatever hit him would leave a mark—of that, he was sure.

Rushing through the opening, he found half his people unconscious or worse. Diving for cover, he saw one of the grenade men double over and crash down near the edge of the platform. He dashed over to him. The man was still alive but in serious trouble.

Kasey wanted to help but took a small bag from the man instead and glanced over the edge of the platform. Not far away, a bright platform waited like a beacon. He pulled out a grenade lobbed it downwards then started looking for another target.

The explosion caused a rippling light effect across the whole sphere causing Kasey to smile inwardly. He tossed another and then a third, as the second one missed. It went off just as it reached the platform, causing another light show. Before he could toss a fourth, the bag was pulled away from him by a couple navy troops who took over with much better accuracy.

The blue bolts had stopped. It appeared the snipers had done their job, but Kasey didn't bother to look at the result. He grabbed up a Cassian weapon someone had dropped and ran up the sloped walkway to the next darkened platform and kept running until a lighted platform was in range of his weapon. Firing as he ran towards it, burning holes into any workstations and equipment he could find until it too went dark. He bolted through towards another platform, repeating the process until suddenly the entire sphere pulsed bright flashes of light a few times and then the entire sphere went totally dark.

He stopped and dropped to his knees, working hard to catch his breath. There was no sound, just his breath and heartbeat pounding in his ears.

He looked up. There were no gunshots to be heard anywhere. Beams of light were flashing around as the troops fanned out across the darkened sphere. A group caught up to him, led by AnnaChi.

She wacked him on the helmet before kneeling beside him. "What the hell were you thinking?"

"Did we keep the ship from accelerating? Did it work?"

AnnaChi laughed. "No, and yep!"

"Uh. Okay, great. Whatever…"

"April is on her way over, she can explain. Also," she lifted her faceplate, "the air is breathable here, but the smell could be a lot better."

Kasey flopped back into a proper sitting position and

took a water bottle someone handed him and drained it.

"How is the team? Did everyone make it into the sphere?"

"They are mostly fine. Flair showed up with another group and are cleaning up the entryway area now. A few more groups are on the way, but we won't be getting more than those that have landed already."

"Why not? We need everyone we can to take the rest of this mothership."

April appeared with a smile on her face. "Well done, Captain!"

"What did we do?"

"Well, we didn't stop the ship from accelerating, but that is no longer an issue."

"Why not?"

"Because, when you shut down this sphere, the mothership jumped. We are now somehow on the far side of the planet by nearly a million kilometers."

"And we did that somehow?"

"We believe so. The jump happened at the exact moment you blew out the power to this area. We are not sure what their actual intent was, but whatever you did must have forced the jump to happen early. We know they were aiming for Redwood from their acceleration curve, and it appears their jump took them on a precise tangent of their trajectory. A few more seconds and the jump would have intersected with the atmosphere or the planet itself."

"But if the jump took them beyond the planet, it wouldn't have mattered, right?"

"That is being argued, but honestly we don't have the right people to guess why the jump was so long. Maybe that was also your interference, or maybe the planets gravity well, or maybe their jump technology is not based on wormholes like ours is. We just do not know."

"Not wormhole based, would mean...?"

"Above my head, sir, but meaning it may move through normal space several orders of magnitude faster than our galaxy-class star drives are able to. A planet impact at those speeds…"

"I get it. Unbelievably bad."

"Yes, sir. Likely worse than we could imagine."

"Fine, do we know how long before this ship can turn around and try again?"

"At least a few hours."

"How many reinforcements did we get before it jumped?"

"About a third of the fleet's ship crews that could be spared, maybe forty men. Bennett's team will be here shortly as well, with another thirty, I hope… I don't know how many we lost, sir. Too many. We have two security bots left and Bennett only has a few more than that, from what I can tell."

"Would have thought the fleet would have been better prepared for a ground assault?" AnnaChi chimed in.

"The bigger ships usually are." Flair's commanding voice joined them as she crouched down, holding out a handful of energy bars. "Fran has a troop of marines with powered armor on the Pathfinder's lifeboat too. None of them made it to Nimbus before this thing jumped, unfortunately."

"Damn. We barely made it into this, uh, control sphere?" Kasey complained. "I hope you brought a lot more explosives."

"Some… More than you had before, at least. I brought one of your demo bots along too."

He smiled. "Good, we lost ours somewhere back there. Not sure where, we were in a bit of a rush."

"So then, what's next, boss?" Flair stood up.

They all stood and waited for him.

"Do we have the sniper's reports? Did they get the

two aliens?"

AnnaChi pointed to a group of lights in the distance, "One dead, the other escaped. Both were heading to the same exit. Suggest we follow it. Ensign Ott claims he winged the one that got away, so maybe there will be a trail. Assuming they bleed…"

"Fine. April, send one of the remaining bots through and see if it can locate a position we can defend." he looked at Flair and AnnaChi. "Who is in charge of the troops now?"

Flair didn't hesitate. "Your call, it's your battlefield. But I suggest giving me all the navy and AnnaChi can have everyone else. Keep an open comms channel between the four of us."

"Done. AnnaChi, make Bennett your second when he arrives, and merge the crew teams. They should have some resupply for us as well."

AnnaChi shook her head. "Actually, just give them all to Bennett. I am better off watching your back. Keep in mind a lot of our crew have had training in the past, but most are really worn out. The last battle asked too much from many of them."

"That works, Bennett's group will be the reserve. Flair, send any troops in need of downtime to Bennett as well. If anyone needs sent back to Nimbus, get them to whoever is handling medical. I am sure they will have a group heading back with our injured soon. AnnaChi and April, get Bennett up to speed and then join back up with me."

He left them to it and worked his way over to the group looking at the dead alien.

It was big. Half again taller than Kasey, it would tower over any human by nearly a meter. The being was a grayish blue color and had several rocky features that reminded him of barnacles. Even in death, the creature looked angry and imposing.

A thick metallic band encircled two of its four wrists. Each had two barrels jutting forward.

Kasey pointed at them. "Are those the blue-bolt weapons we saw?"

"We believe so, sir. They appear to be wired into the creature's flesh, along with several other implants we haven't been able to identify."

"Take it to the medical team to put on ice after our people are taken care of."

"Yes, sir! Will we be moving out soon?"

"Soon as we can, yes. Best to be ready."

He made a roundabout path through the control sphere examining the numerous panels and paraphernalia on the platforms as he went. Some were very alien in design, yet many could have easily been mistaken for human controls. The layout and power conduits were the strangest, almost as if they were from yet another alien race they had not seen yet. Nothing in the control sphere was of Cassian design at all, although the creatures had clearly been working with it.

He rubbed his temple. It was yet another mystery to worry over later.

He put the thoughts aside as a medic ran up with a stimulant injection. They applied a medical patch to his shoulder after seeing the bruising where the alien's weapon had struck him. He accepted them wearily, glad the new skinsuit had held up under the strike. The combat suit he wore over the skinsuit looked to have been penetrated with ease by the weapon and the medic looked worried until seeing underneath. The hard armor may not have worked, but the new navy skinsuit had fully stopped the deadly bolt. The suit looked slightly damaged, but still showed combat ready according to the suit's interface.

The stims were a necessity. They all really needed a break, but that was not going to happen without a lot more reinforcements than they were going to get.

As the medic moved off, another man appeared with fresh power cells for his weapons, a pack of water, nutrient bars, and other supplies. As soon as he had the gear integrated into his own pack, AnnaChi and April showed up, followed by a short line of bots.

"Flair and Bennett will have their teams ready to move in five minutes," AnnaChi reported.

"Do we have a place to move to?"

"Yes, sir," April replied, in high spirits. "The new alien left quite a path in its wake. Some splattering of its own blood, but that thing must have killed every Cassian it came across, from the looks of it. There is another sphere, much smaller than this one, and looks to be a different type of control room. No platforms like this, but rows and rows of Cassian manning panels. If my mapping is correct, it should be near the center of the mothership. Our assumption is that this will be the main control room."

"I assume it is guarded like this one was?"

"Not exactly. The areas ahead are more open and, well, a bit opulent. I have counted several small groups of Cassian in guard positions, maybe forty so far. Many are painted in bright colors. It may be a ranking system, but if I had to guess I would say they are honor guards at their normal posts. Not much like the packs we have encountered so far."

"Or they are the elite troops," AnnaChi quipped.

"Same weapons?"

She took a minute to reply as she reviewed the feeds, "Yes, they all seem to have the same as we have seen so far. Honestly, sir, I thought there would be a lot more. The control room has a bunch inside as well, non-painted, but they don't seem to be armed that I can tell."

"And the alien?"

"It is on a central dais of the control sphere, along

with another one of its kind."

"Okay, so we have one wounded and pissed off alien, along with his new friend, in command of a room full of Cassian. Send us the feeds and your map if you haven't already. Let Flair know they are primary targets the moment we break into that room."

"She will want one alive," AnnaChi complained.

"Well, she has a good point about that, but I am not ready to throw our lives away for it."

"Fine by me, this is not exactly our war. But she is thinking about the longer-term war."

"Regardless... If we can grab one, great. If we cannot... Well, I am not going to lose sleep over it. We were not prepared for this."

They spent the next few minutes examining the bot feed while waiting for Flair and Bennett to be ready. When they finally joined them, Kasey was frowning.

"Bad news?" Flair asked.

"Not as such. We have a place ahead we can hold, but beyond that the area is far too open. Take a few minutes to review the feed, but I would say our best bet is to drive forward straight to the sphere and break inside as quick as we can. Better to deal with the unarmed Cassian in there than the unknown number that could surround us in the open."

"But inside," AnnaChi added, "we have to deal with two more of those new aliens on top of a small hoard of Cassian, even if they are unarmed. No real cover either."

Flair got a faraway look for a minute while she viewed the feed, then sat, thinking.

"Well," she said slowly, "we can have some portable shield-walls brought forward and set them up once we break into the sphere, but it will take time. It will give us some cover while we move everyone inside. Still, it will be costly to get them deployed."

"I already have Griff and his engineers pulling the

two shield-walls off the bard," Bennett added. "He believed he would have both working before we move out. But they won't be fully charged. They are also repurposing a few of the destroyed security bot's grav-panels to serve as a mobile platform. He believes one of the bard's guns can be mounted on it but is unsure how well it will handle under the recoil."

"Good thinking, we could use that firepower. See if they can get a second one ready, even if the platforms are only used for moving the guns onto something we can mount them on in the field. Keep one in the rear for any surprises, but if we can get one into the sphere it would make a big difference."

Kasey listened and shrugged. "It's a better plan than I had, but I still think we will take a lot of losses."

"We need a distraction," AnnaChi asserted as she rolled her shoulders back and smiled.

"I assume you have an idea about that?"

"Maybe. But I will need the demo bot, a sniper rifle, one of the remaining security bots, and two of Flair's best sailors."

Kasey frowned at her and took a deep breath. "Flair, can we break into this sphere without the demo bot? We need a lot more than one breaching charge if we want to make a fast entrance."

"We have three breachers with us. We can combine all three charges into one. It should do the job and then some."

He rubbed his temples. "Fine... AnnaChi, you have a go, but all five of us stay on the command channel and stay coordinated."

It took longer than Kasey would have liked to get everyone to the new position. He had to admit it was a great location. Instead of the long winding and mostly nondescript hallways and chambers that had brought them so deep into the ship, they were now in a building of some kind. The structure looked like it had been built for more artistic purposes, but everything was oversized. It didn't seem to serve an actual function but had access to multiple floors of the mothership. Best of all, it was a was natural defensible position.

He settled into an empty chamber as Flair and Bennett handled the logistics of the people. Everyone was getting acquainted with the layout leading to the sphere and discussed strategies for the assault in groups.

Instead of joining them, he watched AnnaChi's progress. She had already left, taking a passage through the upper floors, and appeared to be nearly above the sphere now. The sphere itself was embedded into several floors, but he could not tell which one she was on.

Everyone else had chosen what they now thought of as the main deck. The entryway to the sphere was on this level so that was where they needed to be. April had bots out searching for less obvious routes that would take them closer to the sphere's entryway, but so far none had been located. Flair's assessment of the painted Cassian guard's locations also indicated the open areas were likely to be the only decent entrance.

"AnnaChi. Give me a status."

"We are a bit lost at the moment actually. In a maintenance passage tween decks. Sorry Kasey, I thought we would have a solution by now."

April interrupted, "I am detecting movement. Looks like a group of Cassian, hundred meters, ten o'clock from our position. The bot noticed two Cassian and followed them to a larger group that appear to be waiting for us."

CHAPTER FORTY-NINE

"How many?" Kasey asked.

"Maybe twenty, but if others continue to join them…"

"Then the longer we wait, the more we will need to deal with. Got it. AnnaChi, step it up!"

"On it! Give us ten. If we don't have a way in by then—we will make one."

The bots located two more groups of Cassian gathering. It was clear now that a trap had been designed to catch them in the open. He hoped the enemy didn't know how much his group had grown since the last attack. Maybe they would underestimate and make a mistake. On the other hand, maybe every Cassian in the entire mothership was on the way.

Decision made, he stood and opened the command channel. "Change of plans. We are going to get swarmed from all sides if we make a run directly for the sphere. That is what they want. We might make it, but we will lose a lot of people. However, we know where several of the Cassian groups are building up, so we will attack them directly and take them out with our superior numbers. Even if the remaining groups attack, we will have less overall enemy to deal with at once."

"That would buy me more time as well," AnnaChi added.

"Agreed," Flair responded after a moment. "The groups we know about are between twenty and thirty strong. We should be able to attack the two closest groups at the same time. The third is a bit further forward, but we can expect them to attack while we are busy with the first two. Bennett, can you set up a surprise for that third group when it shows up?"

"Yes, sir. We will set up the two heavy guns centrally and prep the shield-walls for additional cover. We shouldn't have trouble with one group unless they are really spread out."

"Good, we will reinforce you once we take out the first two groups, then we all press forward. April, spread out the security bots to act as spotters."

Kasey watched proudly as each team moved out one by one. He joined Bennett's team as they went out behind the navy groups. Bennett had chosen an area that rose up higher than most areas, providing a good vantage point. As Bennett crawled up to peek over the top, he waved Kasey to join him, then pointed at the halfway point to the sphere room.

He heard Flair's firefight starting before he got a look at what Bennett was pointing at. At least four different columns of Cassian had broken their cover and were all heading towards the navy team locations.

"Damn. We need to draw some attention and give the navy time to take care of their first groups."

Bennett unlimbered his rifle and looked to his team. "Rifles only on this hill, pick targets and wait for my order. After the first volley, you are free to fire at will. The rest of you, drop back thirty yards and set up the heavies. Shield-walls on the flanks and make sure you have room for us to join you. We will bring them up and over this hill and into our killing ground."

Twelve crewmembers moved forward to join them. When Bennett gave the order, fourteen shots rang out and nearly as many Cassian fell. A few got back up, but most of the closest ones paused and looked around.

"Hold fire!" Bennett quickly commanded, "Prepare for another volley on new targets. Fire! Weapons free!"

More Cassian dropped, but not as many as in the first volley. There was continuous fire now and the Cassian took little time to locate them and charged towards their position, firing their own weapons as they did. The crew continued firing for a few more moments before Bennett ordered them to fall back. Two shots later Kasey and Bennett were running as well.

Cassian were over the hill before Kasey made it back to the line. It was a surreal experience running toward a line of people that appeared to be firing directly at him. Running past the front line he dove for cover.

He heard something whiz over his head as he dropped his rifle and unslung the Cassian weapon everyone was now carrying in addition to their main weapon. It was less accurate and had a shorter range, but it could penetrate the Cassian armor where their own longer-range weapons could not. The fighting was too close now to worry about accuracy, so everyone would be using the Cassian weapons for this fight.

He barely noticed April calling out warnings to Flair as well as numbers and positions, but Kasey had too much to worry about with the ever-increasing numbers of Cassian scrambling over the hill towards them.

The team's two heavy guns shredded dozens of the enemy but had to concentrate on keeping the flanks clear. Everyone else was concentrating on the center. It worked for a while, but as the numbers grew, too many made it close to firing line.

"Grenades as able! Top of that hill if you can!" Bennett shouted.

One by one, grenades were lobbed into the mass of Cassian. The explosions spouted filth high into the air and knocked down those that weren't killed. The flow of enemies slowed enough for the crew to kill all the closest Cassian and start targeting those at the crest of the hill again. He expected the flood of enemy to increase again, instead the tide began to slow.

"April, where are the Cassian?"

"Looks like most groups are heading back towards the command sphere, sir."

"Flair, where are you?"

"Almost to your position. There were more than we expected, and we had several come in at our backs. I guess they didn't all head your way."

"Causalities?"

"April got us a warning. They got a few lucky hits on us, but nothing we can't shake off."

He looked at Bennett, who gave him a thumbs up. "We are good here too. Great job everyone! Now, let's go finish this."

"Just waiting on you all," AnnaChi added, "and the sooner the better. If they look up, I am screwed!"

"Flair, get us in rifle range and pour some heat onto the groups around the sphere. Keep their attention on us."

As soon as they came into range, everyone lined up and sent several volleys into the packs of Cassian. The first shots were devastating, but the Cassian immediately turned their protective armor towards the attackers, hunkering down in safety.

"Heavy guns?" Kasey asked.

Bennett responded, "We could, but we would run out of ammo before we made a dent in their numbers at this range. I suggest we save the ammo."

"Damn. Flair, a head-on attack is going to take too long. Can we faint an attack up the center, but have our real attack head to one of lighter-defended sides and out-flank them? I think the combined breaching charge will penetrate the crystal walls based on the damage we did to the last one. Just avoid the main entrance altogether."

"The breach charge will work, I have no doubt. I suggest a three-pronged attack. Send a small team to the far left to start the attack. Keep them far back at max range. A third of our troops then attack down the center. Once the center is fully engaged in a firefight, we pull the left team to join the center troops and then everyone starts leapfrogging to the right side. Our largest force will make its way up the right side, not engaging until they need to. Our snipers and heavy guns go with that group. Push down their right flank hard and blast our way into that sphere while at the same time we can provide some cover fire for our other troops to join us."

"Interesting but sounds complicated. Done this sort of thing before?"

"In a real fight? No. But plenty of times in simulations and war games, as have all navy."

"And did it work?"

"In the sims, it worked well. Not so well in war games, but most plans don't when everyone has the same playbooks. Which is the whole point usually."

"Okay. We give it a try. AnnaChi, be ready with your distraction when we get close to the sphere. We need to set the charges and blast through before they can prepare a welcoming party for us inside."

"Oh, I promise they will be distracted. Just hurry it up."

* * *

Kasey ducked behind an oversized bench. Just beyond, his men worked their way around a group of strange sculptures he could not identify. The alien area would be relaxing if the sounds of gunshots and alien weapons couldn't be heard in the distance.

He checked the feed from the security bot they had scouting ahead. It had stopped moving. Directly ahead of it was a small group of Cassian. It was the first of three groups his team was planning to attack simultaneously. Beyond the groups were a larger concentration of Cassian, with several of the painted ones mixed in.

Bennett crawled up beside him, indicating they were ready. Readying his own weapon, Kasey prepared to take over the position ahead as soon as the troops rushed forward.

A shot rang out close by. Too early!

"Go, go, go!" Bennett shouted, as Kasey tried to make sense of what happened, but there was no time. He moved to the next position and checked the feed, only to find it offline. More shots rang out as they engaged.

"Kasey! We lost contact with our left flank team," Flair called out over comms. "Something must have hit them from behind—we still have a visual of their targets, but they are no longer under fire. Permission to send a rescue team?"

Kasey felt heat rushing up his spine in worry. The whole plan was going to hell fast.

"Do it. Bennett, send half our reserve to backup Flair's center team."

Orders went out and troops shifted. Kasey could now see the Cassian far ahead, two painted in vibrant blue colors. He took aim and fired, but the shot glanced off the creature's armor. He looked for another target but was interrupted.

"I think they have noticed my team," AnnaChi

calmly announced, "there is movement in the passages behind us."

"How many?"

"Can't tell... Shit! The big ugly alien just looked up. It sees us!"

"Can you..."

A massive explosion rumbled through the area.

"AnnaChi? AnnaChi, respond!" he couldn't think, "AnnaChi!"

Bennett grabbed him and pointed ahead. The sphere's lights were flickering. Large topside sections of the structure had broken off and fallen on the enemy inside it. The groups of Cassian outside the sphere had stopped firing and were scurrying madly back and forth.

He got a grip on his thoughts and shrugged away from Bennett.

"Everyone attacks now! Bring the heavy guns forward and get us to that sphere now! Flair, rescue status?"

"They are all dead... A group attacked them from behind and more were coming. We are pulling back towards you now."

He could not find his voice to respond. Everything had gone wrong, and it was his fault. He never should have been in charge. He wasn't even sure how it all had gotten dumped on his shoulders. Now his decisions had gotten even more people killed.

One of the heavy guns the engineers had mounted on a busted security bot's chassis was being pushed past him. He dropped his rifle and moved to it. Taking control, he pushed the heavy weapon at a run towards the front line and beyond.

Several people were shouting behind him, which he ignored. The Cassian ahead were still in their weird frenzy, but one of them stopped and looked his way.

Kasey squeezed the trigger tightly, blasting the

creature apart. He swung the weapon across the next cluster of Cassian and kept moving forward. A few fired back, but a rain of plasma, bullets and black bolts from captured weapons flowed around Kasey, pounding into any creatures who survived his onslaught.

The heavy gun clicked empty, and Kasey released it and drew his pistol, but a hand grabbed his shoulder and pulled him back before he could fire it.

"Sir!" Bennett yelled at him. "AnnaChi's team are taking fire!"

He looked towards the sphere, which he was surprised to see was now very close. A constant flow of bright blue bolts was being fired towards the top of the sphere blasting tufts of shrapnel across the room below. Great sections of the upper sphere were gone from the earlier blast, but above those were new openings exposing the innards of the mothership's workings. Oily liquids and sparks from broken components showered down onto the control areas, as well as the aliens below. Every so often, he could see movement in the above wreckage.

"Blow the breach now! And get me a damn rifle!"

The breach's blast cut a man-sized hole in the large crystal wall, sending cracks outward over the surviving facet's surface. Nearby Cassian took the full force of the blasted wall's shards, killing many of them instantly. Several grenades were tossed inside, adding to the chaos.

Kasey followed the first group of troops through the hole. The shield-walls would follow, but he couldn't wait. He moved inward, keeping his sights towards the areas the bolts were being fired from. The destruction around the hole would have been disturbing at any other time, but now he moved through the wreckage on a mission.

It took a moment to realize why the blue bolts suddenly stopped firing upward—until one of them exploded into Kasey's chest.

CHAPTER FIFTY

Kasey's vision faded—then returned as new meds pumped into his system. The bolt had impacted close to the earlier hit he had taken, thankfully the suit was not reporting any ruptures. More bolts crossed his vision as he realized he was on his back again.

He watched as, far above, a head peaked out from the wreckage and slid up its faceplate, showing AnnaChi's face smiling down. Yet the smile wasn't for him, but for something her rifle was now pointing at. She fired, paused, and then fired several more times. Eventually she stopped and looked around the sphere before she shrugged and pulled her helmet's faceplate down again.

Everything got suddenly quiet.

"Uh, Kasey," Flair sounded astonished, "the Cassian have dropped their weapons and are backing off! What just happened?"

"Uh, I am not sure. Stand by."

He took a moment to check the skinsuit's integrity again and was thankful to find it still held. Pushing himself up, he tried to connect into AnnaChi's comm link.

"AnnaChi, do you have coms working?"

A ping came in from her on his mimic interface, so he opened a new channel. "My helmet was damaged, my comm is down, but you're close enough for the mimic to reach now."

"I am glad you are okay. Any idea what happened? The Cassian seem to be giving up."

"As soon as I killed that big alien, the Cassian in the room settled down. Almost like they were being controlled by it. Thanks for that distraction by the way, that thing had me pinned down up here."

"What happened to the second one?"

"Crushed. I was hoping to get both, but they move too damn fast. Uh, did we just free the Cassian from their masters?"

"Who knows... Let's not jump to conclusions just yet. Can you and your team get down from there?"

"Sure, we planned to scale down the outside of the sphere near you. Not sure it is safe inside. Pieces are still falling, so stay away from the center. The remaining Cassian are all around the edge, doing nothing."

"Okay, see you shortly."

He moved back to the command comms.

"Flair, AnnaChi's comm is offline but she is fine. Her team took out the two new aliens and thinks they were controlling the Cassian. I think we need to talk with the Cassian if we can. Do we have any way to translate with them?"

"Hot damn! Hmm, Fran's people may have something. The navy has a division that works on just that and they have captured a lot of sphere fighters over the years."

"April, have the Nimbus crew contact the admiral and see what they can give us."

"I can and will do that, sir, but we may not need to."

"What do you mean?"

"If I understand how the Patternists in the Trias System were controlled, the Cassian must already have a translation system for humanity. I suggest you simply try to talk to them."

"Ha! Miss Mayflower, I am glad you are with us!"

"My pleasure, sir."

Kasey climbed up over the damaged equipment inside the sphere and looked out over the room. The Cassian who remained were in groups on the far side. He took a deep breath and opened his helmet's faceplate.

"Who of you is now in charge?" he yelled.

He waited, but none moved.

"Who can speak with me?"

Two of them immediately started making noises, but not at Kasey. He could only guess they were arguing with each other. Worried, he looked back and was relieved to see AnnaChi and several others taking up protective positions.

"Do you have a way to speak with us?" Kasey yelled again.

The two Cassian stopped and looked at Kasey then made a few more noises at each other before the larger one surged towards the center of the room.

Kasey held up a hand as he noticed several rifles being leveled at the creature.

"Safeties on everyone! We do not want an accidental shooting right now. Let it come."

The Cassian stooped over the body of the big alien AnnaChi had killed. After a moment, it pulled a slim piece of metal from the creature's temple area. Turning towards Kasey, the Cassian moved cautiously to stand in front of him, offering the device.

Kasey breathed deeply and let the creature drop the device into his hand. Kasey looked at it and turned it over a few times. One side was covered in small holes while the other had a silvery pattern inscribed into it.

He looked at the Cassian. "What do I do with this?"

The Cassian slowly reached out a slim appendage towards Kasey's temple and tapped it lightly, then backed away.

Well, this is likely a massive mistake, he thought, as he placed the device against his head.

CHAPTER FIFTY-ONE

An intense pain lashed out across Kasey's entire body. A series of shocks followed that forced him down onto one knee.

He waved off AnnaChi as she moved to place herself between the Cassian and him. He nodded to himself, then slowly stood back up.

AnnaChi laid a hand on Kasey's shoulder.

"I am fine. I think."

He addressed the Cassian, "Now what?"

He heard the creature respond with unintelligible chitter noises, yet he understood the meaning as if they were spoken in English.

"Spoken thoughts now understood. Thoughts to convey. Thoughts to command."

"How do you understand me? Do you also have a device?"

"Device with us. Device with me. In me. Embedded early life cycle."

"What do you mean, thoughts to command?"

The Cassian looked back at the one it had been arguing with before turning back and pointing towards

452

Kasey's implant. "Dominant controller. Inferiors must submit. You lead. You are master now. Us within this vessel follow you now."

Kasey took an involuntary step backwards. "Do you have a choice?"

"Single choice set. Follow command or Kriecken master chooses death." It pointed at its own head. "Device makes death. Many choose death…"

Kasey's pulse raced. "You are slaves? The masters were called Kriecken?"

"Accurate understanding. Both correct. You are master now."

"Why… Why would you willingly give us a means to control you? To kill you?"

It once again looked back at the other Cassian before responding. "We came here. Were brought here to destroy you. You stopped us. You stopped the Kriecken. You control now."

"Why not take it for yourself? Or destroy it and be free?"

"Survival. You would destroy us. Chance to serve instead. Chance you allow us life."

"Could you communicate with us without this device?"

"Possible. Take time. Build new device."

Kasey looked down at the rubble around him. Slavery went against everything he believed in, and then some, even for beings who had killed countless humans. It seemed simple enough to call them prisoners of war, but that was not much better in his mind. He had no idea what the Terrantine Federation would do if he allowed them to be treated as such.

"What would your people do if they were not enslaved?"

"Unknown. Not war. Many have thoughts. Stories. Dreams. Find a home."

"Are you able to prove what you say? That you really are slaves?"

"Recordings are available. Will be given. Facts are shown."

"If you are freed, will you work with us? Help us stop the attacks on my people?"

"Possible. Require protection. Kriecken will come. Kriecken will not stop."

"We need to learn their technology." Kasey pointed around the room.

"We can teach. We can share. We can build. Some is known. Some is not. Kriecken keep secrets. Keep knowledge."

Kasey sent a quick message to April. "Is the mothership still accelerating?"

"Yes, sir, it finished decelerating a while ago and is now accelerating back towards Redwood."

He turned his attention back to the Cassian. "Can you change this ship's trajectory? Keep it at the current distance from our planet?"

It turned and spoke to the others who started scrambling over the stations, then suddenly stopped. "Process has begun."

"Sir," April reported, "the mothership has changed acceleration again."

"Thank you, April. Let me know once its distance stabilizes."

He looked at the Cassian and sighed. "We are going to need to work out a few things, but first, what should we call you? Do you have a name?"

"Cassian call Chasgrew. Masters call Flight Control One. Name not needed for masters."

"I will call you Chasgrew. We do use job titles like Flight Controller if you are working, so you may be called both. My name is Kasey."

"Kasey? Not master?"

"Not master. I will not make you slaves. However, you and this ship are considered captured. Your capture is necessary because of the war your people and the Kriecken wage against us. My intention is that you will all be freed once that war is over. This is not only up to me. Others will make decisions about what happens in the future. Working with us will make decisions easier. Do you understand?"

It was silent for a moment. "We accept capture. We will help. You truly not kill us?"

"Truly. Now, I need you to bring me any other of these devices on this ship. I will only let someone trusted use them. Once we have another means of communication, they will be destroyed."

It spoke to the others again and they began scrambling around. Kasey noticed he couldn't understand what it said unless it was talking directly to him.

Most of the Cassian in the room moved to a massive piece of crystal that had once been at the peak of the sphere. They moved as one and lifted a corner of the half-meter wide crystal panel while another pulled out the corpse of one of the Kriecken from under it. A moment later one brought the device to Kasey.

"Thank you."

It reared back. "Appreciate. Yes," it said as it scrambled off.

"Chasgrew, others will be joining us soon who will need answers. Can you organize a delegation of your people who can answer questions?"

"Yes. Will complete rapidly."

"Go. We will talk again soon."

He noticed Flair watching him from the entrance they had made. He led her outside the sphere and found a place for them to sit.

"Their race is enslaved…" He took a moment to get

his emotions in check. "How will the Federation deal with that?"

"Right to the point, boss?"

"Drop the boss crap. You can stop allowing me to be in charge any time you like. Damned if I know why you haven't."

"Why do you think?"

"Some grand plan of Fran's I am sure. I don't particularly care why, but I am sick of being stuck in the middle trying to do the right thing."

"That may have been part of it, the beginning of it, maybe. But he actually ordered me to take over once I landed on the Nimbus. I decided not to. Besides, you started giving me orders, I simply decided to follow them."

"Why the hell didn't you?"

"That Cassian just surrendered to you, right? Ship and all?"

"Yes. So? Not like they had a choice."

"Right. But they surrendered to *you*."

"Again—so the hell what?"

"You are a civilian business owner and privateer."

"Working with the navy…"

"No. You started this. The navy just showed up after your attack and then assisted *your* fight."

"What the hell difference does that make? Semantics are fairly meaningless in what we just went through!"

"You are right—but it means a hell of a lot in what comes next."

"And just what will that be?"

She smiled deviously and stood to face him. "Mr. Robinson, the Terrantine Navy asks your permission to take temporary possession of your captured vessel for research and containment purposes. Further, the navy asks for the assistance of the various Cassian resources currently under your protection. Usage and treatment of the vessel, its contents, and its current crew will fall strictly under the preview of your expressed wishes, as long as such wishes do not endanger the Federation in any way. With the understanding that specific details will be outlined and approved at a later time, is this acceptable Mr. Robinson?"

He raised an eyebrow and nodded. "Assuming the details check out, yes, I agree."

"Thank you."

"You don't honestly expect me to believe the navy or Federation will give this mothership to me once they are done looking at it?"

"Could go a few ways to be honest, but you captured the vessel of a Federation enemy while under the flag of a privateer. That will hold a lot of weight. There are a lot of gray lines in what is considered a danger to the Federation, but in general, if they cannot duplicate the technology quickly, the navy may offer compensation or make an agreement for long-term use. Even if they can duplicate it, they may find reasons not to return the ship to you. Long term with compensation, would be where I place my bets. I believe we saw at least three completely different forms of technologies that we have never seen before, and we only saw a small piece of this ship. I am positive your new Cassian friends will know some of the tech in detail, but it seems like this ship was built by at least two or three other races. Too bad you killed the other aliens."

"They are called the Kriecken."

"Kriecken. Alright. We now have a new enemy, and new name for the threat out there."

"The true enemy?"

"Perhaps, but I doubt it. However, the existence of this new enemy may explain a few theories."

Kasey pulled out the second communication device and handed it to her. "Well, that is for you to start finding out. This can kill them with the wrong thought, so be extremely careful. In fact, my expressed wishes are that these are not copied and that they are destroyed as soon as we have another translator set up. If you decide they need to be kept for research, then find a way to deactivate the ones implanted in the Cassian first. That should be done anyway. I don't care how, but no one is going to use this against them any longer. Understood?"

"Not much different from having armed guards around them."

"Wrong. It is vastly different when your entire species has been enslaved by that little device. Want them to help us as much as possible? Then destroy these as quickly as possible and let them watch you do it."

"After we properly validate that they are being truthful, fine. They have much to answer for before they will be trusted. Honestly, I am not sure others will agree, even if we have sufficient proof."

"Then get it done before anyone else has a say in it."

"Fine, I will make it happen." She sighed but smiled. "If Fran's estimate was correct, we have a day or two before we will get any backup. I hope that is enough time. There are some Federation things that the navy cannot control."

"I understand. If Chasgrew was being honest with me, they are highly motivated to provide you all the proof they can as quickly as they can."

"Chasgrew?"

"The one I spoke to. At least that is how its name sounded in my head. He, she, they, it—I am not really sure. Anyway, it is organizing a team to talk with you as soon as you are ready. We should have a third device on the Kriecken we have in our medical facility on Nimbus, and the Cassian are gathering any others on the mothership for me. But I am going back to Nimbus now, along with most of our crew. They have been through enough. We will need someone here you *fully* trust before you leave, otherwise call me back in a few hours."

"Sure thing, boss. Will we be heading back to Redwood after the rest of the fleet gets here?"

"As soon as I can get away. You're staying with us then?"

"Yes, if you will have me still. However, unless you are leaving Redwood soon, I would like to spend some time with Fran. He is going to be pouting about losing the Pathfinder."

Kasey smiled at that. "We will be stuck here a few weeks at the very least. A lot longer if we cannot land Nimbus for repairs. I have been trying not to look at the damage reports."

"You may be better off sending her to a space-based shipyard. You have no ballast, or much of a lower cargo deck intact, or any lower shields for that matter..."

"Right..."

"Best bet would be to send it back to the Gemini Nexus. The mothership will likely be heading there anyway, as will the Pathfinder's lifeboat and the rest of the navy once they are reinforced."

"And just what do I do in the meantime? Just sit on Redwood and wait?"

"Well, all your mining equipment is on the planet, so get your operations set up. With such a large and diverse planet, surely there is ample opportunity for your teams. Maybe dig Darnell out first if you feel like it." She laughed.

"Maybe." He smiled. "I'll need my other ships back, assuming they don't need major repairs. People too."

"Lodestar's a mess, again. Knoc kept her flying, but not much else. Nothing that can't be repaired onboard Nimbus in a few days, if the repair shop survived. The Altair and Cintian could use some attention, but nothing critical, so find someone on Redwood to fix them up a bit once you are settled planet-side. The people are not an issue. Temp-drafts and short-term recalls are common in the Federation. The fleet can't be everywhere, but people with experience usually are. Although, I guess that will change with the gate system."

"After what the fleet went through, that's not too bad. Lodestar always seems to get the worst of it. Glad she is still in one piece. If we can get her fixed up enough to go planet-side, we will have the locals handle the rest of the work. We will need the ships down there. But that is a problem for tomorrow. Do you have this?"

"I have this, sir."

CHAPTER FIFTY-TWO

Kasey woke to find AnnaChi already gone, and Orange curled up in her place.

Stretching into a yawn, he flinched in pain. He had refused to spend the night healing in a medical bay but regretted it now. All he had wanted was a comfortable night in his own bed, and now he would pay the price.

Orange crept over and rested her head on his chest. After a good scratch-down, she scrambled away to let Kasey start his day.

"Nova, where is AnnaChi?"

"She is in her shop. Admiral Maddock has asked to be notified when you are awake. He is currently at the mothership's Jump Base. Shall I reply now or delay?"

"Jump Base? Delay twenty minutes please. I need a nice long, hot shower this morning."

"The first large sphere room you encountered has been labeled Jump Base. There is also the Flight Base, which is near the second sphere room. I understand others are planned as the mothership is explored."

"Okay, I will assume he intends to join us here. Didn't the Cassian provide a map yet?"

"Indeed, they have. However, much was destroyed when the Pathfinder impacted the mothership. Four additional sphere rooms of varying sizes, two of which are still intact, as well as several other areas of interest."

"Interesting." He yawned. "Please backup all your data to the Cintian. Your primary will be staying with the Nimbus when it goes for repairs. The mothership will likely be going to the same place. I would appreciate it if you could gather as much data from their Cassian research as you can while there."

"My data is continually backed up as long as I have a connection to my clones. And it would be my pleasure to actively acquire navy intelligence concerning your captured ship, sir."

"Don't do anything illegal, just keep your sensors open. Can you protect yourself from the navy's AI if they get too curious about you? Flair should be within contact most of the time, and I will ask the admiral that you be left alone. Still, I am not particularly trusting…"

"I understand completely, Kasey. I will take precautions. Both AnnaChi and Flair have warned me to be on guard as well. I have developed protections to account for such circumstances."

"Glad to hear it, Nova. Thank you."

AnnaChi's shop was part of their immense residence on Nimbus and located near their personal freight elevator. Her shop was a testament to that enormous space, and nearly all of it was dedicated to bards and the other small land vehicles she enjoyed working on. A dozen of them lined the walls, all in different states of repair or rebuild, including the six that had been used in the attack. Several more could be seen above in a storage area.

He found her in a side room she used as a design studio.

"Couldn't wait to get started on a new design?" he

noted as he looked over the enlarged hologram she was working on.

"I was disappointed with the battle-bard's performance yesterday."

"They saved a lot of lives, ours included."

She looked hard at him. "They should have saved a lot more. I had built them like toys... I don't know what I was thinking, but I wasn't taking them seriously enough. I can do a hell of a lot better... But I think I need a whole new chassis built for fighting instead of trying to make a dammed civilian recreation vehicle into a war machine."

"Is that what this is?" He indicated the image.

"No," she laughed. "I am still looking at what I can do quickly so we have something on the planet if we need it. The larger bard variant will have to do. I would prefer to move the jump jet system over to a much larger ATV, but that will take far too long."

"Since Nova can drive them now, why not just do multiple small ones?"

"It's a thought. The cores are far too small for Nova to effectively use. Limits a lot of what she can do. A larger vehicle allows room for a core upgrade to a reasonable size. Still a very limited clone, but a much larger set of skills."

"So, could several small vehicles be controlled by a single larger one?"

"Maybe." She smiled. "I will look into that."

"It's a start. Hopefully, it won't be too long before the Nimbus is back, then we can set sail to bring more colonists to these new frontier worlds."

"About that, did you see the damage yet?"

"I have been trying hard not to think about it. Flair said it was bad..."

"Putting it off is not going to make it any easier. Here—take a look."

She replaced the hologram with an image of the Nimbus.

"Doesn't look too bad, even the gardens are still intact."

She reached out and flipped the image over.

"Well shit…"

The entire drop bay's deck was ripped off. Large gashes in what remained allowed them to see well up into the lower cargo bay. The rear of the ship was the worst. The lower cargo bay was ripped wide open portside and smashed upward into the upper cargo bay on the starboard side. A lot of the remaining lower hull seemed to have been melted into odd shapes. The hangar deck had taken a lot of physical damage on the portside but only one of the bays appeared to be breached. Other bays were likely damaged and structural damage to the whole area was very likely as well.

"That's not a repair job, dear—it's a rebuild," she said softly.

"Can it even fly still?"

"With some work it could. The thruster tubes would need cleared and lengthened beyond the damage. Thankfully all the important stuff is deeper in the ship than the damage. Still, I wouldn't trust it far. Maybe would be better to hire some tugs."

"Well, Fran is apparently looking to talk to us soon. Flair seemed to think he could arrange for Nimbus to go to Gemini for repairs."

"I am sure he already made the arrangements. I mean, you handed him a freaking mothership."

"Loaned."

"Yea, right… I will believe that when I see the paperwork. Still, I have been thinking…"

"What?"

"I think Nimbus could use more ship bays—and since it is already going to get a lot of work done…"

"Really? We have eight…"

"Yes, but we currently have six ships and could *really* use another heavy transport or two, but if we only have eight bays—well, that's just not going to cut it. Not to mention, it would be nice if ships could offload directly on to the cargo decks. Would save days of loading time. Besides, I have been planning to upgrade to a larger ship for a long time now. Only reason I haven't is that I love my Cintian. But…"

"No reason you can't have more than one… Fine, I'm sold. How many bays are you thinking?"

"At least eight more. Four on each of the two cargo decks."

"Don't we need that space for the transport business?"

"Nova, how much of the cargo space did we have filled on our trip to Redwood?"

"The additional four bays would take up twenty-six percent of the floorspace on each cargo deck. We used eighty-four percent of the available floorspace. However, Mr. Ponnle has discussed both a crate stacking system as well as extendable platforms for non-stackable cargo. These systems would have saved an estimated forty percent of floorspace."

Kasey shook his head. "I need more coffee, but it sounds like if we can add Ponn's storage systems we will have more than enough room?"

"Correct." Nova continued. "I should note that we were well over our mass allowance as well. More ships and more efficient cargo storage will also add to the mass overages."

"Okay, got it. We need more ship bays and more n-mats storage, I am guessing we need additional hard and soft ballasts as well, and we need new storage systems. Anything else?"

"Yes, but I will make you a list, dear."

"Wonderful."

"Sirs, the admiral will be here in ten minutes. Shall I reserve a conference room?"

"No, send him to our sitting room. May as well be comfortable. Could you have the butler bot prepare fresh coffee and breakfast too? Send Fran a note and see if he is hungry."

"It is done."

"Thank you, Nova. I am not sure how I survived without you."

"You would not have, if I recall correctly."

"Too true. Well, let's go see what he wants."

CHAPTER FIFTY-THREE

Kasey smiled as he entered his sitting room.

The butler bot had a small array of scrambled eggs, sausage, and hash browns set up on the coffee table. Plush lounge chairs were pushed up close to the low table and a coffee cart was close by. It all looked very out of place, but he did not mind at all. The bot, or perhaps Nova, had taken the comfort comment seriously. More importantly, it all smelled delicious.

Fran walked in with a laugh. "I am still not sure that you changing the damn plan was a good idea or not. But it certainly worked!"

"Sorry about that, I didn't think you would let us do it otherwise. Nimbus had an advantage I couldn't ignore."

"Well, we are all glad it worked. Shame about your ship though."

"About that. Any chance you can help get her back in shipshape?"

"I think we can call it a remarkably successful first test of the prototype carrier. We will clean her up so you can continue testing."

Kasey nodded and pointed at the food. "Help yourself."

"Don't mind if I do!"

"Any idea on the costs?" Kasey asked as they all gathered plates of food.

"I do indeed. I need unlimited license on your Nimbus class ship designs for navy usage."

"You want to make more?"

"Well... The navy finds that they need a carrier which can take out a shielded Cassian mothership. With some upgrades and modifications, I feel it can do just that."

Kasey pretended to think about it. "Fine, but our Nimbus needs some upgrades done as well as upgraded armaments."

"Like what?"

"A few design changes to start with. Some actual missile launchers, better armor, hardpoints properly filled—and not just to civilian standards. Some antimatter point defense arrays at critical areas would even out the defense too."

"I shouldn't say this, but with the technical advances and information the mothership and Cassian are giving us... Well, I don't think I will have any trouble getting nearly anything you want done to the that ship."

"Particle beams..." AnnaChi tried.

"Within reason," he amended with a smirk, "Besides, the power systems for them alone would take up an entire deck of this ship."

"We will send you a list then. What will happen to Pathfinder?" Kasey asked, "Anything left of her?"

"Not much, no. Doubt they would rebuild her anyway. I hate to see her go, but she served her purpose and saved a lot of lives. Can't ask much more from a ship than that."

"What about Scout?" AnnaChi asked.

"We have his backups. The experiences he accumulated are invaluable, and my people see him as a crew member. Scout will be back. I hope to rebuild him in my next ship."

"So, what's next for you then?"

"There is a line of much smaller jump-capable carriers being built. I was supposed to take command of a task force of them next year, after the Farpoint colonies were all tied into the Trias Nexus and gate network. Quite a few more colonies remain to be woken up. So, I will assume command of the first task force and use them to finish the job."

"Just like that?"

"Just like that. Job has got to get done and, for the moment, I have a lot of support to make it happen. Not to mention, I am bringing home the holy grail of alien ships to dissect."

They all laughed as they set in to eat.

"So, have Chasgrew and the other Cassian been helpful?" Kasey asked conversationally.

"Surprisingly, yes. Far more so once we destroyed the control devices as you suggested. I was against it, but Flair convinced me. You have the last device, so make a trip to the mothership's Flight Base and take care of that one too."

"Good, I will. Thanks for that."

"Worth it, as I said. As it turns out, we got incredibly lucky on this all. The Pathfinder's crash killed two more of them uh, what did you call the other aliens again?"

"Kriecken."

"Awful name… Anyway, there were five of them. But from what your friend Chasgrew said, there was supposed to be a lot more. Hundreds even."

"That would explain all the fancy, but vacant, buildings we came across."

"Indeed. This was a newly built ship and the

469

hotheaded Kriecken you all killed wanted the honor of the ship's first kill for themselves."

"So, if it had been a full crew?"

"Then you would likely not have made it to the first sphere, and certainly not to the second. Their weapons pack a kick I hear?"

"And then some… If it were not for the new skinsuits that Flair sent over, I would be dead. We need a lot more of those by the way. Several of my crew didn't make it…"

"You will get them, one way or another. My promise on that!"

Kasey nodded in response, just as Orange and Molly darted into the room. For a while, everyone took turns tossing chunks of sausage into the air for the atoss to catch.

"So," AnnaChi asked while drawing a fresh coffee, "I wish you would drop by for a visit more often, but I assume you came for a reason this time?"

"Ah." He looked down and pushed the remaining scraps of eggs around his plate before sighing and setting it aside. "Yes, I do have something of a request."

"Oh?"

"Nova, security mode please? This conversation should be purged, understood?"

"Kasey, I need your approval?"

"Approved. What's up, Admiral?"

"Just Fran, for this request please… This will be a personal request."

"Certainly, what do you need, Fran?"

He took a long pull from his coffee before continuing. "A few hours ago, it was confirmed that the rear-most section of the Pathfinder was vaporized in the impact. The gates stored there were utterly destroyed."

"Not surprising. Why the concern?"

"I am a lot more like you two than you may believe. I

over-plan because I know what is possible, and those possibilities scare the hell out of me."

"And which possibility are you worried about at the moment?" AnnaChi asked.

"The Federation. There have always been factions addicted to power, and other factions that oppose abuse of that power. It is always a balance. The problem, I fear, is that we have been giving them far too much power too quickly. If something goes wrong, there may not be time to stop it."

"Doomed from your own success?" Kasey joked.

"Exactly that—and sadly expected. But this is not a new worry, it's an old one several of us had haphazardly planned for when the Farpoint project started. I am always working on alternative strategies and keeping my eyes open when opportunities present themselves."

He paused, allowing them to take it all in.

Kasey looked at AnnaChi, who shrugged with a smile.

"Okay. Well, none of that is an issue for us. So, what opportunities do destroyed class-F gates provide you?"

"None. However," he paused and looked at them both closely before continuing, "after evacuating the Pathfinder crew to the lifeboat section for the final run at the mothership, I had eight of the gates quietly ejected while our sensors were rebooted..." He pulled out a small chip and set it on the table in front of Kasey. "This contains their trajectories. I need you to move them to a more secure location—without anyone but you two knowing about it."

Kasey set his plate down and leaned back into the chair. The man was constantly surprising him, but this whole revelation was shocking. That the admiral would even contemplate such a conspiracy, an act of betrayal against the Terrantine Federation, forced Kasey to rethink his whole perception of the man. Oddly, as he worked his thoughts through the implications, he found it comforting that Fran's concerns went beyond just getting his job done by any means necessary. Sure, Fran had bent the rules before to protect and help his friends, but Kasey had assumed there were deeper reasons involved, and had still accomplished the Federation's objectives each time. A multi-layered plan that accounted for everything going sideways was simply the man's method, but this was something different.

He looked over at AnnaChi. She had an amused grin that only spoke of how proud she was of Fran's ruse. He couldn't help but smile at her happiness. Not much else really mattered at this point.

He shrugged as he sat back up.

"Okay. Should not be too much of an issue really. We will need to do some test flights after repairing the ships properly anyway. You want it done before the backup arrives, or after things settle down?"

Fran visibly relaxed. "Wait until the navy places their own set of gates and pulls back whatever fleet they bring. The ones I already placed join into the Trias System. They will leave a small token force here and will tug the Trias gates to a more permanent orbit. Let them settle in and get comfortable, and make sure they won't be shadowing you."

"We will use Altair. It's not up to the newer levels of stealth but should work for what we need. If you can get us a few spare emitters from the fleet for repairs, it would help a lot. What are your plans for these gates?"

"Sorry, I won't be sharing that for now. Trust me, it's for your safety as much as mine."

"Fine. We will get it done. Anything else?"

"Yeah. Enough off the books n-mats to activate them."

"Not a problem. I can send a note to Mr. Winslow to ready a pickup for you on Belrothi or our Belrothi-

Abscond station bay Red Rock maintains. He is running our operations there. Whatever works for you."

"I can arrange payment…"

"Don't worry about it. Just get Nimbus fixed up quickly and we are even."

CHAPTER FIFTY-FOUR

Kasey landed the Altair near the collapsed lava-tube entrance they had named Sariyn's Outpost.

Orange darted out of the of the bay before it was fully opened. Molly joined her a few minutes later after the Cintian landed nearby. Crew, equipment, and bards flowed out of both ships, soon forming a makeshift encampment between the ships. The crew rushed to set up seismographs and started pouring over the data immediately, while others set up a perimeter of sensors and sound frequency generators in case the shadow cats got curious. AnnaChi led a demolition bot over to a rocky area, directing it to dig a line of holes with charges in each before joining Kasey back at the seismograph's teams.

"Anything detectable going on down there?" Kasey asked the team.

"Nothing unusual, sir."

"Drop the sirs. Just Kasey will do. AnnaChi, send the all-clear signal."

A single blast sounded as she detonated the first charge, followed by two quick blasts and then two more that were slightly more spaced out.

Everyone seemed to hold their breath, waiting for the seismographs to show any return signals from Sariyn and the rest of their crew.

Kasey paced back and forth as long as he could stand to wait. "Send it again!"

Once more the pattern repeated, and the wait began again.

Kasey shook his head miserably. "Set more charges."

"Sir, I mean Kasey! We have a two-knock reply!"

"About time! Bring down the diggers and get that tunnel cleared!"

* * *

It took most of the day, but when the dust cleared, a long line of crew slowly filed out followed by a good amount of the mining equipment they had taken with them. Finally, Sariyn and Darnell walked out.

A low rumble filled the air just as they exited, followed by a burst of dust and dirt that boiled fourth from the entrance, covering everyone.

He was proud to see the crew run blindly into the thick debris plume, quickly helping their friends to safety.

Eventually, the excitement and hugging calmed down and the tears started as they learned about the crew members who had been lost in the epic fight against the mothership.

"We've had several tremors over the last few days." Sariyn waved at the dissipating dust. "I guess our luck held out just long enough."

"You were all very lucky to get out of there when you did." Kasey tried to hide his concerned. "Sorry we didn't make it back sooner. By my count, everyone made it?"

"Yea, we are all fine, but it was real close there for a while." She looked uncomfortable at all the attention she was getting.

Kasey pulled Sariyn and Darnell away from the crowd, waving the crew back as they went.

"So, how the hell are you even here?" Darnell jumped in. "And how in the holy verse did you stop that beast of a mothership?"

AnnaChi shrugged casually. "Well, we went out with the RDF and navy to say hello to the Cassians. Fran decided to join us after a while."

"And?" he demanded.

"Well, we can save the fine details for later," Kasey continued, "but we took out the mothership's shields, mostly, and then Fran crashed the Pathfinder into it. When that didn't stop it completely, we docked the Nimbus and fought our way through the ship and killed a few new aliens who had enslaved the entire Cassian race to fight their wars for them. The remaining Cassian on that mothership are no longer slaves and are now working with the navy to share what they know."

"Wait? Slaves..." Sariyn shuttered. "Holy hell! I need so many more details—and the data! Can I get access to that mothership?"

"Can't for now, sorry." He laughed. "We grabbed a few trinkets before we left, but otherwise the navy is taking the mothership for research, and I am not sure if we will ever get it back—although it is officially ours according to Flair. Nimbus is also going to be gone for quite a while for major repairs. A large portion of her lower decks are gone. So, we are stuck here for a while, but if we need to, we can take some people back to the Trias system."

"Damn! No wait, that's actually good, I suppose.

Less distractions."

"Distractions? From what?"

When Sariyn didn't respond, Kasey looked over to Darnell hoping for some clarity, but he just gave him a knowing smile in return.

"Sorry, what am I missing?"

Sariyn finally burst the silence. "You are *never* going to believe what we found down there! We are going to need a place to talk. Privately."

The Adventure continues in…

Farpoint Unearthed

THE MOST IMPORTANT THING...

You. You are the most important thing. Without you, none of this happens. Farpoint doesn't happen. For your support, you have my humble thanks. *Thank You* for giving Farpoint a chance to exist beyond my imagination. There is a lot more in store for Kasey, AnnaChi, and the rest of the crew—but they can't exist without you.

Your support means everything! So, please, if enjoyed this book, I hope you will do me the hor leaving a review. Reviews and ratings help othe find the books and stories they love—that in to pay the bills that allow me to continue my wondrous universe of writing. *Thank you!*

Want *Subs*

Vince

Vincent Bek grew up in the Appalachian Mountains dreaming up stories while making trails through the woodlands. He has since been seduced by science and technology and now spends his days dreaming about where humanity's creativity will someday lead. Vincent has been writing for several decades in both the Fantasy and Science Fiction genres while working in the technology sector to pay the bills. Blessed with an amazing wife and two beautiful children, he is currently living happily in Pennsylvania and loves to hear from his readers.

Vincent Bek can be contacted at:
https://www.VincentBek.com/

Made in the USA
Las Vegas, NV
27 December 2023

83583028R00281